HARRY HUNTER MYSTERY SERIES

Book 1-3

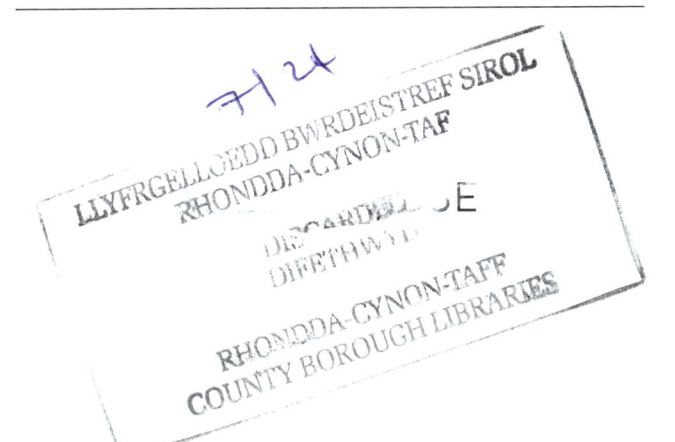

Books by the Author

MYSTERY/THRILLER/HORROR NOVELS

- In One Fell Swoop
- Umbrella Man
- Blackbird Fly
- To Hell in a Handbasket
- Edwina

HARRY HUNTER MYSTERY SERIES

- All The Good Girls
- Run Girl Run
- No Other Way

MARY MILLS MYSTERY SERIES

- What Hurts the Most
- You Can Run
- You Can't Hide
- Careful Little Eyes

EVA RAE THOMAS MYSTERY SERIES

- Don't Lie to me
- What you did
- Never Ever
- Say You Love me
- Let Me Go

EMMA FROST SERIES

- Itsy Bitsy Spider

- Miss Dolly had a Dolly
- Run, Run as Fast as You Can
- Cross Your Heart and Hope to Die
- Peek-a-Boo I See You
- Tweedledum and Tweedledee
- Easy as One, Two, Three
- There's No Place like Home
- Slenderman
- Where the Wild Roses Grow
- Waltzing Mathilda
- Drip Drop Dead

JACK RYDER SERIES

- Hit the Road Jack
- Slip out the Back Jack
- The House that Jack Built
- Black Jack
- Girl Next Door
- Her Final Word
- Don't Tell

REBEKKA FRANCK SERIES

- One, Two…He is Coming for You
- Three, Four…Better Lock Your Door
- Five, Six…Grab your Crucifix
- Seven, Eight…Gonna Stay up Late
- Nine, Ten…Never Sleep Again
- Eleven, Twelve…Dig and Delve
- Thirteen, Fourteen…Little Boy Unseen
- Better Not Cry
- Ten Little Girls
- It Ends Here

HORROR SHORT-STORIES

- Mommy Dearest
- The Bird
- Better watch out
- Eenie, Meenie
- Rock-a-Bye Baby
- Nibble, Nibble, Crunch
- Humpty Dumpty
- Chain Letter

PARANORMAL SUSPENSE/ROMANCE NOVELS

- In Cold Blood
- The Surge
- Girl Divided

THE VAMPIRES OF SHADOW HILLS SERIES

- Flesh and Blood
- Blood and Fire
- Fire and Beauty
- Beauty and Beasts
- Beasts and Magic
- Magic and Witchcraft
- Witchcraft and War
- War and Order
- Order and Chaos
- Chaos and Courage

THE AFTERLIFE SERIES

- Beyond
- Serenity

- ENDURANCE
- COURAGEOUS

THE WOLFBOY CHRONICLES

- A GYPSY SONG
- I AM WOLF

DAUGHTERS OF THE JAGUAR

- SAVAGE
- BROKEN

ALL THE GOOD GIRLS

BOOK 1

Chapter 1

"I DON'T LIKE IT, ROBERT."

"What's that?"

Robert didn't even look up from his laptop. It was late at night, and he was still working, as usual, even on a Friday night.

"I haven't heard from her in hours," Valentina said. "She hasn't responded to any of my texts."

Robert sighed and glared at her from behind the laptop. He was still every bit as handsome as he had been when they met twenty years ago at the annual Vizcaya Ball, which anyone who was anyone in Miami's high society attended. She had been in her early twenties, and he had been ten years older. Still, it seemed like she was the one who looked the oldest these days. He kept himself in shape to a degree that Valentina often worried he might have other women on the side. Robert traveled a lot and was often gone for weeks at a time. Who knew what he did on those business trips?

"It's a dance, Valentina. It's prom. It's a big deal around here, and it is to your daughter too. She won't be keeping an eye on her phone all night, waiting for your texts. Frankly, I would be more concerned if she had answered."

Around here.

Robert always said stuff like that condescendingly like she wouldn't understand because she wasn't from *around here*. Because she was from Colombia…because she had come here when she was in her late teens and never attended an American high school. It was something in the way he said it that made her cringe like she wasn't good enough because she wasn't fully American and never would be.

"Well, she promised me she'd text me," she said with a small snort. "And now it's getting really late."

"She's seventeen; she knows how to handle herself."

"I'm not so sure. Those kids at her school, I don't trust them."

That made Robert laugh. "You don't trust anyone, Valentina. It's in your nature."

And there it was again. Always making sure she knew she was different from him. It was something that had grown in their marriage over the years, coming between them…a disdain toward her. Valentina found it to be odd. Living in Key Biscayne, they were surrounded by people from South America…wealthy people who had nannies and drove expensive cars but spoke Spanish. Living there, Robert felt surrounded, invaded almost, and slowly, he had begun to fight to conserve his sense of being a white American. It was important that his daughter knew she was American, he would suddenly say, and he wouldn't have her speak any Spanish, so Valentina had to teach her when he wasn't at home.

"Well, I don't," she said, lifting her nose toward the ceiling in contempt. "They have never been good to Lucy."

Valentina grimaced when saying the name. It was something they had discussed endlessly when she had become pregnant…what to name their daughter. Valentina wanted to name her a Colombian name; she wanted her to know where she came from, whereas Robert believed she needed to be as American as possible. In the end, Valentina had put her foot down and said she was naming her Luciana after her great-grandmother, and Robert had given in. But over the years, Luciana had become Lucy, and influenced by her father, their daughter insisted that everyone call her that.

Valentina looked at her Rolex, then felt a pinch of deep worry in the pit of her stomach.

"It's eleven-thirty now, and we still haven't heard anything," she said with a slight whimper. "The prom ended at eleven. She was supposed to text us to pick her up."

"They're probably just hanging out after the party," he said, calming her down, or at least attempting to. "You need to relax."

Valentina stared at her phone, checking if there was a signal, then put it down just as the screen lit up. Relief washed over her as she saw her daughter's name on the display. She opened the text.

"They're going to the beach to make a bonfire," she said with light laughter. "She's asking if it'll be okay that she stays out a little later. Guess I won't be going to sleep anytime soon, then."

"Well, there you go," Robert said. "Your daughter is just having a good time for once. High school has not been easy for her, but now she finally seems to be enjoying herself. Don't ruin it with all your worry, please."

Chapter 2

VALENTINA STARED at the clock on the wall. It was past two o'clock now, and still, there was no news from her daughter. She was getting tired now and wanted to go to bed soon. Robert had turned in, and Valentina had also been dozing off on the couch, waiting to hear from Lucy.

She looked at her phone again, wondering if she should call her and tell her it was time to come home. It wasn't like Lucy to stay out all night like this, and by now, Valentina feared the girl might have been persuaded to drink alcohol or do something worse. Lucy was a good girl and had stayed away from all that stuff, so Valentina didn't understand why she'd start now. She usually wasn't interested in partying, and it had actually taken some effort to persuade her even to go to this dance. Valentina had bought her a beautiful lavender dress, but still, the girl had told her she didn't want to go. But then some weeks ago, she had come home and suddenly told Valentina that she had changed her mind…that some kids from the school had asked if she was going and had been friendly toward her. There was also a boy, she had admitted, who had told her he thought she was cute. Valentina had thought it was wonderful and hoped that things were finally shaping up for her like her mother had wanted for so many years. They had gone through so much bullying and so many bad times with no friends in school that Valentina had thought this was an answer to her prayers.

But she hadn't expected her daughter to stay out so late.

Now, she didn't know what to do. She did know, however, that two o'clock was way too late, and it was time to put a stop to it. She walked up the stairs to her bedroom and woke Robert.

"She hasn't texted yet. I fell asleep, but now I think we need to get her home. It's two o'clock," she said.

Robert sat up in bed and cleared his throat. "Really? That is too late. Call her and tell her I'm on my way."

Robert rose to his feet and found his jeans, then put them on. Valentina was about to call Lucy when Robert's phone on his nightstand rang. They shared a brief look; then, he grabbed it.

"It's her," he said. "It's Lucy."

Valentina breathed, relieved. But the feeling was soon replaced by anger over her daughter's reckless behavior. Lucy knew this was way too late. She was being very irresponsible.

Robert picked up the phone and held it against his ear. A voice could be heard on the other end and was yelling loudly, so Valentina could hear it vividly even if she couldn't make out what was being said. But she did realize the voice didn't belong to her daughter.

Robert's smile froze, and his eyes became steel gray.

"Who is this? WHO is this?"

Robert looked at the display as the connection was lost.

"Who was that?" Valentina asked fearfully. "What did they say? Robert?"

But Robert was unreachable at this point. His nostrils were flaring, his eyes ablaze with anger.

"Robert? Who was that?"

He grabbed his shirt and put it on while running into the hallway and down the stairs without uttering a single word to his wife.

"Robert?" she called after him, but he just continued, rushing out the front door, which slammed shut behind him.

"Robert? ROBERT?"

ONE YEAR LATER

Chapter 3

"HEY, you! Yes, you, I'm talking to you!"

I approached the guy in the alley. I couldn't see his face or the young girl's face enough to see their eyes or their features, but I didn't have to.

I knew exactly what was happening.

"This girl is no more than a teenager, and you're selling crack to her?" I said. "What kind of a monster does that?"

The lanky guy stared at me in the darkness. The girl saw the chance to take off and ran out of the alley and into the street. I knew she would probably just run around the corner and find another creep who would sell her whatever she was craving, whatever they had her hooked on. I knew I couldn't save her, but I was doing my part to try and clean out the availability.

"W-what the…?" the guy said. His hand slid back inside his hoodie with the small white rock in it. He puffed himself up in front of me.

I stared down at him. It was one of the advantages of being six-foot-eight. Not many felt superior to you, especially not lowlife drug dealers in Overtown Miami. The guy was about to pull out a weapon; I saw the movement of his hand behind his back, where he probably kept it in the waistband of his jeans. It was most likely a knife since most of these Haitian dealers in this part of town couldn't afford a gun. They were also often searched by the cops patrolling the streets and finding a gun on their body would be excuse enough to shoot them.

We all knew the drill around here.

As his hand moved toward the knife behind his back, I moved my arm just enough for my zip-up hoodie to open up so he could see the gun in my holster inside of it. The sight made him let go of the knife. It also made him realize I was a cop if he hadn't already.

"Hand over the goodies," I said. "I'm confiscating them. You're not selling to any more young girls; do you hear me?"

"No way," the guy said with a sniffle, then wiped his nose. He was edgy, and his hand was shaking. It would soon be time for him to have his next fix. He had to sell to other poor souls in order to keep up with his own demand. It was the circle of life around these parts. And it was a never-ending story.

"That girl is someone's daughter; do you know that?" I asked and reached for his hoodie. I grabbed him by the collar and pulled him upward, closer to my face. "Did you get her hooked, huh? Did you introduce her to crack, giving her the first ride for free, so she'd become a lifelong customer, huh? Don't look at me like that; I know your type. Scum of the earth."

I reached into his pocket and pulled the rock out, still holding him by the collar with the other hand.

"Hey, that's mine!" he yelled.

"Not anymore," I said and put him down.

As I did, he took a swing at me. I wasn't expecting it, and it took me by surprise. His fist slammed into my right eye with such force that I fell backward. The little kid was a lot stronger than I had given him credit for. I roared in pain while the kid jolted forward, trying to get away.

Another awesome part about being this tall, by the way, is that I have very long arms. So, as the kid leaped forward, thinking he'd be able to get away, I simply reached out my right arm and grabbed him by the hoodie, then pulled him backward. His legs were in the air as I pulled him back and threw him down on the pavement with a thud. I then leaned over him and placed my massive fist on his nose, breaking the bone. Blood gushed from it, and he looked at me, confused. I gave him another blow to his face, then reached into his jeans pocket and found another rock that I took before letting him go.

"Might be a chance for you to try something new, make a career move," I said as I let him go. Above me, the warm Florida night was threatening to end in a storm, and I heard thunder in the distance.

"Hey," the kid yelled after me as I walked away. "You can't do this to me."

"I can't?" I said when I reached the end of the alley. "I think I just did."

"It's police brutality!"

That made me laugh out loud as I walked away with both rocks.

"Yeah? Well, good thing I'm off-duty tonight."

Chapter 4

THE *SERENITY* FOLLOWED the current with its prow facing the open sea, pushed by a gentle landward breeze. They had turned off the engine and lowered the anchor just outside of the marina. Behind them glittered the Miami lights in the dark night, and they could no longer see the yacht club.

The four girls listened to the music the waves made when gently kissing the sides of the boat. It was so quiet out there in the open ocean, one of them, Sandra, thought to herself. She, for one, had longed for such peace of mind for a long time. Her friend, Katelyn, was drinking a soda.

"Should we be heading back?" Georgiana said. It was her father's boat they had borrowed, and she was always so worried her dad would get mad at her. They had told him they were going fishing, even though they had no idea how.

"It's getting late."

"No," the fourth girl, Martina, said with a light laugh. "We're eighteen now. We can do as we please. Our parents don't get to boss us around anymore. I wanna stay out a little longer, please?"

Katelyn watched Sandra finish her soda. Martina gave them a

look. "I can't believe we'll be graduating in just a few months, can you?"

"I sure can believe it," Katelyn said and lifted her soda. "I can't wait to…"

Katelyn stopped talking when they all heard a noise coming from behind them. They turned simultaneously to look and spotted someone standing in the stern of the boat, wearing a black diver's wetsuit.

"Who the heck is that?" Georgiana said and rose to her feet, pushing Martina away. "Hey, you! What are you doing on my boat?"

The person remained eerily still and just stood there like it was the most natural thing in the world. Sandra couldn't see a face or make out if it was a man or a woman.

Could it be someone who's lost? Sandra thought to herself for a brief second while Georgiana rushed toward the person. *Maybe this person thought it was his own boat? Maybe he couldn't find his way back in the darkness? Maybe he's in some kind of trouble?*

"You can't just crawl on board my father's boat," Georgiana yelled as she almost reached the diver. Too late did she see the harpoon in his hands, not till it was fired and speared through her chest.

Sandra stopped breathing when she saw what happened. Shock rushed through her body in waves, and she found herself completely unable to move. Martina started to scream and instinctively rush toward Georgiana's lifeless body, but as she did, the diver pulled out a knife. It cut through the air with a hiss, cutting into her skin. The blade penetrated her throat, splitting it open, and she too fell to the deck, landing right next to Georgiana.

Seeing this happen to her friends, Katelyn tried to make a run for it, but the diver had by then pulled out the spear from Georgiana's heart, reloaded the gun, and fired it at her, hitting her in the leg. Katelyn screamed and fell while the diver rushed toward her. Sandra crawled up on the edge of the boat and looked into the dark water beneath. While the diver slit Katelyn's throat, she made the decision.

She closed her eyes and plunged in.

As she landed in the water, she swam for the surface as fast as she could, then spotted the lights from the yacht club. Sandra screamed while trying to swim.

Then she heard the plunge coming from behind her, and panic set in as she realized the diver had jumped in after her. She swam for her life, screaming for help, desperately flapping the water, but feeling like she was going nowhere, like in those awful nightmares she always had where she ran and ran, but never moved. She lifted her head above the water and gasped for air when she felt something grab her. Arms reached up from the ocean beneath her and pulled her downward forcefully into the deep darkness below.

Chapter 5

"YOU SHOULD HAVE SEEN HER; it was like that time when we told her she couldn't start horseback riding because we couldn't afford it. Do you remember that? Of course, you do. How could you forget? It almost broke your heart, having to say no to her. It was embarrassing to her since Amelia, her best friend, got to go. That's the only time I remember you being embarrassed by us not having much."

I reached over and took Camille's hand in mine. It was so delicate, and I was reminded of the day of our wedding when I had put the ring on her finger. I had held her hand in mine and thought it was such a responsibility to have to take care of another person, someone so fragile.

I had no idea how right I had been.

"Anyway, I told her she was grounded for a month, then took it back and said a week instead. But then she started to bargain, and we ended on two days. I know what you're thinking; don't give me that look," I said and chuckled, then leaned back in my chair, running a hand through my hair. My face was still pounding from the beating I had received the night before. "I am weak; I have to admit it. I have a soft spot for our daughter. I never can be mad at her for more than a few minutes. It's those eyes, you know? I can't resist them."

I sighed and looked at my wife. She was still beautiful, so gorgeous. And those eyes, they still had me locked in. Even though they weren't exactly looking at me, but down at the floor while her head slumped to the side and slid downward toward her shoulder. I grabbed it and pushed it back in place on the pillow. I had bought her one of those elevation beds so she could sit up straight from time to time, but her head kept falling, so I lowered it slightly. Her eyes stared right past me as I looked at her beautiful face and caressed her cheek. I leaned over and wiped drool from her chin, then kissed her cheek gently, closing my eyes, envisioning her when she had still been well.

Before the drugs caused her brain damage.

People usually thought that if you overdosed, you either died or you would be okay. But that wasn't always true. Not for Camille. She had been a drug addict when I met her through my job as an undercover cop at Miami PD, infiltrating the underworld of crack, especially in Overtown, the Haitian part of town. She had been hooked back then, and I had taken her to a rehab facility, taken her off the streets, paying for it out of my own pocket. I had visited her every day while she was there, and soon, we fell in love. When she was released, she moved in with me in my townhouse, and the year after, we were married, and she had our daughter, Josie. For years, she stayed clean; at least I believed she was clean. Until one day three years ago, when I came home from my shift and found her. Her head rested on a pillow on the couch, her wrists were bent and fingers contracted into fists. She was rocking back and forth as if to stand up but then collapsed into the sofa. That was when I knew something was terribly wrong. She had taken heroin and fentanyl and that had caused her to stop breathing. I rushed her to the hospital, and they managed to get her to breathe on her own again. Her kidneys had failed and they had then recovered as well. But her brain had been starved of oxygen for so long that it was left severely damaged. Now, she lived in the bedroom upstairs in her new bed, while I slept on a mattress on the floor next to her, making sure I'd wake up in case she needed me.

The doctors said she would never be the same as she used to be. Still, I was determined to make the most of our time together while she was still here. But, boy, I missed hearing her voice. I missed hearing her laugh and seeing her dance with our daughter in the kitchen downstairs. I missed everything about her, but most of all, I missed looking into her deep brown eyes. I hated that she was just lying there in that bed, completely lifeless alongside a urinary catheter, pill boxes, and her feeding tube.

"There you go," I said and wiped the last of the drool away, then tossed the napkin, biting back my tears. "You're as good as new."

There was a small knock on the door, and Jean, my next-door neighbor, poked her head in.

"I think Josie is ready for school soon," she said. "I can take over and give Camille her bath now?"

I smiled when seeing her. Jean wasn't only my neighbor; she was also my savior and helping hand. She was a registered nurse and helped me out with Camille as much as I needed. She was also Camille's best friend and had been very close to her before the overdose. At least, we thought she was, but she had been every bit as surprised as I was to learn that Camille had started doing drugs again.

I walked to her and hugged her. "Thank you, Jean. You're the best. I don't think I would know how to get by without you. I'm sure Camille knows how much you do for her and us, and if she could, she'd thank you."

That made her blush. "Don't give me that," she said and waved me away. "You'll ruin my makeup. I just got myself ready for my shift and all the doctors I plan on flirting with today. I won't have you ruin that. Go and take care of your daughter, and then I'll have a look at that shiner afterward."

Chapter 6

"GOD, please bless this food and the people eating it."

I held my daughter's hand in mine while saying the prayer, then opened my eyes and looked at her while I added:

"And please help Josie not to be so addicted to her darn phone."

I sent her a look as she realized I had caught her with the phone in her other hand.

"Busted," I said and reached out my hand. "Hand it over—no phones at the table. You know the rules. And especially not while we pray."

"But it's just breakfast, Dad. It's not like it's dinner or anything."

"Hand it over, please."

Josie sighed and handed me the phone. I put it in my pocket, and she gave me a look that told me she didn't think this was fair treatment. I didn't care. She was on that thing all the time. Sitting at the table was the one time I wanted her full attention.

"So, what's up for today?" I asked and served her some eggs and a bagel. "Any big tests?"

She shrugged. "Only math."

"Only math, huh?"

"It's not that hard, Dad."

I stared at my daughter. She was in the eighth grade, doing ninth grade advanced class math. I didn't do that when I was her age. Josie was doing really well in school, something I was certain she got from her mother. Camille could have done anything with her life, and almost did. She went to FIT, Florida Institute of Technology, for engineering and would have finished her education if someone—that being the monster of a boyfriend at the time—had not introduced her to crack one day. After that, she had ended up on the streets of Miami until I picked her up one day when we raided an abandoned building in Overtown. I took one look at her and knew I loved her. I still did, despite it all.

"Really? So you're gonna ace it, I take it."

She smiled cunningly. "Don't I always?"

I chuckled and drank coffee, hoping it might soon kick in so I could feel more awake. I had been out until midnight the night before, while my dad, who lived right down the street, hung out with Josie, so she didn't have to be alone.

"So, what happened to your eye?" she asked while shoveling in eggs. She had a healthy appetite, on the verge of insatiable, which was probably needed in order for her to keep growing the way she did. She was closing in on five feet eleven at the age of only fourteen years old. There was no saying how tall she was going to get. That part, she didn't get from her mother. That was my humble contribution. But that was about it. The rest of her was her mother's spitting image, especially her good looks. Josie was gorgeous beyond what seemed possible. Her creamy caramel skin, her light green sparkling eyes, and thick curly hair made most people compare her to a young Tyra Banks. I'd rather compare her to Camille, the most beautiful woman to have walked this earth, in my eyes.

Only she was too good for it.

"Dad?"

I glared at her. I didn't want to answer her question and explain what I had been up to the night before, so instead, I finished my cup and looked at my watch.

"You should get going," I said as I got up and grabbed both our plates. "Bus leaves in two minutes, and you still haven't brushed your teeth."

Chapter 7

"OUCH!"

I jumped up. Jean put her hand on her hip and tilted her head. "If you don't sit still, how am I supposed to help you?"

"I don't want your help," I said. "I'm fine."

"Uh-huh, and I'm a secret Russian spy. Now, please sit back down and let me finish this. Your attacker split open the skin above your eyebrow, and I need to close it with these strips. I can't do that if you keep whining. I told you to hold that cold pack on your eye while I fixed this."

I sat back down and tried to relax while pressing the cold pack against my black eye. Jean placed butterfly strips on my skin, pulling it, so it hurt.

"Sit still; I said. Now, tell me something…how did this happen again?"

"It's none of your business," I mumbled.

"None of my business? Right now, it seems to be a whole lot of my business. Patching you up has been all of my business lately. Were you out patrolling the streets on your own again?"

"Maybe?"

"And what exactly does your boss say to you running around the streets at night like some madman, getting beaten up, chasing drug dealers?"

I looked up at her. "He tells me not to?"

"Exactly. Then why don't you stop? You're never going to find the guy that sold Camille those drugs. He's probably dead from an overdose himself anyway."

I grumbled as she placed another strip on my sore skin. "I might not be able to find the guy that did this to Camille, but I can stop others from doing it. I can stop them from selling this stuff to young kids and ruining their lives."

"Uh-huh…and didn't your boss take you out of the narcotics department?" she asked, giving me that look again. Jean had dark blue eyes like me and dark brown hair that she kept in a ponytail so it wouldn't fall in her face while she took care of patients. She was athletically built and a lot stronger than you'd think. She had been my rock through all of this, the past three years, and for that, I owed her everything.

"He did…but…"

"And why do you think he did that, huh, Harry? Was it because you were doing such a great job?"

"No, but…"

"No, he took you off the streets because you couldn't control yourself—because you kept beating people up and get beaten yourself. He was afraid you were going to get yourself killed one day out in those streets. Now, how about you listen to that boss of yours and don't get yourself killed, how about that? Because there are people here who need you, Harry. People who wouldn't get by without you."

"So, focus on the people I still have and don't run, thinking I can fix things that have already happened, is that what you're saying? Thanks, but we've had this conversation before, Jean, and I still don't think it's any of your business."

Jean answered with a grunt, then finished me up, and then the display on my phone lit up.

"That's the third time this morning," she said. "Don't you think you should answer that?"

I stared at the display, then put it down. "It's just my boss. I'll talk to him when I get there."

Chapter 8

"NICE OF YOU TO show your pretty face for once."

Major Fowler gave me that look above his glasses. He was sitting behind his desk, looking through a file when I walked in. He glared at his watch for a brief second. "Only two hours late. I think that might be a new record for you, Harry…Geez, what happened to your face? You know what? I have a feeling I don't want to know."

Fowler leaned back in his leather chair. His salt and pepper hair had been cut very short, probably by the same barber he had used forever, even before he and I had become friends twenty years ago when we were both rookies at the Miami-Dade Police Department. Fowler had climbed the career ladder and become a major, while I was still the man on the ground, now serving in the homicide unit.

"Listen, Fowler, I am…"

Fowler lifted both of his bushy eyebrows. "No, Hunter, you listen to me. I can't keep covering for you, making excuses for you. You come and go as you please, and you're never at the briefings in the mornings. I know it's been a tough time for you and your family, and I have given you all the rope I can, but at some point, it has to stop. Frankly, I don't know what to do with you, especially not on a day like today when we need everyone at the top of their game."

"Why? What's going on?"

He threw out his arms. "If you'd been at the briefing this morning, you'd know."

"Or if you tell me now, I'd know too," I said.

He sighed, tapping his pen on the desk. He pulled out a photo from the file and slid it across the desk for me to see.

"Four teenage girls were found dead last night."

He grabbed another photo and showed it to me. "Three of them were found on this boat anchored outside the yacht club; the fourth washed up by the yacht club's seawall. Two of them had their throats slit; one had been harpooned in the heart, while the fourth had drowned. We don't know if she drowned while trying to escape or if someone killed her. They had borrowed the boat from one of their parents and had taken it out to fish, the father said. The first body, the girl that drowned, was found just before midnight by the personnel that was closing down the club for the night. Two men spotted something in the water and rushed to see what it was, thinking it could be a manatee or a dolphin. When they saw the girl in the water, they called nine-one-one, and it didn't take the responding officers from our South District Station long to realize the girl came from the boat they could see out on the water. When they got out there, they found the three others. A pure blood bath, they said. Gonzalez is still throwing up, last thing I heard."

I stared at the photos, my eyes scanning them. "Looks like the harpooned girl died first, so you'll have to assume the killer was standing here, at the stern of the boat," I said and pointed. "Before the girl there ran toward her, probably because they were best friends, maybe still assuming that the harpoon went off by accident. But then the killer pulled a knife and slit her throat. That's why her body is pushed a little further back. The killer was making his way, killing them one after another. The third one, the girl here, was trying to escape before she was harpooned in the leg, as you can see, so she couldn't run anymore. The killer took his time to pull out the harpoon from the first girl and reload; that was why she made it all the way to the edge of the boat before she was stopped. My guess is the fourth one made a jump for it into the water, where the killer probably jumped in after her and pulled her under the water. A guy like him wouldn't risk her surviving to talk. I say you're looking for a diver, someone who knows his way around spearfishing and how to gut a fish. If you look at the way the throat was cut, the incision here and here, it resembles the way you'd cut the head off a fish. But I guess that doesn't narrow it down by much around here, where fishing and diving are common hobbies. Anyway, if you want my take on it, then I'd say he came onto the boat climbing up from the stern side while the kids were hanging out, drinking, and weren't looking in his direction. Once they heard him, the girl here, the first one, rushed to him, probably because it was her father's boat they had borrowed, and she felt responsible. Then she was shot in the heart. This was an assassination. And it was carefully planned."

Fowler folded his hands on the desk and gave me a look, then nodded with a small smile.

"You know I have no way of telling if you're right or not," Fowler said. "Forensics is still working out there, and it'll take a few days before we know these kinds of details."

"I am right, and you know it."

He nodded, chuckling. "You always had a nose for the details. That's why I can't fire you. You're just too darn good of a detective."

That made me smile. Compliments from Fowler were rare.

"So…you want me on the case?" I asked.

Chapter 9

"NOT SO FAST," Fowler said, shaking his head. "There's more to the story."

"Isn't there always?"

Fowler nodded. "True, but this is more than usual. Do you remember the story of Lucy Lockwood?"

"Sure. It's only been what...a year?" I asked. "She was raped at some school dance, right?"

"She went to prom and, after the party, she went to the beach with her friends, where she claimed a guy raped her while a bunch of kids watched. The guy later called her dad using her phone and told him that his daughter was 'good at sex.' The dad drove down there and found her in the sand all alone. She reported it as a rape and claimed the guy had forced her."

I lifted my eyebrows. "What do you mean *claimed*? I don't understand. You don't believe her?"

"I...well..."

"Who wouldn't believe a seventeen-year-old girl who says she was raped?" I asked, enraged.

"Listen, I know this is a touchy subject since your...your sister was..."

"Raped?" I said. "You can say it out loud, you know. Yes, she was raped when we were teenagers, and now she suffers mental health issues as a result. It's not something anyone would joke around with. And, no, the police didn't believe her either. Told her it was her own fault for dressing the way she did and flirting with the boy who raped her. Don't be like them, Fowler. Don't be like those jerks who told my sister it was her own doing."

Fowler sighed and rubbed his stubble. "Anyway, the investigation back then didn't lead to anything, and a judge dismissed the Lockwood case. There simply was no evidence that she didn't consent; none of the witnesses would say that it wasn't with her consent. They didn't even admit to seeing it happen."

"And the bruises? They didn't tell another story?" I asked.

"You know how it is. You can't argue that it wasn't a part of the act. Witnesses said they saw her flirt with him, act up to him, leading him on at the party."

I shook my head. "You're too much."

Fowler looked down at his papers for a brief second, then back up at me. "The kid had good expensive lawyers who were able to rip the case apart. We did what we could for her, but it just wasn't good enough. Anyway, the thing is, the four girls who turned up dead last night, they are all on the list of witnesses from back then. When Lucy arrived at the hospital, she gave a list of ten names of people who she claimed watched the rape. Last week, another girl, Lisa Turner, turned up dead in a dumpster, also stabbed to death with a fishing knife. They all go to the same high school, and, according to Lucy, they all were on the beach that night when she claims to have been attacked."

I nodded. "And now you're afraid that someone is killing them because of what happened?"

He nodded. "Yes. Morales and his team are talking to the dad today."

"Obviously, but what about the girl? What about Lucy?"

Fowler took off his glasses and wiped sweat from his upper lip. "That's the thing. She went missing eight months ago. Right after the judge dismissed her case, she disappeared. Her parents reported her missing, and we had a search party out and everything, but she was never found. We finally concluded she had run away from home because of what happened. It's not uncommon in cases like these."

I cleared my throat, sending him a suspicious look. "You don't seriously think that Lucy is killing these kids?"

He exhaled. "I don't know what to think, to be honest. But I do know that she has the best motive."

Chapter 10

"I TAKE it you want me on the case of finding who killed those five girls, right?"

Fowler shook his head. "Wrong. I already have Morales and his team on that one. He investigated the rape back then, and let's be honest, he's here on time and attends all the briefings like he's supposed to."

I stared at my old friend. "You're kidding me, right? You're giving the case to him because he plays by the rules? Murder isn't solved by detectives who play by the rules. You know I'm perfect for this case. You know I'm the only one around here who can solve it."

Fowler shrugged. "You can whine all you want. I need someone I can rely on, someone I trust will pick up the phone when I call. The case is his."

"And what about me? Why did you call me in here if you're not putting me on the case?" I asked.

He leaned back in his chair. His wife and two kids were staring back at him from a picture next to his computer. I knew them all well; we used to be invited over for dinner all the time before Camille got sick. After that, they just stopped asking.

"Well, my first thought was to fire you, but then again, I felt bad because you're the detective with the most solved cases around here, and you're my friend. So, I decided against it."

"Geez, thanks?"

"You're welcome."

"So, what do you have me on?"

He leaned forward and folded his hands on the desk again. "Protection, Harry. I can't have any more kids turn up dead." Fowler pulled out a couple of photos of a young kid no more than seventeen or eighteen. He was wearing the same sly smile in all the pictures like he was keeping some deep secret that he knew he'd get away with. Just looking at him made my skin crawl. It was such a cliché…a white, blue-eyed kid from an affluent suburban area getting away with anything, even rape.

"William Covington was the one Lucy named as her rapist, but who was also later acquitted."

"You've got to be kidding me."

"You say that a lot."

I stared at my old friend, out of words to speak. What the heck was his game? He couldn't be serious about this. He wanted me to be a bloody bodyguard?

"Tell me you're joking. You want me to protect some affluent rapist whose parents' lawyer made sure he could get away with it?"

Fowler nodded. "I don't need to remind you that he was never convicted of any crime, and in the eyes of the law, he is innocent. So, yes, that is what I'm asking of you. If you do your job well, then you might get back to solving cases again soon. If not, then maybe it's time for you to find another line of work more suitable for your needs to come and go as you please."

"You're…"

"Kidding? No, not at all. I suggest you keep this boy alive. Your future depends on it."

Chapter 11

I DIDN'T STAY at the department. I slammed the door to Fowler's office, then stormed out without even a word to any of my colleagues. I jumped back onto my motorcycle, roared it to life and rode it across town while yelling loudly into the warm Florida wind. I drove out to the beach, then parked the bike and went for a long walk, telling God just how unhappy I was right now with how he was managing my life.

"Don't you see me at all?" I asked, feeling let down. "Between taking care of Camille and Josie, I can't possibly put in the fifty-hour workweek everyone else is. How am I supposed to do this?"

I sat down in the sand, waiting for my answer, but all I could hear in my mind was me telling myself to stop feeling sorry for myself, to pick up myself and continue.

People need you. Josie needs you more than ever with her teenage years coming up. You can't allow yourself to wallow in self-pity.

"You can't be pitiful and powerful at the same time," I mumbled, repeating my dad's old mantra. He used to say this to me when I came home from baseball, and we lost or when I got a bad grade, which was pretty often since I wasn't a very strong student and I hated school.

My dad never lost confidence in me, though. He knew I'd amount to something one day. He kept telling me that there was a path for me, one that no one else could walk and that once I found what God's plan for me was, what my talent was, I'd be unstoppable. I thought I had found it when I became a detective. Fowler was right. I had been the one who had solved the most cases in the entire department. Even now, when it had been three years since I had solved anything, I was still ahead of the others. It was my path; it was what I was supposed to do.

Why did I keep running into so much resistance, then?

"Why aren't you making it easier on me if I'm doing what you want?" I asked toward the sky.

I sighed and kept looking at the blue sky above. My dad had been a pastor all my life, and it had seemed so much easier for him. It was like he had this connection with God that I never seemed to be able to find. My dad believed it was because I was still carrying so much anger in me from the time my sister, Reese, was raped when we were teenagers. And he was right about that. I didn't understand why it had to happen and why God didn't protect her. He knew how it was going to ruin her life. Was that his plan for her?

I shook my head. No, I couldn't think like that. I was raised to believe in a good God, and I chose to do so, even with the bad things that happen, even when I didn't understand why Camille had to end up like she did.

My phone vibrated in my pocket, and I looked at the display. It was a text from Fowler. It contained an address and a message:

BE THERE AT 7 AM. BE LATE AND YOU'RE OUT.

I sighed and put the phone back in my pocket, then put my helmet back on.

"If that's how you want to play it, God, then so be it. I'll be a good boy and do as I'm told, but I am not gonna be happy about it. Just saying."

Chapter 12

SHE HAD WORKED the evening shift and didn't come home until after midnight. Jean felt exhausted as she parked her old Toyota on the street outside of her townhouse. She sighed and looked at her neighbor's house. The lights were out in all the windows.

Jean grabbed her purse, got out, then walked up toward her porch when a sound startled her.

"Hello?"

A face peeked out. It was Harry. He was sitting on the porch swing and waved at her. Jean smiled gently and casually waved back. The sight of him made her heart skip a beat.

"Hi there, neighbor," Harry said.

"Why are you still up?" she asked, even though she knew perfectly well why. Harry hadn't slept much since Camille's overdose.

"Thought I'd enjoy the nice evening outside," he said. "Lots of stars out tonight."

She looked up. "Sure are. How's Camille?"

Jean always felt a pinch in her stomach when mentioning her name. Camille and Jean had been best friends. They had hung out almost every day, going to lunch, drinking coffee, and yet she had no idea the girl was doing drugs again. It filled her with such a deep sense of guilt every time she thought about it, especially when she saw how much Harry and Josie were struggling. If only she had known. She was a nurse for crying out loud. She knew what to look for. Were there signs she had missed? Anything different in the way Camille acted or spoke? Jean had thought about it over and over again, yet found nothing she could put her finger on.

Camille had been the same in the days leading up to it. Heck, Jean had even spoken to her that same morning before it happened. She had given her those chairs back that she had borrowed for her party a few weeks before. They had a cup of coffee and a couple of donuts that Jean had brought. They talked about Harry and how Camille was worried about his job getting him killed one day, and how tough it was to be the wife of a detective. She feared she might lose him one day, and Josie would have no father. Jean remembered thinking her fear seemed more consuming than usual and wondering if there was a real threat to Harry's life.

Did that drive her back to the drugs? The fear?

No. Camille was happy. She loved her life and her family. It made no sense that she'd suddenly start doing drugs again.

At least not to Jean.

"She's good," Harry said.

Jean could tell he was trying to sound cheerful as usual. He didn't like that she worried.

"She's sleeping," he continued. "I sat by her side all evening after Josie went to bed. I just snuck out half an hour ago. How was your day?"

She shrugged. "Busy as usual when working in the ER. Lots of patients coming down with the flu."

"It is the season," he said with that handsome smile of his. Harry was one big chunk of man, but handsome as the devil. No one could resist that smile of his, least of all, Jean.

But it could never be them. Not in a million years. He was still married, and Jean was Camille's best friend.

It could never happen. Ever.

"Anyway, I should…" She pointed at her house with her thumb.

"Yeah, me too," he said. "I have work to do early in the morning, at seven a.m. New assignment from the boss. My dad will be over to eat breakfast with Josie and make sure she gets to school on time."

"Then, as your nurse, I'll recommend you hit the sack," she said with a chuckle.

Keys in her hand and purse slung over her shoulder, she walked up to the steps leading to her house, sensing how his stare followed her every move. As she was about to walk up, she turned to look at him, then smiled.

"I'll take care of Camille tomorrow morning. You just worry about your big case or whatever it is you're doing."

He exhaled. "I hoped you'd say that. You're a lifesaver, Jean."

She nodded. It didn't feel like much, not since she was unable to save her own best friend's life.

"Goodnight," Harry said.

She reached her door, then sent him one last glance. He had already left the porch and was walking inside the house as she whispered with longing in her voice:

"Goodnight, Harry Handsome."

Chapter 13

I DROVE up the long driveway to the mansion situated on five acres of oceanfront land and walked up to the front entrance at precisely seven a.m. I wasn't going to give Fowler the pleasure of firing me for being late. While waiting for someone to open the front door of the Spanish mansion, I took a quick glance around me and saw the tennis court located in the corner of the lot.

As the wooden door slid open, I showed the woman behind the door my badge. "Detective Hunter, Miami PD. I believe I am expected."

The small—very beautiful—woman mumbled something in a foreign language, then showed me inside, where a tall blonde woman in a tan dress greeted me.

"Mrs. Covington?" I said. "I'm Detective Hunter from Miami PD. I'm here for the protection of your son."

The woman nodded. She seemed like she was in distress. "Yes, yes, of course," she said. "Please, come on in."

"I just need to know a little more about William's schedule this week," I said, "so I can make sure to keep him safe."

She gave me a half-smile. "He has school from nine to three-thirty every day. He has tennis lessons here at the house on Tuesdays and Thursdays from four till six. His teacher comes here to train him. On the weekends, he usually goes golfing or boating with his friends. He also practices his violin on Wednesdays with a private teacher. She comes here."

I was writing notes on my notepad. "So, he basically only leaves the house to go to school and on the weekends?"

"Yes."

I nodded. That sounded like a pretty easy task. She gave me a look. "So, is there…is there anything we need to do? I understand that you believe there's a threat to him? Do we need to keep him home while this is going on?"

I exhaled and ran a hand through my hair. "I think you should just go on the way you usually do. We don't really know exactly what is going on, or whether your son is in danger or not, but we do know that several other kids from his school were killed, and they were all witnesses in the Lockwood case."

Mrs. Covington's lips tightened. "Oh…that. Awful story. I'm glad the judge realized my boy had nothing to do with it."

I stared at her, scrutinizing her, then realized she fully believed in her son's innocence. Of course, she did. She was his mother. She had to believe it, right? How else could you go on after something like that? How would you ever be able to look your son in the eyes again, knowing he had raped someone?

Mrs. Covington's face lit up as someone approached us, coming down the stairs. I recognized him from the pictures in Fowler's office. He hadn't changed much since they were taken. His light brown hair fell into his face as he walked, and he ran a hand through it to move it.

"William," his mother said as she grabbed his arm and pulled him toward me. The boy let her, probably because I was there, then removed his arm from her grip.

"Meet Detective Hunter from Miami PD," she said. "He'll be protecting you over the next few days, you know…like we discussed. After what happened to…"

The mother received a look from her son, and she stopped talking. William reached out his hand and looked into my eyes while shaking my hand.

"Detective Hunter, nice to meet you."

Shaking his hand made my skin crawl, thinking about how those same hands had touched and abused Lucy Lockwood. I was towering above him with my six-foot-eight to his five-foot-eleven. I kept thinking about Reese and how her rapist had gotten away with it, too, how she had to go to school and see him every day, laughing at her. The thought made me want to beat this kid up right here and now.

"We're glad you're here, Detective," Mrs. Covington said. "It's an awful ordeal with what happened to those kids. William knows them from school and…well…"

"Mom," William said, annoyed. "I'm capable of taking care of myself. I barely knew those kids."

"But William, if there's a killer…if that girl is out there killing…"

He gave her a look. "Mom, stop it, will you? You're being paranoid. I can easily handle some girl."

"But…but William…"

"Stop it, Mom."

William hissed the last part at his mother.

"Anyway," I said, feeling uncomfortable. It felt like I had landed in the middle of something I had no desire to become a part of. "I'm just going to be parked out on the street, so if you see anything or hear anything, then…" I handed her my card. "My cell phone number is here, or you can just come out to talk to me. I'll be staying close to William all day, and I'll wait outside of his school as well."

Mrs. Covington walked me to the door and held it for me. "Thank you, Detective. We appreciate it immensely."

I stopped as I reached the door. "Where is Mr. Covington?"

"He…he's not here."

I stared at her as her eyes avoided mine. "As in he doesn't live here anymore?"

She lifted her eyes, and they met mine. "Yes. He moved out. We're separated."

"I am sorry to hear that."

"Don't be," William said from behind her. Mrs. Covington turned to give him a look. William sent her a sly smile, the very same one I recognized from the photos.

"Don't mind him," she said, addressed to me. "He's angry at us for separating. He blames his father."

"Are there any siblings, or is William your only child?" I asked. "For safety reasons, I need to know how many people are in the household."

She shook her head. "No. There's just William and me here. And Dalisay, of course, the woman who let you in. She takes care of us."

Chapter 14

WHEN SHE TOLD people her name was Sophia, they usually assumed it was because of her Spanish heritage, because of her brown skin, but it wasn't. Sophia was half Jamaican and half German. Her parents had both worked on a cruise ship and ended up loving Miami so much—especially because of the melting pot of diversity that it has—they finally settled there and became naturalized. Today, her dad had his own tech company while her mother ran a rather successful investment company. She was one of the only moms in Sophia's friend group who worked, and that made Sophia proud. She, too, was going to make something of herself one day.

At least that was what she had always told herself while growing up. Now, as she was sitting in class, staring at William Covington's neck in front of her, she wasn't sure she'd even make it that far.

Four of the seats in her math class were empty—four seats where Georgiana, Katelyn, Sandra, and Martina usually sat. Sophia couldn't stop staring at the empty chairs, feeling the chill run down her spine.

Murdered, they had said on TV. *Brutally assassinated.*

The thought made the hairs on Sophia's neck stand up. She, too, was supposed to have gone with her friends on that boat that night, only she had decided not to at the last minute because she had to get up early the next day.

There was a fifth victim; they had also said on TV. Lisa Turner. She had been found the week before in a dumpster, stabbed to death. Back then, they had all believed she had met her killer coincidentally…that she was walking the streets when she met her attacker, that it was some drug addict or maybe a crazy homeless person. It had been terrible, yes, awful, of course, but at least it didn't mean anyone else was in danger. With the four others gone too, that had all changed. She couldn't help feeling this killer was making his way through her entire friend group. It didn't seem possible that it was a coincidence anymore.

And you know perfectly well why, don't you?

Sophia trembled again and looked away from the empty chairs, then shook her head. She almost didn't come to school this morning, but then realized it was no use. She had to go on as usual, even though she was beyond terrified.

The police had sent someone to her house and spoken to her parents. They had told them to make sure Sophia was at home from nine p.m. until six a.m. They were also going to have a patrol car drive up and down the street several times a day and have one outside of the school. That made her ease up slightly, but it didn't really make her feel comfortable. Somehow, she had a feeling this killer would get to her, no matter how many police surrounded her.

It was only a matter of time.

The bell rang, and Sophia gathered her things, then grabbed her backpack, hurrying out of the classroom before William could talk to her.

"Sophia," his voice sounded behind her.

She stopped in her tracks and closed her eyes briefly. She had hoped to avoid this.

Sophia turned to look at him as he approached her, books under his arm. He was so devilishly handsome; it was unbearable.

"Did the police come to your house?" he asked.

She looked around to make sure no one could listen in on their conversation, then nodded.

"Yes. And you?"

"They're guarding me all day. Some burned-out detective who doesn't even try to hide that he'd rather see me dead and couldn't care less. He looked like a drunk with a big shiner and everything."

"It's awful…what happened to the others."

"I think it's Lucy," he said.

Sophia stared at him with her eyes wide. Thinking about Lucy didn't make her feel good. William shrugged as they walked into the hallway toward their next class.

"I think she might be crazy enough, don't you?" he continued.

"I don't…know."

"She's been gone for eight months now," he said.

"So, you're thinking she's back with a vengeance?"

William smiled nervously. "Something like that. She didn't get what she wanted in the first place when the judge denied her case. But she's not done yet. This could be her next step."

Sophia stopped at her locker and looked up at William and into his deep blue eyes. He smiled gently, then placed his hands on both of her upper arms, his glare piercing into her eyes. It made her feel uncomfortable, but she couldn't pull away. He was holding her too tightly.

"We can't let her win. Do you hear me?"

He spat the words out, hissing at her angrily. She shook her head while his hands were hurting her arms, and she was squirming in pain.

"Of course not, William, of course not."

He kept staring into her eyes while crushing her arms with his touch until tears sprang to her eyes. His nostrils were flaring like he was almost enjoying it when finally, his smile returned, and he eased up on her.

"Good," he said and let go. He ran a hand through his hair and exhaled, satisfied. He grabbed her chin and lifted her face upward to make sure he had her full attention. Looking into his eyes made her sick to her stomach.

"We agree, then. We've got to stick together in this."

"Of course," she said, feeling her sore arms. As he turned

around on his heel and left, she ran to the bathroom and into a stall where she closed the door. She rolled up the sleeves on her shirt and looked at the huge purple bruises he had left there where his hands had held her tight. She sat down on the toilet, hid her face between her hands, and began to cry, shaking her head.

"What have I done? What have I done?"

Chapter 15

I SPENT the day in one of the police department's minivans that we used for stakeouts. It was equipped with a computer that was hooked up to our system back at the station, so it was possible to work while spending hours and hours staking someone out.

I spent my time doing a little research. I knew it wasn't my case, but it couldn't hurt anything to take a look, could it?

Fact was, I couldn't stop thinking about this girl, Lucy Lockwood, the girl that had been raped and the one Fowler believed might be killing her old friends. I kept thinking about my sister, then wondering, if that had been her, would she have been able to kill because of what happened to her?

Maybe.

I, for one, wanted to kill the guy back then. I did track him down and beat him up on the street of his neighborhood a few weeks after it happened—nothing serious, just enough for him to feel it for a couple of weeks afterward and be reminded that I was watching him. But killing him? And the people who had witnessed it?

It was hard to tell. The motive was there; I'd give Fowler that much. But in my book, it sounded more like something her father might attempt.

Had they had a chance to talk to him yet?

I opened the case file and read through parts of it, skipping the pictures from the boat since I had seen them thoroughly, and I had a pretty good photographic memory, which wasn't always a good thing, especially not when seeing stuff like that. I couldn't get the pictures out of my mind again once they got in there. They could haunt me for months…maybe even years.

I read the father's statement that Morales and his team had taken the day before. Mr. Lockwood had been out of town all weekend, on a business trip and had all the evidence they needed, including an itinerary and hotel receipts. When asked about the group of teenagers, if he knew any of them, he said that, yes, he knew they were all witnesses to what happened to his daughter, and that it was a terrible thing that they had died. Especially for him. He was still working with the DA to get them to reopen the case, and now his list of possible witnesses was dwindling. He had no interest in seeing them dead. It made no sense for him to kill any of them.

He made a good point, I decided. If there was anyone he wanted dead, it was the boy. Why was William still alive?

I shook my head, feeling a little confused when I received a text from Josie.

I GOT A 98 ON MY MATH TEST.

The message was followed by a sad face, telling me she had hoped for more. I chuckled at my overachieving daughter and texted her back.

GOOD JOB, SWEETIE.

I WANTED 100 THO. I MADE ONE MISTAKE. ONE.

98 IS PERFECTLY FINE, I wrote back.

I couldn't help laughing at my daughter, yet hoping she'd never have bigger problems than that.

I bit my lip when thinking about how hard she pushed herself and that she had done so ever since her mother got sick. She had always done well in school before that, but when her mother overdosed, she took it to a new level. Was she trying to prove something? Was she trying to distance herself from the life her mother had?

Whatever it was, I just prayed that she wouldn't burn out.

I returned to the computer, then read through some more testimonies while the hours passed in front of the school. I opened the latest autopsy report that had come in just an hour earlier and looked through it. Then, I stopped. I reread something again and again, while images and sentences rushed through my mind.

I grabbed my phone and called the Medical Examiner's Office and my old friend Emilia Lopez.

Chapter 16

"WELL, hello there, stranger, long time no see. What's it been, two years?" Emilia said as she picked up the phone.

I exhaled when hearing her voice. It brought back a lot of memories. Emilia had always been a close colleague of mine, always ready to help me with my cases and push me ahead in the line when I needed it. It had been a while, yes, because I hadn't been involved in much detective work over the past couple of years.

"What can I help you with?"

"You found a chess piece on the boat?" I asked.

"Well, I didn't; the techs at the scene did," Emilia said. "But, yes. They found a black rook on the deck of the boat. I didn't know it was your case? I thought Morales and his team had it?"

I cleared my throat and didn't answer. "But there was a chess piece in the pocket of the girl found in the dumpster too, right?"

Emilia exhaled. "Yes, a pawn. We found no fingerprints or any DNA on either of them, though."

"What about the one from the boat. Did you find any trace of neoprene from a wet suit?"

"Yes, as a matter of fact, we did."

I leaned back my head in the car, leaning it against the neck rest while pondering over this. It fit well with my theory that the killer came from the ocean. If the killer had been a diver, swimming to the boat like it was my theory, he'd be wearing a wetsuit. At this time of year, he'd have to. The ocean was warm in Florida, but this was January. This was still puzzling me. Did he come by his own boat? The boat with the girls was too far out for someone just to swim there.

"The killer leaves these chess pieces, but why?" I asked. It wasn't really for her as much as it was for me.

Was there a message to it? It had to have some significance, something this killer was trying to tell us.

Emilia chuckled. "That's your department, Detective."

"Of course. Thanks for the update; I'll leave you to your work."

"How's Camille," she said as I was about to hang up. "And Josie? How's she holding up?"

"She's okay, I think. Hanging in there. Camille is the same."

"I'm so sorry to hear that, Harry," Emilia said. "You know how I loved Camille."

"We all did," I said with an exhale. "We all did."

"Well, it's good to have you back, Hunter," Emilia said. "We missed you; well, I did. I missed you."

I hung up and stared at the display on my phone of an old photo of Camille and Josie that I used as a background. It was taken four years ago on our trip to New York…the last trip we had taken together as a family. I touched her face gently with my finger, letting it run down her smooth features. It hurt to know she would never look at me the way she did in this picture again. I would never get to see her with the love in her eyes that was so familiar.

I miss being the one you love.

I stared at my one true love, missing her, then couldn't stop thinking about Lucy Lockwood. I lifted my glance and looked into the street, then realized I didn't buy into the theory that Lucy had come back to kill everyone involved in her rape. But if she wasn't the killer, then it opened up a whole other can of worms. She could be another victim. Or she could be in hiding because she knew who the killer was.

No matter what, I had to find her, fast, before any more kids turned up dead.

I looked at the school in front of me, then started up the minivan. I knew I was supposed to stay and watch William Covington. But there were still four hours till school was out. That left me plenty of time to get back here in time for when the bell rang.

No one would even notice I had been gone.

Chapter 17

VALENTINA LOCKWOOD'S hands were shaking as she served me coffee. She was a stunning woman in her mid-thirties, originally from Colombia, she told me.

"The detective isn't interested in knowing where you're from," her husband, Robert Lockwood, snapped.

Valentina gave him a look, then shook her head.

"No, of course not. I don't know why I said that."

"Anything might turn out to be useful," I said, addressed to her. "Let me be the judge of what is important and what is not."

"What is this regarding?" Robert Lockwood asked. "I had a couple of your colleagues here yesterday and told them I was out of town when those kids were killed. I had just gotten back. Why are you here again?"

I sipped the coffee. It tasted heavenly.

"This is really good coffee," I said.

Valentina smiled nervously. "Colombian. My mother sends the beans every now and then, whenever she can make it to the post office. Her legs aren't what they used to be."

I smiled, turning up the charm to make her feel better about herself and comfortable in my presence. She was obviously broken.

"Well, it's the best coffee I've had in a very long time; thank you for that."

Mr. Lockwood put his cup down hard, causing my cup to jump. "Why are you here? Could we get to the point? I have a busy schedule, and I already told you people everything I know."

"I'm sorry," I said. "I just…well, when I smelled that coffee, I had to ask for a cup. No, I'm not here to talk about the teenagers on the boat. I'm here because I want to find your daughter."

Mrs. Lockwood's eyes grew wide. "Find her…but I thought you stopped the search; it has been so long?"

I exhaled and nodded. "I know. I know. It has been a long time. But she is still a missing teenager and…"

"They think she's killing them," Robert Lockwood said with a snort. "That's the only reason he's here."

Valentina wrinkled her forehead. "They do what?"

"They think Lucy is back and that she's killing the kids from that night because she didn't get that Covington boy to pay for…what he did. Because they wouldn't speak up against him."

"What? I don't understand?" Valentina said. "They think…you think that my daughter…is…is…"

"Of course, they do," Robert continued. "They think either I did it or she did. It's pretty obvious…as revenge."

"I don't," I said, swallowing yet another sip of that delicious warm substance that made my taste buds dance.

"Excuse me?" Robert said.

"I said, I don't. I can't talk for my police department, but I can tell you that I don't believe your daughter is killing anyone. Why would she kill those people who are her only witnesses to the crime committed against her?"

Robert stared at me, surprised.

"I want to find your daughter, so we can prove that it wasn't her. But I am going to need your help."

The two of them looked at one another. Tears sprang to Valentina's eyes. She reached over to grab her husband's hand.

"You'll have to excuse us," Robert said, "if we find this a little hard to believe…that you are here to help. We've been met only with suspicion from the police department ever since we found our daughter…in the sand, beaten and…"

"Raped," I said, swallowing a knot growing in my throat, remembering how hard it was for my parents to say the word when it was Reese, how deeply it destroyed their faith in the justice system and the world. That was the only time I found my dad on the verge of losing his faith in God.

He nodded, his eyes avoiding mine as they grew red-rimmed. "Yes, that. They never seemed to believe her story. They kept telling her she had been flirting with the boy, that they believed she wanted it to happen, but then she regretted it afterward when thinking about what her parents might say when they found out. They even had the audacity to tell her that she dressed provocatively and sexy to lure him in. No matter how much we protested, they kept on and on about how she had made the whole thing up, that they couldn't find any evidence that she was raped. What about the bruises? I asked them. Still, the judge dismissed it because none of the witnesses dared to stand up for our Lucy. They are terrified of the kid, you know? That's why."

"They're terrified of William Covington?" I asked.

Robert nodded and looked away for a brief second, then wiped his eyes with the palms of his hands.

"It's true," Valentina added. "All the kids are scared of him. He's been bullying them since middle school. No one ever dares to say anything. Lucy told me about him before. He once even made some guy burn himself with cigarettes all over his face, threatening to reveal to the rest of the school that he was gay. In middle school, he cut off a girl's hair and shaved her head in the bathroom because she had told on him to the dean, telling him that William vaped in the bathroom. He never got in trouble, though, because he threatened the dean that if he told his parents, he'd reveal that the dean had an affair with one of the teachers. All the teachers are terrified of him too. No one will ever dare to stand up to him."

I wrote it all down on my notepad while thinking about the look William had given his mother at the house. She, too, seemed nervous around him, and slightly anxious.

"Mr. and Mrs. Lockwood," I said and lifted my eyes to look first him in the eyes, then her. "I need you to be completely honest with me. Do you have any idea where Lucy might be?"

They both shook their heads.

"We don't," she said. "We haven't seen her since August fourteenth. She was at home when the call came from our lawyer. The judge had dismissed the case, he said. We sat down and talked to her about it. She ran to her room, and we let her stay up there for a few hours, crying it out while discussing what we wanted to do next. Robert said he'd appeal the decision and try to get the DA to reopen the case. We even talked about moving away. For months, she had to go to school every day and see her rapist there, laughing in her face, tormenting her while she could do nothing. We talked about signing her up for a boarding school to get her out of here, but we didn't want him to win, you know? We wanted to see him behind bars where he belongs for everything he's done, all the people he has tormented."

Valentina stopped and wiped her nose on a napkin. Her husband took over.

"When we went up to her room later that night, she wasn't there. Her bag was gone, and so were some of her clothes. We realized she had run away, but still hoped and prayed she'd come back soon."

"Did she have any money? A phone?"

"She had taken some cash from my drawer," Valentina said. "But it can't have been more than maybe a thousand dollars."

"A teenager can get pretty far for less," I said. "Does she have any relatives she might have gone to see? Or old friends?"

"They're all around here, and we've called each and every one," Robert said. "I can give you the list we gave the police back then."

"Yes, please, and her phone? Did she take it?"

"She left her phone here," Robert said. "In her room."

"Can I see it?" I asked.

"They already went through it when we reported her missing," he said. "They went through all her stuff, but found nothing."

I nodded. "I know, but it never hurts to take a second look. Also, if she had a computer, I'd like to take a look at that as well, if you don't mind."

Valentina nodded at her husband, and he disappeared upstairs while I finished my coffee. Robert came back with an iPhone in his hand and a laptop under his arm. He handed me both.

"I'll have both things back to you as soon as I'm done with them," I said.

"Please," Valentina said and grabbed my hands between hers. "Please, take your time with it. Just help us find our girl. She's a good girl; you must know this, Detective. She truly is; she does volunteer work at the animal shelter, she gets straight A's, she's compassionate toward her friends and would go through fire for them. She would never hurt anyone, never. She must be so scared right now. Please, just find her."

I nodded, looking at them both. I knew better than to promise them anything, yet I really wanted to. If this had been my Josie, I don't know what I would have done. First, the rape and then this? It was almost too much for one family to take.

"I will do everything in my power," I said. "I can promise you that much."

Chapter 18

A WEARY MAN with a cigarette dangling from his lips answered the door of the second-floor apartment. I was back in Overtown and knew the eyes staring back at me a little better than I was proud of.

"Shoot," the guy said, trying to close the door in my face. I put my foot in it to block it, then pushed the door open so brutally it knocked into the guy's face.

"Ouch!" he yelled and stumbled backward.

I walked inside and closed the door behind me. The guy was known as T-Bone because his body resembled one.

"I haven't done anything," T-Bone said, touching his nose and wiping away the blood. "I've been a good boy."

"I'm sure you have," I said and picked him up from the floor, then dragged him to his ripped leather couch. I sat in a recliner next to it, then handed him a tissue to wipe the blood away.

"I'm serious," he said. "I stayed out of trouble like you told me to. No drugs. You can search the entire place; you won't find any."

"I'm not here for that," I said. "I need your help with something."

T-Bone's face lit up. "Oh, really? You need my help now, do ya? How the tables have turned, huh? What's in it for me?"

"Honor and glory," I said and slapped him over the head. "What do you mean, what's in it for me?"

He made the international sign for money, and I exhaled, knowing it would come. "There'll be a reward," I said. I had talked about this with the Lockwoods when leaving, and they had agreed to pay one if it led to finding their daughter. "It could be quite substantial, actually. The girl I need you to find for me has some very wealthy parents."

That did the trick. I could see the change in T-Bone's eyes. Money always did the trick. It was disgusting. But I needed this guy. He knew every corner of town and every face of the criminal world. He knew what pedophiles lived under which bridge and what mobsters to stay clear of if you wanted to keep living. If the girl were living on the streets, he'd know or be able to find out.

I grabbed my phone and found a picture of her. "This girl. Have you seen her?"

He looked at the picture, then sniffled. "Pretty girl. Wouldn't last long on the streets, though." He handed me back the phone. "Haven't seen her, I'm afraid. But send me the pic and I'll see what I can find. I know the guys down by the port would love to get their hands on a girl like that."

I exhaled, knowing he was talking about the human traffickers. Trafficking was a huge problem in my town and a multimillion-dollar business. Six times last year, smugglers had been caught when trying to bring in girls through the port illegally, and we only saw the tip of the iceberg. Thirty-six arrests had been made last year, but there were more and more traffickers coming too, knowing there was a lot more money being made in trafficking than most other crimes these days. If they had gotten their nasty hands on Lucy, she could be anywhere in the country by now.

I sent him the picture and waited for him to receive it.

"I'll ask around," he said, lighting up another cigarette. "But it better be worth it."

"That's all I'm asking."

Chapter 19

I DROVE THROUGH TOWN, frequenting several of my other informers, spreading the word about Lucy Lockwood and hoping to get some information or at least one sighting of her, but I had no such luck. I also visited her best friend's house and talked to her mother, then visited the shelter where she volunteered and asked around to see if anyone was close to Lucy or might know anything about where she might be hiding. So far, all I got were positive statements when asking about her. Lucy was a well-liked girl, and everyone that knew her kept referring to her as one of the good girls. The same went for all five of the girls that had been murdered. They were straight-A students, members of the Bible club, debate club, or chorus, all taking part in the community, all doing volunteer work outside of school, and being just plain good girls.

I drove to South Beach and into an alley where I parked and took the back entrance into a building. I ran the three stories up and knocked on the door to an apartment.

A woman opened the door, her dreadlocks pulled back and held by a hair tie. She was wearing baggy harem pants and a small crop top.

"Hunter? What brings you here?"

"Can I come in?"

She looked like she had to think it over for a few seconds, then agreed. Her name was Alvita or The Plague, as they called her in the cyber world. I just called her Al. Al was a former CIA hacker who had turned her back on the world after seeing what it was capable of. Now, she hid in this small apartment where no one would find her. Except for me, that was since I had known her for years and used her to do the things our own IT department couldn't do fast enough or weren't skilled enough to do.

"What's up?"

"I need your help," I said.

"I kind of figured that," she said with a grin.

I handed her the computer and the phone. "Techs have been through it all, but I need you to dig deeper, do your magic. This girl is missing, and she needs to be found, asap. Can you do that for me?"

She shrugged and placed the computer on the desk. "Give me the rest of the day. I'll be in touch."

I left her apartment, then ran down the stairs when realizing how late it was. I only had half an hour to get back to the school in time. It was a fifteen-minute drive if there was no traffic, which only happened in my dreams. I jumped into the minivan, closed the door, and stepped on the accelerator, pulling into the street. I hadn't made it far when I spotted a black car coming up behind me. I hadn't noticed it before, but now that it was getting so close, I suddenly saw it very clearly.

"What the heck?" I mumbled. The black Hyundai drove very close to me, pressuring me to drive faster.

"Go around me if you're in such a hurry, you idiot," I yelled at the rearview mirror. The windows on the black Hyundai were tinted, so I couldn't see a face behind the windshield.

Finally, it drove up on my side, accelerating till it was right next to me. I tried to see the driver but couldn't see a face. Then, as I expected it to drive past me, it turned toward me instead, making a sudden move sideways, slamming into my van's front end, causing my minivan to drive off the road. I bumped into the grass but managed to regain control of it just when the Hyundai took up the chase and drove into the side of my van, forcing me to run into the guardrail. As my minivan came to a sudden halt, I flew forward and hit my head hard on the steering wheel.

Chapter 20

I MUST HAVE BEEN out for a few minutes because once I came to, the Hyundai was long gone. I was all alone on the side of the road, my head pounding like crazy.

What the heck was that? Who was that?

Someone sending you a message.

I swallowed, trying to think straight, blinking my eyes to better focus, and looked at my phone. I was more than late now. There was no way I'd be able to make it back to the school in time. I looked at my bruise in the mirror. My forehead was slowly turning purple. My face wasn't a pretty sight.

Jean's gonna yell at me.

I turned the key and was happy to realize that the minivan could start again. The front was pushed in, and the sides severely dented. It made a loud rattling sound that couldn't be healthy when I drove it, but other than that, it was fine. It could still take me places, and that was good enough for me. I didn't even want to try and think about what to tell them at the station once I handed it back. How was I going to explain this to Fowler? Well, I didn't have to worry about that yet. I had the minivan for the time I needed it to protect William. Then I'd make up some story if I had to.

I drove carefully, staying just above the speed limit, then reached the school and stopped the minivan outside. I looked at my watch and realized the bell had rung at least fifteen minutes ago.

"Shoot," I said and looked around to see if I could spot William. Most of the kids had already left, and William's Land Rover wasn't in the spot it had been when we arrived this morning. He had already left.

I shrugged, then drove back to his parents' house and parked on the street outside. I exhaled, then looked at my forehead again and cursed the long-gone Hyundai. If only I had seen the face of the driver or seen the license plate when it took off. But I didn't. I had no way of identifying the car.

I opened my phone and tapped on it, checking my emails, then received a text from Josie, who had come home from school. It was our deal that she texted me as soon as she got back, so I knew she was home and safe. I wasn't really calm till I received those words from her:

HOME.

I answered with a thumbs up. She texted me back.

MOM'S ASLEEP. JEAN IS HERE. SHE FED HER BEFORE SHE FELL ASLEEP. SHE'S COOKING FOR US TONIGHT.

I felt my mouth water. Jean was an excellent cook. She was probably working the night shift tonight, which was my luck. I was already looking forward to it. Fowler had told me I only had to stay at the house till six. After that, he'd have a couple of patrols drive by the street at night. The Covingtons' house had security alarms and cameras, so they'd know if anyone tried to break in.

I, for one, couldn't wait to call it a day.

Once I had been out there for about an hour, the gate opened, and Mrs. Covington stepped out, tapping along on her black high heels. She approached me, looking distressed. I rolled down the window as I realized she was there to talk to me.

"What's wrong?" I asked.

"Where's William?"

My eyes grew wide.

"He's not at the house?"

She shook her head. "No. He never came home from school. I thought you were keeping an eye on him; wasn't that what you were supposed to do?"

I swallowed, feeling an outbreak of cold sweat all over my body. This wasn't good. Fowler would kill me if he found out. No, worse than that, he'd fire me, and then how would I pay the bills?

"He might have gone to the country club for a round of golf or just be hanging out at the restaurant with his friends," she said. "He used to do that a lot. Maybe he's with his friend, Krueger. I'll text you his address and number."

"Okay. I'll go look for him," I said and started up the coughing minivan.

Chapter 21

OF COURSE, the boy was nowhere near the country club, nor was he with this Krueger fellow, and his friend hadn't seen him since sixth period, he said. I should have known it wasn't going to be that easy. I felt like an idiot for driving across town looking for this boy, this eighteen-year-old kid who probably was just hanging out with his friends somewhere, maybe picking up girls. I felt ridiculous like I had suddenly become a babysitter for some affluent wealthy kid, who, by the way, had raped a girl and gotten away with it.

But it was my job right now, and I had to stick with it. I simply had to.

"Come on, William; where are you?" I mumbled as I drove up the street back toward the school. I kept calling the boy's cell, but he wasn't answering. After the twelfth try, I threw my phone on the seat next to me, growling. As I drove past a house next to the school, I suddenly spotted William's Land Rover in the driveway. I hit the brakes so hard I almost hit my head a second time when the minivan stopped abruptly.

I panted agitatedly, then looked out the window and spotted William standing in the driveway, talking to someone. The two of them were obviously in some sort of dispute. The guy was older, an adult. I stayed in my van for a little longer, observing them. William was approaching the guy, and it was very easy to tell that the guy was terrified of him. William had that grin on his face, that sly smile. He reached out toward the guy like he wanted to caress his face when instead, he smacked him across the face. The guy fell backward, as surprised as I was.

"What the heck?"

William was holding something in his hand, and as I opened the car door and was about to jump out, I heard him tell the guy to pull up his shirt. The guy did it, and William, grinning, placed a stun gun on the man's skin. The man screamed in pain as the gun sent waves of shock through his body.

"HEY!" I yelled and began running up the driveway. But as I did, William didn't even look at me. I could hear the sound of the stun gun electrical charge against the man's skin.

"STOP, you bastard!" I yelled and felt for the gun in my holster, taking the grip in my hand, ready to pull it should it be necessary. "What do you think you're doing?"

As he heard me yell, he turned his head to look at me, still continuing to stun the man, then he laughed.

I pulled out my gun. "William, stop that right now!"

William didn't move. He stared at me, still holding the stun gun in his hand, still laughing at me like he enjoyed it even more with me watching him.

"William! Step away from that man right now."

He pulled the gun away, then looked at the man once more, lifting his fist, pretending like he was going to hit him before finally pulling away.

"If it isn't Detective Hunter," he said, walking toward me, the look of a madman in his eyes.

"Stop right there," I said.

That made him laugh again. "Or what? You'll shoot?"

"If I have to."

He kept walking toward me, smiling widely. "But you'd never do that, would you, Detective? Because you are here to protect me. That's your job; isn't it?"

"Not when you're hurting people, William. I'll have to take you in…"

"For what? Mr. James here doesn't want any trouble; do you?"

The man shook his head without looking at either of us. "N-no, sir. No trouble."

"See? No witness, no accusations, no case. You're wasting everyone's time here, Detective."

"I saw you do it."

"So? If the victim won't say anything, I hardly think you have a case. Besides, we wouldn't want your boss to know that you weren't where you were supposed to be today; would we? It wouldn't be much fun if he found out that you left your post; would it?"

My hand was wrapped tight around the grip of the gun, my knuckles turning white. I wanted to hurt him so badly. My pulse was sky high, and my hand holding the gun was shaking with anger.

William smiled and walked up to me, then placed a hand on my shoulder. "I didn't think so."

Chapter 22

"I'M TELLING YOU, Jean, it's hard to protect a kid when you want to strangle him yourself."

I grabbed the spoon and served myself a second round of spaghetti and meatballs. Jean made the best food in the world…the smell alone was heavenly.

"Why do you have to protect him?" Josie asked.

I shrugged. "It's my job."

"I thought you were a detective," Josie said.

I exhaled. "I thought so too."

"Sometimes, you have to do stuff you don't really want to," Jean said. "Just like at my job. There's a lot of stuff I don't enjoy doing, but I have to. I bet there's also a lot of homework you don't want to do."

Josie nodded, then rose to her feet with her plate between her hands. "Speaking of, I have homework to do."

She gave me a kiss, then rushed up the stairs. My dad had come over to eat too. Jean had invited him over as she usually did when cooking for us, and now he left the table and walked to the living room, where he sat in a recliner and turned on the TV. He closed his eyes briefly and grunted with satisfaction. He had gotten old over the past few years since my mom died last year. Seeing him alone broke my heart. Those two had been inseparable.

Jean smiled and leaned over the table while I finished my plate. I had told her everything about the case and William when I got back while she was still in the kitchen, cooking. I had to. She took one look at my forehead and demanded to know what I had been up to.

"I just hope I can find Lucy," I said with a sigh. I patted my very full stomach. "I fear she might be in trouble. I don't like that she has been missing for this long."

"I'm sure her parents are completely devastated," Jean said. "I can't imagine going through first her being raped and then…"

I nodded. "It makes me so mad to think about that poor girl being dragged through all the suspicion when she reported the rape to the police. It makes me want to yell at my colleagues. What the heck are they thinking, telling her she is at fault? Who does that? And now this guy is just running around, harassing people and acting like a bully. I can't believe they're having me protect that bastard. You should have seen him today, Jean. I swear; he did this to me on purpose. To get rid of me, get me off his back. He saw I was gone and then knew he could use it. He is that calculated."

Jean gave me a look. "Really? Do you think he might have killed those kids on the boat?"

I exhaled and leaned back. "I don't know, but he sure fits the profile a lot better than Lucy. Everyone I talk to praises her for being such a sweet young girl, always helpful, taking care of others."

"Could William be getting rid of them because of what they saw? Is that your theory? But they already told the police they didn't see anything, and you said that was because they were terrified of him."

"Maybe they threatened to tell; maybe they changed their minds," I said. "That's my theory."

"Or maybe they have something else on him that he doesn't want them to tell anyone," Jean said.

Josie came down the stairs with a deep exhale and placed a book on the table. "I don't know how to do this."

"What is it, sweetie?" I said, surprised. Josie usually had no trouble with any of her homework.

"I need to do this project for Spanish, but I don't know how to do it."

"Let me have a look at it," Jean said. "I'm pretty good at Spanish."

Jean got up and walked with Josie back up to her room. I grabbed the plates and started to clean up. As I passed my dad in the recliner, he opened his eyes.

"When are you going to do something about it?"

I wrinkled my forehead. "About what?"

He nodded toward the stairs. "About her?"

"Jean? What on earth are you talking about? In case you missed it, I'm still married, Dad."

"She's here every day, son."

"Because she helps out, taking care of Camille," I said, getting annoyed with him. "Besides, I don't think she ever thinks about me in that way. I'm her best friend's husband."

"Open your eyes, son. She takes care of you and Josie, doing homework with her. What woman does that?"

I answered with a growl.

"You know what? I have a wife. I don't need another woman in my life, and besides, it's none of your business."

Chapter 23

I STARED at the one-story gray building, which held about a thousand teenagers, while eating the sandwich that Jean had made for me when she came over earlier. I had spent the morning hours, while the sun rose outside our window, talking to Camille, telling her everything about the case. Jean had said she'd make sure to change the feeding tube and wash Camille, while I had to rush out of the door.

And now I was sitting here with nothing to do with myself, but ready, just in case. Using the computer in the beat-up minivan, I did a little research, looking at chess pieces and their meanings. I also looked through the case files from the boat to see if anything new had come in…if Morales and his team had any breakthroughs, but nothing had changed since the day before. They had added a couple of new interviews with friends and family members, but nothing groundbreaking.

I was reading through one of them when my phone rang. The text on the display simply said UNKNOWN, and I picked it up. As I suspected, it was Al since she always hid her number somehow and made sure she was untraceable. Al was what I would define as slightly paranoid and always believed someone was listening in on her conversations or looking for her.

"Stop by today," she said. "I have news for you."

Then she hung up. Thinking now would be as good a time as any, I started up the minivan and drove out across the bridges to the beachside. I wasn't planning on staying long since I wasn't going to make the same mistake I did the day before and not be there when school was out. William had tennis lessons today, I believed. Or was it violin? I couldn't really care enough to remember.

"Hi there, stranger," I said as Al cracked the door open, staring at me suspiciously before letting me in like she wanted to make sure it was really me and not some robot the government had sent to get to her.

Once inside, I closed the door behind me and walked up to her desk with her five computer screens. Some of them were showing surveillance cameras from some street somewhere in the world where it was way colder than here, judging from what people walking past the camera there wore. In one of them, they drove on the other side of the road. There was even a camera from inside a workplace somewhere, and that had me puzzled. Part of me wanted to ask why she was looking at that but decided against it. She wouldn't tell me anyway.

"So, what have you got?" I asked hopefully.

"I went through all of her stuff," Al said, "and I found that she had been Snapchatting with someone right before she disappeared. Now, your tech department wouldn't know how to regenerate old Snapchat, or they might be too lazy to, but I did. And here's a series of snaps that were sent the day before she disappeared that I think you might find interesting. I made an entire transcript in print as I know you're old-fashioned like that."

She handed me a folder.

"Thank you," I said, feeling slightly old.

"Anytime," she said. "Just let me know."

"You're the best."

I hugged her and held her tight for a few seconds, remembering the day I had caught the guy who killed her sister. After that, I never had to ask twice for her help on anything. I had earned myself a lifetime of favors, she said.

I intended to hold her to that promise.

Chapter 24

SHE HAD SEEN him in the hallway between classes, then run into the bathroom to hide, hoping to dodge him. Heart pounding, she hurried into the girls' bathroom and into a stall, locking the door. Her legs beneath her were shaking, her breath ragged.

She sat on the toilet for a few minutes, then she heard the door leading to the hallway open and shut again. From underneath the door to her stall, she saw a set of white sneakers walk past her and then enter the one next to her, closing the door.

Sophia was still crying, so she wasn't ready to go back yet, but knew she'd have to soon. She just couldn't stand sitting there in Spanish class, where William also was, his eyes staring at her constantly whenever the teacher wasn't looking. She felt his glare on her skin, and it made the hairs stand up on her neck. He terrified her so much; she couldn't focus. It was like it would never stop. Not even after she promised him she'd keep her mouth shut. It was like he enjoyed torturing her…like he wouldn't stop because he was having so much fun. She wasn't sure she'd be able to take much more from him. It was only in this darn bathroom that he couldn't get to her.

In here, she was safe.

But it wouldn't last. At one point soon, she'd have to leave again and face him. They had Spanish together next. Sophia sighed deeply, then looked at her watch. She was going to have to be late for class, even if it got her in trouble. She couldn't risk him talking to her again. He'd only hurt her or threaten her, telling her she was worthless and that no one would listen to what she had to say. Some days, he would tell her how fat and ugly she was, or point out a pimple she had, telling her how disgusting that was. Stuff like that to make sure her confidence dropped so that she would feel worthless.

You can't let it go on like this. You have to do something.

Sophia shook her head. It was no use. There was no stopping William Covington. All she could do was survive, get by the best she could.

Hearing the bell ring, Sophia left the stall, then approached the sink where she splashed water on her face, hoping that it would wash away any trace of her crying. There was nothing worse than when people could tell that you had been crying. It was the worst. You couldn't break down; you had to keep up that happy face, pretending like everything was okay.

It was the unwritten rule of high school. They all did it, no matter how bad they were hurting, you knew never to show it. Whatever you did, this was the most important part.

Sophia breathed in deeply, splashing water on her face, then wiped it with paper towels and looked at her face in the mirror.

She stared at it with small gasping sounds. What she saw in there, who she saw standing behind her in that mirror, made her heart drop instantly.

She shook her head desperately while tears sprang to her eyes, tears she knew no water could ever wash away again.

"No, please," she said. "Please, don't."

An arm reached out and grabbed her around the neck, and a knife was placed on the skin of her throat. The person stared into her eyes as the blade was pressed against her skin. As the swift movement was made, and her throat slit, blood spurted out on the mirror in front of her. Sophia gurgled, her body jolting in spasms before it fell to the ground, rag-doll limp.

The white sneakers walked away, leaving the bathroom and hurried into the crowd outside rushing to class. No one even noticed how the sneakers were now stained with blood.

Chapter 25

I STILL HAD plenty of time, so I drove through South Beach, then found a small park where I stopped the minivan. I grabbed the folder that Al had made, then read through the chats that she had regenerated.

I had to admit; what I read was quite a surprise, and I had to reread it a few times over to make sure I wasn't mistaken. But it did provide me with something very important that I hadn't known before.

I knew where Lucy was.

Realizing this, I put the transcripts back in the folder, then started the minivan back up. I looked at the clock. I had still a few hours before school was out. I was doing fine—no chance of me repeating the same mistake from the day before. I drove back across the bridges, then stopped at a red light when I received a text from Josie.

I JUST SPILLED CHOCOLATE MILK ALL OVER MY SHIRT. PLEASE HELP.

I exhaled and looked at the text once more. I could have told her she'd be fine and not to worry about it, but I knew how much something like this could destroy someone in eighth grade, then wrote back:

I'LL BRING YOU A NEW ONE.

I turned the minivan left instead of right, then drove back to my own house and rushed inside. I ran up the stairs and into Josie's room, opened the closet doors, then stopped. I stared at all the clothes in there, realizing I had no idea what to pick. What did Josie like out of all these shirts? There were so many to choose from?

"Need help?"

I turned to see Jean. She was holding a basket of laundry under her arm. "I was just finishing up a load and putting this back."

"Josie spilled chocolate milk on her shirt and wants me to bring her a new one."

Jean's face lit up. "Look who is trying to be father of the year."

"I just want to help her," I said.

Jean smiled. The sight of it made my heart melt. I loved her smile. It made me feel at home.

"Of course, you did. But now you have no idea what a fourteen-year-old girl would want to wear, do you?"

I grimaced. "Could you help?"

Jean chuckled, then put the basket down and walked to the closet. She pulled out a hoodie with some print on it.

"She wears this one a lot. It's her favorite anime character from *My Hero Academia*."

I stared at the hoodie. "I swear I have never seen her wear this."

Jean gave me a look. "Really? Have you ever looked at your daughter?"

I exhaled deeply. "I guess not enough. Does that mean I'm doing a horrible job of being a father? I mean, I should notice these things, shouldn't I? It's important to a young girl?"

"Eh, you're not doing too bad, Detective. The girl adores you. You're fine."

I grabbed the shirt from Jean's hand, then leaned over and kissed her forehead. "Thank you. You're a lifesaver, again."

She blushed and pulled back.

"I am sorry," I said. "Did I do something wrong?"

Jean stared at me; her lips pulled slightly apart. Then she stood on her tippy toes, closed her eyes, and leaned in for a kiss.

Chapter 26

VALERIE HAMPTON WAS BORED. She grabbed her phone and looked at it under the table in the middle of class. She texted Ronald, and, as he had answered, Valerie raised her hand.

"Yes?" the teacher, Mr. James, said.

"Can I get a hall pass? I need to go to the bathroom."

Her teacher sighed. "That's the third time this week, Valerie."

"I know, but I really have to go; I am sorry." She held a hand to her stomach to pretend to be sick, and he finally gave in.

"All right, but maybe you should have a doctor take a look at this. It shouldn't keep being an issue."

Valerie stood to her feet. "It's okay, Mr. James. It's just that time of the month, you know."

That made the class burst into laughter, and Mr. James blush. He looked away, flustered. "All right but hurry up. I don't want you to miss out on the next part I'm getting to."

"Of course not, Mr. James," she said, batting her eyelashes. "I'll be right back."

Valerie walked into the hallway, a grin on her face. She spotted Ronald as he came around the corner, signaling for her to follow him. They couldn't risk running into any of the teachers or the SRO officer on their way, so they rushed ahead till they reached the lockers, where they stopped behind one. No one could usually see them when hiding there.

"Gosh, I thought Mr. James was never going to let me out," she whispered.

Ronald placed a finger on her lips to shut her up, then pressed her up against the wall behind her and placed his lips on top of hers and forced his tongue into her mouth. Valerie laughed and kissed him back, rolling her tongue around his like he had taught her. Ronald wasn't the first boy Valerie had kissed in the hallways of school, but he was by far the most experienced. He was a senior where she was a sophomore, and he knew a little more about life than she did. And about kissing. He knew a lot about that.

"God, you taste like cherries," he whispered, then bit her earlobe.

Valerie wasn't sure why he did that, but it made her giggle.

"What's going on back there? Who's there?"

The voice was Officer Martin's, their SRO officer. He had to have heard them.

"Shoot," Ronald said with a chuckle. "What do we do?"

Valerie looked to her right. The girl's bathroom was only a few feet away. If she could make it in there, he couldn't follow or accuse her of anything.

She giggled, then kissed Ronald's lips again before she took off, running down the hallway as fast as her legs were capable of, while she could hear Officer Martin yelling behind her.

"Hey, you two, where are you going?"

Valerie wasn't sure where Ronald had gone but assumed he had figured out for himself how to get to safety and not to be found. Or else he could talk his way out of trouble. Ronald was smart like that.

Hoping that Officer Martin hadn't seen her, she rushed into the bathroom, panting, and closed the door behind her. Then she laughed and slid to the floor when she realized she had sat in something liquid. She reached and down to feel it, then lifted her hand

and looked at it. That was when her eyes fell on something—or someone—lying on the floor by the sinks.

"What the…?"

Chapter 27

THE KISS WAS WONDERFUL; no, it was more than that…it was unearthly. Soft and gentle, and Jean tasted every bit as wonderful as I had ever dreamt she would. Everything about this moment was so incredible; I wanted it to last forever.

But it was wrong. It was wrong on so many levels, and we both knew it. I grabbed her by the shoulders and pulled her away. She opened her eyes with a small gasp and looked at me, startled.

"Jean…I…"

She shook her head, clasping her mouth, then pulled away from me. "No…No…I don't know why I did that. I am so…I should go. Your dad will be here soon and take care of Camille till you're done working. I should…probably…"

"Jean…please…"

But she had already turned around on her heel and was rushing out the door. She left me in my daughter's room, holding a black hoodie with some Japanese cartoon character that I didn't even recognize, feeling baffled. I stumbled backward and sat on the bed, then touched my lips gently. I couldn't stop thinking about that kiss and how wonderful it had felt.

But it also filled me with such a profound amount of guilt, it almost hurt.

I grabbed the hoodie and hurried into our bedroom, where Camille was. I sighed with sadness when I saw her in there. The sunlight fell on her face and made her eyes gleam, so I could see that beauty in them that I had loved so much.

I grabbed her hand in mine and kissed it. "I am so sorry, Camille; I didn't mean for it to happen. I am so, so sorry. You have no idea how terrible I feel."

Camille stared into the nothingness, as usual. I touched her cheek while my eyes filled with tears.

"I just wished I knew if it was worth it, you know? If I knew you'd ever come back to me. Is it even a life worth living? Is the life you have right now even worth living? I wish you could tell me, Camille. Because I want to know. Is it a good life? Are you happy? What will happen to you when you grow old? Do you want to if it means just continuing like this?"

I sat there, crying for a few minutes, not knowing what to do. A text from Josie pulled me out of my self-pity.

ARE YOU COMING?

I chuckled and wiped away my tears. Never a dull moment when you had kids. Especially not when you were alone with them.

I leaned over and kissed my wife, then realized a couple of tears had escaped her eyes and were rolling down her cheeks. It happened from time to time, and the doctor said it was PBA, pseudobulbar affect, a neurological condition often seen in patients with traumatic brain injury. It wasn't a sign of emotions or of her being able to see or hear us.

But it still got to me every time.

I reached over for a tissue and wiped them away, then kissed her again before rushing out the door, my phone vibrating in my pocket with the many texts from my impatient daughter, or at least I thought that's what it was.

Chapter 28

I KNEW something was wrong from the moment I turned onto the street leading up to the high school. I had been at my daughter's school and given the shirt to the lady at the front office so Josie could grab it between classes. I had thought I was making good time, that I was doing well when I saw the blinking lights.

What is going on?

They had set up a perimeter all around the school, and I had to park down the road and walk the rest of the way up. A crowd had gathered, women mostly, and I guessed they were mothers who lived close by, and who heard the rumors first.

I found my way through and went up to the officer guarding the entrance. He saw me and recognized me, then let me through.

A sensation of anxiety rumbled in my stomach as I walked in through the doors, nodding politely at the colleagues I met on the way. I grabbed my phone and looked at the display, then realized Fowler had called five times.

This can't be good.

I barely made it inside the hallway before I heard his voice, growling my name. I turned my head and saw him come running toward me.

"Hunter!"

Fowler was a big guy like me, not quite as tall, so I could still look down on him when he spoke, but he was pretty sizable in stature and pretty intimidating, especially with his scowling look. The very same look he was giving me right now.

"Where have you been?"

I opened my mouth to answer, but he had no time to wait for me to find the words before he continued.

"Weren't you supposed to be here? Because I vividly remember telling you to stay with William Covington all day, didn't I?"

I nodded. "Yes, sir. I had an emergency at home."

He huffed. "What else is new, right?"

"I have a sick wife; you know this, Fowler."

He paused, then rubbed his forehead. "I know. I know. I am sorry. It's just…well, I can't trust you anymore. You're always running around, and I never know where you are these days. How could this happen on your watch?"

I took in a deep breath. I hated to use Camille as an excuse, but right now, I had to. I couldn't afford to lose my job. Fowler was trying hard not to let his frustration run away with him. I could tell by the way he clenched his fists.

"Well, I'm here now. What happened?" I asked.

Fowler exhaled. "Come with me."

I followed him down the hallway and to the girls' bathroom. The door was open, and I looked inside just in time to see a young girl being pulled onto a stretcher and rushed out of there by paramedics.

"That's a lot of blood," I said, feeling sick. This was awful.

"He cut her throat," Fowler said.

"Knife?"

"We found this," Fowler said and lifted an evidence bag with a bloody fishing knife inside of it.

I walked closer to the area, then knelt next to the pool of blood. "Same type of knife as on the boat, huh? I almost don't dare to ask…"

Fowler nodded. He pulled out another bag and showed it to me. It contained a small black chess piece, a knight.

"We found it in her hand. He must have placed it there before he took off."

I stared at the chess piece, then wondered if William Covington was a chess player. I would bet my right arm he was.

Fowler escorted me out and down the hallway, then stopped. "Listen, Hunter. You know I love you, man; we've known each other for what feels like forever. But I can't keep covering for you. This happened on your watch, and you weren't here. You've got to step up. Now, it wasn't William Covington who was hurt…this time, so I'll let this one slide, but this is your last chance. Do you hear me? Any more slip-ups and you're out. William's dad is a very important contributor to Mayor Simon's campaign. He's a big deal around here, and if anything happens to his son, we'll all lose our jobs; do you understand?"

"Listen, Fowler; I might have found some important information in the case…"

Fowler raised his finger. He puffed himself up while looking at me, a vein popping out in his forehead.

"There is no case for you; do you hear me? Morales and his team are on it. You focus on keeping the boy safe. That is all. Understood?"

I nodded. "Understood."

"Good," Fowler said and left me. As I watched him walk down the hallway, I spotted someone rushing by me and recognized his face immediately.

"Mr. James?"

I hurried up next to him. He seemed in a rush to get away, but I stopped him. "Please, I need to talk to you. Here's my card. Call me, and we'll talk."

He stopped, then looked around to see if anyone saw us together, taking the card from my hand.

"You're a teacher here, aren't you?" I asked.

He nodded. "Yes. What is it you want?"

"That thing yesterday. What was it about?"

His eyes avoided mine. "Please, Detective, I don't want any trouble. Just leave me alone; will you?"

He began to walk toward the exit, and I followed him out into the parking lot. "I told the police everything I knew. They said I could go," he said. "I don't know why you keep following me."

"I want to talk about last night. Why was William Covington at your home? What did he want, and why was he hurting you?"

James shook his head and crossed the parking lot. "I don't know what you're talking about. I was with my family last night. We had dinner; we watched SpongeBob."

"Come on, Mr. James. I was there. I saw him. I saw what happened, what he did to you. Why don't you report him?"

James stopped in his tracks. He turned around to confront me, his face strained with anger, cheeks blushing, and eyes ablaze.

"You listen to me, Detective. You leave this alone, or I'll report you for misconduct. All I want is for you to leave me alone; do you think you can do that?"

And with that, he turned back around and walked up to his car and got in. He roared it to life, then drove past me, giving me an angry glare through the window. As the car disappeared, I turned around to go back when I spotted William standing by the wall of the school, leaning against it, his eyes lingering on me, a sly smile on his lips. The rage in his eyes made my blood run cold.

Chapter 29

JEAN DROVE TOWARD THE HOSPITAL, thinking about Harry. It wasn't that unusual for her to do that since he was constantly on her mind. She was always thinking about him, but today, a little more than usual. Today, she didn't want to think about him; she wanted to forget he even existed. She was so angry at herself for kissing him like that. It was something she had promised herself never to let happen, yet she had done it anyway. Out of the blue? It made no sense.

Have you no self-control?

Jean felt so ashamed of herself that she, for a moment, considered running away, moving away from town, or at least from the neighborhood, so she wouldn't have to face him again. Could she ever look into his eyes again?

She wasn't sure.

But the kiss had been wonderful. She had to admit it had been better than she had ever imagined it would be, and she had thought about kissing him a lot. She had tried hard not to for years, trying to push the thought away, but it had been on her mind a lot anyway, what it would be like to kiss Harry.

Why couldn't he have been an awful kisser? Why did he have to have such wonderfully soft lips?

Jean wasn't happy to admit it but kissing Harry had been on her mind even before Camille overdosed. That was the worst part of it all. Jean had always liked Harry, and she had always felt there was a connection between them, one she had never had with anyone else in the world. But he had belonged to Camille, and he still did, even if she was foolish enough to take those drugs. Thinking about it made Jean so angry.

Didn't she know she had it all?

"What could you possibly have been sad about? What could you possibly have wanted to escape from, huh?" she said into the car as if Camille were still there. "You weren't lonely like me. You weren't scared of never finding anyone who would love you. You had someone who adored your every step. You had everything…the most wonderful man in the world, the sweetest kid. Why would you do this to yourself? You had everything, literally everything I ever wanted."

Jean slammed her hand into the steering wheel as she drove into the parking lot of South Miami Hospital and stopped the car. She grabbed her purse, then looked in the mirror, correcting her hair and makeup.

"You're such a fool, Jean. You've ruined everything," she told herself with a deep sigh, then left the car and rushed inside.

She had just started her shift when they needed her right away. Jean had barely put her bag down when she had to rush into the ER. A young girl was coming in, someone said.

Jean ran down the hallway and was ready as they rolled her inside.

"Girl, eighteen, someone slit her throat with a knife," the paramedics said as they ran down the hallway. "Luckily, a girl found her right after it happened and tried to stop the bleeding with her shirt. She's lost a lot of blood. I'm not sure she's gonna make it."

Chapter 30

I KNEW I was jeopardizing everything, but I had to follow my instincts, and that was to find Lucy Lockwood as soon as possible. So, I took off, not caring what happened to William Covington, or what he was up to. I knew I had just promised my boss something else, but I'd have to deal with that later.

Instead, I drove downtown, growling in anger, Al's folder lying on the passenger seat beside me. Here, another girl had been attacked, and my boss wouldn't even listen to what I had to say.

I drove over the bridge and north onto the beach, then stopped in front of a condominium where I parked the car. I looked at the building in front of me, then at the folder, and the transcripts from her Snapchat.

I walked out and up to the front entrance, then spotted someone coming out and went to hide around the corner.

The woman didn't see me. She walked past me on her high heels, tapping along on the asphalt, seemingly in a rush.

I turned the corner and approached her.

"Mrs. Lockwood?"

She turned to look at me with a gasp. Then she forced a smile.

"Detective Hunter. W-what are you doing here?"

I smiled back, mirroring her fake smile. "Well, I was in the neighborhood, and I thought I'd stop by and say hello to Lucy."

"L-Lucy?"

Valentina Lockwood was many things, but an actress wasn't one of them.

"Let's cut the crap, shall we?" I said. "I know that she's up there in your apartment that is in your maiden name, Valentina Gómez. I read about it all in those Snapchats you thought had been deleted… the ones between you and Lucy planning this. Your husband doesn't know about it; does he? When did you buy it?"

She stared at me, the mask coming off. Her nostrils were flaring angrily, yet I could tell she knew she was defeated.

"He doesn't know, no. I bought it when I decided to leave him two years ago after he…"

I reached over and pulled the edge of her shirt to the side, revealing a huge purple bruise on her chest.

"How long has this been going on?"

She pulled back. "For as long as I can remember. He's always been like this, but it's getting worse. I thought I could leave him, but I don't know how…I bought the condo with my own money that my mother sent me and kept it just in case I finally managed to gain the courage."

"And she's up there? She's been there the entire time?" I asked. "Let me guess; Mr. Lockwood isn't very happy about what happened to her, and he blames her?"

Mrs. Lockwood looked down, then nodded like she was the one who was the bad guy. I had seen so many women like her in my line of work. They were trapped. There was nowhere for them to go, completely dependent on their husbands who treated them like dirt. I couldn't stand it.

"And the baby? William's child?"

Valentina bit her lip. "Robert wanted to kill it. He wanted her to get an abortion. I couldn't let him."

"So, you faked her disappearance?" I asked.

She nodded. "Yes. Please, don't tell him. Please, I beg of you."

I ran a hand through my hair. "I won't. But I'll probably need to talk to her."

Chapter 31

SHE SURVIVED THE SURGERY. How that was even possible with the condition she was in when she got to the hospital was beyond Jean, but she had. Sophia Fisher was in the ICU now on life-support and in critical condition, but alive.

We saved one of your girls, Harry.

It wasn't hard for Jean to figure out that this girl had to do with Harry's case. She didn't know the details of it, but Harry had told her about the girls who were killed on the boat and the one that was found in the dumpster. This incident had happened at the same school that all the others went to and where Harry spent his day protecting the kid that they believed had raped the girl that disappeared.

"We're gonna get you up and running in no time," Jean said as she checked Sophia's vitals.

Jean worked the ICU from time to time, and since there was a lack of nurses in the ICU today with the many patients that had come in, she had volunteered to help. They had assigned her to Sophia.

Now, she stared at the girl who lay in the bed, her eyes closed, fighting for her life. It was an awful sight, yet Jean found it to be hopeful. The girl had made it this far, and she would do her very best to make sure she made it all the way.

"You and me, we're tough girls," she said to her, "Nothing gets us down."

Except Harry.

Jean sighed when thinking about him again and looked out the window. The sun was setting on the Intracoastal waters, creating a gorgeous light.

"Why can't it be us?" she mumbled as though Sophia could hear or even cared. "She had her chance, and she blew it. Now, she's gone; she just lays up there, a vegetable, and meanwhile, we walk around each other, wanting it to be more, but unable to do anything about it. It's not fair, you know? I know; I know what you'll say… life's not fair and all that. I know, I know. I shouldn't feel sorry for myself, yet sometimes I really do. I take care of that woman day and night. I change her catheter; I wash her in parts only her husband should see. I make sure she's kept alive and that she can stay in the house with him. Why? Because I love him. Because I want to do this for him, I want to help him. And maybe because I feel awful for not being able to help her, for not seeing that she was back on the drugs. But does that mean I should just stop living my own life? Don't I have a right to be loved too?"

Jean felt tears pile up in her eyes and then let the tears roll down her cheeks. She wasn't usually one to feel sorry for herself, but today, she was. Today, she felt like everything had exploded in her face and that there was no turning back. She had kissed him, and that opened up a whole can of worms. There was no taking it back. All she wanted was to be happy. Was that so terrible?

Jean wiped her eyes on her sleeve with a sniffle, then shook her head. "I'm sorry to be telling you all this. It's not really your problem anyway. And, frankly, I'm being a baby. I could just go out and find some other guy, right? I could find someone who is actually available instead of wasting all my time and energy on someone who never will be. You're right."

Jean turned to look at Sophia, then smiled when the girl

suddenly moved in her bed and groaned. Jean's eyes grew wide open, and she approached her.

"Sophia?"

The girl moved her head from side to side, moaning loudly like she was having a bad dream. Was she waking up?

"Sophia?"

The girl opened her mouth and mumbled something. It was impossible for Jean to make out what it was, so she moved closer, so close she could hear her even when she whispered.

And what she heard made her heart race in her chest so violently it hurt.

Chapter 32

THE TWO-BEDROOM APARTMENT on the seventeenth floor had gorgeous views over the glistening Atlantic Ocean. It was nicely decorated in blue and white, making it seem like a truly relaxing beach retreat. A lamp made of shells dangled calmly from the ceiling. A huge painting of a sea turtle brought the ocean inside.

On the floor of the living room was a young girl and a young child, both sitting on the carpet.

"Did you forget something?" she yelled without turning to look at us.

"Lucy?" I said and stepped forward. She turned her head and looked up at me, her eyes confused. I recognized her from the many pictures I had seen in the police reports and in the articles I had read about the rape and her disappearance.

Lucy looked at her mother, who was standing right behind me. "W-what…who is he, Mom?"

"It's okay, Lucy," Valentina said. "He knows. He's not gonna harm either of you or take the child. He just wants to talk to you. It's okay, Lucy; trust me."

Lucy eased up slightly. She still looked at me suspiciously.

I stepped forward. "My name is Detective Harry Hunter. I've been looking for you, Lucy."

Lucy scoffed and turned to look at the baby as she fussed. Lucy helped her get the small wooden toy she couldn't reach. I was suddenly taken back to when Josie had been the same age and remembered her dependence on her surroundings, especially on her mother. It was truly magical that such a small helpless creature could grow into what Josie was today. And, frankly, I hadn't done much but keep her alive.

"Precious," I said and squatted next to Lucy, nodding toward the baby. "What's her name?"

"Isabella, like my grandmother," Lucy said, smiling in that way only a mother could when looking at her child. It was obvious she was tired from lack of sleep and constantly being on watch, but she still had that peace over her that only a new mother had.

"Beautiful," I said. "She's big and sitting by herself, huh? I remember that as being a relief for my wife when our daughter started sitting up on her own. That meant you didn't have to hold her constantly anymore."

Lucy chuckled. "Yeah, that is a help. But she keeps throwing those blocks away and then wanting them back, so I have to get them for her…see? She did it again."

The block dropped to the floor, and Isabella made sounds while drool ran down her chin. Lucy wiped her daughter's mouth, then grabbed the block, and gave it to her again. This time, the girl bit into it.

"Teething, huh?" I asked. "That's probably disturbing her sleep, am I right?"

"Oh, my God, constantly," Lucy said. "She cried almost all night."

"Any of them poking through yet?"

"One of the lower front teeth has just poked through the gums; I think it hurts because she bites into everything these days."

I nodded and chuckled. "You can buy these cooling toys that you put in the freezer; when they bite into them, it helps soothe the pain. Josie used to love those."

"I'll remember that," Lucy said. "So…what can I do for you, Detective? I assume you didn't come here to talk about baby teeth?"

I smiled. "Well…no. I need to talk to you. See, there are a lot of people looking for you. Have you heard about the kids that were killed on the boat? They were all from your school. There was also someone they found in a dumpster."

Lucy nodded. Her eyes hit the floor. "I've seen a little bit about it on TV when Isabella has been asleep."

"So, you also know that all those girls that have been killed were on the list of people who witnessed what happened to you on the beach."

"You mean when I was raped," she said, changing expression, her eyes suddenly filled with deep anger.

"Yes," I said.

"I know," she said sadly.

"Okay, so, now you might understand when I tell you that we have been looking for you in connection with these murders."

She wrinkled her forehead. The baby fussed and started biting her hand instead of the block.

"No, why is that?"

"Well, the killings seem to be connected to what happened that night, and to be completely honest with you…"

She laughed. It took me by surprise. "They think I'm killing them? Because they wouldn't testify? That's ridiculous." She grabbed her baby and held her up. "I have kind of been busy with something else here."

"But, I have to ask you where you were on Saturday night between eight p.m. and midnight when the bodies were found?"

"Where I was? Where do you think I was? Where do I spend all my days and nights? I was right here, of course, taking care of this baby that I didn't ask for because this is my life now. While all my friends are out being young and partying, I'm stuck here with her for the rest of my life. Not that I ever partied when I could, but I would at least like to be able to go out."

"Did anyone see you? Your mom, was she here? Is there a doorman who can say you didn't leave the condo?"

"I was…at home," Valentina said. "And we don't have a doorman. But Lucy only leaves the place when she takes Isabella for walks or when they go to the beach. I bring her groceries, or she orders take-out."

"Did you order take-out that night?"

"I might have. I think I ordered a pizza. It's what I eat most nights anyway before I pass out as soon as she falls asleep. No, wait, I didn't order pizza on Saturday because I had Chinese leftovers from the night before."

I rose to my feet, standing up straight. "I see. I just…well, I need to figure out how to explain it all to my superiors."

"Maybe you just don't," she said and stood up, holding Isabella on her hip. "I don't want anyone to know where I am or that I have a child. Just tell them I left the state, and I won't be back."

"I'm not sure it's that easy. They will find you at some point," I said, walking toward the door. A wooden chessboard with the black and white pieces on top of it stood on a small end table. None of the pieces were missing. "But, I guess I'll just have to come up with something."

I stopped and looked at the boardgame.

"Who plays chess?"

"Lucy was state champion," her mother said proudly.

"That was years ago," Lucy said and looked away. "In another lifetime."

Chapter 33

JEAN TRIED TO CALL HARRY, but as usual, it went straight to voicemail. What was it with him and cellphones? He had to be the only guy in this century that was impossible to reach. Harry never picked up his phone and always kept it on silent; it was annoying, especially now that Jean really needed to get ahold of him.

Come on, Harry, pick up!

When she got voicemail again, Jean growled and put the phone down. This wasn't the kind of stuff you told to voicemail. It was too important. She wondered if she should get in her car and drive down to the high school and look for him, but she still had several hours left of her shift and couldn't just leave. The patients needed her.

"Why do you have to make everything so difficult, Harry?" she mumbled as she put the phone back in the chest pocket of her scrubs. She walked down the hallway, and as she passed Sophia's room, she saw movement. The door was open, so she peeked inside, an uneasy sensation growing inside of her.

"Hello?"

A shadow moved by the wall, and Jean's heart dropped.

"Who…wh…?"

A person wearing a doctor's coat was bent over Sophia's body, and at first, Jean thought something had happened to her, but then she saw the plastic bag wrapped around Sophia's face.

"Hey, what are you doing? STOP!"

Jean sprang forward, grabbed the person by the collar and pulled it forcefully. The person stumbled backward but managed to push Jean off, and she slid backward across the floor, hitting her back against something hard. Sophia's body was jerking in the bed, and Jean began to scream.

"HELP! SOMEONE HELP!"

Jean stood to her feet, then lunged forward, plunging into this person with all her weight. She grabbed the attacker around the neck with her arm and pulled with all her might. The attacker gasped as she pulled and pulled till the hands let go of the plastic bag while she still screamed for help.

"HELP. IN HERE. HELP!"

Jean stared at Sophia while fighting the attacker, who was struggling to hold onto the squirming body. Sophia wasn't moving in the bed; her chest wasn't heaving up and down like it was supposed to.

Was I too late? Is she still breathing?

The attacker tried to fight loose from her grip and managed to push an elbow into Jean's stomach so hard that she let go with a loud yelp. The attacker then turned around, grabbed Jean, and slammed a fist into her face, repeating it three times. Pain shot through her jaw and into her brain. She saw stars and felt her body fall to the ground, then slide across the tiles. She heard footsteps in the distance, then yelling, and sensed her attacker going into panic. She then felt hands on her body. She tried to scream for help, but nothing came out. At least she didn't think it did. As she was put into a wheelchair and rolled off down the hallway, Jean was slowly fading off into the unknown.

Chapter 34

MY DAD WAS SITTING in the living room when I got back, watching the news on TV. I kissed his forehead and then went into the kitchen to unload the groceries. I had promised Josie I'd make my famous meatloaf for dinner, her favorite. Big Daddy's Killer Meatloaf…she had named it a couple of years ago. It was actually my mom's recipe, but I knew that she wouldn't mind if I took the credit.

We sat down to eat, the three of us, with Josie trying to look at her phone under the table, thinking I didn't see her.

"Josie," I said and nodded toward the phone in her hand. "Not at the table."

She put it down with a deep sigh, and my dad blessed the food.

"Thank you, God, for this wonderful food and the wonderful company. Thank you for blessing us all and for taking good care of Ellen till we can be with her again. Amen."

"Amen," I said and nodded at Josie to begin serving herself some food.

"Finally," she exclaimed and cut a huge chunk of the meatloaf and put it on her plate. "I'm starving."

My dad chuckled when seeing her plate getting filled and her throwing herself at it like she hadn't seen food for days. I remembered that kind of appetite at her age when I was shooting up like a rocket too. It was hard to explain to your smaller friends, but you needed loads of food when growing that fast, and being hungry felt like you would die. I often came close to passing out in those days.

"No Jean tonight?" my dad said after a few bites.

I froze when hearing her name mentioned. I had to admit; I was happy she wasn't here tonight. I wouldn't know how to face her after what had happened earlier in the day. What would I say to her? She had rushed out, completely out of it. Not that I felt like she needed to be. It wasn't her fault. We had both wanted this to happen.

"I think she's working," I said, hoping he'd change the subject.

"I'm done. Can I be excused?" Josie said and grabbed her phone. I had the feeling she had hurried up to finish eating as fast as possible, so she could get back on her phone, texting her friends, or watching videos or whatever she was doing. I gave her a concerned look, the "daddy look," as she called it.

"You sure you had enough to eat? You know how easily you get hungry an hour after dinner because you didn't eat enough."

She shrugged and got up with the phone in her hand. "I'll just grab some chips or something then."

She rushed up, running past me, but I stopped her.

"Plate," I said. "It won't find its way to the dishwasher on its own."

She groaned loudly, sounding like she was going to die. I shared a look with my dad, and he lifted his eyebrows while Josie did as she was told. I chuckled as she left.

"And so it has begun," my dad said, drinking his sweet tea. "You ready for total and utter chaos for the next five years or so?"

I ate some of my meatloaf and mashed potatoes. "As ready as I'll ever be," I said.

"It's not gonna be easy being the only one here," he said. "Once those boys come knocking on your door…I remember when they started coming for Reese…"

He paused, then looked down. I felt a pinch in my heart. Reese wasn't doing well. I hadn't spoken to her in weeks, and neither had my dad. We were worried about her, and there wasn't a day when we both didn't wonder what her life would have turned out to be if it hadn't been for that rape.

She had never been the same afterward.

My dad leaned back in the chair and sent me a sad smile. "Anyway, I meant what I said yesterday. You really ought to do something about it before it's too late."

"About Jean?"

"Yes."

I lifted my eyebrows. "I thought we talked about this, Dad. I'm a married man. I have a wife."

He leaned forward and put his hand on my arm. "When will you realize she's not coming back? You have to let her go, son. She's gone. You heard the doctors. She's never coming back. It never happens with people in her condition. Can't you see? You're wasting away, trying to care for her, scrambling to make it all work. Yes, Jean is here to help, but for how long? Once she realizes you don't want her, she's gonna go away. And then what?

Meanwhile, you're missing out on everything. You're thirty-six for crying out loud. You're still young. You need to live your life. I see the way you two look at one another, the way you talk. That kind of love is so rare. When you have it, you should hold onto it for dear life."

I exhaled tiredly. My dad had never been fond of Camille. I don't know if it was her past with the drugs or the fact that she was Caribbean. But he never really connected with her, and my mother didn't either. Still, they had always tried their best. It broke my mother's heart when she overdosed, and she helped out for a long time until she died suddenly of an aneurism while vacuuming her house. I sometimes wondered if seeing me in so much distress after Camille's overdose played a part in the aneurysm bursting.

"Don't waste any more of your life, son," he continued. "You'll only end up regretting it. You don't want that kind of regret in your life."

"So, what, you want me just to forget I have a wife upstairs? I can't do that, Dad."

"Send her to a nursing home, son. They can take care of her there. There'll be someone with her all the time, trained nurses who will be able to give her the care she needs. The way it is now, you're barely keeping it together. You're exhausted. It's too much."

I leaned back in my chair with a surprised scoff. I shook my head. "What on Earth happened to believing in miracles, Dad?"

He put his fist on the table. "She's not gonna wake up, son. You're living in a fantasy if you believe she will."

"Wow," I said as I got up and began clearing the table. I stopped with the plates in my hands, then looked down at my dad. "Well, you can think what you want, Dad. I still believe God will bring her back to me. I have faith that he will wake her up, and I want her to be here in the house, surrounded by her loved ones when it happens."

Chapter 35

WAKING UP WAS PAINFUL. Her head was pounding. The sounds coming from outside her body felt so loud…her head was about to explode. Her entire body was hurting so badly she wanted to scream.

Yet, she couldn't.

Jean tried again, then shot her eyes wide open.

Oh, dear God, no.

She couldn't scream for the simple reason that she had been gagged. A wet cloth that tasted like dirty laundry had been shoved into her mouth and halfway down her throat, making her want to gag.

Help? Someone? Anyone?

She was lying down. Her hands had been tied, and her legs bound together. The place she was in was so tight that she could barely move.

Where am I?

Darkness surrounded her, and she tried to sit up but couldn't. There was no more space above her head, and she knocked into the roof.

What is this place?

ALL THE GOOD GIRLS

While groaning behind the gag, she tried to move around, to turn herself so she might be able to see something, anything, but there was nothing but darkness in the tight space. In the distance somewhere, she thought she heard noises; was someone speaking? No, it was different. It was singing. It was a radio. Somewhere close by, a radio was running.

Hello?

She tried to get a sound out behind her gag, but it was impossible. No matter how much power she put behind it, there was nothing but muffled sounds. The wet cloth in her mouth felt like it would suffocate her. Panic set in at the thought, and her heart began hammering in her chest, knocking against her ribcage. She tried to calm herself, but it was nearly impossible. The feeling that she couldn't move caused her to lose control of herself and she hyperventilated.

She closed her eyes and cried, trying to remember what had happened…what had gone down before this moment. She remembered being in Sophia's room. She recalled there being someone in there, and then the fight. She remembered falling, and then the fist that kept coming again and again.

Was there a wheelchair? Yes, she remembered being put in one, then being rolled away. She even remembered the people she passed, trying to speak to them, to reach out or scream for help, but no sound came out of her. She remembered their eyes focused on something else, some even running, none of them noticing her. And then she remembered drifting in and out of consciousness…that alluring darkness that kept calling to her. She remembered it all like small pieces of film that she now ran for her inner eye, piecing it all together until she finally opened her eyes with a gasp for air.

Just as she did this, she heard an engine turn over and then felt the room she was in begin to move.

Chapter 36

"I'M TELLING YOU, Camille, she's turning into a regular teenager. It's gotta be the hormones. That's the only way I can explain it. Last night, I couldn't get her to go to bed. She kept crying. Finally, I managed to calm her down and get her to talk. Apparently, she's struggling with friends at school. Her best friend, DD, has turned her back on her and is now best friends with some other girl and won't even talk to Josie at school. Now, she thinks no one likes her, that everyone thinks she's weird. It breaks my heart to see her like this. What happened to my girl who could be beaten by nothing in life? She used to be so strong. She never used to care what other people thought about her. I thought our struggle would be her stubbornness. Not this. This is nothing like what I imagined. You should have seen her, Camille. She was inconsolable, and I couldn't help her. I never thought it was going to be like this. I have no idea how to deal with stuff like that, all the drama. I'm a boy. We never had drama like that. At least none that I know of."

I sighed and looked at my wife in the darkness. She was sleeping. At least, I thought she was. It was hard to tell. I grabbed her hand in mine and kissed the back of it.

"Gosh, I wish you were here to help me," I said and wiped away a tear. "You'd know what to do, how to help her. It doesn't matter what I say; it doesn't help anything. It usually only makes her even angrier or sadder."

I leaned back in my chair and looked out the window at the horizon. The sun had begun to rise, and it was getting lighter out. I had only slept a few hours, but I knew I wasn't going to get any more. Instead, I leaned over, kissed my wife on the forehead, then headed into the shower.

When Josie came down, I had made pancakes and bacon, thinking her favorite breakfast might cheer her up. To my surprise, she was in an excellent mood this morning and didn't mention a single word about her friends or what she had been so sad about the night before. She smiled and kissed my cheek as I served her the food. I looked at the clock and realized I had to get going if I was going to make it to the Covington house before William left for school. I was getting pretty sick of playing babysitter, but what could I do? I needed my job.

"Is Jean not coming over this morning?" Josie asked.

"I don't know, sweetie. I haven't heard from her since yesterday. She had called a few times, and when I tried to call her back last night, she didn't pick up. She might be busy," I said, then added: "Eat your breakfast. I'll stay till the bus comes if she doesn't show up."

"Who's gonna look after Mom?" she asked, concerned. "If Jean can't come today? She usually takes care of her till she needs to go to work."

I sighed, not knowing what to say. My dad could come over, but I'd have to change her feeding tube and catheter and turn her in the bed to prevent pressure sores. After that was done, my dad could easily take over.

But that meant I'd be late for work. It wasn't going to make me popular.

"I hope she's all right," Josie said and finished her orange juice. "She usually always comes over in the morning, even when she's worked night shift."

I nodded and took a bite of my pancake as well. "I know. It isn't like her. I don't know what's going on. I'm sure she's all right, though."

But you do know, don't you? She kissed you, and the way you reacted scared her off. What if she never comes back?

Barely had I sent Josie off with the bus when I received a text from a number I didn't know. It said:

I AM READY TO TALK. JAMES.

Chapter 37

I SKIPPED Covington's house completely and drove directly to Howard James's address. It was close to the school, and that's where William was going to be in a few minutes anyway. I drove onto the driveway and parked, then rushed up to the house. I knocked, but no one answered. I grabbed the door handle and opened the door, then walked inside.

"Howard James? It's Harry Hunter. I came as soon as I got your text…"

I walked into the living room and found someone sitting in the kitchen.

"Howard James?"

The guy didn't look up at me. He stared at the tabletop in front of him, his head bent, his shoulders slumped. I walked up to him and sat down in a chair across from him. He finally lifted his glance and looked at me.

"They can never know."

"Who? Your family?"

He nodded. "Julia and the kids can never know."

I shook my head as my eyes fell on a picture of him and his

family on the wall. The kids could be no more than three and five years old—two beautiful girls with light curly hair and broad smiles.

James grabbed my arm with his left hand and clenched it, a desperate look in his eyes. His right hand, he kept under the table.

"You must promise me they'll never know."

I looked into his eyes, then nodded. "Of course."

James eased up slightly and let go of my arm. Tears sprang to his strained red-rimmed eyes. He looked like a man who hadn't slept in weeks. He looked like a broken man about to fall apart.

"Just tell me," I said. "You need to get it off your chest."

He stared at me like he was still undecided whether he could trust me or not, then wiped his nose with his hand, sniffling.

"You're not gonna like it," he said.

"I'm sure I won't, but right now, keeping this a secret is making you sick. You can trust me."

He gave me another suspicious look, then made his decision. He leaned back with a deep sigh.

"I don't know exactly when it started. Or who came on to whom. But it happened. The very thing that can't happen when you're a teacher."

"You fell in love with a student?"

He exhaled, then nodded. "Yes. But I never wanted it to happen. You must trust me when I say that I never meant for it to go this far. It just…"

I closed my eyes briefly, thinking about my Josie. I didn't know what I'd do if I found out a teacher had…I couldn't even finish the thought.

"How far did it go?" I asked, even though I desperately didn't want to know the answer.

He gave me a look. "Too far. It went way too far. We started meeting up in secret and…"

"You slept together; I take it?" I asked.

He swallowed, then looked away.

"Okay," I said. "And I take it that William Covington found out somehow and used it against you?"

"Yes, but it's more than that. I didn't find this out until later, but he arranged the entire thing. He set me up."

I wrinkled my forehead. "How so?"

James breathed raggedly. He was a desperate man at this point.

"He…he…forced her to…to pretend like she wanted to be with me."

"Excuse me?"

"He saw how I looked at her in class, and he told her to play along. She told me this later on when we were alone, and she broke down and cried. He pressured her to sleep with me. He knew a secret of hers that would be so devastating to her and her family that it would have destroyed her life. She never told me what it was, but it was enough for her to do as he said. He trapped me, so I'd do as he told me to."

James spoke through gritted teeth, and I sensed his anger from where I was sitting.

"I'm not justifying what I did," he continued. "I knew what I did was wrong. But to find out that it was all…based on a lie? That got me so mad."

"Only now, you can't do anything about it because William Covington knows."

"He has pictures. He hid in the room. We were in her parents' house when they were out of town, and he was there too when we…and he took pictures with his phone that he has kept."

"And now he's blackmailing you? What does he want you to do?"

"Let him pass my class," James said. "It's as simple as that. He was failing, and he went this far just to pass. He's that despicable. Just for a passing grade."

"But I'm guessing he's not stopping there," I said.

"No. That was just the beginning. Now, he just enjoys torturing me for the fun of it. He shows up here and acts like he owns me. He gets me to fail people he doesn't like, or to get him stuff that he needs like alcohol, sometimes weed, stuff like that. I've become his darn puppet. That's all I am. And it won't end."

"And you can't tell the police because they'll arrest you for having sex with a minor," I said. "Why now? You know I'll have to report you after this."

Tears rolled down his face while his hand moved under the table. His eyes looked at me, pleading.

"Stop him, please. I made a mistake, and now I'm paying the price," he said, sobbing. "My family will be destroyed, and so will I. But he can't hurt anyone else. Please, stop him, please."

Seeing the deep desperation in this man's eyes almost made me lose it. "I…I can't…I mean…"

James shook his head, tears running across his cheeks. "You can't stop him, can you?"

I felt paralyzed. I had no idea what to say to him. Should I just tell him the truth, that a guy like William Covington was hard to stop, especially when no one would stand up to him and tell the truth? When he ran a regime of terror that was built on destroying everyone around him?

"If you come forward," I said. "If you tell the truth, then maybe others will…"

I said the words, but he knew I didn't believe them. I had barely finished the sentence before he shook his head, crying hard, then pulled out his hand from underneath the table. It was too late when I realized it was holding a gun.

Chapter 38

JAMES PLACED the gun on his temple and pulled the trigger. It all went by so fast; I hardly even managed to react. The bullet blasted half of his face to pieces, and he fell to the table with a thud, slamming what was left of him into the wood.

I was paralyzed with shock.

I was barely breathing.

Just like that, a life was over. Just like that, two children were fatherless, and a wife had become a widow.

It was unbearable to even think about.

I stared at the body in front of me, then down at the blood that had sprayed my shirt and my hands. I was shaking, trembling, half crying, half choking. I was hyperventilating, my eyes staring at Howard James lying there, lifeless.

Oh, dear God, no.

When I finally was able to gather myself, I grabbed my phone out of my pocket and called for first responders, frantically tapping the display, speaking through tears as the call finally went through.

It took less than twenty minutes before Fowler was standing in the doorway, looking at me. I had been talking to the paramedics until then, and now my colleagues entered.

"What the heck do you think you're doing?" Fowler asked, raging. "Where's the boy? Where's William Covington?"

"He's at school up the street. I was here to talk to…one of the teachers. He had something he needed to talk to me about. It was important."

"Important enough for you to leave your post?"

I nodded. "Yes."

Fowler growled. "Need I remind you that you're not working a case here?"

"No…but…"

"You're in the business of protecting. Why are you interviewing teachers?"

I stared at him, then shook my head. "You know what? I just watched a guy, a father, take his own life. I am not going to stand here being talked to like I'm a baby," I said. "Fire me if you have to."

I pushed myself past him, out the door, while he turned to look after me.

"You bet I will. You're out, Hunter!"

I paused, took in a deep breath, and closed my eyes for a brief second. I wondered if there was anything I needed to say…if I should ask for his forgiveness for the sake of my family's survival, but then decided against it. I was done with this game. I didn't owe him anything. Instead, I continued on my way outside. The sky had grown dark, and black clouds had gathered above me like they knew how I felt.

I was angry. No, it was more than that. I was good old fashioned pissed off. I was sick of this boy and what I had learned about him. I was done with protecting him. And I was going to make sure he was done terrorizing people. Fowler had fired me. I had nothing more to lose.

If I was going down, then I was taking him down with me.

Chapter 39

I DROVE AWAY from the scene after giving my testimony to one of my colleagues, telling him the details of what had happened. Then I rushed back to my car and took off. Luckily, I had a jacket in the car that I put on to hide the blood on my white shirt. I didn't want to scare people. I then walked into the school and into the front office. I showed the lady sitting there my badge. She stared at it, startled.

"I need to see William Covington. Now, please."

The lady behind the desk nodded nervously, then grabbed the phone and called a number.

"Yes, could I have William Covington come to the front office, please? There's someone here to see him."

I stared at her round face and narrow-set eyes as she listened, then nodded. "Okay, I see."

She hung up and looked at me. "William left early. No one has seen him since third period."

I lifted my eyebrows, surprised. "He left early?"

"That's what they said. He didn't sign out with me, though, as he is supposed to. He's not allowed just to leave."

"So, you don't know where he is?" I asked.

She shook her head. "I'm afraid not."

"And he couldn't be in some other class?"

"He's supposed to be in Math, and he wasn't. When the teacher asked about him, someone said William left after third period. That's all I know."

I exhaled, confused. "Okay. Thank you."

"I'm sorry I couldn't be of more help."

"That's okay," I said, my pulse quickening. Something wasn't right here. I could sense it; something was awfully wrong.

I thanked her again, then left, rushing outside. I was on my way to the minivan when I thought of something. Call it instinct or maybe just a hunch, but something seemed to be very off here. There was one thing I needed to check before I left. I hurried across the parking lot, where I found William's Range Rover still in its usual spot.

"That's odd," I mumbled, then walked up to it, thinking maybe he was still sitting inside and hadn't taken off yet. Or perhaps he had just come back from doing whatever it was he was up to. The driver's side door was left ajar, and I pulled it open. I took a glance inside and spotted something on the seat that made my blood run cold. I picked it up and held the chess piece in the air.

"The Queen? And just what is that supposed to mean?"

I looked around me. The school parking lot was eerily quiet. A flock of pelicans floated above my head while my head spun with the many thoughts rushing through it. Where could he have gone? Why hadn't he taken his car?

Had something happened to William Covington? Had something happened to him while I was supposed to have been protecting him?

Chapter 40

HELP!

Jean had been in the trunk for what felt like an eternity. The car had stopped moving and had been parked somewhere for a long time while Jean was left in there for hours and hours. At first, she had tried to make noise and knock against the lid of the trunk, but the struggle had been so exhausting that she had fallen asleep at some point. As she woke up again, she was still in that small compartment, and fear spun through her body as she suddenly believed she had been left there so that no one would find her before she died from thirst or starvation.

Please, someone, find me; Lord, please, help me!

Jean kicked and moved around the little she could when she accidentally kicked the back of the compartment, and something came loose. A speck of light came in through the crack she had made in the old car, and she could peek into the cabin.

She heard noises from outside of the car, then lay completely still, barely breathing. She heard footsteps approaching, and someone was whistling. Then the door to the car opened and the radio was turned on again, music filling the car.

Jean squirmed up toward the crack she had made in the back

seat and managed to peek into the cabin of the car. The person sitting behind the wheel was whistling along with the song on the radio, and the car took off down the road. The light blinded her slightly at first, but as soon as her eyes got used to it, she recognized the face of the doctor she had seen by Sophia's bedside.

Only this was no doctor.

The car took a turn, and Jean managed to squirm around even more, so she could get a better look. She then waited until the car came to another stop at a red light before she made her move. She kicked the seat hard, and it burst open. The driver still didn't hear anything over the loud music. It wasn't until Jean reached over the back of the seat and wrapped the rope used to tie her hands together around the driver's neck that she was finally seen.

A half-choked gurgling sound of surprise emerged from the driver's throat as Jean tightened the rope around the driver's neck. As the driver eased the foot on the brake, the car started to roll slowly forward into the intersection. The driver squirmed and fought for a few seconds before the body grew limp and lifeless. Jean managed to pull the body back into the back seat, then squirmed into the driver's seat, slid into position, and grabbed the wheel with her tied up hands, then placed both of her tied up feet on the brake just as the car was about to knock into a street sign.

Jean turned the car to the side, then managed to slide her tied up feet toward the accelerator and sped up. She maneuvered the car back onto the road and continued, then took a turn.

She drove the car through heavy Miami traffic while people swerved around her, honking loudly, some giving her the finger, her mouth still gagged, her hands and feet still tied together. Then she found a parking lot in front of a school and drove into it and parked the car, breathing with relief.

She then turned her face to look at her attacker, lying lifeless in the backseat. She reached her hands up and tried to pull the gag out, but it still wouldn't move. Panting behind it, she squirmed across to the passenger seat and managed to open the glove compartment, then sighed with relief as she pulled out a fishing knife. Holding it between her two hands, she reached down and cut her feet loose. The rope used was thick, so she had to grind it for what seemed like forever.

Jean groaned behind the gag when finally, her feet came free, and she could move her legs properly again. She then had to turn the knife toward the rope holding her hands. It was a lot harder than she had expected, and the knife kept slipping out of her hands, but finally, she succeeded, and soon, she could move her hands again. She then lifted the knife to the rope strapped tight around her mouth and neck, holding the gag in place, then cut it, and finally could take out the nasty cloth. She spat and gagged as it was removed, suddenly feeling the pain in her jaw from being in the same position for hours and hours. She took a deep breath, then looked back at her attacker again. She turned around, reached into their pocket, and pulled out a cellphone.

She dialed a number, praying he'd pick up for once in his life.

Chapter 41

I HAD BARELY GOTTEN BACK into the minivan when my phone rang. I pulled it out, then picked up.

"Hunter."

"I've seen the girl," a voice said on the other end. I recognized it immediately as T-Bone's.

"Lucy Lockwood?" I asked.

"Yes. She was just seen in Coconut Grove. I'll give you the address once we've negotiated a price."

"Coconut Grove? What's she doing there? That's where her parents live. Why would she go back there and risk being seen?"

"Listen, man; I don't know. But one of my buddies saw her drive into an address there and told me about it. If you want the address, then you have to pay up."

A million thoughts rushed through my mind in that instant. Lucy had been hiding out beach-side with the baby. If she had come back, it had to be important. It had to be worth the risk of being seen. But what could it be?

"William," I mumbled as my heart dropped. "Oh, my Lord."

"I want five big ones," T-Bone said. "For the information."

I grimaced. I didn't have five hundred dollars I could spare, especially not now that I was probably out of a job, and I wasn't sure Lucy's parents were going to pay up. I mean, the dad would probably do it, but I wasn't sure I wanted to tell him where his daughter and the grandchild he didn't know existed were—not after I saw the bruises on his wife.

"Listen, T-Bone, I am…"

"I get it. You don't have the money, do you?"

"Not really, but I do need to know where the girl is. It's very important. Can I owe you one?"

T-Bone laughed. "It's gotta be a big one then."

"It will be. I promise you."

"Okay. I'll hold you to that. You know, I will."

"I expect you to."

T-Bone sniffled. "All right. I'll text you the address."

We hung up, and I stared at the phone until the text arrived. I then glared at the address, startled, before I started the minivan back up and rushed down the street, cursing myself for not having seen this coming earlier.

I had made it to the neighborhood and approached the address when my phone rang again. I stared at the display. An unknown number, again.

I picked it up.

"Hello?"

"Hello…Harry?"

My heart dropped. "Jean? I…I haven't heard from you… where…I mean…what can I do for you?"

"Harry, I have something I need to tell you. It's urgent."

Chapter 42

JEAN TOLD him everything she knew, everything Sophia had told her while mumbling in her sleep, a feeling of great relief rushing over her as she spoke.

"And you're sure about this?" Harry said, sounding somber. "Not that it surprises me. I had a hunch about this, but it's great to get it confirmed. It all makes a lot more sense now."

Jean sighed, exhausted. "That is good news. I hoped it would. I'm just glad I could be of help."

"So…where are you? I tried to call you?" Harry said. "You never picked up. I was…worried."

Jean felt her eyes fill as she thought about being kidnapped and held captive in the trunk. It was hard for her even to put it into words, as it still filled her with such profound fear.

"I…Sophia was attacked, and then…I tried to help her; I was…"

Jean stopped talking. Not because she didn't know what to say or how to say it or because it filled her with sadness and fear. No, it was because someone had taken the phone out of her hand. Now, Jean was staring at Sophia's attacker, holding the phone in their hand.

She could still hear Harry on the other end.

"Jean? Jean? Are you there? Jean?"

The attacker then reached over and slammed a fist into Jean's face so hard that she fell backward and hit her head into the door.

"JEAN?" Harry yelled somewhere in the distance, drifting slowly further and further away until she almost couldn't hear him anymore.

"What's going on, Jean?"

Jean wanted to answer, but she couldn't. She fought bravely to stay conscious as her attacker lifted the phone again and spoke into it.

"Jean can't talk now."

Her attacker then hung up and looked at Jean while she fought not to see double. The attacker then reached over, grabbed her by her collar, and pulled her closer, then lifted the fist again and slammed it into her face. Jean screamed as more punches fell. She pulled her arms up to cover her face, then lifted a leg and planted it in her attacker's stomach. The attacker flew backward with a shriek, and Jean reached for the handle of the door, then pulled it and opened the door. She crawled out, fighting to see straight, and was almost out when something grabbed her ankle and pulled her back. Jean screamed as she felt the hands on her leg, yanking her backward. When she was close enough, she turned around and placed a couple of fast punches on her attacker's jaw. The attacker screamed and let go of her leg, so Jean managed to slide out onto the asphalt, then kick the door of the car closed just before her attacker could follow her. She fought to get to her feet, then made a run for it. She could hear her pursuer opening the door with a loud grunt, then the footsteps behind her as the pursuit began. Jean screamed and sped up, running faster and faster, pushing herself. Luckily, Jean had always kept herself in good shape and was used to running on the beach. This was to her advantage now as she ran toward a strip mall. She turned a corner, thinking she had lost her pursuer, then spotted a family of four who had just parked their car and were walking up toward a Tropical Smoothie Café.

"Help," she hissed, but not loud enough for them to hear. She tried again, but it sounded mostly like wheezing. She turned her head to look behind her and could no longer see her pursuer. Happy about this, she sprinted to the end of the building where the parking lot started. Just as she came around the corner, someone stepped out in front of her. Startled, she let out a small scream to get the attention of the family across the parking lot, but her pursuer grabbed her, and with her mouth covered, she was dragged back toward the black Hyundai, crying and screaming, digging her nails into her attacker's skin.

Chapter 43

"JEAN?"

I stared at the phone that had gone dead. I tried to call the number back, but it just kept ringing.

What had happened to her? Who was that person on the phone? Whose was that nasty voice?

Heart hammering in my chest, I kept staring at the phone, wondering what was happening. I had to help her somehow. What was it she said again? Before the phone was hung up?

"Sophia was attacked and then…I tried to help her; I was…"

She was what? Attacked? Kidnapped?

I leaned back in the seat of my car. "Oh, dear God, no. If anything happens to her, to Jean, I'll never forgive myself."

Try and think clearly now. If Sophia was attacked, then Jean was most likely attacked by the same person, right? So, all this must have to do with what is happening to the girls at the school. It must be the same person who killed them who has taken Jean, right? And if that is so, then there is only one thing you can do, only one way to find Jean.

I took a deep breath, then stared at the entrance to the mansion in front of me. I got out of the van, then walked up to the gate. Just as I did, a small Mercedes convertible came up to it. The window rolled down, and a hand pressed the buzzer and was let in. As the gate opened, I hid in the bushes, then as the car disappeared, I snuck in afterward just as it was about to close. I then walked up toward the house, stayed hidden by some palm trees and bushes until the young girl in the Mercedes stepped out and walked up to the main entrance, where she was let inside. I waited until the door was closed behind her and then a few seconds more before I snuck up to the house, ran around the back, and found a door that wasn't locked.

Chapter 44

I FELT the gun in my holster and put my hand on the grip, then pulled it out as I walked down the marble-tiled hallway toward the voices coming from the dining room. The voices grew loud and angry the closer I got, and I recognized some of them.

"Okay, you've proven your point," one said. "You won."

Laughter followed. I knew that laugh a little too well.

William.

"No, no, my sweet girls. That's where you're wrong. It's not over yet."

"Please, William," another voice said.

Lucy.

"I thought you asked us to come here today to make a truce."

"You're the ones who wanted to meet," William said. "Not me. You texted me and picked me up at school, remember?"

"It has got to stop, William," Lucy continued. "You've taken it too far."

"I've taken it too far? Me?" William hissed. "Need I remind you what you did to me?"

They all went silent for a few seconds. I stayed hidden by the door, my gun ready.

"When is it ever going to end?" Lucy asked, her voice strained. "I'm sorry for what we did to you."

"I'm not," another voice said. I peeked inside and saw a girl I recognized from William's school. I had seen her in the mornings when we arrived. There were several of them present in William's living room. Some, I had seen before; others were new faces to me. But they all seemed to be about the same age.

The girl from earlier continued as she received looks from the others. "I'm not. He had it coming, and you all know it."

Another wave of silence brushed through the room, and I sensed the rest of the girls there agreed with her.

"It doesn't matter," Lucy said. "What matters is what happens next. William, you have got to stop this. Killing people won't solve this. Trying to make it look like I did it by placing stupid chess pieces on the bodies doesn't make anything better either. What will it take to make you stop?"

That made William stand to his feet. He walked toward Lucy and grabbed her around the shoulders, wearing that sly smile of his.

"You know what I want from you, dearest."

She shivered and pulled away from him. "I can't do that. You know I can't. Anything but that."

William grabbed her by the arm and pulled her back forcefully. He grabbed her around the neck and held her tight.

"That is my price. If you don't, the killings will continue."

William held Lucy tight around the neck, and I heard her gasp for air. The other girls stood like they were frozen and stared at William as he tried to strangle Lucy. That was my cue. I had heard enough. I stepped forward, holding out the gun.

"No, they won't, William. It ends here. Let go of the girl. Let Lucy go. Now!"

Chapter 45

"AH, DETECTIVE HUNTER," William said, grinning. "I was wondering when you'd join us. Did you like the little present I left for you in my car?"

I kept my gun pointed at him. He finally eased up on Lucy's neck.

"It's over, William," I said. "I heard everything. I know."

William scrutinized me. "Do you now?"

"Yes, I know what really happened at the beach last year. Sophia spilled the beans while she was in the hospital."

William's smile grew broader. "Did she really?"

Lucy's face grew pale. I looked at her.

"I realized it when I saw the baby. It was just a question of math, Lucy. If that child were a result of that rape, it wouldn't have been older than three months by now. But your baby sat up on her own when I arrived. She was teething. I have a child of my own and know that babies teethe at around six months old. It's also around the same age that they learn to sit by themselves. It was smart, though, to fake a rape to get back at him. And at the same time, you'd have an excuse to tell your parents how you got pregnant. So, you wouldn't have to tell them that you had slept with a teacher… with Mr. James."

"That's right, Detective," William said. "All these *good girls* were in on it. They all seem so innocent with their straight A's and volunteer work, but they did that to me. They planned this to get me sent to jail."

"And why did they do that, William? Because of what you did to them. You terrorized them. You forced Lucy to sleep with Mr. James, so you'd have something on him to be able to control him. You told her to do it, or you'd go to the immigration authorities and reveal that her mom was in the country illegally before she married Lucy's dad. Marriage is no longer a security from deportation in the times we live in. Not if you have been ordered deported before you were married. Lucy would do anything to protect her mother from being deported. And she did."

Lucy's eyes landed on the tiles beneath her, and she sat down in a recliner. Tears sprang to her eyes.

"It was the most humiliating I ever had to do. And now…now, I have a child."

"So, you decided to punish William for how he was treating everyone," I said. "All of the girls got together and agreed to stop him; am I right? Except you forgot a couple of things. First of all, when something like this happens in this day and age, there'll be video. From the beginning, it puzzled me that not one kid who had witnessed the rape had recorded it. It's nasty, but it would have happened. Second, when a young girl is raped, she's changed forever. When I met you at the apartment, you were strong and composed, not broken the way my sister was when it happened to her. That's when I began suspecting you had been lying."

"It's not like it was a total lie," another girl said. "He did rape someone. He raped a girl from school who didn't dare go to the police because her dad works for his dad, and she feared it might hurt her family. William knew this; that's why he picked her."

"So, you just faked one," I said. "On a girl who needed an excuse for her pregnancy. Bruised her up and left her in the sand to be found by her own father. Who made the call to Robert Lockwood, pretending to be William?"

"I did," a girl said. She had a deep voice, and it made sense that it could have been mistaken for a boy.

"But then when it came down to it, you didn't dare to testify, did you?" I asked. "You all backed out. You were supposed to tell what happened, to tell the police how you had seen William rape Lucy on the beach after the party. But you chickened out, didn't you, all of you?"

Eyes across the room avoided mine.

"I was scared," one of them said. "I'm sorry, Lucy, but I was terrified of what he might do to me. He came to me at school and threatened to kill me if I talked. Look what happened to Lisa, Georgiana, Sandra, Katelyn, and Martina. And what about Sophia?"

William laughed. "Look at you all. So pathetic."

I lifted the gun closer to his head. "That might be. But you're under arrest."

"For what?" he grinned.

"The murders of Lisa Turner, Sandra Barnes, Martina Hernandez, Katelyn Patterson, Georgiana Nelson, the attempted murder of Sophia Fischer, and the kidnapping of Jean Wilcox."

William stared at me, grinning even more.

"You think I did all that? I didn't kill anyone. No, you've got it all wrong, Detective. I didn't hurt any of them. I mean, I've wanted to, several times, but I didn't. Besides, murder isn't really my style. I prefer torturing people, seeing them suffer. That's my thing."

Chapter 46

"WAIT. YOU DIDN'T KILL THEM?" Lucy said, standing to her feet again.

William shook his head. "You really need me to repeat it? No. I didn't. I didn't kill anyone. You just assumed that I did."

Lucy snorted. "Then why did you pretend like you were the killer just before when we asked you to stop?"

"Because it was fun," he said. "Thinking that I had killed your little friends gave me power over you. I enjoyed that, especially after what you did to me. I thought you deserved to fear me."

Lucy shook her head, narrowing her eyes. "You're a sick monster."

William laughed. "I'm not denying it. At least I know who I am, and I'm not afraid to show it."

I scrutinized him while trying to understand. Something was off here; something wasn't right. I lifted the gun again.

"Nope. I'm not buying it," I said. "You might not have killed them, but you know who did. Why else would you put that chess piece in your car? You wanted me to think that it was Lucy. Just like the one who killed the other girls wanted me to think that too…to get back at her. She tried to frame you for rape and you—and whoever is killing for you—wanted her to go down for murder. And you know perfectly well who this person is, don't you, William?"

He shrugged. "Maybe I do; maybe I don't. What are you going to do about it, Detective? You're gonna arrest me and try to drag it out of me, huh? Is that what you're going to do? Take me down to the station and play tough guy?"

I walked closer, the gun pointed at him, then grabbed his arm and twisted it till he fell forward with his face against the dining table. I placed the gun to his head, then responded while smiling.

"Oh, I forgot to tell you. I was fired today. So, I guess I don't have anything to lose anymore, do I? I can act just as crazy as I want to."

That wiped the smirk off his face.

"Tell me who did the killings; tell me now," I said, pressing the gun into the back of his head.

William didn't answer. He whimpered slightly as I tightened my grip on his arm, pulling it up behind his back, hard.

"Tell me where Jean is."

Still, he said nothing. I pulled his arm again, and he screamed in pain. My hands were shaking in anger as I pressed the gun harder against his head, my finger uneasy on the trigger, ready to pull. I wanted to, boy; I wanted to finish him off right here and now. Two bullets. One for Reese, one for Jean. He could sense my eagerness to fire the gun. Still, the boy shut up like a clam, refusing to speak. But then he did something else that helped me. He glanced toward the kitchen for a brief second, and that was when it occurred to me.

Of course.

It all made sense now.

Chapter 47

SHE WAS BEING PULLED by her hair. Jean screamed in pain as she was yanked forcefully across the floor.

"Stop, stop, please, just stop!"

As the pain finally eased up on her scalp, she felt her body plop down on the tiles and managed to look around. All she could make out was that she was in a kitchen somewhere. Her attacker was doing something behind her back as Jean spotted a set of kitchen knives hanging on the wall and decided to make a run for them. Ignoring her aching body, she jumped to her feet and reached out her hand to grab one. But as she could feel it in her hand, her attacker grabbed her by the ponytail and pulled her back, hard.

Jean flew backward, screaming, and landed on the tiles. She slid across the floor until her back slammed against the wall. She looked down in her hand and realized she still had the knife. As her attacker stood above her, bending down, she lifted it. The knife slid through the skin on her attacker's cheek. Her attacker pulled backward with a shriek, then felt the cheek and the blood.

"What the…You…"

"Please, don't; please, don't hurt me anymore," Jean pleaded, trying to cover her face with her hands.

Her attacker tried to grab her, but she swung the knife again and cut her attacker on the upper arm. The sound of the knife going through the flesh made the hairs rise on her neck. Blood gushed out on the attacker's white shirt and dripped down on their white sneakers.

I can't believe I just did that.

Her attacker screamed in pain but didn't let go of Jean. A fist whistled through the air and landed on Jean's nose, then another on her cheek, while her attacker lifted her, then threw her across the room. As Jean landed, her attacker came down on her, ready to throw more punches. But somehow, Jean managed to swing the knife again and cut her attacker in the thigh. This one went deep, and she almost didn't get the knife back out. She had to pull really hard to keep the weapon in her hand.

Her attacker screamed, then felt the wound. Seconds later, more punches fell, and Jean kept cutting her attacker in the leg, then the arm, until her attacker finally managed to grab the arm that she was using for the knife, and bent it back so hard Jean dropped the knife. Her attacker then picked up the knife, turned it against her, and stabbed Jean. Jean screamed loudly. Her attacker grabbed the knife and pulled it out again, then raised it above Jean's chest. She swung it toward Jean when the door suddenly shattered to pieces, and someone stormed in. Next, a gun was placed to the attacker's head.

"Don't you even dare," sounded Harry's deep voice.

Jean felt a wave of great relief run through her as she saw his handsome face tower up behind her attacker. Harry stared at the woman holding Jean, his nostrils flaring, his eyes ablaze.

"You make one wrong move, and you're gone. Do you understand?"

Chapter 48

DALISAY RAISED her hands in the air and let the knife fall to the tiles with a clang. She turned to look at me. Jean moaned and tried to move away from her attacker but was in too much pain. She had been stabbed in the leg and was losing blood, a lot of it.

Lucy came up behind me, then gasped as she saw Jean in a pool of blood.

"Call 911," I said. "Quick."

Lucy did. I heard her leave with the phone against her ear, talking to dispatch. I had Dalisay cuffed to a chair, then told one of the girls to keep an eye on her and let me know if she moved.

I took off my shirt and used it to try to stop the bleeding, but blood was gushing out, and Jean was turning pale. She didn't have long. It felt like the ambulance took forever to arrive.

"Harry…I…," she said, squirming in pain. Her eyes were matte and weak. My heart pounded in my chest. I wasn't losing her today.

"Shh," I said. "Don't say anything. We can talk later when you're better."

She grabbed my hand in hers. She squeezed it tight. I looked into her eyes and tried to calm her down, caressing her cheek gently.

It was hard not to cry, seeing her like this and knowing it was all my fault.

"H-how?" she asked, looking into my eyes. "How did you know?"

I glanced at Dalisay, sitting on the chair. "Her tattoo. When she let me in the first time, I saw she had this tattoo on her arm by her wrist. I used to travel in the Philippines. I knew that tattoo was the mark of the Bahala Na Gang, a Philippine gang known for their brutality and terror regime in the country. When I found out it wasn't William who had killed them, I knew she was the only one here capable of murder. It suddenly all added up in a strange way. When I met her the first time, there was also something else that I noticed in her. She spoke to me in Filipino, but her dialect reminded me of how they spoke on an island I had visited when I traveled there. Jeju Island, where a community of women, some as old as eighty, goes diving ten meters under the sea to gather shellfish without the use of oxygen masks. Her dialect reminded me of them, and I guessed she grew up there. I knew the killer needed to have good diving skills and be more than an excellent swimmer. Finally, it was also something William's mother said when I first came here; she said that Dalisay took care of them all. That struck me as an odd choice of words, but I didn't make it out till just now. Dalisay would literally do anything for William, probably because he made her. She was the one who killed the girls, one after another. She also tried to run me off the road so William could use the fact that I wasn't on my post to get me off his back."

Jean tried to chuckle, but then something else happened, something that terrified me to the core. Her eyes rolled back in her head, and her body went limp.

"No, Jean, no," I said, slapping her cheeks to try and wake her. "Don't you dare leave me now, Jean! JEAN!"

I shook her, trying to wake her, but she was gone. Panic erupted inside me. Suddenly, I was taken back to that day, years ago, when I held Camille in my arms the very same way, shaking her, screaming her name as she hung lifeless in my arms. My heart felt like it was going to explode as I relived everything from that terrifying day. I screamed her name, while I frantically shook her, tears spilling from my eyes.

"Don't do this to me, Jean. Don't you dare leave me too."

Chapter 49

I WAS STILL in the waiting room at the hospital when Fowler came to see me. He wasn't exactly who I wanted to see at this point, but he didn't seem to come here to fight. He didn't have that look in his eyes as he walked closer. He sat down in a chair next to me, then gave me half a smile before asking:

"How's she doing? Any news?"

I shook my head. My nails were almost gone. I could still barely breathe. So much of this reminded me of when I brought in Camille. I never thought I'd find myself in this position again. It scared me like nothing else. Would I ever get to see Jean again? The thought of losing another woman I loved was unbearable.

"Nothing," I said, my voice shivering. "It's been hours."

Fowler nodded and gave me a sympathetic look. "We took the maid in and are in the process of interrogating all the girls. What a story this is turning out to be. It's a terrible mess."

"And William Covington?" I asked.

"That's why I came," Fowler said. "He wasn't there when we arrived. He must have escaped at some point in all the chaos."

I stomped my feet in agitation. "No! Argh, it's all my fault. I was so focused on Jean that I didn't keep an eye on him. How could I have been so stupid!"

Fowler placed a hand on my shoulder. "It's okay. We'll get him. The girls are finally talking, telling us everything he's been up to. We're getting a lot of stuff on him. He's still just a young kid; he can't have gone far."

I exhaled tiredly and rubbed my face. "You don't know William very well, then. He's capable of a lot of things."

"We'll get him. I've put up roadblocks all over town, and we have searches out everywhere. He can't leave town without me knowing; be certain of that. If he as much as farts, I'll know about it."

I nodded with a deep exhale. "I sure hope you're right. I wouldn't be able to stand it if he got away with what he has done. He's slippery like a snake, never getting his own hands dirty. Is the maid talking?"

"Not a word," Fowler said. "But we'll get her to."

"I sure hope so. Get her to tell everything, especially how William got her to kill for him."

Fowler smiled and blinked. "There's the detective I know so well. Determined and relentless. Welcome back."

He patted me on the back with a laugh.

"I missed you, bro. I knew you could solve this case."

I lifted both eyebrows. "Did you now?"

"Never doubted it for a second. Morales and his team are good, but who am I kidding? They couldn't catch a killer like that. Once Jean is better, and you've rested for a bit, then come to see me. I'm putting you back in homicide."

I nodded and gave him half a smile. "Thanks. I appreciate it."

Fowler rose to his feet with a sigh. "Now, I have to get back. Lots of work to be done in the coming days. Let me know when you hear news, okay? We're all rooting for her."

"Thanks, Fowler. That means a lot to me."

He left, and I was once again all alone in the waiting room, sitting in the uncomfortable chairs, waiting. I closed my eyes, then slid off the chair and onto my knees, folding my hands. I remembered sitting in that very same position when Camille was fighting for her life and then realizing that she had survived yet suffered brain damage. I remembered how angry I got at God after that. I hadn't prayed like this since.

"Please, dear God, let Jean live," I said. "I know it's selfish, but I need her. I know I've been angry with you. I was so mad at you when you took Camille away. I felt like it was a cruel joke. You let her live like I prayed about, yet she never really came back to me. This time, I pray that Jean will survive and that she'll recover and be herself fully. Please, dear God, don't take her away from me too…I beg…"

I was still on my knees, literally, when the doors opened, and the doctor came into the room. I rose to my feet, heart hammering against my rib cage as I walked to him, just as I had done three years ago when I received the news about Camille.

"Doctor?"

I swallowed, pressing back my tears. So many bad memories, so much fear and anxiety I had to face at this moment; it was overwhelming.

If she doesn't make it, I don't know what I'm going to do.

"She's going to be fine, Detective," he said with a soft smile. "She lost a lot of blood, but she's no longer in critical condition. She's gonna be okay. You can breathe again."

Chapter 50

IT WAS late before I got home. I walked inside and found my dad sleeping in the recliner, the TV running loudly. He woke up as I slammed the door shut.

"Harry?"

He sat up straight and turned off the TV.

"She'll be fine," I said. "I even got to talk to her briefly before she had to go to sleep. I stayed for a little while to make sure she was good."

My dad pulled me into a deep hug, then patted me on the shoulder. His worried eyes lingered on me, and he tried to hide it behind a smile. He, too, had been concerned about Jean, no doubt about it. He was very fond of her.

"Da-a-ad!"

Josie came tumbling down the stairs and threw herself into my arms. "How is she?"

"Like I texted you earlier, she'll be fine. But she's tired. She's lost a lot of blood. She told me to tell you that she misses you, though, and she'll be back as soon as possible."

"Were you scared, Daddy?"

"I was, sweetie. I really was."

"I was praying for her, Daddy," she said.

"That's why she's fine," I said. "God listens to you. Now, go and get ready for bed."

Josie's smile vanished. "Could you tuck me in tonight? I got really scared when I heard about Jean."

That made me smile. Josie hadn't wanted me to tuck her in for a long time since she felt she was too old for that now. I poked her nose.

"You betcha. Now, go, get ready."

She kissed my cheek, then ran up the stairs, and I turned to face my dad, suddenly feeling the exhaustion and hunger from a very long and intense day.

"There's pizza on the counter," my dad said like he read my mind.

I grabbed a piece and bit into it, then went for a beer in the fridge and opened it. I sank into the couch next to my dad with a deep sigh, eating my pizza, and drinking my beer. Later, I tucked my daughter in, and, as my dad left, I went to our bedroom and sat by Camille, then told her everything that had happened that day.

I must have dozed off in the chair because, when I woke up, the clock by the window said three a.m. I felt sore from sleeping in a chair and moved my upper body when I heard a noise. It sounded like someone struggling. It came from across the hallway.

Josie!

I sprang to my feet and stormed toward her room. The door was ajar, and inside, I saw a shadow move. I opened the door completely.

"Josie? Are you all right?"

Inside, I saw something that made my heart stop.

"William?"

He had pulled Josie out of bed and was holding his arm around her neck in a tight grip. He held a gun to her head.

"Dad?" she whimpered.

I reached out my hand toward them. "William, don't do anything stupid. We can talk about this."

"One step closer, and she dies," William said, speaking through gritted teeth. He had a look in his eyes that told me he was desperate enough to kill her if he had to.

"What do you want?" I asked. "I assume you didn't come here to kill my daughter. You want something from me, am I right? Put the gun down, and we'll talk."

William grinned, but he didn't put down the gun. "I do need something from you. You're right about that," he said. "But, I'm going to do the talking, and you'll listen."

"I am listening," I said. "Just, please, don't hurt her. What do you need?"

"I can't get out of this town since they have these darn roadblocks everywhere. I need you to help me get out of here. You help me, and I might let her live."

Chapter 51

"I CAME HERE ON FOOT," William said. "I don't have any means of transportation."

We had walked outside my townhouse. He was still holding Josie tightly, the gun to her head.

"All I have is a motorcycle," I said. "The minivan I drove while protecting you belonged to the police department, and they took it back while I was at the hospital. I took a taxi home."

"Don't detectives have unmarked cars?" William asked.

"Yes, but mine broke down two weeks ago."

"I guess we're going on a bike ride, then," he said. "Let's go."

I took the bike out and got on it. William approached, still holding Josie. I shook my head when realizing what his plan was. My daughter realized it too.

"Da-ad?"

"No, no, we can't ride this with more than two people," I said.

He gave me a suspicious look. "Of course, we can. The girl takes up no space."

"It's too dangerous," I said. "Not to mention illegal. The police will stop us if they see us."

"So, you'll outrun them. You're faster than they are. I'm not letting go of her. She's my security that you'll do as I tell you. I'm not letting her go."

"Dad?" Josie said, whimpering.

I shook my head. There was no way I could allow this. I usually never allowed Josie on the bike. It was too dangerous, especially with three people on it. If we crashed, Josie would most surely die. I didn't even have enough helmets for three people.

But William wasn't going to budge.

He stared at me, pressing the gun against Josie's head. "Either we all get on that bike, or she dies. It's your choice."

I exhaled, terrified. "All right. All right. But at least give her your helmet."

"No way," he said and urged Josie to get on the bike behind me. She reached her arms around my waist and hugged me, then leaned her head against my back. I could feel how her body was shaking with fear.

I took off my helmet and handed it to Josie. "Here, put that on, and hold on tight. It might get bumpy."

Chapter 52

MY BIKE ROARED to life underneath me, and we soared into the dark night, my worried heart pounding in my chest as I swung the bike out onto the road. Josie held onto me tightly and hid her face behind my back. I wanted to comfort her so badly, to take her in my arms and tell her it would all be fine, that soon everything would be okay again. But I couldn't. I knew William probably had the gun pressed against her back, and she had to be beyond terrified.

"There's a roadblock coming up at the end of this road," I said as we had reached the end of 19th Avenue and turned down Flagler Street, driving past the seafood market where I used to take Camille when we were younger.

"What do you want to do?"

"Show them your badge. Don't they know you?" he asked.

"Doesn't matter," I said. "They'll never let us through with three people on a bike."

"Take another road," he said. "One that doesn't have a roadblock."

"I don't know all the roadblocks, if that's what you think," I yelled through the noise from my bike.

"Do it anyway."

I did as he told me to and swung down 22nd Avenue. There was no roadblock, so we continued further down 22nd until we reached Dixie. William told me to speed up, so I did, hoping that a patrol car would see us and stop us. I rode past a place where I knew a patrol usually kept an eye out, and I was right. It was there, as usual. I roared past the car, speeding excessively past it, making as much noise as I possibly could.

It worked. Seconds later, the cruiser followed.

"Shoot," William said. "They're following us. Lose them!"

"I'm going as fast as I can," I yelled back.

I felt the gun pressed against my neck. "I don't think you are."

"It's dangerous to go faster," I said. "I risk killing us all if we crash."

"I'm willing to take that risk," William said. "Are you willing to risk your daughter's life?"

I exhaled and took another glance at the police cruiser behind me, almost catching up to us.

"I am sorry," I said, then sped up, and seconds later, I saw the cruiser become smaller and smaller in the mirror. I bit down on my lip, trying to press my fears away, then roared forward, taking a turn a little too sharply, not taking into account the extra weight I was carrying, making it harder to turn. The bike skidded sideways, and Josie screamed, but I accelerated just in time to get it around the corner without losing our balance or control. I got it back and running, then ran it down another street when we saw blinking lights in the distance.

"Another roadblock," I said, going fast toward it. "What do you want to do?"

William looked behind us, where the cruiser was still trying to catch us. It was now joined by two other patrol cars that came from side streets.

"What do you want to do, William?" I yelled.

"I'm thinking!" he yelled back.

"Gotta think fast! It's coming up!"

"Go through," he then said. "Drive right through the roadblock!"

I swallowed hard. I was afraid he was going to say that.

"All right," I said and accelerated as we came closer and closer to the block. "Hold on, Josie!"

The officers behind the block were yelling at us, but I couldn't hear anything. Then I saw them jump for their lives as they realized I wasn't going to stop. I slammed the motorcycle right into the barricade. When we hit the barricade, William was slung into the air. He flew into one of the parked cars and crashed into it.

I lost control of the bike, and it tilted to the side, then skidded across the asphalt, Josie screaming behind me until we finally came to a stop. Completely out of it, I tried to figure out what was up and what was down, then spotted Josie lying on the asphalt behind me. Blood was running from my legs, and I was in pain, but it didn't matter. All that mattered was her. While police surrounded William with guns, I crawled to my daughter and reached out my hand to touch her shoulder and turned her around.

"Josie," I whispered, then yelled: "Josie!"

ONE WEEK LATER

Chapter 53

"I'VE GOT another one ready. Who's the taker?"

Josie raised her hand in the air, the one that wasn't bandaged. My dad placed the patty on her plate. We were in the backyard of my townhouse. It was a nice seventy-three degrees out, and, as true Floridians, we believed that was perfect for barbecuing, even if we were at the beginning of February.

Josie grabbed a bun, then made her burger and ate it with one hand. She had been lucky and had just broken her arm, along with receiving a lot of scrapes and bruises. Nothing that wouldn't heal eventually, as the doctor had put it.

I had been lucky myself. Nothing was broken, but lots of road rash and a burn on my arm. My dad said we had guardian angels to protect us.

William had survived, too, but was in critical condition. They were doing all they could to keep him alive, so he could stand trial. Fowler and his crew were building a case against him, and it was beginning to look promising. More than twenty people had come forward so far to tell what he had done, and they were all prepared to testify in court against him. Sophia was one of them. She had woken up and was ready to talk, even though she knew it meant getting in trouble for what they had tried to do to him. She and Lucy had both agreed to tell the entire truth. My colleagues had even gotten Dalisay to admit that William had pressured her to make those kills. Dalisay had a sick mother who was dependent on the money she sent back to the Philippines. Dalisay had earlier stolen a pile of cash from William's mother's drawer, and William recorded her doing it with his phone. He promised to keep quiet only if she promised to do everything he said. If she went to jail, her mother wouldn't survive without the money that she sent home. Now, she was going to jail for what she had done for a lot longer than if she had just been punished for taking the money. Hopefully, she was taking William down with her. I had great faith that he would be going down for a very long time. His parents had cut him off, so there were no more expensive lawyers to fight for him. It was time he paid his dues.

"I'll have a hot dog if you have one," Jean said. She was sitting in a lawn chair, a set of crutches leaning against her chair. She had been home for a couple of days, and we were finally beginning to feel like ourselves again.

"This is so much better than hospital food," she said, her mouth full of the last hot dog that she had barely started to swallow before she asked for another one.

My dad handed her one, and she smiled, then put it in a bun and bit into it. I had a burger like my daughter and plastered it with ketchup. It was my second burger, so I was getting there, but still felt like there might be room for a hot dog as well.

After we were done eating, Josie ran back inside to play on her computer, while my dad said he'd go watch some TV.

Jean and I were finally alone. We hadn't been since the day of the kiss. And we hadn't talked about it. It was about time.

"Listen…Harry…" she started. "About that kiss, I don't know why I…I mean, I know you can't, of course, you…"

I stopped her. She looked up, and our eyes locked.

"I think it's time I move on," I said.

"What?"

I exhaled and took her hands in mine. "I have given this a lot of thought, and my dad is right; I need to enjoy my life. Camille would want me to. She wouldn't want me to sit here and whither."

"What are you saying, Harry?"

"I'm going to put Camille in a nursing home. I've already taken a look at some here in the area. I can visit as much as I want. She'll have care twenty-four-seven, and I won't have to always depend on you and my dad. I'm back in homicide, and they actually expect me to show up to the briefings and such. I think it's time for me to focus on my job if I want to keep it."

"Sounds smart," Jean said. "But a tough decision."

"The hardest I've ever had to make. But I think she'll be happy there, as happy as she can be. They can give her what she needs. But this also means that…"

I paused because it was hard to say.

"Yes?"

"That we could…maybe try to…I mean…how about we start by dating? How do you feel about that?"

Jean looked at me, then smiled. "I would like that very much, Harry."

"I realized this when I almost lost you, Jean. But I think I could possibly love you; maybe I already do."

Jean smiled again, then leaned over and placed her lips against mine. She caressed my cheek gently and looked into my eyes. A tear escaped her eye and rolled down her cheek. She parted her lips as if to speak, but I placed a finger on them, then kissed her instead. As our lips parted again, we heard a scream coming from inside the house.

"Josie!"

I stood to my feet and rushed to the back porch, then ran inside. Jean came up behind me, humping along on her crutches.

"Josie?" I called once inside. "What's going on? Why are you screaming?"

Josie came down the stairs. She looked like she had seen a ghost.

"What's wrong, Josie?" Jean asked as she came in behind me, panting.

Josie stood like she was frozen at the top of the stairs. "I...I...I wanted to check on Mom and then..."

"Is something wrong with Mom?" I asked, my heart hammering in my chest. My dad came in from the living room and stood in the doorway.

"No...I mean...yes, I think so."

I ran up the stairs while Jean humped up after me, taking a little longer on her crutches. "What's wrong with Mom, Josie?" I asked, holding her shoulders between my hands.

"I was sitting with her, holding her hand in mine, singing that old song, you know the one we used to sing before bedtime when suddenly...she...she looked at me, Dad. She lifted her head and looked directly at me!"

"She did what?"

"I think you should look for yourself," she said and pointed at the door.

I didn't think about it twice. I grabbed the door and opened it. Behind it, I was met by the sweetest sight I had ever seen in my life. Camille's beautiful brown eyes were looking directly at me. I gasped, startled, then stood and stared at her for a long time, trying to figure out whether I was dreaming or not. So many nights and days, I had sat by her bedside and dreamt that she'd suddenly look at me, suddenly wake up.

"She also spoke, Dad. She said my name. At least, it sounded like she said it," Josie squealed excitedly.

Camille stared at me, blinking. Then her lips parted, and a whistling noise emerged from between them, shaping a word:

"Josie."

I just about lost it. I gasped for air, my heart hammering in my chest. "Oh, my God, Camille, you're awake. I have never...I never..."

"It's...a miracle," my dad said, coming inside. "Just like you said, remember? You told me you still believed it would happen, even though the doctors said it wouldn't, and now...look at this?"

"She's awake, Dad; look, she's looking at you, see it, Daddy?" Josie said, almost screaming.

"I can't…I can't believe it," I said and took her hand in mine, tears spilling from my eyes. As I looked across the room, my eyes fell on Jean, who was still standing in the hallway, and my heart dropped instantly. Seeing this, Jean turned around and walked away. Startled, I stood for a few seconds, not knowing what to do, then let go of Camille's hand, and ran out after her.

"Jean."

She stopped at the top of the stairs. She didn't turn to look at me.

"I'm…I'm…"

She turned to face me, tears in her eyes. "You're what? Sorry? How can you be? This is what we prayed for over three long years. This is what we wanted, Harry. Josie has her mother back; you have your…wife. You can be a family again. This is a good thing, Harry. Go. Be with your family. I'll catch you all later."

"But…"

"Harry, go."

I felt awful, yet so confused. I turned around and ran back into our bedroom, where my daughter was sitting on the bedside, crying her little heart out. Camille was just staring at her, whispering her name. I grabbed both of them in my arms and pulled them into a deep hug, hoping I would never have to let go again. As we hugged, I heard the front door slam shut. My heart ached for Jean, but I tried so hard not to think about it. I closed my eyes and decided to enjoy the moment. Jean was right. This was what I wanted. This was what I had dreamt of happening for three years. It was the best ending to a terrible journey for all of us. Now, we could finally begin the healing process. We could finally become a family again.

My prayers had finally been answered.

THE END

RUN GIRL RUN
BOOK 2

Chapter 1

AT LEAST THEY weren't literally living *on* the street. At least they had a roof over their heads and a place to sleep. Even though it was tight inside the car, Emilia García didn't think it was as bad as when they had stayed in that apartment with three other families, sharing one bedroom, one bath, and one small kitchen.

"I'll pick you up at two-thirty, as usual. If I'm not here, then just wait a few minutes, okay?"

"Okay."

Emilia looked out the window of the station wagon as her mother drove up in front of the school. This was the tough part—getting dropped off. The other kids, on their way into school, always stopped and stared at the towels in the windows and the old rusty car. She feared that they could see all their belongings stashed in there when Emilia opened the door.

It was the fourteenth school Emilia had attended in just her eleven years on this earth.

"Have a great day, honey," her mother said as she stepped out of the car, keeping her head down and avoiding any eye contact at all cost.

Emilia sent her a smile, hoping to brighten up her mother's day.

They had been living in their car for three months now, while her mother looked for a new job. Emilia's mom and dad had split up two years ago, and after a while, her mother hadn't been able to keep up with the bills. After that, they were constantly on the move. They were sleeping on friends' couches or in shelter after shelter. In one of the places where they stayed, a roommate tried to kill a neighbor while they were there, so finally, they had found out they liked sleeping in their car better than any of those places.

"You too, Mom. I love you."

"Love you too, baby."

Emilia slammed the door shut, then watched as the old station wagon drove away, making all kinds of odd noises as it went. A couple of girls from Emilia's class giggled as they passed her, and she looked away. She let them walk inside first before she followed them. Most people might think that school would be terrible for Emilia, since she didn't have any friends, and no one ever talked to her. But the fact was, Emilia loved school. She loved walking into the airconditioned building and feeling like a normal kid for a few hours. After a night in the warm car, she was usually sticky and sweaty and sick of the muggy Miami air. Inside the school building, no one knew she had been up at five o'clock, so they could go to a McDonalds to use the restroom and wash themselves. They didn't know she had been awake every hour during the night to make sure they were both safe, that no one was trying to steal what little they had or attack them. They didn't know that Emilia laid awake at night, listening to her mother's crying in the darkness.

"Welcome to class, students; please find your seats," the teacher said to the class while smiling at Emilia, who was her favorite student.

Emilia smiled back, feeling that strange soothing sensation like she was finally at home.

Here, she was just like everyone else. She was a student who had come to learn. And usually, she was able to forget—at least for a little while—how terrified she was of summer break, of her mother getting hurt when she wasn't there to protect her, or of not surviving another night. Here, she was able to forget all those things for a little while.

Though, there was one thing that she couldn't escape no matter where she went, no matter how much she tried.

The terrible thought of *that* guy finding them, the one with the steel-grey eyes and the big rough hands who kept reaching out for her in her nightmares.

Chapter 2

"EAT UP. YOU NEED IT, BABY."

Emilia looked down into the can of beans. She had only eaten half of its contents and could barely get herself to eat more. The smell alone made her want to throw up. Cold beans eaten directly from the can was her least favorite meal. Not that she could afford to be picky; she should be happy that she even got any food.

Emilia forced a smile and looked at her mom across the cabin of the old station wagon. They had turned the back into a living area by putting the seats down and hanging towels in front of the windows, so no one could look in. It was so hot in there all afternoon, and they couldn't wait till the sun went down. Emilia and her mom had spent the afternoon walking the streets and going into stores to cool down. That way, they didn't have to get in the car till just before sundown. The AC only worked when the engine was turned on, and they couldn't afford the gas to drive around except when going somewhere important like to school or looking for jobs for her mom.

Emilia took one more bite, then swallowed, closing her eyes, barely chewing, so she tasted it as little as possible.

"I'm not hungry anymore," she said and handed her mother the can. Her mother gave her a look.

"Are you sure? It's all we have."

She nodded, even though she felt her stomach rumbling. The school served breakfast, and she still had half a muffin in her backpack she could eat at night if she woke up starving as she usually did. Emilia felt bad for not telling her mom about the muffin, but she needed it to make it through the night.

"Yes."

"Suit yourself."

Her mother ate the rest of her beans, shoveling the last part into her mouth, tipping the can upside down. Some of the red sauce ran down her chin, and she wiped it with her finger, then licked it.

Emilia winced when seeing this. Everything about them and the way they lived was so embarrassing.

Emilia leaned back and closed her eyes in shame, hoping the temperature would go down soon. They had popped both windows open in the front to let in some air. But no wind moved outside, so it didn't help much. Emilia was sweating heavily and felt tired. She peeked out from behind one of the towels and looked into the parking lot where they had decided to stay for the night. They usually shifted around, so the police wouldn't realize they were living there and chase them away. Tonight, they had chosen to park at the port. Emilia never liked sleeping there much. She preferred the parking lot at Walmart, where she felt safer. Down here, it was so vacant. They were surrounded by huge containers and enormous ships, but it all seemed so big and scary. Emilia thought about her day at school and was looking forward to going back the next day. But with every day that passed, they came closer to the weekend, and Emilia hated the weekends. The days drifting around with nothing to do were long and painful.

"Do you have homework?" her mother asked.

"Already did it at school," Emilia said. She failed to mention she had to do it at school since it was required to be done on a computer. She didn't want her mother to feel like a failure more than she already did.

"Maybe we should just call it a night, huh?" her mother said. "Get some sleep? It seems to be cooling down a little now already. There's a breeze coming from the water. I think it'll be real nice in a minute or two. I'll leave the windows cracked open for the night."

Emilia nodded. There was no point in staying awake because they had nothing to do. Emilia was exhausted anyway from waking up so many times the night before when her mother was crying. She really hoped she could just doze off now and not wake up till it was light out again, and the day had begun. She needed to drift off into the world of her dreams, where she'd forget about how miserable her life was.

They used a toilet on the port to brush their teeth and go to the bathroom before bedtime, then got back inside the car and locked the doors.

Her mother leaned over and kissed her in the darkness before she grabbed her pill bottle and took a couple. They were sleeping pills, which her mother often took before bedtime because she needed to sleep heavily. She couldn't afford to take them often, so it only happened on some days.

"Good night, sweetie. See you tomorrow."

"Good night, Mommy," Emilia sighed while secretly praying for sleep to come quickly. "I love you."

"Love you too."

Chapter 3

EMILIA WAS SLEEPING SOUNDLY when it happened. She was dreaming about her father, about the time before he and her mom split up, and those were the best dreams she could have. He was holding her in his arms, swinging her around like he always used to do when she was younger. And he was laughing. Emilia barely remembered him laughing anymore since, in the end, before her parents split up, no one ever laughed in her house anymore. And her mother had barely laughed since.

They were in the middle of a deep hug, her father and her, when she felt movement. In her dream, it resulted in an earthquake, and she felt herself getting stirred up with fear. Her dad didn't seem to feel it. He just kept hugging her and laughing, and she had to yell at him to let him know there was an earthquake. Still, he didn't let her go, and she felt so safe in his arms, even though the entire earth shook beneath them.

"Dad?" she said in the dream. "I think something is wrong."

"No, sweetie; we're fine. We're safe here," he said, smiling. The sight of his smile calmed her. But then another thought struck her, one she couldn't escape.

Mom? Where is Mom?

Her heart began to race in her chest as she realized her mother was nowhere to be seen.

"Mom?" she called out as the earth shook even stronger beneath her. "Mom?"

Now it felt like it wasn't just the ground beneath them that shook; it was the entire universe.

"What's happening? Dad? What's going on?"

As she turned to look in her dream, she spotted her dad suddenly far away as the ground opened up and swallowed him. She watched him disappear, screaming, then woke up inside the car, heart pounding in her chest, gasping for air.

"Dad? Mom? Mom?"

She opened her eyes just in time to feel the push. She gasped and pulled the towel aside, only to see the edge of the dock disappear behind them and someone standing on that dock looking down at her. A face she knew a little too well.

A face with deep-set steel-grey eyes.

Emilia gasped fearfully and then heard the loud sound of the car plunging into the water. Paralyzed with panic, Emilia stared into the darkness as the car sunk. It took a few seconds for her to figure out what was going on, that this was no longer a dream.

Then, she screamed.

"M-O-O-O-M!"

She reached over and shook her mother, but she wouldn't wake up. The sleeping pills had knocked her out completely, and when that happened, Emilia knew there was no way she could wake her.

"Mom, please," she moaned as the car sunk deeper and deeper into the water, and some of it started to spurt in through the cracks. It was creaking and making all kinds of scary noises outside the car while Emilia panicked inside.

"Please, Mommy; please, wake up! I think we're drowning, Mommy. I think we're…please, wake up."

But her mother didn't wake up. Emilia whimpered and held her tightly as the water slowly filled the cabin of the car. She cried and tried to open the door, but it wouldn't budge. Emilia kicked and screamed as her clothes were soaked, and soon, she could barely keep her head above water.

THREE WEEKS LATER

Chapter 4

"GIRL FOURTEEN, ACUTE CARDIAC ARREST."

I was running behind the stretcher as I heard the paramedic give the message to the nurse in the ER. I don't know if it was hearing him say the words that made me finally break down and cry, or if it was the sight of them rushing my daughter down the hallway, asking me to stay back, that did it to me.

I leaned forward, hands resting on my knees, still panting, when Jean came out to the waiting room and saw me. We hadn't seen each other for weeks, and as her eyes fell on me, I started crying even harder.

"Harry!"

She rushed to me, grabbed me in her arms, and helped me sit down. It wasn't an easy thing to do with a big guy who's six-foot-eight and weighs more than two hundred and thirty pounds. Especially not for a small woman like Jean. But Jean was a lot stronger than you'd think. She spoke with a shivering voice.

"What happened? I saw them rush someone down to surgery. It looked like... Was that Josie?"

I nodded, gasping for air. I could hardly get the words across my lips and struggled to tell her.

"Sh-she fell. They have an important volleyball game next week. She had just been out running, then came back into the yard where I was sitting, then she just fell. It was like she deflated. I…I don't understand. I…I…she wasn't breathing; she was completely gone. There was no pulse or anything, Jean; she was just lifeless. I frantically performed CPR. I was so scared; you have no idea. But I got her heart beating again while my dad called for help. The paramedics came and rushed her into the ambulance…her heart kept shutting down, they said, and they barely managed to keep her alive." I looked into Jean's eyes. They were filled with worry and fear. She was breathing heavily. Jean cared for my daughter almost as much as I did. I continued, my voice cracking:

"What's happening to her? She was fine this morning, and then she said she'd…go for a run…and now this? What's happening to my baby?"

Jean grabbed my hands in hers, and I leaned my head on her shoulder. I could tell she was moved too. Jean was a nurse at the ER, but she was also my neighbor, and we had been very close until recently. Until my wife, Camille, woke up from her brain-injury coma due to an overdose three years ago, Jean had been the one taking care of us all. But now that my wife was better and was awake, Jean had pulled away. Maybe because we had kissed, maybe because we had decided to start dating the moment before Camille awoke.

Sitting here, I suddenly missed Jean more than ever.

"What's happening to her?" I asked. "Will she be all right?"

Jean took a deep breath. It was obvious that she was shaken. "She's in good hands. That much, I know. They took her into surgery right away."

"Tell me she's going to be all right, Jean. I won't be able to live without her. She's my everything."

"I know, hon," she said. "I know. They're doing all they can."

The doors to the ER slid open, and my dad stepped inside, looking distressed. My dad, the retired pastor, who was always there for me…who was always there with an encouraging word or ready to step in when I needed someone to look after Camille or my daughter, Josie. He was, in many ways, the rock I leaned on, and I wouldn't know how to do all this without him by my side.

"I drove here as fast as I could," he said and hugged Jean when he saw her. "Any news?"

"Not yet," Jean said. "I'll go check now and keep you posted, okay?"

"Thank you; you're an angel," my dad said, holding Jean's hands in his. He had always been very fond of Jean, so much so that he was the one who pushed for me to start dating her, even though Camille was lying upstairs in a vegetative state.

"I told Camille," he said when Jean was gone. "Before I left."

"And?"

"She seemed upset, but I'm not sure she fully understood."

I nodded. Camille was awake, yes, and had been for about a month. It was an answer to our prayers, a miracle even, but she hadn't been the same since she woke up. She was still unable to control her body and could only be pushed around in a wheelchair. She could barely speak and mostly just said our daughter's name; that was all, and she struggled to understand what was going on around her and things we told her. The doctor told us it would require lots of rehabilitation, and that we shouldn't expect her ever to be completely herself again. He also said that her reaction would be different to things, and we couldn't always count on it. She could be smiling yet be sad without us knowing it because she couldn't control her reactions the way other people could.

"She might have understood it," I said. "But she just couldn't react the way you thought she would."

My dad sighed and put his hand on my shoulder. "I'm sure you're right, son. I'm sure you're right."

I knew how he felt about Camille. He still believed I should put her in a nursing home, where they'd know how to take proper care of her. I think he still had a hard time forgiving her for doing drugs again, when she had been clean for years, and thereby ruining my life and Josie's. I was struggling with that part as well if I was completely honest. Even though I didn't like to admit it since she was the one with the brain injury, she was the one trapped inside of her body. I had hoped to get some answers out of her when she finally woke up, but so far, I knew nothing about what happened or why she had started to do drugs again when we were doing so well together. Our life had been perfect up until that point.

Why would she risk destroying our family?

"Here's the doctor," my dad said as the door opened, and someone came inside wearing a doctor's coat. We were the only ones in the waiting room, and the man in the white coat turned to look at us, then approached us with worried eyes.

The way he looked at me made my stomach churn. It didn't seem like it was going to be good news.

Chapter 5

"MR. HUNTER?"

"That's me. How's she doing, Doctor?"

"Not good, I'm afraid," he said. His nametag said, Dr. Scott. He was about half my size and had lips that turned down at the corners, giving the impression of a permanent pout. "She suffered sudden cardiac arrest a second time after she was brought in. We were able to get her stabilized. I'm afraid she has ARVC, a type of inherited Cardiomyopathy. It can cause sudden heart failure, especially in teens and young adults. We were lucky that she was brought in so quickly. In many of these cases, which often occur in young athletes, they don't make it to the hospital alive."

I barely breathed or blinked.

"Heart failure…but…her heart has always been fine. She's been running and playing volleyball for years?"

Doctor Scott sighed and smiled politely. "Unfortunately, it's the same story that we often hear in these types of cases. Does your family have a history of heart disease?"

"Not mine, but I don't know about my wife's. She has no contact with her family, so we have no way of knowing."

"You might want to ask her or have her heart checked as well."

I stared at him, not knowing what to tell him. I couldn't possibly ask Camille about her family history of illness. I mean, I could, but she wouldn't be able to answer. I felt so lost.

"But what does this mean?" my dad asked. "Is Josie going to be well?"

Doctor Scott sighed again. "Not unless she gets a new heart. I'm putting her name on the transplant list, and due to the urgency, she'll get to the top of the list, but unfortunately, it can take months to find one. I'm not sure she has that long. I'm sorry. I wish I had better news."

"Is there nothing else you can do, Doctor?" my dad asked.

"Normally, I'd say we could try the implantation of a ventricular assist device, a mechanical pump attached directly to the heart. Though the device can provide improved circulation support until a donor heart is found, the surgery would be particularly risky, due to the condition of Josie's heart. I wouldn't recommend it."

"Doctor Scott," a nurse called when coming through the doors.

"Listen, we'll do everything in our power to find your daughter a new heart," Doctor Scott said, ending the conversation, "but right now, I'm needed elsewhere. You can see her as soon as she wakes up in the ICU, which shouldn't be too long. The nurses will take you to her."

"Thank you, Doctor; thank you for all you've done." I shook the doctor's hand, and he left. I stared after him, my heart sinking. My daughter had heart failure? How did I not know this till now?

God, please. Find a heart for Josie. Save her!

I sat down, feeling heavy, hiding my face between my hands, praying under my breath for a miracle when Jean came out to us.

"She needs a new heart," my dad said. "You just missed the doctor."

"I know," Jean said. "I heard."

She sat down next to me and placed a warm hand on my shoulder. "I am so sorry, Harry."

"He said it could take months to find one, even though she's so sick that they'll put her at the top of the list. Is that really true?" my dad asked.

She nodded with a deep exhale. "I'm afraid so."

I shook my head. "I can't believe it. She survived, and now she might die…because they can't find a heart?"

"Many patients die while on the transplant list, I'm afraid." Jean swallowed. She looked around her briefly, then said. "Listen, we might have one here locally at the hospital."

I raised my eyebrows as I lifted my head and looked at her.

"What do you mean?"

She grabbed my hand in hers. "Come with me. I'll show you."

Chapter 6

JEAN TOOK us down the hallway to the ICU, then opened the door to one of the rooms. Inside lay a girl, a couple of years younger than Josie, on full life-support. Her eyes were closed, her breathing orchestrated solely by machines.

"She's been here for three weeks," she said. "She's been declared clinically brain dead by our doctors. She'll never wake up, they say. There's no brain activity, and she can't even breathe on her own, but her heart is working fine."

I stared at the young girl, feeling awful. I felt terrible for her; she was nothing but a child. Her parents had to be devastated.

"What happened to her?"

"She drowned," Jean said. "I don't know all the details, but I do know that they pulled her and her mother out of the harbor three weeks ago. I heard they were in their car. The mother was dead when they pulled them out, but the girl's heart was still beating, so they brought her in. They don't know what to do with her since no relatives have claimed her. They can't shut her off till someone gives their consent."

"So, what are you thinking?" I asked. It was strange to look at this girl when my own was fighting for her life as well here in the same hospital."

Jean gave me a look. "Well, she has a perfectly functioning heart, and Josie needs one, right? She's the right blood type too. I checked."

"Is she a donor?"

"Not yet."

"But you just said that she has no relatives, and they can't do anything without their consent," my dad said.

Jean smiled and tilted her head.

"She wants me to find them," I said, "then persuade them to donate her heart, and hopefully, it'll be given to Josie, who is at the top of the transplant list."

"You're the detective, aren't you?" Jean said. "I bet if anyone can find them, it's definitely you."

I exhaled and nodded. It was tough to have to make a decision like this, especially for me, a pastor's son who believed in miracles and the power of prayer. But I also believed in my daughter's survival and would do anything to make sure she didn't die. It was an ethical dilemma that I couldn't afford to have.

"I say it's worth a try, at least," Jean said. "They can always say no."

"I don't know about this," my dad said skeptically. "Haven't the police looked for them already?"

"Probably," Jean said. "But so far, they haven't found them, and I have a feeling Harry can. It's a long shot, but better than nothing, the way I see it."

"A long shot is better than no shot at all; that's for sure. Do you have a name?" I asked. "The name of the girl?"

"Emilia García."

"And the mother?" I asked. "The one that died?"

Jean shook her head. "I'm afraid I don't know."

I nodded pensively.

"I'll find it and the relatives, if it's the last thing I do."

Chapter 7

I OPENED the door without knocking. My boss, Major Fowler, lifted his eyes and looked at me as I burst into his office, located on the third floor of the building housing the Miami Police Department on 2nd Avenue. It was Sunday, but I knew he always came in for a few hours to get ready for the coming week. He liked the quietness of the office on Sundays, he had told me.

"Hunter? What are you doing here? Isn't this your day off?"

I stepped toward his desk. "It is. But something's come up. I need your help."

Fowler leaned back in his chair. We had known each other forever, and even though he had gone from dark brown to salt and pepper over the years, the way he lifted his eyebrows when looking at me was still the same.

"What's going on?"

"I don't have time to explain everything, but to make it quick, Josie was put in the hospital today. It's her heart."

Fowler went pale. "Oh, dear God. I am so sorry, Hunter. Let me know if I can do anything for you."

I rubbed my face, feeling sweaty from rushing to the police department downtown on my motorcycle. It was February, but

Miami didn't care. The air outside was heavy, and the sun scorched from the clear blue sky.

"You can."

Fowler threw out his hands. "Name it."

"Who was on the case of the car that was pulled out of the harbor three weeks ago? Emilia García was the girl's name. The mother died."

Fowler gave me a puzzled look.

"I don't have time to explain," I said.

He shrugged. "All right, it was Detective Ferdinand."

"Got it," I said, then turned around and left, forgetting to shut the door behind me.

"You're welcome," Fowler yelled behind me, but I barely heard him.

I hurried down the hallway until I reached Ferdinand's desk. I had known the guy for ten years and worked on several cases with him. He was known to be a good detective and one I trusted.

"Hunter?" he asked and closed a drawer, looking up at me from behind his reading glasses. Ferdinand was pretty much my opposite. Small and chunky, and standing next to my six-feet-eight, he looked almost like a child. He had a handsome face behind the glasses and kind eyes. He was around ten years older than my thirty-six years and had been in the force for twenty-five years. From his computer screen, his wife and two adult children looked back at him, smiling on a beach somewhere. He liked to work weekends so he could take time off during the week instead when his wife had to work.

"I thought this was your day off. You never work Sundays."

"It was. I need your help."

Ferdinand nodded toward the chair, signaling for me to sit down. I did, even though everything inside me screamed that I was running out of time.

"What's on your mind?"

"Emilia García."

"The girl we pulled out of the harbor?"

"That's her."

"What about her?"

"I need the details of the case."

Ferdinand nodded. He turned around and opened a drawer behind him, then looked for a few seconds before he pulled out a file that he placed on the desk in front of me.

"This is all there is on them as of now. It was pretty straightforward. The case was closed after three days."

Chapter 8

"IT WAS SUICIDE," Ferdinand said with an exhale. "They had been living on the streets for some time, sleeping in their car, and we figured the mom simply couldn't take it anymore and decided to end it for both of them. We found sleeping pills in the car, and the toxicology report stated that the mother had taken enough of the pills to knock out a small horse. We concluded that she popped a couple of pills, then ran the car over the edge, taking the daughter with her. Such a tragedy."

I stared at the file, flipping through the pages. "And the dad?"

Ferdinand bit his lip, then shook his head. "We never found him. They divorced two years ago, and he fell off the face of the earth."

"Do you have a name?"

"Luis Martinez, a fairly common name. Right after we identified the mother, we sent a patrol out to his last known address, but they said he didn't live there anymore. They didn't know where he moved to. He might have left the country."

I nodded while looking through the pictures taken of the inside of the car. I paused at a picture of the mother.

"Have you looked for any other relatives? What about her

parents?" I asked and tapped on the mother's picture. "Do you know anything about the grandparents? If the dad is nowhere to be found, they're the next of kin."

Ferdinand threw out his hands resignedly. "I know that she came down here from Dallas, Texas, so my guess is they're up there. I've spoken to Dallas PD and asked them to try and look for them, but that's all. I haven't heard anything. To be honest, I haven't had the time to dig deeper into it. You see this pile over here? All cases I have neglected over the past few months. I'm swamped here, Hunter. I simply don't have the resources to go chase down a father or a set of grandparents who may not even live in this state. No matter how much I want to."

I lifted my eyes and met his.

"Can I try?"

Ferdinand furrowed his eyebrows.

"Sure. I just don't seem to understand why. Why would you? Don't you have enough to do with the Four Seasons case?"

The Four Seasons case was the story of five men being found dead in a hotel room at the Four Seasons Hotel six days ago. I had been put on the case and had been buried in it for days. So far, it looked mostly like a drug deal gone wrong, but I had a feeling there was more to it than that. I just hadn't been able to break the case open yet. Everywhere I went, I was met with closed doors.

Today was Sunday, and I always take Sunday off to go to church with my family and then rest. I had been looking forward to this day. It was supposed to be a relaxing day with my family, and now it was turning out to be the most hectic day ever, trying to save my daughter's precious life.

I nodded. "I do. But this is something else. I'm not reopening the case, just trying to find the relatives."

"Be my guest," he said. "There was nothing I'd like more than to find the poor girl's relatives and let them know what happened. It would give final closure to this entire affair."

I grabbed the file and rose to my feet, sending Ferdinand half a smile.

"Thanks."

"If you succeed, then I'm the one thanking you," Ferdinand yelled after me as I hurried out to my motorcycle.

Seconds later, I was rushing across town toward the beach.

Chapter 9

"HUNTER? On a Sunday? This gotta be serious."

Al, alias Alvita, alias The Plague, opened the door and let me inside. I hurried past her, then put the file on her desk with the five monitors showing surveillance cameras from all over the world. I had never asked her what she used those for, or if it was even legal for her to be monitoring people in all those places. Some of them were obviously placed in people's homes, and others were in workplaces. We had an understanding. She helped me out, and I didn't ask any questions. Al was a former CIA hacker, and I had no idea how she made a living now. I wasn't sure I even wanted to. I had once helped find her sister's killer and earned myself a lifetime of services from her.

"It is," I said. "Josie is sick. I don't have time to explain in more detail, but she needs a new heart asap."

Al looked at me from underneath her heavy dreadlocks. She was probably the shortest person I had ever known, but she still drew more attention to herself in a room than anyone I had ever met, even though she desperately didn't want to.

"And you think I have one?" she asked.

I shook my head. "No. There's a donor at the hospital, well

maybe there is, but we need to find her relatives. She's a young girl who has been declared brain dead, but her heart is fine. She's a match, they say, but we can't find her family."

Al nodded. "I see. And you want me to find them?"

"Yes, please. I have the name of the dad."

She lifted her eyebrows. "A name? That's all?"

I grimaced. "I'm afraid so. The mother and the girl were homeless, living in their car. The parents are divorced. I have the last known address on the father, but he doesn't live there anymore."

Al nodded pensively while rubbing her dreadlocks that were pulled back into a thick ponytail. "All right, an address is good. We're starting to get somewhere. What about the mother. Did she have a phone?"

"She did, but it was destroyed in the water."

She looked at me, startled. "The water?"

"The mother and daughter drove into the harbor three weeks ago. Suicide. The daughter survived but is brain dead; the mother died."

"And the phone wasn't waterproof?" she asked.

I shook my head. "I asked down in forensics, and they said it was completely destroyed. It was an old one."

Al's face lit up. She grabbed the file and opened it. "But if there was a phone, there is a phone record with a provider somewhere. Let me see what I can do. There's coffee in the pot in the kitchen. It's bulletproof coffee, but you don't mind, right?"

"Any coffee will do," I said, even though I wasn't very fond of Al's health keto power coffee since the fatty butter always threw me off a little. I had to admit, though, that it did give me extra energy from my first sip, and I needed just that. I sat on her red velvet couch that looked like something my grandmother would have in her living room, then tapped impatiently on the side of my cup as I drank, watching Al do her magic. I tried my best to pretend like I wasn't counting the minutes anxiously.

Chapter 10

"CAN I GET YOU ANYTHING?"

Jean looked at Josie in the bed. The girl looked so weak and pale; it was awful. Josie was usually such a strong girl, and Jean had never seen her like this.

Josie smiled feebly. "How about a new heart?"

Looking at her brought tears to Jean's eyes. She tried to stifle them since she didn't want the girl to see them.

"Your dad is working on that one," she said and took Josie's hand in hers. Harry's dad had been with her all afternoon but had just gone out for a coffee and a bite to eat. Jean felt worry in the pit of her stomach, gnawing at her insides. It tormented her to see Harry and Josie in this type of distress.

It had been a month since Camille had woken up, and Jean had snuck out of the house to leave them alone for the reunion. It wasn't without some pain that Jean had seen Camille come back to life. She was thrilled that she had; of course, she was. Camille had been her best friend. And it was what was best for Josie and Harry. But while Camille was sick, Jean had fallen in love with Harry. She had tried desperately not to and fought every urge, but it had happened anyway. And now, she had to push her feelings away every time she saw him, and that was painful. She had avoided him at all costs, taking extra shifts at the hospital to keep herself busy and away from the house. Yet, she still found herself standing in front of their house at night when coming home from her evening shift, staring at the porch, wondering what they had been up to that day, if they were getting proper food to eat, or if Josie needed help with her Spanish. She was simply missing being a part of their lives. While Camille was sick, she had been over there constantly when off from work. She had taken care of Camille, changing her feeding tube, her catheter, and making sure she didn't get pressure sores. She had cooked for Harry and Josie and often Harry's dad—who lived right down the street—too. She had plunged in headfirst and gotten herself too involved with them. And now it was all over. It was like she had lost her family. And the worst thing was that she wasn't allowed to feel the way she did. She had to be happy for them; she had to be thrilled that their prayers had been answered. Heck, she had even prayed for Camille's recovery herself on many occasions. She really shouldn't be feeling this way, this deep pain.

Yet, she was.

And now they were all here again, in trouble, needing her assistance yet again, ripping open the old wounds.

It didn't feel fair.

"I know," Josie said hoarsely. She closed her eyes briefly and seemed to be dozing off, but then opened them again and looked at Jean, squeezing her hand.

"I missed you," she whispered.

At first, Jean stared at her, startled, thinking she might have heard her wrong, but then the girl repeated it.

"I missed you, and so did Dad. He just won't admit it."

Jean swallowed hard, pressing back the tears. She sniffled and touched Josie's cheek gently, fighting her tears.

"You rest now, sweetie. You need it," she said, her voice shivering. "You need it to keep you strong."

Chapter 11

"HA. That was a lot easier than I thought."

I looked up from my coffee cup. I had been staring into the black glistening substance for a few minutes, dreaming myself away while thinking about Josie and then—guiltily admitted—Jean. Seeing her again today had made my heart jump, even though I felt ashamed about it. I missed her terribly and was so glad she could be with us at a time like this when we needed her the most. I felt terrible for what I had done to her, for turning my back on her just when we were about to be more than just friends and neighbors. I had broken her heart, and now my excuses were no good. But what could I have done differently? My wife had woken up after three years in a vegetative state. I couldn't very well turn my back on her now. What kind of a person would that make me? It didn't matter what my feelings were for Jean. I was a husband and a father before anything.

"You found something?" I asked and stood to my feet.

"Not just something. I found him, the dad."

I hurried to her desk. "Really?"

"Don't look so surprised," Al said. "I am actually quite good at what I do."

"I know you are…it was just really fast."

"I went through the phone records and internet browsing on her phone, which the phone company registers, even though they'll tell you they don't. Here, I found out that the mother had an old Facebook account. There are a lot of Jennifer Garcías out there, so finding the right one was a lot easier this way. She didn't use her profile much and hadn't posted for years, but she did post pictures of her husband and daughter three years ago before they were divorced. And bam, here he is."

She clicked and showed me a picture of a man holding a child of about seven or eight years old.

"This is Luis Martìnez?" I asked and pointed at his face.

"Bingo. So, now that we know what he looks like, we just need to find him. I ran a face recognition program, and *ba-da-bing*, look what came up."

Al scrolled on her computer and then stopped. "He changed his name one year ago, about the same time he moved from the address we have. If your little detective friend had thought about looking into it, maybe digging a little deeper, he'd have easily found the court documents. His name is now David Smith, one of the most common American names you can find. Probably had a hard time finding work and changed his name to make it easier. Or he got himself in some trouble and needed to hide."

"David Smith?" I asked.

"And there's more," she said.

"I hoped you'd say that."

"He lives right here beachside. Here's his address. Now, just like there are a lot of Garcías and Martìnezes around here, there are also a lot of David Smiths, so finding him wasn't straightforward. I found pictures of him from surveillance cameras downtown, places he seems to frequent, based on how many times he appears on them, especially on the one from an ATM at his local bank. That way, I could narrow it all down to a radius, then I searched for David Smith in that area, and I found him. Here's his address."

I stared at Al. I could have kissed her at this moment. Instead, I gave her a big hug, even though I knew she wasn't someone who enjoyed physical contact much.

"Thank you, thank you, Al."

"No problem," she said and pulled away as I let her go. "Now, go find him and save Josie."

"Let me know if there's anything I can do for you in return," I said.

"Something might be coming up," she said. "But not now. Go!"

Chapter 12

THE ADDRESS LED me to a small unit on top of a Cuban restaurant. A woman of Spanish heritage opened the door, and I asked for David Smith. She gave me a suspicious glare before she stepped aside and let me in. I followed her down a small hallway with rooms on both sides. All of them had people sitting or standing in them and voices speaking, some yelling loudly. There was a TV on somewhere and kids playing. The condo was no more than two bedrooms, but there seemed to be three or four families living there.

"David?" the woman said as we walked into what would have been a kitchen, but with all the mattresses on the floor, looked more like a shelter.

A man looked up from the back of the room, and all eyes were on me now. I recognized the face from Al's computer screen, where I had seen him holding his daughter tightly. He seemed ten years older than in that picture.

The woman nodded in my direction, and David stared at me, his eyes loaded with suspicion. I knew most of these people could tell I was a cop from far away, and David sure looked like he smelled it on me.

"I'm here about your daughter," I said, trying to soften him up. "Emilia?"

It worked. His eyes grew tender, and his shoulders came down. He approached me quickly.

"Is there a place we can talk privately?" I asked.

He nodded and showed me out on the balcony, where he lit a cigarette and blew out smoke. By the way he looked at me, I could tell he knew I wasn't bearing good news.

He puffed his cigarette. "How do you know my daughter? You a cop?"

I nodded and leaned on the railing, looking down on the street. Music rose from the Cuban restaurant below.

"I am sorry…"

He stopped me, raising his hand and turning his head away. "Please, don't…"

"But I have to," I said. "We've been looking all over for you. It happened three weeks ago, and no one has been able to find…"

He turned to look at me. "Three weeks ago?"

"Yes, the police have been searching for you to tell you…"

He shook his head, then slammed his hand into the railing. He bit back tears and took a deep inhale of his cigarette.

"How…how did it happen?"

"It was suicide," I said. "She drove the car into the harbor with them both in it. She took pills first. Jennifer didn't survive, and…"

He held his breath. "And Emilia? She's alive?"

I swallowed. This was beyond hard. I tried not to put myself in his situation, but that was even more difficult because it could be me in a short while. The thought brought tears to my eyes.

"Yes, I mean, not really."

He smoked again, looking at me with confusion. "I don't understand. She's alive, or she's not?"

My eyes hit the ground below. "She is…but she's not. She's been declared brain dead, and she'll never wake up."

A sob emerged from his lips as he could no longer keep it together. He brought a hand to his mouth while his torso shook. I placed a hand on his shoulder and let him cry for a few seconds, fighting to keep it together myself.

"Can I…Can I see her?" he finally asked.

I nodded. "Let me take you there."

Chapter 13

SHE WAS PRACTICING HER VIOLIN. Still, it didn't help her escape the odd feeling that she'd had all day like someone was watching her. Savannah Hart was worried she might be going crazy. She had been a little paranoid lately and felt an unease deep down in the pit of her stomach. Not even being inside her own home could help her feel at ease, and that was puzzling to her. Savannah stopped playing and walked to the window, then looked outside. A car was parked on the other side of the road. Was someone inside it? Was that the person who was watching her?

Savannah took a deep breath, then closed the curtains tightly, shaking her head. No, it was crazy. Besides, she had to practice for her concert next week. Savannah played in the Miami Symphony Orchestra and had since she was nineteen.

During the day, she was a music teacher at the local elementary school. It was a job she enjoyed more than anything. Giving away her joy of string music to the young ones was a privilege.

Savannah didn't have any children of her own and was never going to. Cancer had forced the doctors to remove her uterus when she was fifteen, and that put an end to that dream. It was a great sorrow for Savannah to know she'd never be a mother, and she had devoted herself to her strings instead, making that her passion.

She had barely begun playing her music again when her phone rang. She grumbled and picked it up. It was—of course—her mother. Just checking in, as usual, three or four times a day, depending on her level of paranoia. She had been like this ever since Savannah had been diagnosed with cancer as a teenager. She was constantly terrified that Savannah would drop dead, or worse, get kidnapped or killed in the big city.

"Hi, Mom," she said with a sigh.

"Oh, good, you're home," her mother said, her worried voice vibrating. "I thought you'd call as soon as you got home from work."

"Well, I forgot. I needed to practice. Besides, we spoke this morning, remember? You told me to check the romaine lettuce in my fridge and throw it out if it was from California where they had found E Coli."

"Yes, well, did you? Lots of people have gotten sick from this lately. You really should be careful."

"Mom, I don't even have romaine lettuce in my fridge."

Savannah closed her eyes tiredly. It was on days like these she wanted to leave the country and move to some small island somewhere, where they had no phones, where it could just be her playing her violin and nothing else. She was sick of having to deal with her mother every day like this. She constantly worried. It was probably all her concern that had made Savannah paranoid and feeling like she was being watched all the time.

It was exhausting.

"Listen, Mom, I gotta go."

"Oh, really? You haven't lit any candles, have you? I just read that the fumes are toxic…"

"Goodbye, Mom. I need to practice. I'm sure I'll talk to you later."

She hung up with a deep sigh, then rubbed her forehead. She put the violin back up on her shoulder, then closed her eyes and disappeared into her music, trying to get that feeling of unease to leave her body by playing it away.

Chapter 14

"SO, she's basically just lying there and can't do anything at all? She can't even hear me?"

David stood by his daughter's bedside and looked down at her, shaking his head. Doctor Scott had come in with us.

"I'm afraid not, Mr. Smith," he said. "There has been no brain activity detected over the past three weeks, and she has been declared brain dead. That means her brain is no longer working in any capacity and never will again. I am sorry."

David touched her arm gently, running a finger up against the skin. "She's grown so much, you know? I can't believe how tall she's gotten. She looks just like her mother now."

He wiped his nose with his hand, then sniffled, pushing back more tears, looking at the ceiling.

"I never should have left them. I don't know what I was thinking. I thought…I thought it was best for them. You know what I mean?"

I nodded like I did.

"Me and Jen, we were…fighting every day, and I thought they'd be better off without me. I was in no state to take care of them. I got in with the wrong group and I…well, I feared for their lives, for our lives. I didn't know that things were this bad. I didn't know they were sleeping in their car. I mean, when you first came to me, I thought maybe they had been in a car accident, or they had been shot or something. It was a bad neighborhood where we used to live. I hoped that if I left, the gangs would leave them alone. I owed money, you know? I got myself into a lot of trouble, and there was no other way out. I had to do it. I had to go into hiding. That's why I changed my name and left and have kept hidden for years, not even contacting my daughter on her birthdays and missing all the Christmases. I thought they were safe this way, at least from me and my problems. I didn't know they had lost the house and were living in a car. I didn't know they were in trouble. And I have to say; I never thought that she would…that Jen would…kill herself. She was such a survivor, you know? A true fighter. I've known her for fifteen years. She never struck me as someone who'd do that."

"Living in the streets, sleeping in your car can be tough," I said. "She might have grown hopeless, not seeing another way out."

"Still…" he said, quietly looking down at Emilia. "I don't know why she'd do that, and do this to…to our daughter?"

"Depression and hopelessness can lead people to do things we never thought they'd be capable of," Doctor Scott said, then signaled for me to leave.

I walked outside the room, breathing raggedly, my heart breaking. The doctor began his chat with David while I closed the door and left them to it. I walked down the hallway, my heart sinking. I was fighting to keep the anxiety at bay. I stood in the hall, closing my eyes briefly, sliding down with my back against the wall, squatting while praying for the right results, praying that David would make the right decision.

This was the moment when Doctor Scott would speak to David about shutting off the girl's life-support and ask if he'd consider donating her functioning organs, and especially her heart. This was the moment my daughter's future would be determined.

David Smith held it all in his hands.

Chapter 15

ONLY A FEW MINUTES LATER, the door slammed open, and David Smith stormed out into the hallway. I rose to my feet and looked at him, heart hammering in my chest.

I didn't like the expression on his face.

"You want me to kill my daughter so you can save yours? Is that why you came to find me? You didn't think I'd figure that one out, did you?"

I swallowed hard while staring at the man in front of me. Then I nodded. I had told him about Josie before we drove to the hospital and how she was waiting for a donor heart. Of course, he would know it was for Josie when the doctor asked him to consider donating, even if he wasn't allowed to say who would receive the heart. David was many things, but stupid wasn't one of them.

"You're right," I said. "That is why I came looking for you. Because my daughter needed your help, but please understand. My daughter's life depends on her getting a new heart."

He snorted. "And so, you thought she could get my daughter's heart, huh? And tell me, why is your daughter more important than mine, huh? Why is her life worth more than Emilia's?"

"It's not...believe me, I never thought it was. But my daughter has a chance—a very small chance—of living, but only if she gets a new heart."

"How can you be so sure that my daughter doesn't? Do you know the future? Do you know what will happen tomorrow?"

"Of course, I don't."

"I know what the doctors say about her, about her being brain dead and all that, but do they really know for sure? I mean, there are always stories about people waking up, right? It could happen; it could be a miracle. How can you ask me to shut her off and deny me the possibility of a miracle happening?"

That hit me where it hurt. Who was I to say that God couldn't perform a miracle on the girl, even though the doctors had said it was impossible? Was I robbing Emilia of that opportunity? I had seen one happen in my own house. I had seen my wife come back from a condition they said she wouldn't.

David stared at me, nostrils flaring, then calmed himself. He gave me a compassionate look.

"Listen, man…I am sorry about your daughter; I really am. If anyone understands what you're going through, it's me right now. If I could give you any of my organs to save her, I'd do so willingly. But I can't do what you're asking me to. I simply can't. I am not going to kill her. I can't do it."

My heart dropped when hearing those words. I knew it had been a long shot from the beginning, but I had to admit, I had believed in it to the end. I had truly thought he would see the sense in saving my daughter.

"I understand," I said, my voice breaking.

He placed a hand on my back. "I'm sorry. I'm sure there is another heart out there for her."

I didn't look at him. I just turned around and walked away, trying to hide my tears. I wasn't angry with him. I truly wasn't. He was right. We didn't know tomorrow. We couldn't know for sure that something amazing wouldn't happen. Fact was, I knew I would have done the same. I, for one, believed in miracles and would never dare to take God's matters into my own hands. How could I ask him to do something I never would?

Chapter 16

MY DAD PROMISED to take care of Camille, so I could spend the night with Josie, holding her hand. She felt so weak and feeble, and her eyes were filled with concern as she looked at me.

"There'll be another heart, Dad," she said, speaking with a small, still voice. It was so typically Josie to worry more about me in this situation than herself. "I'm sure they'll find one in time. God won't leave me or let me die like this, and you know it."

I exhaled and smiled. I had to admit I admired her faith in this crucial moment and wished I could have just a piece of it, just enough to make it through the night. But the fact was, I was losing all my faith and with it my hope that things would end up all right. It was hard to believe in miracles when sitting and holding your dying daughter's hand, everything screaming inside of you.

Where are you, God? Why is this happening to me? Don't you care about me? You can't let her die. You can't let her die!

I held her hand in mine till she dozed off, then decided to go to the vending machine to quiet my screaming stomach. I had gotten some chocolate when an alarm suddenly sounded. I immediately glanced toward my daughter's room, only to see nurses rushing about.

Josie!

I dropped my chocolate bar and ran to her room. Inside, nurses were yelling, and the machines sounded like they were screaming.

"What's going on?" I asked.

"Please, stay outside," a nurse told me and closed the door.

I stared at the closed door, my heart sinking. I didn't even see Jean come running down the hallway. She came up to me, her face strained. She was holding papers in her hand that she held up in front of me.

"What's going on?" she asked, perplexed.

Tears sprang to my eyes. "I…I don't know. All the alarms went off and then…they told me to wait out here. I fear her heart has…"

Jean's eyes grew wide. "Oh, no."

She held the papers up so I could see them. I didn't understand.

"He signed them," she explained. "The consent forms. Doctor Scott left them in Emilia's room, and the dad signed them and left them in there. I came straight from there. I went to check on her vitals and saw that he was gone; her father was gone. On the table, he had left the papers and this note. It has your name on it."

She held the note up and showed it to me. It read:

IT'S ALL MY FAULT. I KILLED HER. I KILLED MY DAUGHTER. NOW YOURS WILL LIVE. TREASURE EVERY MOMENT YOU HAVE WITH HER.

I read it a few times to make sure I had read it right, then looked up at Jean. "So… that means…?"

She nodded. "That was why I came down here…to tell you that you got the heart. You got it, Harry. Josie has a new heart."

I stared at Jean and felt so confused. I didn't know what to think. Was Josie saved? Or was it too late?

That was when the door of Josie's room burst open, and she was rushed out on a stretcher and soon disappeared down the hallway. Jean followed them, leaving me behind, feeling completely helpless.

ONE MONTH LATER

Chapter 17

"DO WE HAVE ANY AVOCADO? I am in such a mood for avocado."

I turned to look at my daughter. Josie was out of her bed and sitting in the kitchen. She was getting bored with being at home all day long, and I was about ready to send her off to school again soon.

The school had been really great and understanding. They had let her do online school as much as she was capable, and luckily, she was a bright kid, so she'd catch up soon enough when she got back.

Her breastbone still wasn't entirely healed after the transplant, and we still had to keep a close eye on her incision wound, cleaning it often so it wouldn't get infected. Other than that, she seemed to be fit for fight. The first two weeks after the transplant, she was still weak and got tired really easy. But now she was my good old Josie with the big brown, gleaming eyes. She was slowly gaining weight again, even though she had to watch her diet to speed up the recovery and make sure she didn't eat too much fat and stayed with lots of greens. She was going to have to take medication for the rest of her life to make sure her body didn't reject the heart, but that was a small price to pay.

"Avocado?" I asked puzzled. "You don't like avocado. I never buy them because you hate them?"

Josie shrugged. She had taken her sketchbook out and was drawing some strange creature with only one eye. She had been into a lot of creepy stuff lately, and I figured it was a phase. Josie looked at her finished product, then turned the page and began a new drawing.

"Well, now I do," she said.

I dried my hands on a dishtowel. "I'll buy some when I shop later. They're good for your heart."

My boss, Major Fowler, had also turned out to be great through this time of hardship for me. He had let me work from home a lot while taking care of Josie. That, along with my dad's help, stepping in when I needed it, ensured I was able to manage through this past month.

I was still working on the Four Seasons' case and had to admit I hadn't gotten anywhere with it. Not that I wasn't trying; I guess my focus was just somewhere else these days. Not that anyone blamed me. I had dodged a major bullet here. No wonder all I wanted was to be with my daughter and enjoy still having her.

Meanwhile, Josie spent most of her time during the day sitting with her mother, talking to her. Camille still hadn't improved much, but she did say Josie's name often, sometimes repeating it several times in a row, other times yelling it out, and that made our daughter feel like she was listening to what she said. Even though we all knew it was the only word Camille could say and that it could mean a lot of things. It still made Josie feel like she was special to her mother.

Jean had started to stop by again regularly since the operation, and I liked that. She checked in on Camille and was bugging me about getting Camille to a rehabilitation center so she could start getting her legs and arms to function again along with her speech. I had been looking at a couple of places that were within my budget, but there was a waitlist. It would take a few months, they said. Once again, we'd have to be patient.

It was hard for me not to think about David Smith. Every time I looked at my daughter, I felt such profound gratefulness to the man, and it pained me that I didn't know where he was. I wanted to do something for him in return; I just didn't know what. What would make you feel better after doing something like this? Maybe it was more my desire than it was his because I felt awful that his daughter had to die for mine to live.

"Also, buy some root beer," she said while still drawing.

I paused. "Excuse me? Root beer?"

She looked up and nodded, mocking me. "Yes, root beer, Dad. You know…the sodas."

"I know what root beer is, but you hate root beer, remember?"

She gave me *that* look, the one only a teenage daughter can give you and get away with.

"Well, not anymore. Things are changing, Dad. Keep up."

And with that, she let go of her sketchbook and left me. I stood back, smiling. Just watching her walk up the stairs made my heart so happy. She was no longer out of breath easily, and she seemed to be growing stronger and stronger each day that passed. It was hard to believe that it was the same girl who had been so weak just a short while ago, lying in her hospital bed.

It had been the last minute, they said. Josie's body had given out right before Jean brought me the signed papers. They had told me afterward that her organs were shutting down . If David hadn't signed the papers when he did and Jean found them when she did, it would have been too late.

"God might not be early, but he is never too late," my dad had said. Once again, I had to say he was right. Even though I still struggled with the fact that it had to happen in the first place.

I walked to the kitchen table, grabbed her sketchbook, and was about to close it when I paused. I stared at the drawing Josie had made, puzzled. Not so much because of how good it was, that surprised me too since Josie wasn't usually very good at drawing because she was too impatient.

It was what she had drawn that made my blood run cold.

Chapter 18

I FLIPPED the pages in the book and looked at the previous drawings, then grabbed the sketchbook in my hand and walked up the stairs. I knocked on Josie's door, then walked inside.

"You forgot this downstairs," I said and held up the sketchbook.

"Oh, thanks," she said.

I opened it to the drawing that had gotten my attention. "What's this?"

She looked at it. "Oh, it's nothing."

"It must be something since you've drawn it several times. Look. It's the same scene over and over again. Where did this come from?"

"It's just this nightmare I keep having," she said with a sigh. "It's nothing, really. Calm down."

I looked at the sketch again. It showed a car in the water, sinking into the harbor, and a little girl inside the car looking out the window.

"You're dreaming about this?" I asked.

"Yeah, almost every night."

"How long has this been happening?"

"Since I got back from the hospital, I guess, why?"

I shook my head. "No reason. I was just wondering."

I stared at the sketch again, my heart pounding in my chest. I had never told Josie about the girl whose heart she received…about Emilia. She couldn't possibly know that was how she died, could she? Had she heard it somewhere else? Maybe at the hospital? But only Jean would know that the heart came from Emilia. It was usually kept anonymous. And Jean would never tell her about Emilia. I couldn't imagine why she would.

"Who is she?" I asked, to figure out if she knew.

Josie shook her head with a shrug. "I told you. I don't know. Just someone from my dream."

I stared at the sketch, then back up at my daughter, wrinkling my forehead, wondering. How was this even remotely possible? How could she know the details about Emilia's death so well? The station wagon in the sketch was even painted a bright green like the real one had been, the one I saw in the case files.

"Why are you so interested in some silly dream anyway?" she asked with a scoff.

I ignored her remark. I couldn't stop looking at the drawing, my pulse quickening. It wasn't just the details that spooked me. There was more to it than that. What had me totally freaking out was something else in the drawing, something—or someone—standing on the dock.

"Who is he?" I asked.

She exhaled. "I don't know who he is. It starts with me waking up inside the car, and it's moving, and then I look out the window and see him standing there, looking at me with these steel-gray eyes. I just know in that instant that he's the one who somehow made the car fall into the water."

Josie shivered as she spoke. I could tell it was unpleasant for her to talk about it, and I wondered if that was why she hadn't told me.

"It freaks me out every time," she added, "and then I usually wake up."

Chapter 19

I TOOK Camille out for a walk, pushing her in a wheelchair. She enjoyed getting outside and going for a stroll around the neighborhood, looking at the flowers. She pointed at a big red rose, and I pushed her close to it, then plucked it and gave it to her. She smiled at me, then started to cry.

"Oh, no, sweetie," I said and bent down. "Are you okay?"

Her head tilted sideways, while tears were still running down her cheeks.

I smiled and hugged her. "I know. I know. You can't help it. You can't control your reactions. We'll get you better soon, I hope."

I pushed her down the street, letting her cry while dangling the rose in her hand. I felt tears coming to my eyes as well while wondering if I would ever see the Camille I had loved so dearly again. I was ashamed to admit it, but this didn't seem like her. This felt like a completely different person.

I stopped at a park so she could watch the children play while I sat on a bench next to her. Camille liked watching them play; at least, I believed she did. It was hard to tell. At least it was a change of scenery from the bedroom, and she had to enjoy that.

We looked at the young children playing while sharing a snack.

She was eating better on her own now, and that was a huge improvement. I just wished I knew what was going on inside that mind of hers behind those beautiful eyes. If only I understood what she needed, what she wanted.

Did she still love me? Did she remember anything from our life together?

"Why did you do it?" I suddenly asked out of the blue. I hadn't planned on saying anything, but it had been on my mind for so long, it just burst right out of me. "Why did you start doing drugs again?"

I stared at her, feeling stupid. The woman couldn't speak a single sentence. What did I expect to get out of her? Maybe nothing. Maybe that wasn't why I asked. Maybe I just needed to get the words across my lips.

She lifted her glance, and our eyes locked. I stared into them, wondering if she even had understood the question at all.

She parted her lips, and a word left her lips.

"Josie."

It was pretty much the only word she had said since she woke up. That and *ba-ba*, which she said a lot too, but I had no idea what that meant yet either. The doctor had said there was damage caused to her speech, language, and swallowing, and it could take years for her to rehabilitate it all. I just hoped we could start her rehabilitation therapy soon. I hated that we'd have to wait.

Camille's face looked confused as she repeated the word "Josie."

I nodded and took her hand in mine.

"Yes, Josie."

But her eyes remained bewildered as she kept looking at me, barely able to lift her head enough to do so.

"Josie."

"Yes, Josie," I repeated.

She shook her head and looked like she was really trying to say something, then almost yelled out into the park:

"JOSIE!"

She was getting agitated now, and I took her hand in mine, trying to calm her. It was obvious that I had upset her with my question. She yelled it again, repeating it over and over:

"JOSIE! JOSIE! JOSIE!"

People were turning to look at us, concerned looks in their eyes, some even pulling their children away fearfully. I got up, smiling awkwardly at them, then started to push her back toward the house while she still kept yelling our daughter's name.

Chapter 20

"SHE WAS YELLING, YOU SAY?"

Jean looked at me over the steaming cup of coffee. After my walk with Camille, I had put her back to bed, where she had finally calmed down and fallen asleep. I needed to get out, so I walked next door and knocked. Jean served us coffee and a piece of chocolate pie she had baked that smelled divine. Two of my favorite things were chocolate and pie.

"Yes, everyone was staring, and I couldn't get her to stop. I feel terrible for admitting this, but I was really embarrassed. I can't stand seeing her like this. I hate to say it, but it's almost like it's worse than when she was just a vegetable, you know? Now, she's awake, but not much has changed, really. I still can't communicate with her, and I can see that she is trying to."

"It sounds like she was trying to tell you something, and the words just wouldn't come; her brain wouldn't cooperate. I've seen it before in patients who suffered brain injury. I think she might be trying to tell you something. Maybe you need to give her some time, and then it'll come."

She sipped her cup, and I mine while feeling awful in my stomach. Had Camille sensed I was embarrassed about her? Had she simply been frustrated because I didn't understand her? Was that why she was yelling?

I shook my head. "I'm sorry for coming here like this. You must think I'm…"

"No," she said, placing her hand on my arm. "I am glad to be here for you. For all of you. You know I am."

I looked up, and our eyes met. On another day, in another lifetime, I'd have leaned over and kissed her in this instant. Instead, I pulled my arm away and leaned back.

"There's something else on your mind, isn't there?" Jean said. "I know you, Hunter. Something is going on in there. What is it?"

I exhaled. Jean knew me so well.

"It's Josie."

She sipped more coffee and ate her pie.

"What about her? Is she having trouble?"

I leaned forward, at first debating if I wanted to tell her this, then decided if anyone would understand and wouldn't laugh at me, it was Jean.

"She started having these dreams. Ever since she got the new heart, she's made drawings of them. It scared me half to death, to be honest."

She gave me a look. "Why?"

"Because they showed how Emilia died."

Jean put the fork down on the plate. "Her donor?"

I nodded. "Yes. You know how her mother drove the car into the water down at the harbor. She's drawing that, and I don't know where she got the information. I haven't told her how Emilia died, have you?"

Jean shook her head. "I couldn't see why I or anyone would tell her that."

"And there's more in the picture than what we know, and that's what has me puzzled, to put it mildly."

"What is it?"

"A man. There's a man standing on the port, up on the dock, looking down at them. Josie says he's always standing there in the dream, and he scares her. She also says that he somehow made the car fall in the water."

"I see," Jean said. "And now you're worried that maybe it wasn't a murder-suicide, that it was, in fact, something else, am I right?"

I nodded.

"I fear they were both murdered, yes."

Chapter 21

"I JUST CAN'T UNDERSTAND how on earth Josie would know about this. That's what I'm struggling with," I said and sipped more coffee. "I mean, if I choose to believe this, to believe that they were actually murdered, then what do I do next? I can hardly reopen the case based on my daughter's dreams, can I? They'll all think I've gone nuts. More than usual."

Jean thought it over for a few seconds.

"It's actually not that uncommon. There have been lots of reports of organ transplant receivers claiming they seem to have inherited the memory, experiences, and emotions of their deceased donors, even though they never knew anything about them. I know they did a huge research project recently where a doctor found sixty-something transplant patients and collected their accounts. He wrote an entire book about it, which I read; I just don't recall the title. But it was quite stunning how they had changed in personality, and how they carried memories that, when it was researched, turned out to have belonged to their donors. A woman who had never liked beer started to drink beer and eat green peppers and chicken nuggets suddenly after receiving a heart from an eighteen-year-old man. She kept dreaming about him too and knew his name was Tim and ended up going looking for him. Others say they have suddenly developed a taste for classical music…stuff like that. There was also a girl who was gay before the heart transplant, and after, she wasn't. I think I have the book here somewhere," she said and got up. She walked to the living room, then came back with a book between her hands.

"This is the one." Jean opened it to a page. "Here's one that is very similar to Josie's story. This is a woman who says that she dreams about her donor's accident every night. She says she can feel the impact in her chest as the car slams into her. She also says she hates meat now, even though she loved it before. Here, you can take the book home and read it if you like."

Jean slid the book to me across the table.

I stared at her, then down at the book in front of me.

"So, it's really a thing?"

"Yes, Harry. You're not going crazy, and neither is Josie. The theory behind this phenomenon is that memory is accessible or processed through the cells, and since the heart possesses cells similar to the brain, and it has been proven that the heart sends information to the brain, it may be possible that information about memories and traits may be transferred to the recipient's brain."

"So, let me get this straight," I said. "You're telling me that heart transplant recipients can receive information through the donor's heart after it has become part of their body?"

"That's the theory, yes," she said, "but read the book and you'll know more. I found it very interesting."

Jean looked at her watch.

"Anyway, I should get to work. I have the evening shift tonight."

I left her house and walked back to mine, book in my hand. I made myself another cup of coffee, then sat with the book in the living room, reading through all the accounts, one after another, startled and pushed in my beliefs of what was possible for the human body. I had to admit, it all made a lot more sense: the sudden cravings for avocadoes and root beer, her sudden ability to draw, and her new-found interest in creepy stuff that she had never had before.

It all made so much more sense.

But it also meant that, if this was true, if what Josie was dreaming actually happened, then somewhere out there was a murderer who had killed Emilia and Jennifer García, and who was getting away with it.

Chapter 22

THE RAIN DRUMMED on the roof of the car and poured on her windshield so hard the wipers almost couldn't keep up. It was a typical Florida afternoon thunderstorm, and it always clogged the traffic through downtown. People slowed down, some almost till they came to a stop, and now Savannah was barely moving forward.

She looked in her rearview mirror at the car behind her to make sure it kept its distance. In the back, she had her case with her violin. She had been at practice with the orchestra, and now she felt tired. It had been a long day. The kids at school had been impossible. They were so loud, and their instruments sounded awful. There was especially one kid who always gave her trouble. His name was Jarrett. As usual, he hadn't practiced for today and kept stopping when they just got into it. He was the only one in class who played the double bass, and that meant he had to know his stuff; otherwise, he threw them all off.

Savannah finally reached the intersection where she had to turn to get to her small street, then drove down the wet road through the puddles. As she parked the car in front of her townhouse, she looked in the rearview mirror again and thought she saw the same car that had been behind her all the way home.

Savannah turned her head to look, but the car continued past her, accelerating down the street, where it took a turn at the end.

"That was odd," Savannah said and wrinkled her nose. She could have sworn she had seen the same car parked outside her house several times this week. Was it following her? Was someone watching her?

You're being paranoid again. You're turning into your mother.

She walked inside and put down her case. She hung her keys on the hook, then walked into the kitchen, where she grabbed herself some water that she drank while looking into the street. She didn't like it. It had been going on for weeks now, this paranoia, this feeling of constantly being watched.

Maybe she should see someone about it?

Except there was something that made her think she wasn't completely off, that it wasn't her going crazy. She knew she had a reason to be cautious, a reason to fear for her life.

Because of what she knew. Because of what she had seen.

Savannah shook her head in distress. She didn't like to even think about it. It made her so anxious, it almost hurt. Yet, as she stood there in her kitchen, she couldn't help herself. No matter how much she tried, she couldn't escape the images in her mind…images of the man with the steel-gray eyes and big hands. Of the dead body on the ground. Of the blood on the ground.

Savannah dropped the glass she was holding. It slid out of her grip and fell onto the tiles below, where it shattered. Small pieces of glass were everywhere, and she began to clean them up but cut her finger on one of them. She stared at the blood from the tip of her finger, while images of the body and the blood on the ground flashed through her mind, making her lose her balance. She reached over for the kitchen table and closed her eyes, trying to replace the images with something nice, something pleasant.

She looked over at the violin case, then wiped the blood off on a paper towel, opened the case, and took out her beloved violin. She touched it gently, then took out the bow and placed it on the strings.

She closed her eyes and started to play, drifting off into the world of music. She played like this for hours and hours on end, not even realizing it had become dark out and nighttime was fast approaching. Savannah kept playing, pressing her tears and fears back till her fingers hurt, and she had no more strength in her arms to hold the violin.

Then she finally put the violin down with a loud exhale. She slid into a kitchen chair, thinking she ought to feel hunger, but she didn't. She was too upset, too exhausted for that.

As she decided to call it a night and turned off the lights in the kitchen and walked to the stairs, she heard a noise coming from behind her. She gasped and looked toward the back entrance leading to the yard. A shadow was standing there, wearing a raincoat. The water from his jacket was dripping on the floor.

Chapter 23

I WAS UP MOST of the night reading the book Jean had given me, taking notes along the way. There was so much of what these patients said that was similar to what I had experienced with Josie. Mostly the small quirky changes in personality. Yet, I was still skeptical and not completely ready to cry bloody murder. Josie could, after all, somehow have heard about the child and mother being pulled out of the water at the port before she had her heart failure...before she got the heart from Emilia. It happened three weeks before the heart transplant, and she could have seen it on TV or read about it online. Maybe she had even forgotten that she had heard about it.

I did some research online and read up on the details that had been told in the newspapers and on TV from when the car was found in the water. No one had witnessed it drive into the water, but someone at the port, working on a container ship close by, had heard the splash and seen the roof as it went down. He had called nine-one-one, and they had sent in divers to pull Emilia and her mother out. But no one had seen it go in.

At least no one that had come forward.

I dozed off at around three a.m., reminding myself to get some work done on my Four Seasons case the next day. Fowler had called earlier and left a message, asking me how things were progressing. I hadn't called him back because I didn't have any news to tell. The case hadn't been on my mind much lately, but I knew I had to get back to it soon, or Fowler would get in one of his moods and start talking about taking me off it. I needed to prove my worth to him, and that I was still one of the team. It wouldn't be long before Josie would be back in school, and then I'd be able to get back to work properly. Camille wasn't as dependent on me anymore, and she could easily spend the hours alone while I went to work. My dad said he'd be able to take her to therapy every day once she started.

I was dreaming of seagulls for some reason, seagulls hovering about my head, trying to grab food from my hand when I heard the scream. I opened my eyes with a gasp, then jumped out of bed and ran to Josie's room.

Inside, I found Josie sitting up in bed, lights on. She had pulled the covers up over her head, and she was shaking badly.

"Josie? What's going on? Did you have another nightmare?"

I sat on the edge of the bed. She didn't answer, just kept trembling. I pulled her covers off, then pulled her into a hug. I held her in my arms, caressing her hair.

"My heart, Dad, it's racing so fast."

"Shhh, it's gonna be okay, sweetie. It was just a dream."

Josie shook her head. "N-no, Dad. This wasn't just a dream. You don't get it. This was…so real."

"Was it the one where you're inside the car again?" I asked. "The one from the drawings where the car ends up in the water?"

She shook her head. "No. This one was different. Completely different."

I nodded. "Okay, and what was it about then?"

She looked up at me, her eyes wide and scared. "A…It was a body, Dad. A body lying on the ground. There was a shot, a loud bang…actually, three of them, and then…there was this guy on the ground with blood around him."

"Okay? And then what?"

"That's it. I…I think I know where it happened. I think I know where the body is buried. There was a hole in the ground. Someone had dug a hole."

"Excuse me?"

She looked down like she was certain I wouldn't believe her. "I think it's real, Dad. I have this feeling…"

I didn't know what to tell her. Did I say that she was nuts? That her mind was playing tricks on her? Or did I indulge her? What if what she was seeing was, in fact, real like the people in the book? Many of them had seen actual events in their donor's lives, things that turned out to have actually happened.

Was this what it was?

There was only one way to find out.

"Get dressed," I said and threw a shirt at her.

"Why?"

"We're going for a little drive."

Chapter 24

JOSIE'S HANDS were clenched tightly around the coffee cup from Starbucks. We had stopped at a drive-through for a couple of necessary lattes and chocolate croissants to help keep us awake. Bugs were dancing in the beam from our headlights of the Chevrolet given to me by the city. I could tell Josie was uncomfortable doing this, but I still thought it was the best thing to do.

We had to know.

"Take a right over there," she said and pointed.

She had told me she didn't know the address of the place from her dream, but she knew exactly where it was.

I drove up in front of the City of Miami Cemetery, and she asked me to stop the car. I looked at the sign above the entrance in front of me.

"Here?"

She nodded. "Yes. I remember that sign from my dream. Come."

I got out of the car and followed my daughter as she walked up to the pavement and continued toward the entrance to the cemetery. She stopped by the bars and the closed gate.

"It's locked," she said.

"Of course, it's locked. Cemeteries are locked at night," I said. "Says here, it closes at ten."

She turned to look at me. Her eyes were gleaming in the light from the streetlamp above. A mosquito bit me on the neck, and I slapped it.

"In my dream, the gate was open when the man was killed. He was shot in the head and fell to the ground, limp as one of those rag dolls. We need to get in there."

I pulled the large gate. "But we can't, Josie. We'll have to come back later."

She shook her head. "No, Dad. I remember it now. I have it fresh in my memory exactly where the hole had been dug in the ground and where the man was shot. We have to do it now. We'll climb the fence. It's not that hard, see?"

She grabbed the bars and started to climb, pulling herself upward.

"Josie," I said. "This is too hard for you. You have to be careful with your heart; you know this. No strenuous activity."

"I'm fine, Dad, look," she said as she reached the top of the fence, then jumped down on the other side. I watched her hit the ground, my heart nearly stopping at the sight of her flying through the air and landing in the grass on the other side.

"Are you okay?" I asked.

She rolled to the side. "Yes, I'm fine."

"And your heart? Is it okay?"

"It's fine, Dad. Geez."

"Okay, I'm coming in after you."

I grabbed the bars and started climbing. I jumped down on the grass, then helped Josie get to her feet again.

"I'm fine, Dad, really. I feel fine. You're doing that worrying thing again."

"Okay, just let me know if you feel faint or lightheaded or anything out of the ordinary, okay? Shortness of breath? This is important."

I looked around us and into the dark cemetery. A sea of old tombstones was surrounding us.

"Okay, and where do we go next?"

She pointed.

"Right over here, come."

Chapter 25

"HERE," she said and showed me the place, lighting it up with the flashlight on her phone. The beam slid over a tombstone.

"*Timothy Wilson. Beloved father and husband?*" I said, reading from it. "This looks like a normal burial place, Josie."

"I know," she said. "But I remember this stone from my dream. I was watching…she turned around and let the light shine on a stone behind us. "From over there, covered by that tombstone, hiding behind it. I remember my hands were shaking. I also remember hearing my ragged breath. I remember being scared," she said and pointed with the light at the ground where I was standing. "Someone was standing here, and another man was with him. Then the first man pulled out a gun and shot him in the head. Three times. *POP-POP-POP*. I saw him fall to the ground, dead in a pool of blood. Next to where you're standing, there was a big hole."

"But this guy, Timothy Wilson was eighty-eight," I said. "He died in two thousand and one."

"Look at the ground," she said and lit up the burial ground.

I knelt by it. I had to admit; the grass seemed very new on the grave. Much fresher than on the graves surrounding it, even though some of them were newer. There was also more dirt on it than the others. The grass was only partially covering the area.

It looked like it had been dug up not too long ago.

Josie knelt next to it, then dug her fingers into the dirt.

"What are you doing, Josie?" I asked.

She kept digging dirt up and moving it to the side.

"Help me," she said.

I looked around us, feeling sweat prickle on my face. If I were caught here, it wouldn't look good.

"This is vandalism, Josie," I said. "Timothy Wilson's family has paid for this place, for their beloved father and husband to rest in peace. You can't just dig up a random grave."

"Well, I don't care," she said. "I know what I saw is true, and I need to prove it to you. And to myself. Help me or not; I need to see what is down here under this dirt."

I stared at her, contemplating whether I should yell at her and drag her home like a good father would at this point.

But something held me back…the part of me that wanted to know too.

"Josie, you have to stop. Stop it now," I said. "You're gonna get us both arrested, and I could lose my job."

"Then help me so it'll be done faster," she said, panting agitatedly as she removed a huge chunk of dirt. I didn't like her working herself this hard. She had to be careful and preferably be in bed, not out digging holes in some cemetery at night. This wasn't good. This wasn't good at all.

"Josie," I said, exhaling, then knelt next to her and dug my fingers into the soft dirt as well.

Twenty minutes later, we had dug a small hole and were sweating like crazy.

"We're not getting anywhere without a shovel," I said, wiping my forehead with the back of my hand. "Maybe we should just call it quits."

"No," Josie said and continued. She dug in deep and pulled out a lot of dirt. Then, she stopped moving.

"What's wrong?" I asked.

"I think I touched something," she said. She reached down and pulled away more dirt when something came to light. Josie's face lit up, then her eyes turned terrified.

"I told you."

She kept digging till the arm was completely free from the dirt, and soon I helped her dig a body out till the torso and waist were visible, and we could pull it the rest of the way out of the ground.

I let the light shine on the face, or what was left of it. Maggots were crawling in the empty eye sockets, and the body had started to liquefy like they tended to if they'd been in the ground in a wet environment for more than a month. Still, I could easily tell who it was, and as I realized it, my heart dropped.

Chapter 26

IT WAS the ring on his finger that gave him away: a golden ring with a blood-red stone on the finger of his right hand, or the little that was left of it. I stared at the ring as the crime scene techs removed it from the bones and secured it for evidence, my heart sinking.

I had looked at that very ring so many times in my life when I had been in this man's office. The mere thought brought tears to my eyes.

"Hunter!"

I turned and spotted Fowler as he came up toward me. The crime scene techs had put up lamps to light up the area, and I could see his face clearly. He held an evidence bag up with something inside it.

"They found his wallet," he said. "It was in the jacket he was wearing when buried. It's him, no doubt."

I was the one who had called Fowler to tell him of our find. I thought he deserved to be the first to know. After all, he had known our former Major Wolfe better than any of us. Fowler had been Wolfe's protégé, and his only natural successor once he retired eight years ago. Those two were like family. Heck, we all were. But those two had been closer than any.

"I am sorry," I said. "I am so sorry."

Fowler paused. He, too, was fighting to keep it together. He bit his lip excessively while looking at the body.

"Yeah, well..." He stopped and gazed up at me. "You know how it is."

I nodded. "I didn't even know he was missing. Had you heard anything?"

Fowler rubbed his stubble. "Yvette called me about two weeks ago. She told me they had split up a few months earlier and that she hadn't heard from him in a while. He didn't pick up when she called, and she needed some stuff from the house. I figured he was angry at her and told her to keep it cool for a little while. I knew the divorce would have been hard on him; you know how much he worshipped Yvette."

I nodded. I did. She had been his everything. Yvette was French, and he had met her in Paris when they were both in their twenties. They had moved to Miami due to his career. But Yvette didn't like Florida. She didn't enjoy the lack of culture and history, as she put it, and she never grew fond of us Americans. Those two fought like cats and dogs, yet I always thought they loved each other deeply. It seemed like it. But apparently, it hadn't been enough after all.

"Anyway..." Fowler said. "I never followed up on it. I tried to call him once but then forgot about it. It never occurred to me that something might have happened to him. And especially not...this."

I nodded.

"So, what's your take on it?" he asked, nodding toward the remains of our former boss.

I swallowed and took a deep breath. "Burying his body on top of another grave is a clever way to make sure no one notices. Few people actually stop to look at the grave, especially when the guy is old and has been dead for a long time. Most people won't notice the new grass or that the dirt has been dug up. That's why the killer believed it was okay to leave the ring and wallet there...because he assumed Wolfe would never be found in a place like this. Three very distinct holes in the skull tell me he was shot three times in the head. I'd say it was an act done in sudden anger."

Fowler looked at the body and the crime scene techs who were taking photos and video of the scene. He then nodded.

"And you still stick to the story that it was Josie who led you out here?" he asked. "That she dreamt this because of her new heart?"

I nodded. "I know it's hard to believe, but as I told you, according to the book I read about this, it's been known to happen before. Earlier cases are very similar to what she's experiencing."

"I still don't quite buy it," he said. "But you did find the body."

"I'd also like to look into the death of Emilia and Jennifer García," I said, knowing I was overstepping here. But I had to give it a go. "Josie says she believes they were murdered."

Fowler chuckled and shook his head. "I think you have enough on your plate as it is. I can't have you chasing ghosts. I'm not reopening the case because your daughter had some weird dream about the girl who gave her a new heart. Come on, Hunter. How would I ever explain it to my superior? Everyone would think I had gone nuts. The case is closed, and you should let it go too. I know you cared for Wolfe, but you're too involved in all this. I'll have Ferdinand take this one."

I bit my lip, repressing my desire to get angry with him.

"Let it go," Fowler said and placed a hand on my upper arm. "For your own sake and Josie's."

The way he said it, it almost sounded like a threat, and it threw me off. Fowler was gone before I could confront him about it.

Chapter 27

I KNOW I was supposed to be doing something else. I was supposed to be working on a different case. Yet, there I was, defying all orders from my boss by being at the police impound, showing my badge to the guy at the window along with an evidence number I had taken from the García case file.

"Yeah, I know that one," the guy behind the glass said and got up from his chair. "It's right over here. Follow me."

I did, and we walked through a carpark of impounded cars. Cars that had been parked in wrong places, cars that had been held back for evidence, and cars rusting away because no one knew what else to do with them.

He stopped by a rusty old green Ford Escort station wagon that looked like it had been young in the late nineties. The type you just didn't see on the roads anymore. Rust was eating it up, and it hadn't helped that it had been submerged underwater before being pulled out with two people inside of it.

Two people my colleagues assumed had killed themselves. Two people I had a feeling had been murdered.

"There she is," the guy said. "Not much left of her, though."

"It's all I need," I said. "Thank you."

The guy gave a sniffle, then left me.

I stared at the old rusty car, while a million questions welled up in my mind. There was so much I needed answers for that I hadn't gotten from reading through the case file. There was especially one thing I believed they hadn't examined. Was the front door locked? No matter how much I had read through the files, it didn't say anywhere. When they pulled it out of the water, did they have to break a window to get the bodies out? It didn't say that either.

I reached over and grabbed the front door, then pulled it open. It sure wasn't locked now. And no windows had been broken. Had the divers been able simply to open the front door and pull them both out?

And what about the keys? Had they been in the ignition? It didn't say in the report, but they weren't there now. I grabbed the case file in my hand and flipped through the pages, looking for my answer. And there it was, right in front of me in black and white in the forensics report.

The keys were found inside the mother's jacket.

"How do you drive an old car like this one with the key in your pocket?" I mumbled and looked inside. I knelt by the driver's seat and looked under the steering wheel. Two small wires were sticking out, and as an old Miami cop, I knew exactly what that meant.

The station wagon had been good old-fashioned hotwired.

I took a photo with my phone, then leaned inside and took a few more of the inside, while wondering about another thing, the very thing that had me puzzled from the first time I read the report.

I then grabbed my phone and called Detective Ferdinand.

"Yes?"

"How come they were in the back seat when they were found?"

"What are you talking about?" he asked.

"The García files. It says in there that they were both pulled out from the back of the station wagon that had been arranged like a sleeping area because they lived in the car. It says both the mother and daughter were in the back when pulled out. Wouldn't the mother at least be in the front if she drove the car into the harbor?"

Ferdinand sighed on the other end. "You've got to be kidding me. Of all the days, you choose today to bother me with this? Do you have any idea how busy we are right now with what you found last night?"

"I am very well aware," I said, not backing down. I demanded answers now. "But this is important too."

"All right, all right," he said. "I guess they were pushed back. That's what one of the forensics techs suggested, that the mother could have been pushed back by the water when they went in."

"What if that's not what happened?" I said, staring at the station wagon in front of me. "What if someone broke into the car and hotwired it, then drove it to the edge, got out, and pushed it into the water?"

Ferdinand exhaled. "Listen, Hunter. I don't have time for this. They were two homeless people; they drove into the harbor either to commit suicide or maybe by accident because the mother had taken drugs. I don't know. But I do know the case is closed, and I suggest you leave it that way if you know what's best for you and your family."

With that, he hung up, and I stood back, feeling like I had once again been threatened by someone I thought I knew well.

What the heck was going on here?

Chapter 28

JEAN HAD BROUGHT Camille into the kitchen and had her sitting in her chair. Harry had bought her a brand-new wheelchair, one that supported her head, so she could lean back now and then when she needed to rest or couldn't hold it up properly herself.

Camille looked up at her, then smiled, using only one side of her mouth. It was all the gratitude she was capable of showing; Jean knew that much. She handed her a fork, then placed the cut-up meat in front of her and sat down. Camille struggled to put the fork into a piece of meat and missed a few times.

Josie was there too and stared at her mother while she fought to get just one piece of meat into her mouth.

"It's crazy, right?" Jean said when seeing the sadness in the girl's eyes. "How she has to learn everything from scratch again. Learn how to walk, how to eat, and one day, hopefully, talk again. But she's making progress every day. I haven't been here in a while, so I can really see the difference."

Josie nodded, biting her lip. Jean could tell a lot was going on in the poor girl's mind. It couldn't be easy to see her mother like this.

"Will she ever be the same, the way she was before?" she asked.

Jean sighed and helped Camille guide the fork closer to another piece of meat. "Probably not exactly the same," she said. "But she can get close."

"It just takes so long," Josie said.

It was Harry who had asked Jean to stay with Josie for a few hours today while he was at work. He didn't want Josie to be left alone in the house with Camille after what they had discovered the night before. He felt she needed to be with an adult, and his father, old Pastor Bernard, was out of town for the day. Jean still felt a little strange being back in the house, and with Camille now being aware of her surroundings. It had destroyed her chances of ever being with Harry, but she was still happy for them that they had gotten their mother and wife back…or at least some version of her, that was.

Jean reached out and grabbed Josie's hand in hers, then smiled warmly.

"Give her time. I know it seems like it's going slowly but think of her as a baby who has to learn everything. It takes time. But I think she can do it. Your mom is strong."

Jean looked at Camille, realizing she actually didn't know how much Camille understood. She didn't seem to be listening to what they were saying, but there was a tear in her eye that rolled down her cheek. Jean wiped it away with a tissue, then squeezed Camille's hand as she let go of the fork, and it fell to the plate with a loud clang.

"Are you tired, Camille?" she asked. "You look tired. I think it's time for your afternoon nap. Here, let me help you with…"

She grabbed the napkin she had placed under her chin and tried to wipe Camille's mouth with it, but Camille turned her face away and gave Jean a push. She then let out a wail of sorts, sounding like a wounded animal.

"What's happening?" Josie asked.

"I think she's upset."

"Was it something I said? Was it because I said I thought it was taking too long, because I didn't mean it, Mom. I'm just happy to have you back, really."

Camille stared at them, shaking her head and torso violently from side to side.

"I think I'll take you to your room to get that nap," Jean said.

She grabbed the chair and rolled Camille to the small bedroom in the back that used to be Harry's office, but now was the room Camille slept in, so they didn't have to get her up and down the stairs. Just till she could walk them on her own, which Harry believed wouldn't be long. Jean helped Camille get into bed, then put the covers on top of her and held her hand in hers while squeezing it.

"I know you're in there, Camille, and I want you to keep fighting, okay? For Harry and Josie. They need you to get well. I know you can do this, Camille. You don't get to give up, do you hear me?"

Camille lay still with her eyes open for a little while and groaned like she was trying to speak. It was something she did a lot. Earlier in the day, Jean had tried to hand her a pencil and a paper, thinking she might be able to write what she wanted to say, but so far, Camille hadn't been able to hold the pencil still enough to write anything. If only there were some way for them to communicate.

"It'll come," Jean said. "The words. Just be patient, okay?"

With that, Camille closed her eyes and started breathing heavier. Jean rose to her feet and walked to the window to close the curtains when she spotted a car with someone sitting inside it on the street across from them and realized it had been there all morning.

Chapter 29

JEAN WAS on the porch outside when I drove up to the house. She gave me a nervous look as I got out and walked up the stairs.

"What's going on?" I asked anxiously. "Did something happen?"

She pulled me closer, then pointed across the street. "That car."

"What about it?"

"Someone is sitting inside it, and they've been there all day. I have a feeling this person is watching us, watching this house."

I stared at the gray Buick, scrutinizing it. I had seen it parked there in the morning when I left for work. I hadn't noticed that someone was sitting inside of it, but I did now.

"I didn't say anything to Josie. I didn't want to scare her. That's why I thought I'd wait for you out here, so I could tell you before you went in."

Jean's blue eyes looked up at me. I felt like hugging her close to me. I didn't like seeing her in distress like this.

"Go inside," I said. "I'll deal with it."

She nodded, still looking deep into my eyes. I stared at her lips, remembering the kiss we had shared a little over a month ago. I could still feel it, and often it was the last thing I would think about before falling asleep at night. I couldn't forget about it. It was impossible.

"Okay," she said, then pulled away and walked back inside. I watched her go, and as the screened door slammed shut, I felt for my gun in my holster and kept my hand on the grip as I walked down the stairs with my eyes focused on the grey Buick. I walked quickly toward it, hoping to get to it before it could take off. Using my long legs to take big steps, I rushed toward it, and the driver didn't see me until I was almost there. He started the engine, then drove out of the parking spot.

"HEY!" I yelled and tried to step out in front of it to stop it. But the driver didn't intend to stop. He stepped on the accelerator and rushed toward me, forcing me to jump to the side of the road in order not to be hit.

I rolled in the grass, then lifted my head just in time to see the license plate and memorize it. I got to my feet and brushed off the grass, then hurried back to the house and slammed the door shut behind me, locking it carefully. I took a few breaths to calm myself. I didn't want Josie to notice that anything was wrong.

"Dad!" Josie yelled as she saw me. She hugged me, and suddenly a sweet aroma filled my nostrils.

"I've made lamb for dinner," Josie said. "Well, not completely by myself. Jean helped me."

"It smells heavenly," I said and kissed her forehead. I stared at Jean, who was checking on the meat in the oven. Lamb was one of my favorite meals, and Jean knew this. Seeing her in my kitchen cooking again made my heart overflow with happiness. I had missed her terribly over the past month. She used to take such good care of all of us, and I guess I hadn't appreciated her enough.

"Dinner will be ready in half an hour," Jean chirped. "I called your dad, and he'll be over shortly. He just got back."

I smiled happily. *Just like old times*, I thought, then felt guilty. I couldn't do this to myself. I couldn't romanticize the time before Camille woke up.

"I'm sorry I was late today," I said as I put the keys down and opened my laptop. "It wasn't my intention to ruin your entire day off."

Jean smiled. I hadn't seen that smile in quite a while, and even though I didn't want it to, it filled me with warmth.

"It's okay," she said. "I actually enjoyed myself. It feels good to be here again. Josie and I had some catching up to do."

I looked into her eyes, feeling all kinds of sadness. Why did I feel like this when looking at her? Why did I have all these emotions that I didn't have when looking at Camille? Was my dad right? He was the one who told me he believed I loved Jean more than Camille, even before Camille overdosed.

He couldn't be right, could he?

I shook my head and looked down at my computer. It didn't matter. There wasn't anything I could do about it now anyway. I was married, and my wife was sick. She needed me more than ever.

Chapter 30

WHEN SAVANNAH WOKE UP, she was lying on the floor. Her face felt sore, and her lips tasted like blood when she licked them. She felt drowsy and had a hard time opening her eyes. It was so hot; she was sweating like crazy. What was that awful smell? She tried to recall what had happened before she ended up there.

She remembered playing the violin. She remembered it getting dark and that she had decided to go to bed. Then she remembered there was a noise and then there was something else. A man, yes, that was it. A man had entered her house and was standing by the back door. Then what had happened?

"Who are you? What are you doing here?" she had asked.

The man had stepped into the light, pulling down the hood on his raincoat. That was when she had stopped breathing. Recognizing the eyes staring at her, she knew he had come for her. He had finally found her.

"I never told anyone," she said. "I kept it to myself."

But the man didn't seem to care. He rushed toward her, and as she saw that, she went for the front door. She turned around and made a run for it, but the man was faster. He grabbed her by the collar and pulled her back, then put his arm around her neck and dragged her backward.

Savannah had screamed, but he was too strong. He had punched her, then put his hands around her neck, holding tight till she had fainted.

Why am I not dead?

She asked herself this as she took a couple of breaths, trying to get back to reality. Her eyelids still felt heavy and hard to lift, so she focused on her hands, trying to move them. They weren't strapped down. The same went for her legs, and she could move them with ease. But the stench was getting worse, and it was getting harder to breathe.

What's going on here?

She finally managed to lift her eyelids and look. But all she could see was deep darkness.

Savannah sat up and tried to look around, trying to figure out where she was. She reached out her hand, and it hit something, and she felt it, then used it to lean on, to get to her feet. She recognized her bed, and leaned against it, then felt her way to the nightstand with the lamp, found the button, and turned it on. Except nothing happened. There was no light. She flipped the button again and again, but nothing happened. She then felt her way past the dresser to the door, where she flipped the switch on the wall next to it.

Still nothing.

Did the power go out?

There was like a rumbling noise coming from outside the room. Savannah walked to the window, then grabbed the thick velvet curtains that had been closed to shut out all light. As she pulled them aside, she suddenly saw light, and lots of it, in the shape of flames licking the side of the house.

Startled, Savannah pulled back with a scream.

Oh, dear God, it's a fire. Someone set fire to my house!

She backed up to get away from the window, then ran for the door. She grabbed the handle, but the door was locked.

Who locked the door? I can't get out!

Savannah pulled it, again and again, shaking the door, but it wouldn't budge. A huge pop startled her as the windows shattered, and the fire soon grabbed the curtains inside and spread to the bed, moving faster than seemed possible. Savannah screamed at the top of her lungs, then shook the door handle again and again, then started kicking the door till it finally broke open. Thinking she had found a way out, Savannah crawled through the opening she had made and into the hallway when she realized it too was surrounded by flames on all sides.

    She was trapped.

Chapter 31

AT DINNER, Camille sat in her wheelchair next to me, so I could feed her to make sure she got enough to eat. She seemed very insistent on trying on her own, so I let her eat by herself, at least till she gave up and let me take over.

After dinner, Josie, my dad, and I cleaned up while Jean took Camille to her room and put her back in bed. I told Jean she didn't have to do that, but she wanted to, she said. She loved Camille and enjoyed taking care of her again. Camille got exhausted quickly these days, but at least she was present now. It was an improvement, and hopefully to her life as well, even though there still was so much she wasn't capable of doing.

"At some point, you have to forgive her," my dad said.

Josie asked if she had helped enough by now and would be allowed to go back upstairs. I nodded and let her leave. My dad handed me a plate, and I put it in the dishwasher. I turned to look at him once I was sure Josie was completely out of sight and wouldn't be able to hear us.

"What do you mean?"

"Camille," he said. "You're angry with her for doing drugs again and for causing this overdose, but at some point, you have to let it go, son. It'll only eat you up and come between you two."

"I've already forgiven her," I said.

"Have you now?"

I gave him another look. My dad, the former pastor, always had a way of seeing straight through me to a point where it annoyed me.

I smiled. "It's a work in progress."

"It always is," he said. "It's rarely something that happens instantly. It takes time, and sometimes it's a process that lasts an entire lifetime. But letting go of that resentment and anger toward her is vital if you want to move on."

"I know," I said, sounding like an annoyed teenager. "I just…it's still hard for me to understand why she would do it, why she would hurt us all like this."

"Pray about it," he said and handed me the last dish. I placed it in the dishwasher, then turned it on. My dad and I each grabbed a glass of iced tea and sat in the living room. I poured some in a glass for Jean and gave it to her as she came out to join us. My dad turned on the TV and watched the news, while Jean and I sat in silence for a few minutes.

"So, did you figure out who was in that car?" she asked, using a low voice. "Did you see him?"

"No, he drove off. I didn't even get a look at his face. But I did get the license plate and called it in and had them run it in the system before we ate dinner."

"Did you get a name?"

I nodded.

"So, who is it, anyone we know?"

I nodded again. "You won't believe it; I hardly did myself. It doesn't seem to make much sense. I've been pondering about it all night."

"Try me."

I leaned forward.

"David Smith."

She wrinkled her forehead. "As in the same David Smith, who is the…"

"The father of Emilia García, yes, the girl who gave Josie her heart."

Jean leaned back and took a sip from her glass of iced tea, a puzzled look on her face. "He was here? Keeping an eye on us? But…why?"

I shrugged. "Beats me. But he sure was in a hurry to get away when I approached him. I had to jump for my life so he wouldn't hit me. Scraped my arm."

"Do you want me to take a look at it?" Jean asked.

I chuckled. "I think I'll survive."

"Why do you think he was there all day? It is strange, don't you think?"

I sighed. "I don't know. There's a lot I can't seem to figure out right now. But I intend to dig deeper into it. Something is very wrong in this town, and I don't like it one bit."

Chapter 32

WHEN MY DAD LEFT, I told Josie to get ready for bed and walked Jean home. She lived right next door, but with what she had seen earlier in the day, with Emilia's dad watching us, I didn't like for her to be out on her own. I felt uneasy at the thought of him lurking out there. I was extremely grateful for what he had done, giving my daughter a new heart, and I still wanted to thank him for it, but showing up like that, sneaking around my house? Running off when I approached him? It made me very uncomfortable. I couldn't figure out why a man like him would do that. Why didn't he just come to our door if he had something he wanted to talk to us about?

Why did he rush off in such a hurry?

But if I was completely honest, it wasn't just that. I had another reason that I wanted to walk her home. I had enjoyed her company this whole evening, and frankly, I didn't want it to end.

"So…" she said as we walked up her stairs and stopped by her door. The old porch swing was moving in the wind, the chains squeaking. There was a nice breeze tonight, and it felt good on my skin.

"This is me."

"Thank you," I said with a deep sigh. "For everything. For

helping out today with Josie and Camille, for cooking, for just being there and for…well… being who you are."

That made her chuckle. "Wow. That was a lot."

"I just…I don't know how to thank you enough. I know the past month has been…well, it's been terrible, to be honest. I missed you, and I know it's selfish and I…I want to make sure you understand that you don't have to hang around us if it makes you uncomfortable. I don't want to force you to come over if it's too unbearable; I hope you know this."

She placed a hand on my arm. "I know, Harry. No one is forcing me. I do it because I enjoy it. You never meant for any of this to happen. It's not your fault. None of this is. It's just…bad timing."

I nodded, pressing back tears. I looked into her eyes, feeling my emotions stir again. She smiled, her sweet eyes narrowing, creating small lines in the sides. For a second, I thought I'd kiss her, and leaned in slightly, but then pulled back.

"Maybe this isn't such a good idea," she said, and let go of my arm. "Us hanging out too much."

I nodded. She was right. What we were doing was dangerous. The more time we spent together, the more I was falling for her. But being without her this past month had made me miserable. I didn't want to go back to that.

"I'm sorry," I said. "I am so, so sorry…for everything."

She chuckled, but it didn't sound happy. She then lifted herself onto her tippy toes and placed a kiss on my cheek. I closed my eyes as her lips met my stubble, genuinely wishing it could have been on the lips.

"Good night, Harry Handsome," she whispered, her eyes closed, leaning in against me. I grabbed her wrists and took in a deep breath, smelled her, trying to take as much of her back with me as I could.

She sighed. I sighed. I could feel her warm breath against my skin. I wanted to stay like this forever. I wanted to hold her in my arms forever.

"I should go," she whispered, but she didn't pull away, and I didn't let go of her. Neither of us dared to move because, in doing so, we'd ruin the moment; we'd rip our lives apart yet again.

"I'm gonna go now," she said, finally pulling away from me. It felt like someone pulled away the very ground I stood on. I took a deep breath and looked at her again when out of the corner of my eye, I spotted someone coming down the street. A guy walking his dog. He gave us one look, then said:

"Did you guys see the fire? It looks like it's only a couple of blocks down. It looks big."

I turned around, walked down the stairs, then looked behind Jean's house where the man was pointing. And there it was. What looked like a few streets behind ours, a thick pillar of smoke reached the sky.

"Oh, dear Lord," Jean said. "I hope no one is hurt."

"I'm gonna go check it out," I said, grabbing my phone and calling nine-one-one.

"I'll go with you," Jean said and followed me into the street.

Chapter 33

FLAMES WERE LICKING the windows of the house. A window popped as we approached it, sounding like gunfire. The thick smoke was hanging deep from the ceiling, emerging through doorways and the vents. The heat greeting us was immense, like a brick wall, the air thick with toxic components from the burning synthetic materials like furniture and paint inside the house.

A couple of neighbors were outside in their front yards, looking at it, and in the distance, I could hear sirens. I had talked to dispatch, and now the firetrucks were approaching.

"Do you think whoever lives there was home when the fire started?" Jean asked.

"I hope not," I said. "With a fire like this, you'd have barely two or three minutes to get out."

As we stood there, staring at the flames, listening to the sound of them devouring the old house, we heard a sound. One so terrifying, it made my heart stop.

"Did you hear that?" I asked.

Jean gave me a look of distress.

"Yes. It sounds like…knocking."

"Someone's in there," I said. "Hammering on a door somewhere."

I looked around me, realizing the firetrucks were still at least a minute out. If this person, whoever it was, was trapped inside, there wasn't time to waste. A minute could mean the difference between life and death.

"I'm going in," I said.

"Harry, no," Jean said. "You'll only get yourself killed; the smoke alone is poisonous. You know better than this. Harry, are you listening?"

I wasn't. I had already left her and was rushing up toward the house. Thick smoke emerged from all the passageways behind the front door. The door handle had to be too hot to touch, so instead, I kicked the wood again and again. It broke into pieces, and thick warm smoke hit my face. I turned away but was still blinded by it. I coughed as the heat forced me to my hands and knees.

"Hello? Is someone in here? Hallo?" I yelled.

I crawled forward into the house, staying close to the walls. I had been through training programs for situations like this when I was just a young police officer in the force, but that was years ago now. Yet I remembered the important stuff, like staying low, and as I was inside, I found an umbrella in the hallway, grabbed it, and used it to sweep the floors since I couldn't rely on my eyes. They were burning badly, and I kept them shut most of the time while searching the surroundings.

Then the umbrella hit something.

There was something about the sound a human body made when being hit with an object. It was one you'd recognize anywhere. I knew I would, and at this moment, I did.

I reached out my hands and felt to be certain. My fingers touched clothing. The feeling was sickening. There was no mistake; this was a person, a body. The question was whether this person was still alive.

I grabbed ahold of the body and pulled it up on my back, then began to carry it out through the thick smoke. The body was heavy, a lot heavier than you'd think. I grabbed the arms to hold it steady, but the burned skin slipped off, and I couldn't hold on properly. I crawled forward toward the door with the body on my back, crying because my eyes burned so badly, but also because of all the emotions in this instant, not knowing if this person was dead or alive.

Once I reached the porch, I fell forward onto the wood and heard voices around me. People were yelling something that I couldn't understand. Soon, black boots and yellow uniforms had surrounded me, and the weight was lifted off my back while other hands then grabbed me and lifted me as well. The last thing I saw was the ground disappearing right before I passed out.

Chapter 34

JEAN WENT with Harry in the ambulance. Her heart was throbbing in her chest as she watched him on the stretcher. He was breathing, yes, but he was completely out. Jean had seen many patients in her life as a nurse come in after a fire, then die shortly afterward. Usually, it was from inhaling carbon monoxide or other poisonous gases from burning synthetic materials on furniture or having the insides of their breathing passages burned. Harry had been inside of that burning house for way too long, without being equipped for it. It wasn't just dangerous; it was stupid and so typical of Harry.

Risking his life for some complete stranger.

It made her so angry that he'd do that. But she couldn't really be mad at him, could she? How could she be mad at a hero?

As they arrived at the hospital, Jean ran inside with them. It was strange to be on the other side in a situation like this, seeing her colleagues come running out, grabbing the stretcher, and rushing off with him. The ambulance with the woman Harry pulled out had arrived shortly before them, and she knew they were already fighting to save her life. She had heard the paramedics yell that she was still alive right before she was rushed into the ambulance. The question was for how long. Jean had seen the damage the fire had done to her body. She had been severely burned on most of her body, and Jean knew her chances were slim, very slim.

Jean was shown inside by her colleague, Tina, into the waiting room. It was so eerily silent in there, more than what Jean could bear. Time seemed to stand completely still. She stared at her phone while tapping her leg, then called Harry's dad. He didn't pick up. She tried again, but it went straight to voicemail. She knew he had a landline, but she didn't have that number. Jean sighed, then tried again before giving up. She knew Harry's dad, old Pastor Bernard, liked to go to bed early, and once he did, there was no waking him. Jean stared at the phone, then found Josie's number and was about to call her when she stopped herself. How could she explain this to the girl? They had been through so much lately, and she was not supposed to get too agitated with her new heart and all.

I need to know he's all right first. I need to have something to tell her.

Jean rubbed her forehead, then walked into the hallway, looking for anyone she could talk to. A nurse or a doctor, someone who could tell her if Harry was okay or not. It felt like she had been in that waiting room forever.

Jean walked down the hallway. She spotted one of her colleagues, then called out her name, but she continued and ran into the operating room. She wondered if Harry was there. Had he suffered burns?

The doors suddenly slammed open, and Jean stepped aside. They rushed someone out of the room, and Jean gasped when she realized it was the woman Harry had helped out of the house. As they rushed her out and down the hallway, Jean locked eyes with her, and she saw such deep terror in them, her heart almost stopped. The woman was breathing in puffs; her skin so burned it was falling off in flakes. It was a gruesome sight. It was hard to see that she was even human behind the disfigured skin.

As her eyes met Jean's, it was like she tried to get Jean's attention. Jean held her breath and stared at her as she passed, while the woman's mouth moved. As Jean looked at her, she realized the woman was speaking, that her mouth was shaping two words.

Two words that would stay with Jean for the rest of her life.

The woman had barely let them leave her lipless mouth when her EKG monitor flatlined, and all the alarms sounded.

Chapter 35

"STOP FUSSING OVER ME; I am perfectly fine."

I growled at the nurse. She had just told me they wanted me to stay at the hospital for a few hours. I had told her a million times that I had to get home to my daughter and that I was all right.

"So, this is where you're hiding."

"Jean," I said, smiling as I saw her gentle eyes lingering on me from the doorway. "Tell her I'm fine; will you?"

She gave me a look, lifting her eyebrows.

"Are you?"

"Yes!" I groaned. "I'm perfectly fine. You can read the darn report yourself. It'll tell you I'm great and ready to go. No severe burns, only some mild ones to my leg, but it's nothing. And I have no signs of smoke inhalation. They took an x-ray of my chest to see if there was damage to my lungs; they checked my oxygen levels and the levels of carbon monoxide in my blood. The doctor said it's all good."

Jean sighed. I could tell she wasn't sure she believed me. She always thought I exaggerated just how fine I was. She grabbed my phone from the table next to me.

"Here. You need to call your daughter and tell her where you are and don't forget to mention how you got yourself into this trouble."

"All right," I said and grabbed it, "but then can you do something for me?"

Jean rolled her eyes with a sigh, then smiled as I pleaded with my hands clasped together.

"There's always something with you, isn't there? Like what, might I ask?"

"Find out how she's doing."

"Who."

"The girl I pulled from the house."

"Oh, Harry..." Jean's face went blank. I sank back in the bed, leaning against the pillow at my back.

"Oh. Are you su..."?

Jean shook her head, her eyes overwhelmed with despair. "I am sorry. She died just now in the hallway. They were transferring her to the Burn Center. They resuscitated her, but her heart failed. And that was it. She's gone."

Tears welled up in my eyes. I couldn't believe this. It had all been in vain? I had risked my life...for this? Only for her to die in the hospital? The thought was unbearable, cruel.

"What...what was her name?" I asked.

"Savannah Hart."

"Savannah Hart," I repeated pensively. I wanted to remember her.

"But there is something else," Jean said as the nurse left us. She closed the curtain around me so no one could see us. She sat on the edge of the bed.

"What?"

"She said something to me right before she died."

I made a face. What was she talking about?

"You were there? When she died? I don't get it."

"I saw her when she was being transported down the hallway. Our eyes locked, and then she mouthed two words to me that I can't forget. Her eyes were so insistent; it still gives me goosebumps to think about it. It was like she knew she was going to die, and it was important for her to get this message across to someone before she went. I can't explain it; I just knew it was important."

"And what did she say? What were those two words?"

Jean leaned over and whispered in my ear. As she spoke, my eyes grew wider, and my heart started to pound loudly. I could barely believe her. With two small words, shaping a name, some of the pieces in my puzzle suddenly fell into place. Not all of them, but enough for me to understand that this woman wasn't in an accident. She was killed by the same murderer that had killed Major Wolfe, and if Josie's heart told the truth, the same person who had also murdered Emilia and Jennifer García.

Chapter 36

"TIMOTHY WILSON."

I kept repeating the name over and over again in the Uber on my way home. Jean was sitting next to me, yawning. I couldn't blame her. I was exhausted too. I had called and spoken to Josie, then told her not to worry and just go to bed, that I'd be home soon. I just hoped she had been able to fall asleep. She needed all the rest she could get.

"I remembered you told me that was the name on the guy's grave," Jean said, "the one where you found your old boss. That's why it startled me so much. Do you have any idea why she'd say that name?"

I shook my head. "Not really, other than she must have known Major Wolfe was buried there. Just like Emilia knew."

"Do you think she might have seen who killed him and buried him?" Jean said as the driver drove up in front of my house. I thanked him for the ride, and we both got out.

"That is exactly what I think. You have a very sharp mind, Miss Wilcox," I said, teasing her. "We could use someone like you on the force one day."

She scoffed. "I'll just end up having to patch you all up when some tough guy roughs you up. I'd end up babysitting all of you."

I exhaled as the Uber disappeared down the road.

"Thank you…again," I said. "For staying with me tonight when I was in the hospital. That means a lot."

She smiled, "Ah, don't go all soft on me, Hunter. You know I'll always be there for you. Besides, I had to make sure you were all right and that you didn't drive the nurses crazy. Now, remember, if you have any signs…"

"I know, I know. Cough, shortness of breath, headache, any changes in my skin…if it turns blue or pale due to lack of oxygen, if I feel confused, if I faint, if I experience chest pain…did I leave anything out?"

"Maybe just vomiting blood; that's something to look out for too."

"Isn't it always?" I asked with a grin.

"This is no joke, Harry Hunter. You listen to me. You come knocking on my door if you have any of those symptoms, okay?" she said. "Or call nine-one-one right away. It's up to you. But don't ignore it; you hear me?"

I nodded. "Yes, ma'am. Loud and clear. Now, goodnight."

Jean sighed. Her shoulders came down slightly. It had been a tough night for her too. I hated that I made her worry.

"Good night, Harry. Take care."

I sent her one last look as she walked up to her porch and I to mine. I smiled as I saw that she looked at me too, right before we both walked inside. I still felt like I could smell the darn smoke everywhere, and my throat was scratchy. I went to get a glass of water in the kitchen first, to bring with me up to bed.

I had barely turned on the light in the kitchen when I heard a loud bump coming from upstairs. When I looked out in the street, I saw the gray Buick parked a couple of houses down under a streetlight.

What in the…?

Wasting no more time, I hurried into the hallway and grabbed my gun from the safety box in the closet, using my fingerprints to open it. With the gun held out in front of me, I walked as quietly as possible up the stairs.

Chapter 37

THE GUN WAS steady in my hand as I was reminding myself to be cautious not to overreact. After all, the bumping sounds could easily have been Josie going to the bathroom, or maybe she hadn't gone to bed at all after we spoke. But the sight of the Buick in the street made me suspect otherwise, and I wasn't taking any chances.

I reached the top of the stairs when I saw a shadow move across the hallway...the shadow of a person who looked nothing like Josie.

"Stop right there," I said.

He did as I told him.

"Hands where I can see them, behind your head."

The person obeyed. Hands were placed behind the neck.

"Now, turn around."

As I suspected, I was looking at David Smith. He was shaking heavily.

"What are you doing in my home?" I asked and stepped forward, holding the gun out. I felt such anger swell up inside of me and had to keep my cool so it wouldn't run away with me. It was one thing that he was watching us from the street, but having him break into my house where my daughter was sleeping all alone was something completely different.

"Answer me! What are you doing here? Did you hurt my daughter?"

He shook his head. "N-no."

"What's going on?"

Josie came out through her door and looked at us.

"Are you okay?" I asked. "Did he touch you?"

Josie shook her head. "No. I didn't…who is he, and why is he here…Dad?"

"She was sleeping," David said, stuttering. "I was just…watching her."

"You were watching her sleep?" I asked. "Why?"

David sank to his knees, crying. "Don't you understand? She's all I have left of her. She's all I have left of Emilia. She has her heart…pounding in her chest, my daughter's heart."

"What?" Josie asked. "He's her dad?"

"Is that why you've been watching us?" I asked.

He nodded, sobbing. "Yes. That and because I needed to protect her."

"What do you mean protect her?" I asked, confused.

David pressed back tears and swallowed before he spoke. "Someone wants her dead."

"Someone wants my Josie dead?" I asked. "Who?"

"I don't know," David said, crying.

I stepped forward and placed the gun to his head, then yelled: "WHO?"

David was trembling beneath the gun. "I don't know him. I don't know his name or who he is, but I know he works at the harbor. I've done a couple of gigs for him, you know…transport. Stuff like that, illegal transport. He imports appliances, fridges, freezers, washer and dryers, stuff like that under the radar. Avoiding taxes and stuff like that. I don't know much about it except I sometimes drive one of their trucks. That's all. I owe money, a lot of it, and they pay me well. Better than any other driving job. As long as I don't ask any questions. Anyway, I heard him talking to someone about it a few days ago, about the girl, the daughter of a detective and how the heart, my Emilia's heart, had led them to find the body of some guy that they wanted to stay buried. I knew it could only be Josie they were talking about. They talked about cutting that heart out of the girl, getting rid of her. I thought I could protect her. As I told you, she's all I have left of my girl, my sweet daughter."

"Why didn't you just come to talk to me? You could've warned me instead of hanging out in the street like that," I said, still angry, but easing up slightly.

"I panicked. I wanted to see Josie, to see her with my daughter's heart, and then when you came out to the car, I freaked out. I panicked, and then I thought you wouldn't talk to me after I almost ran you over."

"Well, you're right about that. No one listens to someone creeping around like some snake. I'm not even sure I believe half of what you're saying right now."

Josie came up behind me. "Dad, listen to the man. Look at him. He doesn't look like much of a threat, does he? Don't forget what he did for me."

"He broke into our home, Josie. This is our sacred place. Here, I expect you to be safe. He violated that."

She placed a hand on the gun and lowered it while looking into my eyes. I eased up. No one could soften me up like Josie.

"Who were these men?" I asked David. "The ones you heard talk about Josie?"

He shook his head. "I don't know their names."

I lifted the gun again. "You're gonna help me catch them. But not till we've gotten Josie to a safe place."

Chapter 38

"WHAT'S THIS?"

Al stared at Josie, her eyes squinting. She was fully dressed, even though it was three a.m.

"It's my daughter. Josie, this is Al; Al, meet Josie. Get used to one another. She's going to stay here for a little while."

"She's what?"

Al stared at me, but I pushed past her inside and walked to a couch, then told Josie to lie down on it.

"Do you have a blanket? Josie needs rest. Her heart, you know."

Al stared at me, her mouth still half open. She slammed the door shut behind us and put the many safety locks back on.

"Now, wait a second, I have never…I'm not…children and I are not a mix."

"Blanket, please," I said, ignoring her.

Al walked to her closet, grabbed a blanket, then handed it to me. I used it to cover Josie, then kissed her, and told her to sleep. It didn't take a second before her eyes were closed and she was breathing heavily. She needed it.

"Are you even listening to me?" Al said.

I pulled her to the other end of the room, so our talking wouldn't wake Josie. "Listen, I get it. You don't like children. But Josie is fourteen. She's not a child. Christ, she's twice your size, if you haven't noticed."

"A lot of children are taller than me; that doesn't mean they don't cause trouble or make a mess," she snorted. "I'm not the motherly type."

I sighed and ran a hand through my hair. "I need this."

She gave me a look.

"Remember your sister and how I found the guy who killed her?"

Al groaned loudly. "Oh, you're gonna pull that one on me, huh?"

"You said a lifetime of help."

"I meant on computers. Hacking stuff. Not babysitting."

"She's in danger," I said. "They want to kill her. I can't go into too many details, but she helped find a body that was supposed to stay hidden. You're the only one I trust right now. No one knows this place even exists. It's a freaking fortress."

Al exhaled and fiddled with a dreadlock. "All right, I guess. But I'm not cooking or anything like that."

"You don't have to," I said and handed her a one-hundred-dollar bill. "Buy a pizza. Buy several since Josie eats a lot. She's still growing."

"I wouldn't think it was possible for her to get any taller, but I'll take your word for it," she said and took the bill.

"Just don't let her leave the apartment, okay? I need her to stay hidden," I said, about to walk to the door.

"I haven't left this place in years, at least not in full daylight," Al said. "I think I can manage. But, hey, be safe out there, will ya?"

I chuckled. "And you say you're not the motherly type. That right there was some pretty deep motherly stuff."

"Get out of here," Al said. "Before I kick you out."

"Oh, before I forget," I said and stopped myself halfway to the door. "There is one more thing I need you to do for me, something I know you're very good at."

Al rolled her eyes at me. "You're the gift that just keeps on giving, aren't you? Okay, Hunter. Spit it out. What is it?"

Chapter 39

I KNOCKED ON THE DOOR, then poked my head inside. It was the next morning after only a few hours of restless sleep. I had a pounding headache but ignored it, knowing Jean would kill me if she knew.

"You got a minute?"

Fowler was on the phone when he saw me. He nodded and signaled for me to give him a minute while he finished his conversation. Then he hung up.

"Hunter." He looked at his watch. "This early? Something must be up."

I sat down in a chair across from him.

"I know that look," he said and leaned back in his leather chair, folding his hands in front of him. "It usually means trouble."

"It's the Wolfe murder," I said. "You know how Josie helped find where he was buried, right?"

Fowler chuckled. "Allegedly because she dreamt it, yes, how could I forget? Has she had any other dreams recently?"

"None that she has told me about, but I have reason to believe she's in danger."

"Really?"

"Yes, whoever killed Wolfe is trying to get to her."

He got a serious look on his face. I thought about David and how he was doing back at the house where I had cuffed him and put him in the pantry, then closed the door. Camille was the only one in the house, and she would be sleeping most of the day. I reminded myself to start looking for a nurse for her. Jean was wonderful, but it wasn't healthy for any of us that she came over so often. It broke my heart to think this way, but it was necessary.

"And you're certain about this?" Fowler asked.

"I'm not making this up, if that's what you're suggesting," I said. "I have this from a reliable source."

He nodded. "Okay. Have you gotten her somewhere safe?"

I nodded. "She's staying with Al."

Fowler smiled. "I remember her. You still see each other?"

"Occasionally," I said.

Fowler had been my partner back when we had been on Al's sister's case. It was around the time he received news of his promotion, and I had ended up solving it alone while he moved up the ranks instead.

"Okay," he said. "And what do you need my help for, then?"

"I need to re-open the García case. I think they were killed because the girl knew who killed Wolfe. These two cases are deeply connected, and I want the means to solve them. I also think it's connected to the death of Savannah Hart, who died in a fire last night. I believe she was murdered too."

He wrinkled his forehead. "Do you have any evidence to back up this claim? It takes hard evidence to reopen a case; you know that."

"I'll have it hopefully by the end of the week. I have a hunch I will."

Fowler nodded. "Okay, then. You've always had good hunches. If you can provide proof enough, then the case is all yours, but it won't make you popular with your colleagues. You're basically questioning another detective's work and claiming he didn't do his job properly."

I rose to my feet, phone in my hand.

"I'm a big boy. I can take it."

Chapter 40

"DO YOU HAVE ANY SODAS?"

Josie looked at Al, the strange woman in harem pants who was sitting by her many computer screens, staring at them steadily, her fingers tapdancing across her many keyboards.

She didn't answer…maybe because she had on that big headset. Probably listening to music or speaking with someone at the other end of the world. She had been like this for the past four hours, ever since Josie woke up, and she was beginning to get bored. Her dad had taken her phone, so she couldn't be traced, and she didn't have her computer or her sketchbook with her either. There was nothing to do. Plus, she was starving. Al had been awake when she woke up, and she wondered if she had slept at all. The constant tapping on her keyboard was annoying, and she didn't like the way her eyes didn't look away from the screen…not even once. It was like she was hypnotized by that blue light like her very soul was sucked into the screen in front of her and couldn't let go. Josie had asked for food, for cereal or even some bread, but Al hadn't answered her.

Now, Josie rose to her feet and walked to the kitchen, then looked in the fridge. There was nothing much in there. Just some pomegranate, some kind of weird looking juice, and a pineapple. Was that all this woman ate?

No wonder she was the size of an ant.

Josie filled a glass of water from the fridge, then drank it, but it didn't help anything. She felt weak because she hadn't eaten for so long. It wasn't good for her heart to be fasting. She wondered if she should go and ask Al about food, like go up to her and get in her face to get her attention. Maybe pull off the headset.

Nah, she's busy and doesn't have time to take care of you. You heard her last night. She didn't want to babysit. She doesn't like children.

Josie didn't like to impose or be in the way. She wasn't one to demand much of people around her, and especially not if she sensed they didn't like her or want her around. More often than not, she was certain that if she didn't do things right or behave well enough, she'd lose people—like her dad would get mad at her and leave her. It was a real fear she'd had ever since her mother overdosed. She'd always felt it was her fault, that it was something she'd said or done to upset her enough to make her start doing drugs again. She often feared she was the one who had driven her mother to do the drugs again somehow, and now she was terrified of doing the same thing to her father. That's why she hadn't told him about how she felt that something was wrong with her heart before all of this happened. Before she passed out, she'd feel weak from time to time, especially when doing sports; she could get very dizzy. But she didn't dare to tell him. She didn't like for him to worry about her. Worry wasn't good for anyone. It made people sick. She knew that more than anyone because she worried a lot herself. She worried about her dad getting shot at work; she worried her mother would never get back to normal again. She worried that God would take them both from her, and she'd end up all alone. She worried about those things too much.

Josie felt a pinch in her heart as her stomach rumbled. She grabbed the strange juice and poured herself a glass of it, then took a deep sip. It tasted awful. She spit it all out in the sink, then washed her mouth with water. She went to the fridge, stared at the pomegranate, then decided it wasn't worth even trying. She looked at her watch.

"Could we order pizza?" she asked. "My dad said we could?"

Al was deeply into her work, and, of course, she didn't hear. Josie sighed deeply, then walked back to the couch where she had slept. The couch was way too short, and she woke up with pain in her legs and hips.

If only she had her phone, she could call her dad and ask him to bring her food. Had he completely forgotten about her? It was one in the afternoon, and she was starving.

Josie sat down with a deep sigh, and looked at the door, willing him to come.

Bring pizza. Bring pizza!

As she sat there, staring at the door, it was like it suddenly exploded. Josie screamed as men entered the apartment, men wearing black masks and holding weapons. They pointed them at Josie and hit Al with a stick on the back of her head, so she passed out.

Next, a man entered, a man in a black suit, walking toward her with a grin on his face, his haunting steel-gray eyes glaring down at her.

"Hello, Josie," he said. "I think it's time you and I met properly, don't you think?"

Chapter 41

I RAN my bike across town, zigzagging through traffic, making sure that if anyone followed me, I'd lose them easily. I made a quick stop at one of my favorite pizza places on the beach. I asked them to make me a large pizza with ham and cheese, then drove up the small alley toward Al's building. I grabbed the pizza, ran up the back entrance and up the stairs, whistling. I had a good feeling about this case. I was going to solve it with the help of David Smith, who was still cuffed to a pipe in my pantry. I was going to him next, making sure he didn't starve to death in my house. I knew it wasn't very nice of me to cuff him like that, but I had to make sure he didn't leave. I needed his help to catch this killer. Without him, I was lost. He knew when the next delivery was due down at the harbor, and that was when they'd be there again, those men that had spoken about Josie and cutting her heart out. He had told me he was hired to do the next job tomorrow night. I just hoped Al would find me some evidence I could use against them. If all went well, I could have a team with me at the harbor and nail them once their delivery came in. But the illegal import of appliances wasn't exactly enough for me. I needed them to go down for the murder of Wolfe, and hopefully, Savannah Hart, along with Emilia and Jennifer García as well. I just didn't have all the pieces put together yet, and I hoped Al would provide me with that.

Knowing her, she'd been at it all day and had completely forgotten to feed my daughter. That was why I brought pizza. I felt compelled to, somehow. Maybe it was just my common sense.

I ran up the first flight of stairs, pizza balancing on my hand, the intense smell of it in my nostrils, making me realize I was actually starving. It wasn't exactly heart-healthy food for my daughter, but it was the best I could do right now. It was better than her not eating.

As I reached the top of the stairs, my heart suddenly dropped. The door to Al's apartment was gone. I could barely breathe when I saw it. Al never left it open. She locked it with at least five locks. As I approached it, I realized the door was on the floor inside the apartment, splintered to pieces.

Inside, I saw Al lying on the floor, blood smeared in her hair.

I threw the pizza down and ran to her.

"Al!"

She groaned something and tried to lift her head but couldn't.

"Careful," I said. "You've gotten a blow to your head. Come, let me help."

I helped her back up into her chair, where she sat for a few seconds, staring at me like she couldn't focus properly…like she had to figure out who I was. I grabbed her some water, and she drank.

"Josie," I said nervously. "Where is she?"

Al seemed to have to think it over for a few seconds. "I was… working on that thing you asked me to and didn't…I wasn't looking. I wasn't paying attention. Suddenly, there was movement; someone approached me faster than I could react, and I felt something hit the back of my head. I am sorry, Hunter. I completely blacked out."

"Who was it? Who took her?" I asked, my voice shaking in despair. "Who took my Josie?"

"I didn't get a look at them, but I have cameras. The entire place is covered."

Wincing in pain, she leaned over her computer, then clicked a few times with the mouse and wrote a passcode to something. A picture showed up on the screen, a picture of the door. The door was then kicked in, and two men in black masks and clothing entered, pointing big guns at Josie. Then, a man entered, wearing a suit. With fists clenched and heart throbbing, I watched him talk to Josie. Then the men grabbed her and carried her out, kicking and screaming. Al stopped the video right before the man in the black suit turned around and was about to leave.

"There you go," she said. "That's your guy."

"I can't believe it," I said and rubbed my hair. I stared at the face, my nostrils flaring and blood boiling.

"There's more," she said, wincing again in pain. "I found this for you. It had been deleted from Savannah Hart's cloud on the night she died, but I managed to recreate it. Here you go. This is what this guy is so eager to cover up. This is why both Savannah Hart and Emilia García had to die."

Al pressed play, and I watched the shocking video for a couple of seconds, then asked her to play it again and again. Then I asked her to send the file to my phone before I left in a fire of rage. I couldn't believe I had been so stupid all along. I had been trusting the wrong people.

Chapter 42

"GOD, give me the strength to not blow his head off because I will do it if you don't stop me."

I mumbled the words as I ran up the stairs and burst inside. I threw my helmet on the couch, then grabbed my gun, and pulled it out of the holster. I grabbed the door to the pantry, then pulled it open, pointing the gun at David, who was still sitting inside on the floor, cuffed to the pipe on the wall behind him.

He gasped when he saw me. My six feet eight could be very intimidating when I wanted them to be.

"You betrayed me, why?" I asked. "How did you know where to find her? How did you know where Josie was? Because I don't remember telling you."

David stared up at me, his hands shaking. "I don't know…what are you…I've been here the whole time."

"Cut the crap," I said and walked closer with the gun, finger steadily on the trigger. Boy, I wanted to kill him, right then and there. Just pull the trigger and get it over with. I was that angry at this point, and sick of being deceived. I had truly believed this guy, trusted that all he wanted was to protect Josie and Emilia's heart. I had believed that he was just a grieving father who wanted to be close to whatever was left of his daughter. I had even felt sorry for him.

I felt like the biggest fool on earth.

"I'm sick of your lies. I saw you," I said. "On that video that Savannah Hart made before her death. The one from the graveyard where you shot Wolfe. I saw you, and then I saw Emilia, your daughter. You were arguing, weren't you? You had asked Wolfe to meet you there, hadn't you? And then you were arguing. Emilia was there, playing. Being homeless after you left them, her mother often let her run around in parks and at the cemetery while she was passed out on pills, sleeping in the car. That evening, she had parked next to the cemetery, and Emilia was playing around when she suddenly heard voices and hid behind a tombstone. Someone was arguing, and one of the voices sounded familiar. The girl then peeked up and, seeing her father, the man she hadn't seen in a very long time, she called out to him just as the shots were fired. Terrified, she realized she had just witnessed her own dad kill someone, and she screamed. Then, she took off running.

Seeing this, you ran after her, trying to catch her. Meanwhile, Savannah Hart was out on one of her evening jogs, as she usually was at that time of the day, when the air is cooling down after sunset. She was in her own thoughts when she heard the shots go off and found herself right outside the cemetery. She heard the scream that followed it and realized something was very much off. Thinking she was unarmed, and her only weapon was her phone, she pulled it out and started filming between the trees. She filmed the body on the ground and then turned it to film you as you ran for the girl and grabbed her just as she reached the exit. On the video, I saw how you were holding the girl's mouth, covering it, and I could hear you hushing her, telling her it was all right and just to make sure she stayed quiet. Seeing this, Savannah knew she had to do something to save the girl, so she yelled at you. Filming you and coming up toward you, she told you to *let go of the girl*. On the video, you can clearly hear her tell you that she is live streaming it, probably thinking that will make you stop, which she is right about. You let go of Emilia, and she ran off. *Run, Girl, Run,* Savannah yelled after her. But as she made it into the street, Emilia ran into someone else, a buddy of yours. He was waiting by your car, waiting for you to finish the business he asked you to do, killing Wolfe. He's a guy with steel-gray eyes, who Emilia didn't know. Savannah was filming the encounter, and the guy saw her and forgot about Emilia, who ran with all she had while the man approached Savannah, yelling at her to stop filming.

That's when the filming stopped, and I assume Savannah ran off and later made it home. But you and your buddy then decided to go after them both, didn't you? He said he'd take care of Emilia, your daughter, and you could focus on the runner, on Savannah. So you kept an eye on the area for a little while, and one day you saw her running again, then made sure you followed her home and to work, and knew all of her routines before you made your move, didn't you? You burned down the house with her inside of it after you had made sure to remove the video from her phone and computer. But the thing is, those things never really disappear."

I raised my phone and played the video clip again. I let him watch as he saw his daughter run, and right when he grabbed her, I paused it. "There you have it. Now, I've made sure that this clip is safe somewhere in cyberspace, so if anything happens to me, the clip will be the evidence. You can't outrun it."

David's eyes didn't leave the screen and the picture of his daughter. Tears sprang to his eyes.

"She was your own daughter, for crying out loud," I said with disgust. "What kind of man are you?"

"I swear to God; I never meant for this to happen," he said. "This is a nightmare. I told you I had gotten in with the wrong crowd. I was in trouble. I owed money, and this was my way out. I feared it might end up hurting my family; that's why I left them. To protect them from these people."

"Yet, that's exactly what happened anyway," I said. "You sure messed that one up."

David's eyes were spilling over with tears, and he was shaking his head like he had trouble believing it all, like the realization of what he had done hadn't sunk in until now.

"Please," he said. "Please, don't… They said they'd kill me if I didn't kill her. They were both witnesses, both girls were. They couldn't let them live to tell what they saw. These people, you don't joke around with them. I comfort myself with the fact that I didn't kill my daughter or my ex-wife."

"Yes, you did. You just let someone else do the dirty work for you. It doesn't make you innocent. You might as well save it for someone who cares. I don't have time to listen to your self-pity or excuses," I said, stopping him before he began pleading for my mercy on his damned soul because I had none left for him right now. It was out of my hands.

"You can repent in front of God, and He'll take it from there," I said. "But for now, I need you to tell me where Josie is. You take me to her right now. I *will* shoot you if you don't. This is your chance to make something right again or die here. And don't doubt I will do it. It'll be the easiest thing in the world for me. See, without my daughter, I'm nothing. If anything happens to Josie, I will lose any will to live. The way I see it, I have nothing to lose at this point."

I pressed the gun against his forehead, and he whimpered.

"All right, all right. There's a warehouse on the port. That's probably where they have taken her."

"What warehouse? There are tons of them down there."

"It has a number on the side, two-eighty-one. It's a blue building. You can easily find it."

I shook my head. "You're coming with me. You'll show me which one."

I reached over and released his cuffs, then placed them back on his wrists while keeping his hands behind his back, so he couldn't surprise me. I was done trusting this guy. I was done trusting anyone.

Chapter 43

SHE COULDN'T SEE ANYTHING. The man with the steel-gray eyes had blindfolded her and gagged her, then tied her hands behind her back and tied her legs. They had then put her inside of something like a box. She lay curled up into a ball in this compartment, and she couldn't move. Josie had never been more afraid in her life, except for the time she had come home and found her dad and mom in the living room, her mom with foam coming out of her mouth, her dad screaming for her to call nine-one-one. That was the worst day of her life. This came in as a close second.

Dad will find me. Of course, he will.

But he might not even know she was missing. Maybe he was still at work and wasn't planning on stopping by Al's apartment till tonight? Who knew where they might have taken her at that point? She didn't even know where they were going, only that she was moving, swaying along inside her bubble.

Where are they taking me?

The man with the steel-gray eyes had touched her chest before she was taken away. He had touched it gently, then placed an ear against it like he was listening to it. Then he had laughed and told her how amazing the human body was and what it was capable of.

"To think that it could tell you about me, huh?" he had asked while gently caressing her cheek. "Yes, I know your heart snitched on me. Aw, what's that face? Don't look so upset; it'll only hurt when we take it out. After that, you won't feel a thing. I promise."

The last part was said with a huge grin, and then his men had picked her up, blindfolded her, and taken her away. She had tried to scream and fight them, but it was no use.

Now, as she lay there inside her own darkness, all she could do was pray…pray like her dad had taught her to when in trouble. Pray the same way she had when her mother had overdosed. Pray the same way she had every day for three years while her mother was nothing but a vegetable. Josie had fought not to lose hope during that time, but it had been a tough fight. It was so hard to believe that a miracle could happen after all this time, and she kept fearing it wasn't going to. She had remembered her granddad's words every time doubt hit her like a freight train: "Sometimes our lives don't turn out the way we want them to. That's when we need faith to kick in. Trust that God knows what he is doing. Trust his timing."

Back then, she hadn't understood much of what it meant, but now she did. Once her mother had finally come back, it had been such a big miracle; it almost seemed impossible.

As she lay inside that small compartment she was being transported in, thinking about her mother and the miracle they had experienced helped strengthen her faith. She was afraid, yes, scared to death. But she also knew what God was capable of. And she had to trust him once again. Even though it was hard to, she had to do it. She simply had to because it was all she had.

Without faith, there was only fear.

Without hope, she was lost.

Chapter 44

"IT'S that one right over there, the blue one."

David nodded to show me which building it was since he couldn't use his hands or fingers to point. I spotted the building and then the number on the side of it. Two hundred and eighty-one. I parked my city-issued Chevrolet behind the neighboring building and got out. I walked to David's door, opened it, and helped him out as well, holding my gun into his side, making sure he understood the rules.

"No games," I whispered in his ear, pressing the gun hard into his side.

I let him lead the way as we approached a big white truck and walked past it. I looked into the back of it before we continued to make sure Josie wasn't in there or anyone who might surprise us from behind. The truck seemed to be in the process of being filled with appliances…what looked like a couple of fridges, several dryers, and at least one washing machine. It wasn't even half-filled, so I knew someone would be there soon, probably bringing in more, and hurried past it toward the blue building before we were seen.

"No, not the front," I said and stopped him as he was about to lead us to the big opening of the warehouse. I heard the sound of a forklift coming from in there; maybe there was more than one.

"There must be a side entrance or a back door or something," I said.

"Over there," he said and nodded. I turned to see a small door in the side of the building.

"Perfect," I said.

I opened it as silently as possible and pushed David in first in case there was a guard in there, but he just walked straight in, gun placed against the back of his head.

"Now, take me to him," I said.

"Are you sure?" he whispered back. "I mean, there's one of you, and he has his own army."

"I don't care," I said.

"I sure hope that God of yours is keeping an eye out on you today," he mumbled. "You're walking straight into the lion's den."

"And I won't even smell like smoke when I come out," I said, "now, show me the way."

"It's your funeral," he said, then walked forward. He stopped at another door that I had to open for him, one that led into the big hall where the forklifts were working, grabbing the brand-new still wrapped appliances one after another, transporting them out to the truck. There was a lot of noise, and no one noticed that we entered. The first guy who did see us went for his gun immediately, and I pulled mine from David's head, pointed it at him, then fired. I hit him in the shoulder, right in the spot that I knew would make him drop the gun. And it did. The gun fell to the cement floor below, and the guy fell to his knees in pain, holding his bloody shoulder.

Now, all eyes were on us.

The forklifts stopped what they were doing, and anyone working there stared first at me and then at David. I placed the gun to the side of David's head to make sure they could all see it.

"I need to see him," I said. "Now."

Chapter 45

"WHAT'S GOING ON HERE? Why have you stopped working?"

Ferdinand came out from behind the glass window leading to the back office. He took one glance at me with his steel-gray eyes, then nodded.

"Ah, I see."

He looked at me, then at David before he stepped forward.

"Stay where you are," I said. "One step closer, and he's toast."

"What do you want, Hunter?" Ferdinand asked with a deeply annoyed sigh. "Why have you come?"

"I want my daughter back," I said. "Where is she?"

"Your daughter?" he said with a grin. "You've come here looking for your daughter? Well, she's not here. I don't have time to have young girls running around here. It would be way too dangerous, anyway."

"I know everything," I said. "I know what you two did. I have the video. The one Savannah Hart took on that night at the cemetery. I know you killed Emilia and Jennifer García. I know David killed Savannah Hart and Major Wolfe."

The grin on Ferdinand's face had faded. He still stared at me like he was contemplating what his next move should be.

"What did you do with her, Ferdinand? And don't tell me she isn't here because I know she is. I know you took her."

"Well, you're welcome to have a look around," he said. "See if you can see her anywhere."

I threw a glance around the warehouse, my heart pounding in my chest. Where could he be keeping her? A couple of his goons had their hands inside their jackets, waiting for me to make a mistake so they could pull their weapons and finish me off. They had all seen what happened to the first guy who tried and didn't dare to yet. But it would only take me letting my guard down for a split second for them to make their move.

"No? Well, then, let us get back to work, will you?" Ferdinand said. "We have a shipment that needs to be in Chicago by tomorrow night."

I stared at the appliances, all gathered up against the wall across from me. One forklift had stopped not far from me with a dryer barely lifted off the ground. I kept staring at it while so many questions piled up inside of me. There was so much I still didn't understand.

I bit my lip, then turned to look at Ferdinand.

"It's not just appliances, is it? I mean, I keep wondering what's so lucrative about importing appliances illegally. Is that worth risking your career? Risk going to jail?"

I walked to the dryer on the forklift, holding David close to me. He was my collateral. My theory was that he and Ferdinand were partners in this, and Ferdinand needed him. At least I hoped he did. I let go of David, then reached over and pulled the bubble wrap off the dryer just enough to be able to open it. I pulled the door open, then peeked inside.

The sight that met me from in there almost made me lose it. I had a lot of theories as to what they were, in fact, transporting, but I could still barely believe what I was seeing.

Chapter 46

JOSIE GASPED FOR AIR. It was getting tight where she was, and she was fighting to breathe properly. It was hot too. Unbearably hot. She was constantly sweating, and her throat was scratchy from thirst.

She hadn't moved for quite some time now and was getting anxious and restless. It was hard not to panic when you couldn't move.

Please, God, have someone find me. Lead my dad to find me. I know he'll listen to you. Don't let me down. Don't forget about me.

Josie laid still while sweat trickled down her forehead and landed on her lip. It tasted salty and made her feel even more thirsty. Josie would do anything right now for something to drink. After hours inside this place, she was beginning to feel dizzy and like she couldn't stay awake much longer. She kept dozing off and waking up again, and she knew dehydration was starting to set in. It wasn't good for her heart, and she had more than once felt a huge pinch, one that made her cry out behind the gag. And now she felt it again. A stabbing pain went through her chest, and she was certain she was running a fever too. The tiredness, the weakness, along with shortness of breath and tightness of her chest were some of the symptoms she could feel if her body was rejecting the heart, she had been told.

She was feeling all of that right now. All of it.

This was too much strain and stress on her heart. Her body couldn't cope with it anymore.

Hurry up, God. It's getting serious now. I'm running out of time. Get my dad to me, please.

A few tears rolled down her cheeks as she dozed off, then woke up again, only to realize she was still in the same darkness but feeling even more tired now. She closed her eyes again and thought of her family, of how happy they had been once, how happy she had been when she was just a child. Before everything went bad. Before her mom had…

Josie dozed off once again in the middle of a thought, no longer having the strength to fight the luring sleep calling for her.

In the distance, she thought she heard her father's voice, but she didn't know if it was just part of her dream.

A few seconds later, it didn't matter anymore.

Chapter 47

THE ANXIOUS BROWN eyes looking back at me from inside the dryer blinked a few times while deciding whether to trust me or not. They belonged to a young boy, nine, maybe ten years old.

The realization of what I had found made me cry out with distress. I pulled back and looked at Ferdinand, shaking my head in disgust.

"A...a child?"

He narrowed his eyes while looking at me. "Maybe you ought to stop now, Harry. Before you go where there is no way back."

"Oh, I think we've reached that point, don't you think?" I asked, biting back my tears. "I think we're way past that."

I turned to face the stacked appliances leaned up against the wall in front of me, on top of one another, as high as the ceiling. How many were there? One hundred? Two hundred?

Heart throbbing in my chest, I ran to the front of the stack, ripped off the bubble wrap, and opened a freezer. Another set of anxious eyes was staring back at me while the mouth gasped for air. The woman reached out her hand toward me. It seemed she was more dead than alive. I kept the lid open, then ripped the cardboard off the next one, where I found another young boy, maybe fourteen.

Who were these people?

"Where do they come from?" I asked while opening the next, frantically pulling at the wrapping, tears streaming across my cheeks. The cruelty in this seemed impossible.

"Who knows?" Ferdinand said. "Where do any of us come from? We help them to a better future."

"Refugees?" I said addressed to him. "You're smuggling refugees? How many of them arrive alive, huh? After hours, maybe even days inside these things, how many survive, huh? What did you promise them? A better life? If they only gave you their savings, is that it? They gave you all they had, thinking you'd help them get into the promised land? And then what? They'll get arrested and sent back? Or end up in the streets? If they make it that far."

He shrugged. "They know the risks."

I stared at him, startled, appalled. These were human lives he was talking about. How could anyone be this cruel and still call themselves human?

"Was Wolfe in charge of it all and then handed it down to you?" I paused. "No, wait…he didn't know about the refugees, did he? You added that part later when he retired from the force. He was the one who had made a little extra through selling these appliances and making sure the port authorities looked the other way. He had made a small business out of it, then handed it down to you when he left and couldn't take care of it anymore. But you changed it, and he didn't like it. That's why he had to go. He wanted you to stop what you were doing; it had gotten out of hand. Maybe he even threatened to expose you, am I right?"

"You expect me to answer that?"

"You don't have to. I know when I'm right. So, you had David kill him, but there were witnesses, and you then had to remove them too. But you hadn't counted on Emilia's heart causing Josie to dream about you and how you killed her, and about where to find the body."

"That was an unfortunate turn of events," Ferdinand said. "Everything else was going so smoothly and had for years."

One of his goons made a move, and I grabbed David again, then pulled him close to me, placing the gun against his temple.

Ferdinand signaled for his goon to stand back. "It's too bad, Hunter. You could have been in on it. I would have cut you a deal. We could use someone like you on our side."

"Who else is in on it?" I asked. "Who do you work for?"

That made Ferdinand laugh. "You don't seriously expect me to answer that, do you?"

I pressed the gun against David's temple, hard.

"WHO?"

He laughed again. The sound of his laughter felt like knives to my skin. I couldn't stand the sight of the man. He made me sick.

Still grinning, Ferdinand reached inside his jacket, pulled out a gun, and shot David three times in the chest. David's body went into spasms, and he slid out of my hands. I stood behind, blood smeared on my clothes, then looked up at Ferdinand, eyes wide with shock.

"He ratted me out," Ferdinand said. "He was supposed to kill the girl. That's why he came to your house. But instead, he warned you. Probably because he wanted you to take me down, so he could have everything to himself. I've been expecting him to make his move for a little while now. Now, he can't. And neither can you."

With that, Ferdinand lifted his gun again, pointed it at me, and fired.

Chapter 48

I THREW my body to the ground. The bullet whistled past me, grazing my shoulder as I fell. I landed on my side with a loud thud, panting for air as a regular gunfight broke out.

Once the goons saw that I was still alive, they all simultaneously pulled their guns and shot at me. Luckily, I managed to jump behind a dryer. I heard the bullets hit it on the other side and ricochet off it, causing the bullets to fly everywhere while I crouched down, covering my head.

Once the shooting stopped, I peeked out. That was when I realized the goons hadn't been the ones doing all the shooting, and now most of them were on the ground, some in a pool of their own blood, others screaming in pain, while some were on their knees, holding their hands above their heads, pleading for their lives.

Behind them all stood someone I knew very well. He smiled from ear to ear as he saw me.

It was Fowler.

"Hunter!"

Seeing him, I dared to get out from behind my cover. I walked to him while the officers he had brought moved in and arrested the ones that were still alive. Fowler pulled me into a hug. It felt awkward since he was never much of a hugger; yet it was by far one of the best I had ever gotten.

"Al told me where to find you," he said. "She was worried and had you tracked down, then called me with your exact location. She said you might require assistance. Boy, was she spot-on. We arrived right after you did, SWAT team and everything. We were ready to move in until we heard you two talking. I decided to wait to make sure I heard everything."

"I don't think I have ever been this glad to see you," I said and hugged him back.

"Whoa there, soldier. Don't crush me," he said as I let go of him.

I looked around, then realized something.

"Ferdinand. I don't see him anywhere. Did you book him?"

A SWAT officer came up to us. Fowler asked him, and he shook his head. "Haven't seen him, sir."

My eyes grew wide, and I frantically looked around us. "Could he have gotten away?"

We ran outside, then around the building. There was a big empty space in the parking lot.

"The truck," I said. "There was a big white truck parked here. Where is it now?"

Fowler growled loudly, then turned to his officer. "I thought we had this place surrounded. How did he get out?"

The officer looked confused.

"It doesn't matter now," I said and ran to my car parked behind the next building, then jumped in and roared it to life. I backed out, swung it around, then floored it while calling Al on my phone.

"Al, I need your help."

"Hunter! Where were you? Have you found Josie?"

"I need you to track down a white truck for me using your surveillance cameras. It's leaving the harbor now or left within the past few minutes. Can you do that?"

Chapter 49

"I ALREADY HAVE IT TRACKED DOWN," Al said on the other end.

Putting the siren and lights on, I raced down the road, took a sharp turn, then continued, going down the only road leading out of there.

"What? How?"

"I have it right here on my screen, showing it's driving down MacArthur Causeway, and going onto I95 now, northbound.

"That's great, Al, but how do you know this already?"

"Well, it isn't exactly the truck I'm chasing as much as it is Josie."

"Josie? You know where she is?"

"Yes, she's in the truck, moving up I95."

"What? Why didn't you tell me sooner?"

"Because I didn't know sooner, you fool."

"I don't understand. How do you know now then?"

"Take a right now and get onto I95, continue north," she said.

"Okay," I said and did as she said.

"Listen, I didn't know this till now. I didn't know she was on a truck. I just knew she was at the harbor. When you brought her to my place, I had a feeling I might end up losing her somehow. I told you I'm no good with kids, no matter the age or size. I knew I couldn't keep an eye on her constantly. So, I put a transmitter in her pocket while she slept, one so small she can't feel it, and no one can see it."

"So, you knew she was at the harbor when I left your place?"

"I knew I could track her, and I tried to tell you, but you rushed out of there so fast I didn't get to. Now, if you would have picked up your phone for once in your life, I would have been able to tell you this sooner, but you didn't, and so I called Fowler. He was my last resort since I can't stand the guy, but I had to make sure you were safe."

"So, you're my guardian angel," I said, smiling at the phone, eyes focused and determined on the road ahead.

"Take the exit now," she said. "Get off I95. I found a shortcut. The truck is about a mile ahead of you now, but there's a small traffic jam. You're gaining on him, fast. But you need to get around the jam."

I took the exit, roared across an intersection while cars cleared the way for me, as I came blasting through with sirens blaring and drove back onto I95. I had barely made it when I spotted something in the distance, something sticking up between the cars.

A truck. A big white truck.

"I see it," I said. "I've got him!"

I floored the accelerator once again and came closer still, forcing cars in my way to move to the side. Now, there were only two cars between us. Snorting in anger, I pressed the car to perform to its utmost, and soon I was right behind it, then I pressed up on the side of the truck.

"Come on; come on," I said to the old car as I nudged it along, praying it would soon surpass him.

"You're almost there, Hunter," Al said on the other end. "Now, give it all you have."

But Ferdinand had seen the lights and heard the sirens by now, and he sped up, pressing the truck to go faster. Still, I made it up on his side and could now look directly at him next to me.

"That's right, you bastard," I mumbled while looking straight at him. "I'm coming for you!"

Chapter 50

I SIGNALED for him to stop, to pull over, but he refused. No surprise there. I could hear a chopper approaching in the distance and prayed that it was Fowler, sending assistance.

"STOP, you idiot!" I yelled at Ferdinand, waving my arm wildly. "Before you get us all killed!"

And worst of all, my beautiful daughter.

We approached a car that was driving slower than us, and I had to slow down significantly so that I wouldn't ram into it. Growling, I watched as Ferdinand took off on the inside lane, while I had to wait a few seconds for the car in front of me to shift lanes and let me pass. I groaned and yelled something I knew I wouldn't be proud of afterward, then floored the accelerator. I heard a sound from above and looked up, then realized it wasn't a police chopper, but a news helicopter.

"Where the heck is my backup?" I yelled into the radio. "I need all roads closed on I95 northbound, and air support!"

Dispatch confirmed they were on their way, and as we passed an entrance to the highway, I spotted two police cruisers racing out behind us, just as I drove past them. I reached the back of the truck and sped up to get back up on his side. Seconds later, I succeeded and could once again see his sweaty face inside the cabin, grinning back at me, his eyes manic and crazy.

As I pressed the Chevrolet to its utmost, I finally caught up with him. I pulled the wheel forcefully to the side and rammed into his front left side, knowing very well he was the biggest, and I would probably be the one ending up getting hurt. I just knew I had to try and stop him before Josie was hurt. If he had trapped her in one of those appliances in the back, chances were that she was running out of air, or at least exposing herself to an amount of stress her heart couldn't take at this point. I feared another heart failure, one that would prove to be fatal this time.

The truck swerved to the side but returned to the road just as quickly, this time knocking me forward. My car skidded sideways, turned to the side, and as I looked out the side window, I saw the truck roaring toward me.

I closed my eyes as Ferdinand blasted toward me, then turned the wheel fast and got the car back into its own lane just as the truck roared past me.

Sweat springing from every pore in my face, I stepped on the accelerator once again and drove up on the side of the truck again, trying to repeat what I did earlier. Ferdinand looked down at me, still grinning, then pulled the wheel and knocked into me instead. My car bumped sideways and hit the guardrail. The noise of the car scratching along it hurt my ears, and I let out a loud scream as I tried to regain control of my car. Meanwhile, Ferdinand had been so busy watching me, he hadn't noticed the cars in front of him, and soon he knocked into one of them. There was a terrible noise as he tried to brake, and the truck skidded sideways and crashed into a couple of other cars in front of it before it ran off the road and into the grass.

I held my breath as it roared toward a line of trees, knocking a few of the lighter ones over, cracking them like sticks before it finally met its match in an old magnolia tree and banged into it. The truck came to a sudden halt with a loud crash, and everything stopped inside of me.

Chapter 51

"JOSIE!"

I pushed the door but couldn't open it. I then leaned over and grabbed my Swiss Army Knife from the glove compartment before I crawled to the passenger seat, opened the door, and jumped out into the road. I ran for dear life toward the truck on the side of the road, barely able to breathe because of the fear rushing through me. I knew Josie was onboard that truck somewhere since Al had told me. My only guess was that she was in the back somewhere.

Smoke was emerging from the front of the curled-up truck, but my focus was on the back. The cargo had fallen to the side when it hit the tree. I ran to it, unlocked the hatch, then pulled the doors open and jumped inside.

"Josie?"

The appliances had been tossed around in there like were they nothing but light Lego blocks in a box. A big fridge was right by the door, and the first thing I did was to grab the cardboard box wrapping and cut it open with my knife, then pull it off with everything I had, but it still felt like it was too slow, way too slow. It took forever before I could finally pull it off and open the door to the brand-new fridge.

A set of eyes stared back at me. Someone was in there all right, but it wasn't my Josie.

Leaving the door open so the young woman could crawl out, I exhaled, then climbed over the fridge and moved further inside the truck. I cut open a washer, a dryer, and more people crawled out, some—especially the children—I had to help out. One little girl couldn't even stand on her own two feet; she was so weak. I had to carry her outside, where I hoped and prayed one of her parents were among those that I had set free. Seeing the girl, a woman made a squeal and grabbed her in her arms, and I breathed a sigh of relief.

I then returned inside and found the last box that hadn't been opened. I cut open the wrapping around it, then the box it came in. Thinking there was no way my tall girl would ever fit inside of that small washer, I prepared myself for not finding her. Frantically, I removed the Styrofoam, throwing it everywhere while crying heavily.

Where are you, my sweet Josie? Where are you?

I pulled open the washer forcefully, then peeked inside. The sight that met me was at once sweet and more frightening than anything.

There she was. My wonderful daughter was curled up into a tiny ball inside the washer.

"Josie?" I said, crying. "Josie?"

She wasn't moving. She wasn't opening her eyes.

I reached inside to touch her, then tried to pull her out. Her lifeless body was heavy and hard to move, but finally, I managed to pull her out completely.

That was when I realized she wasn't breathing.

I shook her.

"Josie? Josie? JOSIE?"

I felt for a pulse but found none. Her heart wasn't beating.

I placed her on the floor, then performed CPR, frantically fighting to get her heart back to life again, while calling for help over the radio. Sirens were blaring outside, and more than one chopper was hovering above us.

Josie felt so fragile, so small under my hands; I feared I'd crush her. Yet, I continued, forcefully trying to pump her heart back to life.

"Don't leave me, Josie; please, don't leave me!"

Chapter 52

"DAD?"

It happened so suddenly that I had no idea when or how. I just knew it had happened. At some point, her heart had started beating again, and she was now looking at me with those gorgeous brown eyes of hers.

Never had there been a prettier sight.

I pulled her into a deep hug and held her so tight she started to complain that I was crushing her. I cried and kissed her cheeks over and over again.

"Are you okay?" I asked, looking into her eyes.

"I…I think so."

"Are you sure? You have to be honest with me here, Josie. Does anything hurt? Shortness of breath? Anything?"

She shook her head. "I think I'm fine, Dad."

"You're still going to the hospital. I'm not taking any chances."

"What happened?" she asked, confused.

That was when I remembered Ferdinand. My eyes grew serious as I realized my business here wasn't done.

"Stay here for a sec. Can you do that for me?"

"Where are you going, Dad? Dad?"

I grabbed my gun, then hurried outside. All traffic had been stopped on the highway. Not a car was moving. Firetrucks were parked in the road, and their blinking lights were lighting up the sky, while they were fighting to get someone out of one of the crashed cars.

Police officers were busy attending to the refugees, trying to make sense of the mess. Several of them were leaving in ambulances. I hurried to the front of the truck, then looked inside, wanting to make sure he had either died or that they had gotten him.

The cabin was empty.

I looked around, feeling anxious and worried he might have gotten away in the confusion. I hurried to an officer who was attending to a refugee.

"The driver of the truck," I asked. "Did you book him?"

The officer shook his head. "Not that I know of."

"Did someone else?"

I looked around me, then noticed something on the side of the truck, a handprint of blood like someone had leaned against it.

Someone with blood on their hands.

I hurried back to the cabin, then noticed a trace of blood in the grass that led between the trees.

"Oh, no, you don't," I said, as lifted the gun and followed the tracks.

I ran through the trees, my eyes scanning the area thoroughly for any sign of Ferdinand. He couldn't have gone far, I concluded. He was hurt, and there really weren't that many places to go.

I took a few more steps when something came at me from behind a tree. A metal plate of some sort that Ferdinand could have taken from the crash site slammed right into my face. I felt the pain, and everything disappeared for a few seconds while I tumbled backward before my sight returned, and I saw him standing right in front of me, blood dripping from his arm.

I had barely gotten my focus back when he leaped at me.

Chapter 53

PUNCHES RAINED DOWN ON ME. They were hitting my jaw, my nose, my cheek, shooting pain through me. I managed to get one of my own in, then reach up and grab his chin and push him backward, away from me. I had dropped my gun when he hit me with the metal plate, and I could see it on the dirty ground, but it was too far away for me to reach.

Ferdinand jumped me again and punched me hard on the cheek. My head swirled to the side, and I heard a crack in my neck, but the blow didn't knock me out, and soon I was the one placing one on his nose. The sound of it cracking underneath my knuckles made me wince before I planted a second blow straight to his chin with such great force that he flew backward and slid across the dirt.

This time, he didn't get up again.

I rose to my feet and approached him, looking down at him. His eyes were closed, his mouth open, blood gushing from a wound on his lip. I walked to my gun and picked it up, then turned just as he woke.

I walked back and placed the gun on his head, my nostrils flaring, spitting out blood on the ground.

"It's time for some answers, Ferdinand. I don't believe for one minute you and David were alone in this. Who else is in on it? Who do you work for?"

He mumbled something, then spat out more blood.

"What was that?" I asked.

"I said, you really expect me to tell you?"

I pressed the gun closer to the skin on his forehead.

"Yes."

That made him laugh, but I could tell it hurt to do so. "You want me to snitch, huh, Detective? You think I'm gonna answer your questions, let myself be interrogated, cut a deal, do what's best for me, huh? Is that it?"

"Yes. That's exactly what I expect you to do. You know how these things work better than most people."

He exhaled. "I do, Detective. I know how things work, all right. Especially around here."

"So, tell me now, and I might let you live. You know I could just tell them you were trying to escape, which is actually the truth. At least close enough for me to get away with it."

He looked up at me again, grunting and annoyed, then grinned. "Why don't you ask your wife?"

"Excuse me?"

"I said…why…don't…you…ask…your…wife?"

I shook my head, unsure if I had heard him right. What kind of a sick game was this?

"What are you talking about?"

He grinned, showing off his bloody teeth. He had knocked out two of the top front ones, probably from the impact when driving the truck into the tree, and strings of blood were dangling from them.

"You heard me."

"You're lying," I said.

"Really? Think about it. How much do you really know about her?"

I stared down at the pathetic man. I wanted to hurt him so badly, to slap him across the face, but I didn't. Instead, I stared at him, my hand with the gun shaking with anger.

"You don't know anything about my wife," I said. "Absolutely nothing!"

"Probably not then," he said, still grinning. "My mistake."

Faster than I realized what he was up to, he then reached up, grabbed my hands, pressed down on my finger on the trigger, and fired the gun.

Chapter 54

THEY KEPT Josie at the hospital for twenty-four hours to monitor her heart, then sent her home, telling me that everything was as it should be. The heart was functioning as it should, and as long as she stayed away from stressful situations for a few weeks, she'd be fine.

Needless to say, I was very relieved to hear that.

I brought her home and put her to bed so she could take a nap. I sat on the edge, then folded my hands.

"Dear God, thank you for protecting Josie. Thank you for letting me have more time with her here. I wouldn't know what to do without her."

I felt Josie's hand on my arm and opened my eyes. "God knows. He knows you need me."

That brought tears to my eyes, and I kissed her cheek, then sat with her till she dozed off. I liked just looking at her. Jean was downstairs, preparing dinner, and as I walked out into the hallway, I could hear her rummaging around down there. It was a sweet sound. I had told her she didn't need to cook for us, but she had insisted. We had enough on our plate today, she said.

I didn't protest.

I walked downstairs and entered Camille's room. Her eyes

lingered on me as I walked in, and I stood for a little while, simply staring at her. She was sitting in her wheelchair; her head leaned against the backrest. She moved her mouth to speak, but nothing but grunts came out.

I had gone through all her stuff upstairs in our bedroom the night before, not sleeping even a little bit. I took every box that belonged to her and went through it, trying to make sense of things. But it had gotten me nowhere. The worst part was that I had no idea if what Ferdinand had told me just before he shot himself had any truth to it…if Camille really knew anything, or if it was just his way of making sure to ruin my life on his way out. If so, he had succeeded. He had gotten to me; that was sure. So many questions piled up in my mind, and I had no way of finding answers.

Yet, I still had to try.

"Why?" I asked her like she understood and knew what I was talking about. "Ferdinand said you knew about those refugees being smuggled in the appliances. Why did he say that? What did he mean?"

Camille stared up at me. Her mouth was open, and a little drool ran from her lip. I felt so helpless. I had loved her; I had cared for her. We had a child together. She had been the woman for me. And now this? Now, I had no idea what to believe anymore. I hated the way I was looking at her now. I was terrified of the knowledge I had received. Would it make me resent her? Would it make me push her away? And even if Ferdinand was right, could I still judge her for her previous actions? Could it have been something from her past he referred to? Back when she was a drug addict? So much had happened since then. She had changed. At least, I thought she had until she overdosed. But then she had suffered a brain injury; could that have changed her? Or did she belong in jail for what she knew or had done?

And most importantly, could I still love her?

The door opened behind me, and Jean entered. Camille turned her eyes to look at her.

"I'm sorry," she said. "Are you guys talking? Am I interrupting something? I just wanted to take Camille out of her room. I thought she could sit in the kitchen with me. I know she likes to do that from time to time. And it gets her out of this room."

I nodded and wiped away a tear.

"That's very nice of you."

Camille made a loud squealing noise as she usually did when she wanted something. Jean turned to look at her.

"Oh, it looks like she wants the sketchbook. I gave her Josie's a few days ago when I was alone with her, and she seemed to enjoy scribbling on it. Nothing I could make anything of, but I think with a little practice, she might be able to write real letters and maybe, in time, tell us what she wants."

Jean reached over and grabbed the sketchbook, then handed it to Camille along with a pen. Camille groaned, then held the pen in her clenched fist and drew something on the paper.

Jean turned to look at me, then smiled compassionately. "Are you okay? You don't look okay."

"I'm just…pondering about things; that's all."

"Is it the case? About the refugees? Did they not catch everyone involved?" she asked.

I swallowed, then shook my head.

"We're not sure. Some might have been in on it that we don't know about. Those types of things usually spin a lot deeper than what you'd think."

She nodded. "A lot of those they arrested out at the warehouse were officers, right? That's what they said on TV. Some were hired help, but a bunch of them were cops. Bad seeds."

"Yeah, apparently it's been going on for quite some time and reaches deep within the force. It's a mess. I'm not exactly popular in the halls these days for taking down a bunch of my colleagues."

"And Fowler?"

"What about him?"

"You think he was in on it too?"

"No, why?"

She shrugged. "I don't know. It's just that…well, the former major was. Maybe he took over the torch if you know what I mean. They were close, weren't they?"

"I don't think that's the case…" I said. "I've known Fowler for years. I don't think he'd ever…"

"Okay, so let me ask you this. Did you ever find out how they knew where to find Josie when you were hiding her with Al? Did anyone else know where she was? Did you tell anyone else besides Fowler?"

"No, but…he could have told someone; maybe he told Ferdinand?"

She gave me one of those looks. "You really believe that?"

"I don't know, maybe because…"

"And how did Ferdinand get away from the warehouse at the port?" she continued. "The SWAT team had the area surrounded, yet he got to the truck and drove away? Are you telling me someone isn't helping him? I think you have a mole, someone on the inside helping him. Someone high in the ranks. That's what I think."

I exhaled, annoyed. "You watch too many movies."

I said the words in order to stop this conversation, hoping to sweep it off the table. I didn't want to talk to her about this anymore. I wanted this to be over and all the bad seeds found.

Yet, I couldn't help wondering if she was right. She made a strong point. Not one that I liked much. But something wasn't right about this story, and I needed to get to the bottom of it, even though it wasn't going to be easy.

"Anyway, do with it what you want," Jean said, then walked to Camille. "I told you what I think…say, what's that?"

She grabbed Camille's sketchbook, then studied it.

"I think you should see this," she said, showing it to me.

I approached them, looking at the scribbles on the paper. To me, it didn't look like anything, at least not at first. But as I got closer, I could make out what looked like two single words.

KILL ME

I looked up at Camille, then back at the words.

"Kill Me?"

Jean nodded, a sad look in her eyes.

"You want me to kill you?" I asked Camille. "Are you crazy? That's not gonna happen."

Camille groaned loudly, her hand with the pen in great spasms. She was getting agitated, and when she was like that, it was even harder for her to control her movements.

"She's upset. I don't think that's what she is trying to say," Jean said. "Could it be something else?"

"Like what?" I asked, confused. "I don't see what else it could be? She wants to kill me?"

"No, you dummy," Jean said. "I think it means someone tried to kill *her*. Someone tried to kill Camille. It wasn't an accident. She wasn't doing drugs. She didn't overdose."

Hearing this, Camille suddenly yelled, almost screamed at the top of her lungs: "JOSIE! JOSIE!"

I stared at her, puzzled. Jean snapped her finger.

"She keeps saying that, yelling it out. Maybe that's what it means? That's what she's been trying to tell us all this time when yelling out Josie's name? What if she was really trying to tell us that someone tried to murder her?"

My eyes locked with Jean's, and I felt more mystified than ever. Was she right? Had someone tried to kill my wife? Did it have anything to do with what Ferdinand had said? With what Camille knew and maybe had been a part of?

As more and more questions piled up, I felt more confused than ever, especially about who to trust in this town. But one thing was certain. One thing Ferdinand had been right about.

I didn't know my wife at all.

THE END

NO OTHER WAY

BOOK 3

STATEMENT OF KRISTIN HOLMES

INCIDENT # 2010-141345

CARSON: Today's date is April 15th, 2010; the current time is 1209 hours. I am Detective Gary Carson, along with Sergeant Steve Bailey. We're here at Monroe County Sheriff's Office at 5525 College Road, Key West. We're talking to Kristin regarding the disappearance of Kate Taylor, who was last seen on April 13th, 2010, at Sloppy Joe's Bar at three a.m. All right, uh, Kristin, would you mind repeating your name and spelling it for me, please?

KRISTIN: Oh, okay. My name is, uh, Kristin Holmes. That is K-R-I-S-T-I-N H-O-L-M-E-S.

CARSON: All right. And what do you do, Kristin?

KRISTIN: I am a therapist. Pediatric therapist.

CARSON: All right. Now, Kristin. Tell us why you are here.

KRISTIN: Well, I was, uh, me and my two friends were…

CARSON: (Fiddles with pages, then moves microphone) That is Joan Smith and Kate Taylor, right?

KRISTIN: Right.

CARSON: Go on. Please, speak into the microphone.

KRISTIN: Well, we wanted to go on this trip, this road trip, to Key West and Key Largo. It was Kate's thirty-fifth birthday, and we wanted to treat her to something, uh, special, and so we thought we'd come down here to party and then later swim with dolphins. All Kate wanted was to try that, so we thought this was the time.

CARSON: Without your husbands? You live in Miami, right?

KRISTIN: Well, I'm not married, but the other two are, and yes. We all live in Miami. Kate needed to get away on her own for a little.

CARSON: And why is that?

KRISTIN: Well, she… I don't know, she was… she and Andrew have been fighting a lot lately; I don't know the details, but she told me she really needed to get away.

CARSON: Do you think she was scared of him?

KRISTIN: (long pause) No. I think she was just bummed out about the marriage. She never told us much about it, just that she needed to blow off some steam or something like that.

CARSON: Was that the term she used? Blow off some steam?

KRISTIN: (sighs deeply) I don't…I don't remember exactly how she put it, but yes, that was the idea. To get away.

CARSON: Okay. And then what happened?

KRISTIN: Well, we drove the long way down here and spent the first night at some hotel downtown, then went to the sunset festival and later Sloppy Joe's.

CARSON: Did Kate meet anyone there? Talk to anyone?

KRISTIN: (sniffles) She talked to a bunch of people. It's how she is, you know? She likes to talk to people.

CARSON: Was there anyone in particular that she spoke with?

KRISTIN: (long pause) Well, there was this guy, uh, but I don't think that…

CARSON: And this guy, can you give us a description? Did he give her his name?

KRISTIN: Matt, his name was Matt. That was all she told us. He was tall, had brown hair and blue eyes. A little young, in my opinion, but Kate liked him.

CARSON: And what did Matt and Kate do?

KRISTIN: They danced and maybe they, uh, kissed a little.

CARSON: Uh-huh, and what else?

KRISTIN: What do you mean?

CARSON: Did she sleep with him?

KRISTIN: (pauses) Well, no, I don't think so. We all had a little too much to drink, so I don't really know. She was all over him, though, and kept saying she was crazy about him. She could have gone off at some point and… you know, without us knowing it.

CARSON: Is Kate the type who would do that?

KRISTIN: Yes.

CARSON: But she didn't go home with him?

KRISTIN: No, she wouldn't do that. She was supposed to come back to the hotel with us. We were going to leave early in the morning to go to Key Largo and swim with the dolphins.

CARSON: But you never made it that far? You never made it to Key Largo, and you didn't go swimming with dolphins?

KRISTIN: (Sniffles) No. She wasn't in her bed the next morning. We think she never came back to the hotel. She stayed longer at Sloppy's than Joan and me.

CARSON: And that was two days ago, right?

KRISTIN: Right. At first, we thought she might have gone somewhere, maybe gone home with this Matt guy, and we waited for her to come back, calling her phone, but she didn't pick up. When she didn't come back last night, we went to the police, to you, and said we couldn't find her. We filed a missing person's report, and the officers on duty said they'd look for her. They also said she was probably out partying still and that she'd show up eventually, that they got a lot of disappearance cases like this, especially around spring break. Usually, they'd show up on their own. We went looking for her everywhere around town. Then, you called us this morning and told us to come in at noon.

CARSON: And you have no idea where she could have gone? She hasn't hinted anything or maybe told you something like she wanted to run away or anything like that?

KRISTIN: I don't know. Maybe.

CARSON: What does that mean?

KRISTIN: She did tell me once in the car on the way here that she wished she could just disappear. But people say stuff like that, right?

CARSON: Some people might, but very few actually do it. Now, did she leave a note, a text, or anything?

KRISTIN: No. We called Andrew, and he hadn't heard from her either. He's on his way down here now.

CARSON: Okay, Kristin. Is there anything you'd like to add to your statement?

KRISTIN: I don't think so. I'm just…I'm really worried about her, you know?

CARSON: Okay. All right, Kristin, uh, I'm going to go ahead and conclude this interview for now. It's 1250 hours.

STATEMENT OF JOAN SMITH

INCIDENT # 2010-141345

CARSON: Today's date is April 15th, 2010; the current time is 1304 hours. I am Detective Gary Carson, along with Sergeant Steve Bailey at Monroe County Sheriff's Office at 5525 College Road, Key West. We're talking to Joan Smith regarding the disappearance of Kate Taylor, who was last seen on April 13th, 2010. Joan, do you mind repeating your name and spelling it for me, please?

JOAN: Joan Smith, J-O-A-N S-M-I-T-H.

CARSON: And what do you do, Joan? What's your profession?

JOAN: Me? I don't do anything (laughs nervously). I am what you'd call a professional housewife. My husband is a lawyer in Miami. I take care of the kiddos, is what I do. But between you and me, I'd much rather be working.

CARSON: And what can you tell me about the reason that you're here today?

JOAN: Well, you asked me to come in, didn't you? I was hoping it was because you would help me look for Kate.

CARSON: That's what we're trying to do.

JOAN: So…? Have you looked for her?

CARSON: We have patrols out searching for her.

JOAN: So, why are we here?

CARSON: Tell me about why you've come to the Keys.

JOAN: Kate wanted to do something special for her birthday; it's her thirty-fifth, so she's beginning to feel a little old, you know? She wanted to have fun, go out for a night with the girls, then drive up to Key Largo and swim with dolphins.

CARSON: But she didn't want to go with her husband, and I believe she has a child too?

JOAN: Yes, and no. She needed some time off, some time to herself. Us girls need that every now and then too, you know? Just like the boys need to hang out and belch at the TV or look at women in a bar.

CARSON: Were you coming here to look at men?

JOAN: Heck, yeah. Kate needed to see something other than that dull husband of hers. She needed to feel wanted again.

CARSON: And her husband didn't make her feel wanted?

JOAN: Listen, Andrew is as sweet as the day is long, but he is just as dull too. She was tired of him and wanted to blow off some steam. Who can blame her?

CARSON: Blow off some steam? Was that the term she used?

JOAN: I guess. Maybe not in those words, but that was the gist of it, yes. She wanted to get away.

CARSON: Get away from what exactly?

JOAN: I think she was just bummed out about the marriage. She never told me much about it, but I know when a girlfriend is in a bad marriage.

CARSON: So, was it a bad marriage?

JOAN: No more than most marriages, I guess. No more than mine. We all have our issues, don't we?

CARSON: But she wanted out of her marriage, is that it?

JOAN: Yes, she said so several times. She wanted to get away.

CARSON: Could her husband have hurt her?

JOAN: Andrew? No, please. He is many things, but violent is not one of them.

CARSON: Is he the jealous type?

JOAN: What do you mean?

CARSON: Would he get angry if she was unfaithful?

JOAN: She would never do that. Not Kate.
CARSON: So, she didn't cheat on him?
JOAN: No.
CARSON: That isn't her character?
JOAN: She wouldn't.
CARSON: She didn't meet anyone while you were down here?
JOAN: No.
CARSON: She didn't talk to anyone while you were partying?
JOAN: She talked to a lot of people. Kate loved to talk to people.
CARSON: But no one in particular? There wasn't one person she spoke to or danced with?
JOAN: No. I don't think so. I would have noticed if she spoke to someone in particular.
CARSON: (papers rustling) Because your other friend mentioned a man, someone named Matt? Does that name ring a bell?
JOAN: (pauses, then chuckles nervously) Ah, Matt, that guy, yes. I forgot about him.
CARSON: Can you describe him?
JOAN: I don't know, uhm, he was bald, I think, or maybe that was some other guy.
CARSON: So, you don't remember what he looked like?
JOAN: We had a lot to drink. I'm sorry; I don't. I don't think Kate liked him very much, and she got rid of him quickly.
CARSON: (clears throat) Did she ever talk about leaving her husband?
JOAN: Yes. I think she was tired of him. She did say in the car on the way here that she wished she could just disappear.
CARSON: So, you think that's what happened? She just left?
JOAN: (long pause) How the heck am I supposed to know? All I know is that she wasn't in her bed the next morning like she was supposed to be. We shared a room and thought she'd come home on her own. She didn't want to go back with us, so we left her there at the bar. At first, we thought she might have gone somewhere, and we waited for her to come back, calling her phone, but she didn't

answer. After we had waited for a very long time and she didn't come back, we went to the police and said we couldn't find her. We filed a missing person's report, and the officers on duty said they'd look for her. They also said she was probably out partying still and that she'd show up eventually. Then, you called us this morning and told us to come in at noon.

CARSON: Okay, Joan. I think we're about done here. Is there anything you'd like to add to your statement?

JOAN: I don't think so.

CARSON: Okay. All right. I'm going to go ahead and conclude this interview for now. It's 1402 hours.

TEN YEARS LATER

Chapter 1

MY DAD WAVED from the front pew, and we rushed up next to him. Josie plopped down in the seat next to me with an annoyed sigh, staring at her phone from underneath the pulled-up hoodie.

"What took you so long? It's about to start," my dad said.

"I'll have to tell you later."

I glared at Josie, then shook my head. She had an outfit breakdown this morning. That was why we were late for church. Those weren't unusual these days, but today had been worse than the other times. She had cried and said she looked stupid in everything and that she felt like a hobo because she was wearing sweatpants. I told her not to wear sweatpants, that it was silly anyway because it was eighty degrees outside.

"But I want to wear them," she had answered.

"Then wear them. I think you look great."

"Are you kidding me? I look like a homeless person, or some druggie," she had then said.

I had stared at her in confusion, not knowing what to say next. It didn't matter what I tried to say anyway. It would be wrong, no matter what. So, I had shut up, with the result that she had growled at me and told me I didn't care about her. In the end, I had just told her to get a move on, probably yelling it a little too loudly. And here we were, almost missing the beginning of the service.

Yes, it was true what they said. Age fourteen is a nightmare year for a girl. I had never had a boy, so I couldn't say what that was like, but this girl was enough teenager for me for the time being.

It'll pass. She'll grow older and then it'll get better.

The worship music began, and we rose to our feet. Josie stayed sitting, and my dad noticed, then pushed my arm and nodded toward her.

I leaned down so she could hear me. "Josie, stand up, please."

"Why?" she whined. "I don't like this music."

"We're at church, and we stand up and worship just as we stand in respect for God's word. Come."

"I can't. My legs hurt."

"Your legs hurt?"

"From volleyball, remember? Besides, I can worship just fine while sitting down. God doesn't care."

I took a deep breath, trying to remain calm. She had been testing my patience for the past few weeks, and to be honest, I was getting a little tired of it.

"Josie, I need you to get up right now and put that phone away. Now."

"But…"

"Josie!"

"I just don't understand why I can't just sit down and…"

I gave her a look, *that* look, the one letting her know she had reached the end of the rope. If she continued, she knew that she'd end up getting grounded and her phone privileges taken away.

Reluctantly, she put the phone in the pocket of her hoodie, then rose to her feet. I took in another deep breath, feeling everything but victorious, then closed my eyes.

God, I need all the strength you can give me today. Please. And tomorrow too and the rest of the week while you're at it. I have no idea how to deal with this all by myself.

Josie's mother, my wife Camille, had overdosed three years ago and was left with a brain injury that she was still trying to recover from. She had started rehabilitation, and I had hired a fulltime nurse for her, even though both were way above my budget. She had regained some of her speech and mobility but was still bound to a wheelchair. For three years she was bedridden and in a vegetative state until two months earlier when she suddenly woke up, and we started to communicate with her. She still only said a few words, but her vocabulary was slowly growing, and she was beginning to understand more of what we told her.

But we still didn't know exactly what happened to her. She had recently managed to communicate to me that someone had tried to kill her, but we hadn't come any closer as to who or why.

I, for one, was determined to do everything in my power to find out and bring them to justice.

My favorite worship song was next, and I sang along while tears ran down my cheeks. I was so grateful to God for bringing my wife back and for getting my daughter a new heart when she needed it. But there was still so much I didn't understand, and I felt my faith diminishing as the days passed.

When God, when? When will we get the answers we need? When will these people be brought to justice?

The worst part was that I had also recently discovered that my wife wasn't who I thought she was. I had stopped a group of human traffickers, taking down a group of my colleagues, smuggling refugees through Miami Harbor from South America and the Caribbean inside appliances. But before he had killed himself, one of the guys I believed was in charge had told me Camille played a role in this. Or that she at least knew it was happening and who was behind it. I wondered now if that was why they had tried to kill her.

The only person I shared these things with was my neighbor, Jean. She was a nurse and had helped us out from the beginning once Camille got sick. She used to be best friends with Camille, but now she was so much more than that. She was family, and to me, she was even more than that. I had realized I was falling for her, and that maybe I had been in love with her for a long time. But as Camille woke up, I had to distance myself from her, so I wouldn't hurt her. Still, she was the only one I trusted enough to share my thoughts with, even though I tried not to.

When did life get so complicated?

I wiped the tears off my cheeks and looked briefly at my dad, who worshipped with his hands in the air, eyes closed, and sang his dear heart out. My dad was my rock, and without him, I wouldn't have been able to go through all this. He helped me when in need, and as a former pastor, he was always ready with an uplifting and faith-building word for me when I struggled, which was a lot these days.

The music stopped, and the pastor took the stage.

"Give it up for our worship team," he said. "Aren't they amazing?"

People clapped. Josie had sat back down and was on her phone once again. I decided not to say anything. The last thing I wanted was for her to hate going to church as she got older. I had to pick my battles with her at this age; my dad had taught me that. It was easier said than done, but I was trying to live by it.

"Please, be seated," the pastor said, and we did.

Chapter 2

THE PASTOR STARTED his sermon about the prodigal son who returned, and how the father's love for him made him run toward him and how our father's love for us was the same.

Big enough to forgive all we have ever done.

I enjoyed the sermon and tried hard to listen while the pastor spoke, but someone sitting in front of me kept talking loudly. It was a young boy and a man whom I assumed was his father. I couldn't see their faces, but they were obviously quarreling, and their voices were growing louder.

"I knew you'd say that. Why can't you just tell me the truth for once," the boy said, hissing at his father.

"Keep it down," the man said.

A woman sitting next to them hushed them, and they went quiet for a few minutes until it started all over again. I was suddenly very pleased with my own daughter's behavior. We never yelled at each other that way. It's like they say; there's always someone who has it worse than you, right?

"What do you mean you can't trust me?" the man said, turning his head, looking at his son.

The boy scoffed loudly. "Don't give me that. You know perfectly well what I'm talking about."

The man shook his head and looked away. "I'm not having this discussion here. Not now."

That made the boy rise to his feet. "Yes, you are. I need to know, Dad. I deserve to know the truth. NOW! You've been lying to me all of my life! It ends here. Do you hear me? It ends HERE!"

"What on earth are you talking about?"

By yelling, the boy had attracted the attention of everyone in the church, even Pastor Johnson, who had stopped his preaching. He was looking down at them, a surprised look in his eyes, a look that seemed mostly concerned. He was only displaying what the rest of us were feeling—concerned and uncomfortable. Like spectators to a show we weren't invited to. This was clearly a discussion that wasn't meant to be had in church. It was the kind of thing that should stay behind closed doors.

"Sit down, son," the dad said, speaking through gritted teeth. "You're embarrassing me."

"No," the boy said, on the verge of tears now. "I am done doing what you tell me. I am done with you."

And with those words, he reached inside his hoodie and pulled out a gun. He held it between both hands, and it was shaking as he placed it against his father's head.

If he didn't before, then he most certainly had the church's attention now. A wave of panic rushed through the crowd, and someone yelled:

"Gun! He's got a gun!"

I felt Josie's hand on my arm as she raised her head.

"Dad?"

"Get down," I told her, and she ducked behind the pew, arms above her head.

The boy with the gun was shaking violently as he sobbed and pressed it against his father's temple. The father had raised his hands above his head and was tilting his head, trying to get away from the gun while whimpering lightly, his terrified eyes lingering on his son at the other end of the gun.

"Please, Nick."

"Don't do this," I said to the boy, approaching him. He didn't look at me. He stared down at his dad, his lips quivering.

"Stay out of this," he suddenly said to me. "You don't know anything."

"Then, let's talk," I said. "Tell me all about it. But don't ruin your life by doing this. If you pull that trigger, there's no going back. Your dad will die, you'll go to jail, and you'll have to live with the fact that you've killed someone for the rest of your life. And believe me; that's not something you'd wish for yourself."

"Yeah?" the boy said as he sniffled. "And just how do you know? You ever killed anyone?"

"As a matter of fact, I have," I said.

That made him turn his head and look at me.

"Really?"

I nodded, then pulled out my Miami PD badge. "One of the downsides to the job. It doesn't matter how bad these people are; it still haunts you for the rest of your life. Now, God will forgive you, but you'll never be able to forgive yourself. You'll always keep wondering if there wasn't some other way, always wish that you had done something different. It doesn't matter if the guy you killed is a murderer himself or even someone who has hurt children. They'll still visit you in your nightmares. The question is still there; couldn't it have ended differently? Did he have to die?"

The boy stared down at his father while the church was slowly being cleared out around us. People were running for their lives, storming out of the emergency exits, some were crying, others screaming. Nick didn't seem to care. He wasn't there to perform a mass shooting. His focus was solely on his dad.

"Nick," I said. "It might give you ten seconds of relief to shoot him because of whatever he has done to you, but it's not worth it. Trust me."

The boy glared down at his dad, the gun still shaking in his hands. I was sweating heavily, my heart pounding in my chest.

"Just give me the gun, Nick. Just hand it to me."

I could tell he was contemplating it; he was considering doing as

I told him, at least for a few seconds. He lifted his head and looked at me, our eyes locking. I saw nothing but deep despair in them. The gun was lowered slightly, and he leaned over like he was about to do as I told him when there was movement from the other side. I turned to look as a local police officer entered. I had seen him outside the building when entering. Like all other churches in the area, they had a police officer guarding the entrance when we came and left, and sometimes they even had a car on the street and officers directing traffic outside.

"Drop the gun!" he yelled, holding his gun pointed at Nick. Seeing this, my heart dropped.

"Please," I said, lifting my badge. "He was about to hand it over to me."

But Nick was confused now. I reached out my hand and said to him. "Nick, just give me the gun. Please, before this officer finds it necessary to shoot."

Nick stared at me, then at the officer. The gun was no longer at his father's temple, so the dad saw a chance to get away. He sprang forward, leaping for the end of the row. Seeing this, Nick gasped, then panicked. He turned around and fired a shot at him. This prompted the officer to fire as well, and a second later, I stood with Nick in my arms as I grabbed him when he fell, blood gushing out on my white, newly-ironed church shirt.

Chapter 3

IT HAD BEEN A PRETTY quiet day so far at the ER. Jean was working the morning shift and had just helped a little girl who had fallen off her bike. She had gotten a cast on her arm, and now Jean was handing her a lollipop for her braveness. That's when they got the message.

They were bringing in two victims of a gunfight.

After that, there was not a quiet moment. As soon as they were rushed in, Jean didn't sit down for the rest of her shift.

The young teenage boy was in the worst shape. His father, who had also been shot, had suffered a gunshot wound to his upper arm and was brought into surgery right away, where they managed to remove the bullet and patch him up. The bullet hadn't fractured any bones or hit any organs.

The young boy was a completely different story. He had suffered a gunshot to his chest, and they fought for his life in there for hours and hours. They had asked Jean to assist. It broke Jean's heart to see such a young man going through something like this at his age. He had his entire life ahead of him.

At least he was supposed to.

He had lost a lot of blood, and they brought in bag after bag of O-negative, while the doctors shook their heads, unsure how this was going to end. Dr. Harris, who Jean often worked with, had that look in his eyes that she didn't care much for, the one that told her he was close to giving up hope.

"We're losing him, Doctor," she told him as his blood pressure suddenly dropped rapidly. "Doctor?"

The sound of the heartrate flatlining was possibly the worst in the world, and as she heard it, Jean's heart knocked against her ribcage. She pulled out the defibrillator, and the doctor resuscitated the boy's heart. The heart rate came back up, but only to flatline again. They did the same things all over again, and the same thing happened. The third time, they succeeded in keeping his heart pumping, and Jean breathed again for the first time in minutes.

She knew she wasn't supposed to get emotionally invested in patients, but it was hard not to, especially when it involved those whose lives you had fought for. She wanted this boy to live so badly; she almost cried when his heartrate flatlined again a few minutes later.

"Not today," Doctor Harris said and used the defibrillator once again. "We're not losing you today."

The boy's body jolted as the electric shock went through him, and Jean turned to look at the monitor, praying for a heartbeat.

Come on; come on.

A second later, one came. And this time, it continued. Sweat sprang from her forehead as the doctors continued their work and were finally able to patch the boy up before he was taken to the ICU.

At the end of the day, she stood by his door, peeking inside and watching him. She then grabbed her purse and left the hospital, tears streaming across her cheeks. Not because she was sad, but because she loved her job so much. She loved being a part of saving lives. But at the same time, she hated how much bad stuff she had to witness every day. She hated that she lived in a world where young boys and their fathers got shot.

As she drove down her street, she saw a shadow on the porch of her neighboring house, and she breathed heavily. She parked the car and got out, then spotted Harry sitting on his swing.

Chapter 4

"HEY THERE, NEIGHBOR."

She wasn't supposed to since they were trying to stay away from one another, but something compelled her to walk up the stairs, up onto the porch where he was sitting. And as she saw his face, she realized why.

He had been crying.

"Are you okay? Harry?"

He shook his head, then bit his lip and leaned back in the swing. She sat down next to him, grabbing his hands between hers. His eyes were red-rimmed, and he didn't look at her.

"Oh, Harry. What's going on? What's happening? Is it Josie?"

He shook his head, then sniffled. He leaned his head against her shoulder. It was odd when a man as big as Harry, who was six-foot-eight and weighed around two hundred and thirty-something pounds, leaned against a small woman like Jean. It had to be an odd sight.

"Is it Camille? Is something wrong with Camille?"

He lifted his head and wiped his eyes. "I'm sorry. I'm just..."

She smiled. 'Tell me, Harry. What happened?"

"There was this kid. In church. He was fighting with his father in the row in front of us. He then pulled out a gun. He wanted to shoot his dad but ended up getting shot himself. I was so close to helping him. He was so close to handing me the gun, and then… well, it all went wrong."

"I think I know who you're talking about," she said. "He was brought into the ER, and so was his dad."

"I am afraid to ask, but…"

Jean squeezed his hands. It killed her to sit there with him this close and not be able to kiss him ever again.

"He is alive, Harry. It was a close call, but he is still alive. The doctors say he has a good chance of recovery."

"Oh, God, that makes me so relieved to hear," he said. He chuckled, grabbed her face between his hands, leaned over, and placed a kiss on Jean's lips.

It took them both by surprise and, startled, they both pulled away. Jean rose to her feet and walked a few steps toward the stairs, her heart pounding in her chest.

What the heck?

"I'm…" Harry said. "I'm sorry, Jean. I was just so happy. I didn't think."

She shook her head. "You can't do that, Harry. You can't just kiss me and then regret it. It's not fair to me."

He got up. "And I don't want to. The fact is, I don't regret it at all. I want to be able to kiss you every day, Jean. I think I…"

"Don't you dare. Don't even think about going there," she said, raising her hand to stop him.

"But why not?" Harry lowered his voice. "I want to do the right thing, but the fact is, I'm not sure I love Camille anymore."

Jean shook her head. "I don't want to hear anymore, Harry."

"I could divorce her," he said.

"No!" Jean said. "Don't you even say that. Camille is not herself. She might get better with treatment, and then what? You're a family, remember? What about Josie?"

That made Harry stop, and she knew he hadn't thought any of it through. He was acting on impulse, and that wasn't good enough for Jean. She loved him, she truly did, and she'd give anything to be with him. But she couldn't be the one to break up a family, especially not when she loved his daughter and wife so dearly. She couldn't be that person. Plus, she knew Harry would never leave Camille when she was at her most vulnerable. It was never going to happen. It simply wasn't in his nature.

He stared at Jean, and she shook her head.

"I'll forget this even happened. I need to go to bed now. Go and be with your family. Goodnight, Harry."

Chapter 5

I WATCHED her walk down the stairs and toward her own house, cursing myself. I had blown it, hadn't I? We were doing so well, and now I had ruined everything. Why did I have to kiss her?

I had acted on impulse, and I hadn't thought about it. It was an accident, except it wasn't. Because accidents weren't something you usually really wanted to happen, were they? I wanted this to happen; I longed to kiss her so terribly.

The thing was, I felt more and more detached from Camille lately, especially since I felt like I hadn't even known her back before she overdosed. When I met her, she was a drug addict, and I helped her get clean, and we fell in love. But she had never told me much about herself. I barely knew anything about her childhood or her life before she met me. I had never met any members of her family or even friends. Her excuse was that they all lived in the Caribbean, in the Dominican Republic, and the only friends she had here in Miami were related to her drug abuse, so she didn't want anything to do with them. But I knew she went to FIT at one point; there had to be at least someone decent that she knew from back then, right?

I walked back inside and went into her room, where she was

lying, staring at the ceiling. Josie was sitting in there, holding her mother's hand in hers.

"Are you okay?" I asked. "With everything that happened today. Must have been scary."

She sighed and nodded. "It was pretty scary. Mostly when the shots were fired. I thought they'd hit you."

I smiled. "So, you were worried about your old man, huh?"

She nodded. "I'm always worried about you."

I nodded pensively. Josie wasn't fond of the fact that I was a detective. She was terrified I'd get shot one day, and she'd lose me too. I couldn't blame her.

"I don't feel like she's getting any better," Josie said and looked at her mom. "Are you sure they know what they're doing at that rehabilitation center?"

"I'm pretty sure, yes. But I've recently heard of a different type of treatment that I am willing to try. They've had some pretty interesting results with cases like your mother's."

"Really?"

I nodded. "A nurse at the rehabilitation center told me about it and gave me a number. I'll call them tomorrow and see what they might be able to do for all of us."

"That sounds awesome, Dad." She looked at her mother, who was drifting in and out of sleep now.

Josie whispered, "I really miss her, you know?"

"I know," I said.

We stared at Camille in silence, each of us thinking about her when she had been herself…back when we had been a real family. I could hardly remember those days or what our relationship was like. Had I loved her? I knew I had. I just couldn't really find those emotions again. I kept wondering who wanted to kill her and why. Was it the people behind the trafficking ring? And did they still want her dead? There was so much I didn't understand, and maybe it was wrong of me, but it made me resent her. I couldn't help being angry with her for somehow putting Josie and me in this situation, for breaking our daughter's heart like this. If she had been involved with the wrong crowd and kept it a secret from me, I didn't know if I would be able to stay married to her.

"Why do you think he did it?" Josie suddenly asked, breaking my train of thought. She got up from her chair, and we walked out of Camille's room. Her breathing had gotten heavy, and we knew she was asleep.

"Who?" I asked, closing the door behind us.

"That kid. At church? Why do you think he pulled the gun on his father?"

"That's a very good question, honey."

"I mean, I know what it's like to be angry with my dad, but it takes a lot to go where he went…if you know what I mean."

I looked at my gorgeous daughter as she walked up the stairs to her room. The thought had crossed my mind too while thinking about what had happened earlier.

What would make a young teenage boy try to kill his own dad?

THREE WEEKS LATER

Chapter 6

I KNOCKED and opened the door to my boss's office.

"You wanted to see me?"

"Come in, Hunter," he said and signaled for me to enter. "Close the door behind you."

I did, then went to sit across from him. Fowler and I had known each other and worked together all of our adult lives. He was the one who climbed the career ladder while I remained on the floor and in the field. I preferred it this way as I was never cut out to be a leader. I'd rather be out there getting my fingers dirty. But that wasn't Fowler. He seemed to thrive being in this big office and carrying the weight that came with the title of Major.

"I need you to be careful out there, Hunter," he said, folding his hands on the desk, with serious eyes, his eyebrows furrowing.

"Me? I'm always careful," I said.

"Listen to me. You need to watch your back out there," he said and pointed at the door. "You're not exactly the most popular guy around here."

"I know," I said. "Not everyone likes what I've done, seeing their colleagues go down like that. But I'm sure I'll be fine. It had to be done."

Fowler placed a small bag on the table, then slid it toward me. "I had someone I trust sweep my office. They found this. They bugged me, Harry. That's how they've stayed on top of things, staying out of trouble. That's also how they knew how to find Josie. You know when you thought you'd put her in a safe place with Al and told me about it, remember?"

Remember? How could I ever forget? My daughter had been kidnapped and almost murdered by my ex-colleague, Detective Ferdinand, before he ended up killing himself. He and several others from my precinct were all part of the human trafficking group, smuggling refugees into the country from Guatemala and the Caribbean. The case was still ongoing, and the FBI was working it with my cooperation. Right before he died, Ferdinand was also the one who had told me that Camille was somehow involved in all of it. I had wondered if Fowler had been in on it as well since he was the only one who knew where Josie was, and yet they found her anyway, but this little bag on the table explained everything. I could trust Fowler again, and that made me feel good. But it could also mean that there were still people around here that we couldn't trust… people that wanted us gone.

"I'll be all right," I said and reached over to grab the bag with the microphone. "Can I borrow this?"

"Be my guest," he said.

I looked at it in the light, then put it in my pocket. "The kid."

"What kid?"

"From the shooting at my church three weeks ago. What's gonna happen to him?"

"He's recovered," Fowler said. "He's in custody now. They're gonna try him as an adult."

"An adult? He's fifteen?" I said.

Fowler shrugged. "He brought a gun to church. He shot his own father. You know his dad is the State Attorney, right? They can't go easy on the boy. He knew what he was doing. He's old enough. Besides, that's not our department."

"Still. He's just a kid. One year older than my Josie. Is he talking? Has he explained anything?"

Fowler shook his head. "He won't say a word to anyone. Not even his lawyer."

I nodded. "Can I have a go at him?"

Fowler chuckled. "I wouldn't know why you'd want to."

"Just indulge me, will you? I think I connected with him at the church. I feel bad for him. At least give him the chance of telling his side of the story, right?"

"I will never learn to understand you, Hunter. But if you really want to, then knock yourself out. I'm not stopping you."

Chapter 7

THE TREATMENT CENTER was located in a three-story yellow building north of Miami. Doctor Kendrick, who was a small blonde woman with comforting eyes, greeted us in her office. I rolled Camille's chair inside and sat down.

"Okay," she said and looked at the papers I had brought her. It was Camille's medical file.

"As you can see, the doctors didn't think she'd ever wake up and become responsive again," I said. "But she did."

"And that was three months ago?" she asked, looking at Camille, whose eyes were on her as well. Her right arm had a couple of spasms, and she tried to speak, but it didn't make any sense.

"Yes. Approximately. Unfortunately, I don't think there has been much improvement over the past months, even though she goes to rehabilitation therapy three times a week. She does speak a few more words, and she does seem to be more responsive when I talk to her, but she can't control any of her movements, let alone do simple tasks like eating on her own."

"I see," Doctor Kendrick said.

"I don't know if I'm just being impatient or…" I said.

"It's only natural, Mr. Hunter," she interrupted me. "Once we begin to see progress in the ones we love, we expect things to move a lot faster than what they do. With that being said, I do think we can help her. Looking at her file, she seems to be a perfect fit for what we do here. Now, there are a few things I want to make sure you understand before we begin anything."

"Yes, of course."

"Now, treating Anoxic Brain Injury with hyperbaric treatment, in a hyperbaric chamber, is not FDA approved yet. We have research suggesting it works, and we have seen cases where it does work. Recently, we had a little girl who nearly drowned and had been dead for two hours, with no heartbeat and, therefore, no oxygen flowing to her brain. She was—like your wife here—unresponsive for months, till she came here. That doesn't mean it's some miracle treatment. There are doctors out there who will claim we were just lucky. That there is no evidence that it was due to our treatment. Now, since it is not FDA approved, your insurance won't pay."

I nodded. "I'm well aware of that. I'll pay out of pocket, even though it will drain my budget."

"Very well, Mr. Hunter," she said, smiling. "Now, the way the treatment works…what your wife has is Anoxic Brain Injury, as you are very well aware. It's a type of brain injury caused by oxygen deprivation. This can cause serious damage as the brain depends on oxygen to function properly. We know now that brain cells without oxygen will begin to die after only six minutes. There are several ways to suffer anoxic brain damage. Nearly drowning, experiencing a lack of oxygen due to a heart issue, or like in your wife's case, an overdose of drugs. Now the use of Hyperbaric Oxygen Therapy can promote healing by restoring oxygen levels and improving the flow of oxygen-rich blood to the brain. This can help blood vessels to grow and repair damaged tissue. The treatments are designed to help her injured brain cells shrink, expose healthy neurons, and 'wake them up' with pure oxygen. We provide oxygen to the patient in a pressurized chamber, giving her the same air pressure as air at sea level for forty-five minutes twice a day. Now, as I said, we can't promise you anything, but we have seen great results in other patients like her. Like the girl I talked about who is now functioning at almost a normal level for her age, which is quite remarkable."

I exhaled nervously. This was a big decision, one that I had to make all alone. "And what are the side effects?"

"She might feel slight discomfort in her ears because of the pressure, kind of like in an airplane. It can get very hot in the chamber while it's being pressurized, and she might feel fatigued, lightheaded, and hungry after the treatments. More severe complications can be lung damage, fluid buildup or rupture of the eardrum, sinus damage, and changes in vision causing nearsightedness, or myopia. There's the possibility of oxygen poisoning, which can cause lung failure, fluid in the lungs, or seizures. But side effects are normally mild as long as the therapy doesn't last more than two hours, and the pressure inside the chamber is less than three times that of the normal pressure in the atmosphere. Now, we will take her temperature and do a general health check before we begin the treatment, just to make sure she's in good health, that she doesn't have a cold or any respiratory issues. After that, we should be good to go."

I looked at Camille briefly, then exhaled. "I think we're in. Right now, we'll take anything we can get if there is even a remote chance of improvement."

Chapter 8

I WORKED on my computer while Camille was in the chamber, receiving her first treatment. I was nervous as they slid the lid on top of her and closed the chamber. I could see her face through the small glass window in the chamber from where I was sitting, and she seemed comfortable enough. It was always hard to tell with her, and I worried that she was scared or maybe even in pain. But Doctor Kendrick, who was in the room with us the whole time, assured me that she was doing very well, that there was nothing to worry about.

Once she was done, they helped me put her back in her wheelchair, and I was told to be back the next day, early in the morning. They wanted us to come in every morning and every evening, so I was going to have to work my schedule around her treatments. It wasn't going to be easy, but if it provided any results, it would be worth it.

"How did it go? Is she any better?"

Josie was all over us as soon as we came through the front door. She looked at her mother, but as she saw no improvement, she gave me a disappointed look. Typically, the impatient teenager had expected an immediate response.

"She looks the same," she said.

"Josie, sweetie. It will take a while before we'll see any results," I said, then helped Camille get back into her room and lay her down on her bed. She was exhausted and fell asleep right away.

"But..." Josie said.

"We have to be patient," I said, grabbing her by the shoulders. "I have great confidence in the doctor and this treatment, and in God, naturally."

Josie sighed as we walked back into the kitchen, and I started dinner. I was making spaghetti and meatballs, and seeing this, Josie wrinkled her nose at the meat.

"So, how long do you think it'll take?" she asked.

I found an onion and started to cut it up, then exhaled tiredly. It had been a long day for me as well. I dreamt of lying on the couch and putting up my feet.

"I don't know, honey. To be honest, I need..."

I stopped when a foul smell hit my nostrils. Josie noticed it too.

"What's that smell?"

"It smells burnt," I said.

We both turned to look toward the front door, where something lit up the darkness outside by the windows leading to the porch.

"Stay here," I told her, then walked to the window and peeked out. Out on the front lawn, I spotted something that made me almost lose it.

"What is it, Dad? Dad?"

"Stay here!"

I hurried back into the kitchen, grabbed the fire extinguisher, then ran to the door and pulled it open. I rushed down the stairs into the front yard, where someone had put my trash bins and set them on fire. I ran down there, opened the extinguisher, and put it out, covering everything in the white foam. The smoke hit my face, and it smelled awful, so I turned away.

As I did, I saw a word written in red paint on my garage door. The letters were covering the entire surface, making them as tall as I was. The paint was still wet and running, but the message was clear enough:

RAT

Chapter 9

"WHAT WAS THAT?"

Josie stared at me as I hurried inside and closed the door behind me. "Why were our trash bins on fire?"

"It was nothing," I lied. I didn't want her to worry. I closed the door to make sure she didn't go outside and see the writing.

"It looked like something, Dad."

"It was just kids, okay? Pranks, you know."

She calmed down. "Oh, okay."

I smiled, then continued my cooking, shaping the meatballs. Josie stayed with me for a few minutes more, seeming like she wanted to talk, but then eventually giving up.

"I have homework," she said, then walked upstairs. "Call me when dinner is ready."

Normally, at a moment like this, I would have told her to help me set the table, but not this time, not today. As soon as she was gone up the stairs, I grabbed a bucket of soap and water, then ran out to the garage door and started to wash off the paint, scrubbing it. I got most of it off and was about to walk back inside when Jean came up behind me.

"What's going on?"

I turned to look at her, my heart jumping at the sight of her.

"What's this?"

"Someone set our trash bins on fire and wrote RAT on my garage door. I think they're trying to scare me off from talking to the feds."

She nodded. "The trafficking case, huh. So, you think it might be your colleagues who did this?"

I shrugged. "Could be. I'm not exactly popular around the station for doing what I'm doing. But they don't scare me. I will not stop till all of them are brought to justice, that's for sure."

Jean smiled and nodded. "I wouldn't expect any less from you. But what about Josie?"

"What about her?"

Jean pointed toward the burned-out bins in my front yard. The smell of melted plastic was still thick.

"Did she see this?"

"She saw the fire, but not the writing. I told her it was a prank. I'm not sure she believed me. She's getting too smart for me. I just don't want her to worry about this too. She has enough with her mother and all. She even says she's constantly worried about me getting hurt or killed while at work. It's too much for such a young girl. She should be worrying about her friends and boys and stuff like that."

"So, what are you going to do about this?" Jean asked.

I shook my head, then poured the last soapy water on the garage door. I had managed to wash away most of it, even though you still could see the trace of what had been written.

"Ignore them. That's what you do with bullies."

Chapter 10

THE PRE-TRIAL DETENTION center was located right across the street from the Richard E. Gerstein Justice Building on 13th Street. A handful of security guards in green jackets stood outside the entrance to both buildings as I drove through the gates and into the detention center, known to be one of the toughest in the nation. In there were the most hardcore criminals, awaiting their trials.

And then there was Nick. Fifteen-year-old Nick Taylor.

I was shown into a room with benches and tables that were bolted to the floor, so they couldn't be moved or lifted in the air and used as weapons.

Nick entered, heavily chained on his hands and feet, then sat down across from me while the guard stood only a few feet away. I tried to smile, but it was hard to be sincere in these circumstances. The boy had lost a lot of weight since I had last seen him in the church, and he was paler than the barren white walls behind him.

"Nick?" I said, trying to look into his eyes, but he kept staring at the floor beneath him.

"My name is Harry Hunter. I'm a detective with Miami PD, and I've come here to help you."

No reaction. I hadn't expected one, but it didn't make it less uncomfortable.

"I was there when you pulled the gun out. I was sitting right behind you. Maybe you remember me? I tried to persuade you to hand me the gun. I was the one who tried to tell you not to ruin your life. Do you remember, Nick?"

No reaction. I tried another approach.

"I want to help you, Nick. They want to try you as an adult, and you're looking at some serious charges here. If you tell someone why you did it, then maybe we could be…"

I stopped myself. I didn't know if telling his story would actually help him or not. The fact was, he had attempted to kill his father, and in a public place on top of it, where he risked the lives of many others. The media was all over his story—the State Attorney's son being tried for attempted murder. They had practically already convicted him. I was no attorney. I couldn't promise him anything. I saw him do it, so there was no doubt of his guilt. But I could be there for him; I could listen to his story.

"I've read up on your background, Nick," I said and found his file. I placed it on the table, then opened it. "Your mother, she died ten years ago, didn't she?"

Still, no answer.

"It says here she disappeared on a road trip to Key West ten years ago. Her body was discovered three days later in the water down there, hidden underneath the mangroves. A fisherman spotted her, it says here."

The boy remained still even though he was now fiddling with a loose string on his orange jumpsuit. I couldn't tell if he was reacting at all to what I was saying. My guess was that he was hurting too badly even to be able to look at me.

"What did he do to you, Nick?" I asked, closing the file with a deep exhale. "See, I don't believe a boy like you did this without a valid reason. I think your father did something to make you do this." I slammed my palm onto the metal table between us. The sound was louder than I had intended it to be and bounced off the walls.

"What did he do to make you so mad? Come on, talk to me."

That's when I finally got my reaction. Nick lifted his eyes and looked into mine while I continued, "The way I see it, you had enough. You got angry, maybe you were even scared of him, and that's why you pulled the gun. And you might not want to tell me or anyone why, but I'm not letting him get away with it, you hear me?"

The guard signaled for me that my time was up and went to grab Nick. He stared at me, his green eyes piercing through me. Then as he rose to his feet, he finally spoke while being pulled away, "I remember you, Detective. I remember you."

Chapter 11

"I THINK he was about to talk just when they took him away."

My dad looked at me. We were sitting at the dinner table and had just finished our pizza. I had been to late afternoon therapy with Camille, and Josie was in her room doing her homework.

"And what did he say?" My dad asked and grabbed another slice of pizza, even though he had stopped eating minutes ago. My dad was very fond of food in general, especially the unhealthy kind.

"He said he remembered me," I said. "From the day he shot his dad, he remembered me. I made a connection with him, which no one else has been able to do."

My dad chewed and swallowed. He washed it down with iced tea. "So, what will you do next?"

"I'm gonna go back in a couple of days and see him again," I said. "Maybe he'll finally open up to me and talk then; maybe I can get the whole story. I don't feel good about this case, especially not about the father. Something is off, and the boy is the one taking the fall."

"So, you believe the father might have hurt the kid, is that it?"

I leaned back with a deep sigh. "Maybe. In my book, it takes a lot for a fifteen-year-old to try and kill his own dad. And I remember he said stuff to him before he pulled the gun out."

"What stuff?"

"Like he had been lying to him all of his life, that he was done trusting him. Something like that," I said and sipped my own iced tea.

"So, you believe it has to do with his mother's death, am I right?"

I exhaled and drank again. "Yes. Of course, I do."

"Did they suspect foul play in her death?" he asked, reaching over for yet another slice and biting into it. My dad had gained a lot of weight in the years since my mom died. She was the one who reminded him to stop eating and to exercise. He kept himself fit for her sake, but now that she wasn't here anymore, he had let himself go. I wondered if I should say something. I decided not to. He was in his seventies and didn't have to look good for anyone. He could have his pizza and enjoy it if he liked. I just wanted him to live long and stay with us for many years and not develop heart issues or anything like that.

"They concluded that she drowned, but the case was never closed. I found it when looking around a little and had the files sent up here from the Key West archives. Kate Taylor and two of her best friends were on a road trip to Key West. According to these women, it was Kate's thirty-fifth birthday, and she wanted to spend it with her friends, partying in Key West and then go swimming with dolphins in Key Largo. But they only made it to Key West. They partied that night, and she was seen dancing with some guy—they searched for him for a long time. All they knew was that his name was Matt and that he was tall and had brown hair and blue eyes. That's it. The girl's friends reported her missing the next day when she didn't come back to the hotel. At first, they thought she was out with this guy, and that she'd come back eventually, but when she didn't, they went to the police. The police searched for her for several days, and three days later, a fisherman found her floating in the shallow water, hidden under the mangroves. They concluded she had died from drowning. Maybe she went swimming at nighttime and got in trouble."

"But the case was never closed, you say?"

"No. They kept looking for this Matt guy, thinking he might be able to shed light on how a very good swimmer like Kate could suddenly drown. Was she pushed in? Did she fall from a boat? She had no bruises on her body, so there was no sign of being forced. So, what happened? It ends there."

My dad nodded pensively. "So, you think the dad might have killed her? The Miami-Dade County State Attorney?"

I shrugged. "She was away without him, dancing with another man. He could have followed her there; he could have gotten jealous, who knows?"

"You think Nick knows, don't you?"

I nodded. "It would explain a lot, wouldn't it?"

Chapter 12

I WAS RUNNING LATE for Camille's afternoon appointment and rushed in through the doors, pushing her wheelchair ahead of me.

It had been two weeks since we started coming to the treatment center, and I was finding it increasingly more and more difficult to be everywhere I was needed. Josie was complaining because I was never at home anymore, while Fowler was complaining because I didn't show up in time for morning briefings, even though I had told him I had to be at the treatment center every morning at nine and every afternoon at five. My cases were being neglected as I seemed to be trying to be several places at once, ending up being nowhere. At least, that's how it felt. When I was at work, my mind was constantly at home, thinking about all the stuff I needed to do, all the laundry I hadn't done, all the dishes in the sink, and the dental appointments for Josie, along with her volleyball games and practices, trying to figure out how I was supposed to drive her there while going to the treatment center with her mother. On top of it all, I had to remember to make a lunch for Josie every day and figure out what to cook for dinner.

It was a lot to balance at once.

While Camille received her treatment in the hyperbaric chamber, most of my thoughts were with Nick Taylor. I had been going through the old case files of his mother's death again and again and read every article that was ever written about her disappearance, and every time, it came down to the mysterious Matt. The guy she had been with on the night she died. No one seemed to know who he was or had even seen him when the police asked them back then. Not even the bartender at Sloppy Joe's, where they were drinking and dancing, could remember him. It was just the two friends.

Or was it?

While Camille was inside her chamber, I suddenly realized something. I flipped a couple of pages in the case files until I reached the two statements taken by the police—the first interviews with Kate Taylor's two friends, Joan and Kristin. There was something about them that had rubbed me the wrong way from the beginning when I first read through them.

They weren't a match. And in the places they were a match, they were too much of a match, too similar, down to the choice of words. I didn't like how they both said that she was *bummed out about her marriage* and that she needed to *blow off some steam*, and she *wished she could just disappear*. They were some very distinct sentences and sounded almost rehearsed…like they had memorized them. And then there was the thing about the guy, Matt. Only the first woman, Kristin, spoke about him on her own. She talked about him like he had been there all evening and said that Kate was *all over him*—that she was crazy about him. Whereas her other friend Joan didn't even remember him when asked, or maybe she didn't want to mention him? Could she be covering for him? Did she know him? While Kristin described him as tall, brown hair and blue eyes, Joan called him bald and stated that she couldn't really remember him and that she didn't believe that Kate was very interested in him and that she wouldn't cheat on her husband. Meanwhile, according to Kristin, she would definitely be able to cheat on her husband.

It didn't match up.

Who was telling the truth?

Was Joan lying to protect this guy?

I leaned back, running a hand through my hair, wondering

about this and why they hadn't looked more deeply into this ten years ago, when Doctor Kendrick came in, smiling. Her blonde hair was in a ponytail today, and it made her look younger. Her brown eyes smiled at me.

"I think she's done for today. You ready to take her home?"

Chapter 13

I DROVE up in front of my house, my mind still occupied by Kate Taylor's death, going through the many possibilities, always returning to the one theory I couldn't escape: That Andrew Taylor, Kate's husband and Nick's father, killed her in a fit of jealous rage, angry that she spent the night with some other guy, dancing and maybe even sleeping with him on her thirty-fifth birthday, and that Joan somehow knew this Matt guy and wanted to protect him.

I turned off the engine with a deep sigh, then got out and grabbed the wheelchair from the back and rolled it up to the door, then opened it and looked in at Camille. Usually, she would be half asleep at this point, tired from her treatment, but not today. Today, she looked at me and smiled, almost laughed as I peeked inside to help her out. Seeing this and hearing her light laughter, I couldn't help laughing too.

"What's so funny?" I asked. "Was it something I said?"

Knowing she couldn't answer, I bent over to get her seatbelt off, but as I did, she reached out her hand and grabbed mine. With a light gasp, I lifted my head and looked into her eyes. She was smiling widely while we were holding hands, lifting them in the air.

It was a coordinated maneuver that I knew she hadn't been able to do before. Our eyes locked, and then she spoke, "Th-Thank…you."

I almost lost it at this moment. Until now, she hadn't been able to utter more than one word, and usually, it would make no sense and be completely out of context. Like when she told me someone had tried to kill her, she simply yelled out our daughter's name. This was different. This was her actually speaking to me.

"What did you say?" I asked, my eyes watering.

"Thank…you," she repeated, then much to my surprise, she continued: "For…for all you h-have done. I don't deserve it."

The words spoken were so clear and flowed from her mouth like it was barely difficult at all. Tears sprang to my eyes as I stared at her, still while we were holding hands and she moved hers in a coordinated fashion, pulling both of our hands up and down.

"I…I don't know what to say. Camille. The hand…the movements…and you're speaking!"

I said it while almost squealing. She smiled and nodded, tears spilling onto her cheeks.

"It's working," I said, shaking my head in disbelief. "I can't believe it. The treatments. They're really working!"

She nodded again while crying.

I lifted my head, then grabbed her head between my hands and looked into her eyes.

"You're back, Camille."

She lifted her hand and touched my cheek, then wiped away a tear that had escaped my eyes and rolled down my cheeks. The movement was small and seemingly insignificant, but not to me. To me, it was bigger than any moonwalk. I grabbed her hands and pulled her out of her seat, then stood with her in my arms for a few seconds, letting her stand on her feet; then, once I sensed she had balance, I let go. She stood for a few seconds, staring at me like I had abandoned her, but then realized she was standing on her own, actually standing on her own two feet. She wasn't leaning on the car, and not on me either.

I nodded, then reached out my hands.

"Come."

Camille took one step toward me, then another before she fell forward into my arms, her legs deflating beneath her due to the lack of muscles after years of not being used while she was stuck in a bed and chair.

I grabbed her, placed her in her chair, grinning so loudly that Josie must have heard it inside the house because she came running out onto the porch.

"Dad? What's going on?"

"Your mom," I yelled as I helped Camille sit in her chair. "She…she walked! She actually stood and then walked two steps toward me on her own."

Josie shrieked and ran down the stairs toward us.

"Really? She did?"

I couldn't hold back my tears as Josie threw herself into her mother's arms. Camille chuckled and cried at the same time, while Josie held her close.

"And she spoke," I said, wiping tears away from my cheeks. "She spoke real sentences, several of them."

"Really?" Josie said and looked at her mother. "Is this true? You're better now, like really better?"

Camille nodded. "I…am."

Chapter 14

JEAN WAS SITTING in her kitchen, eating Ramen noodle soup since she wasn't in the mood for cooking. She hadn't been for quite a while now, probably ever since she stopped cooking for Harry and his family. It was like it was pointless now that it was just herself and not an entire family who needed her.

She missed being needed.

Jean sighed and looked into her soup. A lot seemed pointless these days. She was staying away from Harry, giving him his space and letting them be a family, but what did that mean for her? Where did that leave her?

Destined to be alone for the rest of her life?

You fell in love with the wrong guy.

That's what her mother would have said if she ever told her about him, which she never would. Her mother could be very judgmental when she wanted to, and she wanted to…a lot. It was like she enjoyed watching Jean lose confidence and feel like a child again. It was one of the reasons Jean never involved her in anything in her life. She kept her mother at a distance so she wouldn't be able to criticize her for her choices in life.

But this one, she would have been right about. You blew it, Jean. You wasted your love on a man that wasn't available.

She had barely finished the thought, feeling sorry for herself, when she heard the screaming from outside in the street. It made her rush to the window and look out. There they were, Josie, Harry, and Camille.

Jean walked out on the porch, then looked down at them. As she stood there, Harry spotted her and called out to her.

"Jean! It's amazing!"

Jean walked down the stairs and approached them, heart pounding in her chest like a hammer.

"She walked," Harry said as Jean came close. He had tears in his eyes and his voice was breaking.

"And talked," Josie added. "God is healing her. God is so good!"

"He sure is. Isn't it wonderful?" Harry asked.

Jean looked at him. She wanted to scream. Of course, it was wonderful. Of course, it was a miracle and worth celebrating.

But it also shut down her hope of ever being with Harry, of him ever putting Camille in a home. If Camille was really coming back, Jean didn't stand a chance. She knew it was selfish to think like this since she should be thrilled for them, and in a way, she was. She just wasn't thrilled for herself, for her own sake.

She was devastated.

Jean forced a smile through her tears. "That is wonderful news, Harry, really. I am so happy for y'all."

"It's the new treatment," Harry said. "I've seen little improvements every time we've gone. Like her being more alert, her looking at me more when I spoke, and smiling more. Little things. And today, she took a huge leap forward. I have to say it was hard to believe that there would ever be any improvement. But here we are. I can't believe it, Jean."

Jean swallowed and nodded while looking into his sweet eyes, the very eyes she loved so dearly. She felt her eyes tear up and bit her lip.

"I should…I have to get back. But congratulations to all of you. It's amazing; it truly is."

While still speaking the last few words, Jean turned around and hurried toward her home. She walked up the stairs, then turned to look at them. As they rolled Camille back into the house, she made her decision.

It was time to move on.

Chapter 15

"THANK YOU, God, for bringing Camille back to us. We pray we'll continue to see improvement in her and that she'll recover completely. We know you can and will do it because you love us so much. Amen."

"Amen," Josie repeated.

She was lying in her bed, PJs on, and I realized that she had grown out of them again. We'd had a nice evening together, eating pizza again. Camille had lasted for only about half an hour before her head started to slump and I had to put her to bed. Before she dozed off, she looked at me, then grabbed my wrist.

"I…am…sorry," she said.

I shushed her. "You need to sleep."

She had dozed off before I finished the sentence, and I had watched her sleep for a few minutes, wondering what the coming days and weeks would bring. Would I finally get some answers? Would I finally get to know what really happened to her and how it was all connected?

Would she tell me the truth?

Would I like what she told me?

Would I love her again?

It was hard to tell. I knew I would go far for Josie's sake. I just didn't know how far I was willing to go.

"Good night, Daddy," Josie said as I turned out the lights and left her room.

"Good night, sweetie."

I closed the door and walked back into my own bedroom. I brushed my teeth and got out of my clothes. I liked to sleep in my boxers as I was usually very hot at night, so I ducked in under the covers and turned the lights off. Then I just laid there in the darkness while a million thoughts rushed through my mind. I was excited and frightened at the same time. It was a strange sensation. Was I ready for this? Was I ready to get Camille back even if it meant I got to know the truth about her? Could I handle the consequences?

I believed so.

I sighed and thought about Jean. I had been so excited earlier; I hadn't even stopped for a second to think about how she felt about it. It had to be tough on her, even though she pretended to be happy for our sake.

The thought made me feel terrible.

No matter what I did, no matter how this ended, someone's heart was going to be broken.

I closed my eyes and tried to sleep, willing myself to think about something else. But then Nick Taylor showed up, and I couldn't help feeling disillusioned. He didn't belong in with the adults, among the most dangerous criminals in this country.

If only I could find the connection. If only I could get him to tell me what made him so angry at his dad.

I got up and opened my laptop, then logged into the police database, searching for the boy's name. Something came up that I hadn't seen before, and suddenly I was looking at what might be exactly what I was searching for. At least it was a step in the right direction.

If only I knew where it led.

I closed the lid of the computer, then looked at the clock. It was almost three a.m., and I had been at it for hours. I turned off the light and was about to turn back in when I heard a bump from downstairs and my heart stopped.

Chapter 16

I GRABBED MY GUN, then walked into the hallway, holding it out in front of me. I walked to Josie's door, then peeked inside. She was sleeping soundly, so it wasn't her bumping around.

Another sound followed…footsteps across the wood.

Someone was down there.

I walked down the first few steps of the stairs, then paused to listen. When there was no sound, I took another few steps down, holding out the gun in front of me.

I reached the living room, then scanned the area quickly with my gun held out, but couldn't see anyone. I walked to the light switch and flipped it, then looked at the wall behind the couch.

Three big letters were painted in red. The paint was wet and still running, spelling one word:

RAT

Anger rose inside me, indescribable, uncontrollable anger. It was one thing that they wrote this on my garage door and set a trash bin on fire outside. But entering my home? My house? My sacred place, where my family and I believed we were safe?

That was something completely different.

I heard another noise, then turned to look. I found myself face to face with a man. He was wearing a black ski mask, and I couldn't see his eyes. He was standing by the door to Camille's room, holding a gun in his hand.

I pointed my gun at him.

"Hold it right there."

The man lifted his gun as well, and that was when I noticed. As he moved his jacket, attached to his belt, I saw a golden badge that looked very similar to mine.

He was a cop.

Realizing this, I lowered my gun slightly, then tried to look into his eyes, but he was too far away, standing in the darkness by her door.

"Who are you? What are you doing in my house?" I yelled and walked forward, letting my anger drive me. "Why have you come here?"

"Stop talking," the voice said. I didn't recognize it. He had to be from another department. "Stop talking to the feds, or you're a dead man."

"Says who?" I said, still approaching him, hoping to see his eyes better if I got a little closer. "Who are you, and why are you threatening me, huh? You think I'm scared of you, huh?"

"You're a dead man, Hunter," he said, lifting his gun. "We'll take your entire family if you don't shut up."

The mention of my family angered me further, and my finger on the trigger was hard to control. If I shot this guy now, I would have the law on my side. He was in my house, threatening me and my family.

"I'm not scared of you. Who do you work for?" I asked. "Who is behind all this?"

The guy looked at me, then backed up, turned around, and ran down the hallway. I was after him right away, springing toward him, grabbing him by the jacket and pulling him back. Just as I was about to pull the mask off, he reached up and punched me hard on the nose. I fell backward, still holding him, but he had the upper hand now, and the punches were falling on me, hard. This guy knew how to fight. I grabbed him in an armlock, holding him tight when a gun went off.

Chapter 17

JEAN WOKE UP WITH A START. She was gasping for air, heart pounding, and sweat springing to her forehead.

What was that? It sounded like a shot!

"Harry!"

She jumped out of her bed and stormed out the door, down the stairs and hurried toward Harry's house, heart in her throat.

Please, don't let them be hurt. Please, let them be all right.

She rushed up the stairs, grabbed the door handle, and tried to push it open, but it was locked.

"Shoot!"

Jean hurried back down the stairs to the front lawn and found the key inside the sprinkler that didn't work, where Harry kept it under the loose lid in case of emergency. Then she ran back up on the porch and unlocked the door.

She stormed inside.

"Harry? Josie?"

She almost screamed their names, worried sick. Someone appeared at the top of the stairs.

It was Josie.

"Josie," Jean said. "Are you okay? I heard a noise. What happened?"

She looked as confused as Jean felt. "I...I don't know. I woke up. There was a loud noise. Was it a shot I heard?"

"I don't know. I heard it too. Is your dad okay?" Jean asked, panting and agitated. "Is he all right?"

"I don't know," Josie said. "I don't even know where he is. He's not in his room. The door is open, and I can't see him in there."

Jean scanned the living room. The lights were on.

"Harry?"

Josie came down the stairs toward her.

"Da-a-a-d?"

Her voice was trembling. Jean struggled to keep calm, as well. She stared at the big red letters on the wall.

"Harry?"

Josie stood in front of her, staring up at the tall red letters, her hands shaking.

"W-what is this?" she asked. "Jean? What does this mean? Who did this? Who painted this?"

"I don't know," Jean said, then looked toward the hallway leading to Camille's room, where the door was left ajar.

"Harry?" she asked, then walked toward it, her hands shaking. If someone had broken into the house and hurt Harry, they could still be here; they could still be here, hiding out.

As she approached the hallway, Jean saw blood on the wooden floors. A trail of blood led away from Camille's room toward the back entrance. Jean paused and stared down at it, heart pounding in her chest.

What happened here?

"Harry?"

She pushed the door open with a shaking hand. Inside Camille's room, she saw someone. He was sitting in a chair next to Camille's bed. Harry was only in his boxers, bent over Camille, his fists clenched. He had blood on his chin and chest.

"H-harry?"

He lifted his glance, and their eyes met.

"A-are you okay? We heard a noise, and it sounded like a shot being fired…?"

He nodded. "I shot him. By accident."

"Who did you shoot, Harry?"

"The intruder. We fought; the gun went off by accident. I think he was shot in the leg. Probably just a graze since the bullet was lodged in the wall."

"So…where is he now?"

"He escaped. When the shot went off, he punched me hard, and I blacked out for a few seconds. When I came to, he was gone. I hurried in here to make sure Camille was okay. She took an Ambien before she went to bed. She couldn't find rest, so I gave her one. Luckily, I think she slept through it all."

Jean approached him, then bent down. Her eyes filling, Jean bit her lip and leaned her forehead against Harry's, holding a hand behind his neck.

"I was so scared," she whispered. "I thought I lost you."

He closed his eyes and exhaled. His breath felt warm on her skin. His soft lips moved closer. She could feel them brush against hers.

"Dad?"

Josie showed up in the doorway, and Jean let go of Harry and pulled away with a light gasp. Josie stared at them, her eyes concerned and confused. Whether it was the blood on her father's body or because she had seen Jean and Harry in an intimate moment, Jean didn't know.

"Dad?"

He smiled. "I'm fine, Josie."

"You don't look fine."

"Well, you should have seen the other guy," he chuckled, trying to sound cheerful for his daughter.

"You're not hurt?" Jean asked. "Nothing I need to patch up?"

He shook his head. "Couple of bruises, but I'll be fine. I'll be sore tomorrow, but nothing else."

"You sure I shouldn't che…"

"Hello?" a voice sounded from the front door. "Hunter? You here?"

Harry lifted his gaze.

"That'll be Fowler," he said and got up.

"You called Fowler? You didn't call the police?" Jean asked, concerned. What was going on here? What was he not telling her?

"He is the police," Harry said, walking past her. "He's the only police I trust right now."

Chapter 18

"YOU DIDN'T GET to see his face or eyes at all?"

Fowler looked at me across the living room. I had sat down on my couch, Fowler in my recliner. He was scribbling notes on his pad. Up until now, I had been reasonably collected, but now that I was telling him everything that had happened, it was getting harder to keep my anger at bay.

I shook my head.

"He wore a ski mask. I was never close enough to see his eyes. I didn't recognize his voice."

"But you're certain he was one of ours?"

I nodded with a sniffle. Jean and Josie were in the kitchen, where Jean had served Josie some ice cream. They were both eating it, sitting at the breakfast counter, chatting. Every now and then, she'd throw me a glance, and our eyes would meet. She was trying to calm Josie down and make her think about something else, and I was very grateful for that.

"He had a badge, Fowler."

Fowler glared at the red letters on the wall, shaking his head. "I told you to watch your back."

"This was in my home," I said. "They were in my house, Fowler. In my own darn house!"

He lifted his hand. "I know. I know. We'll get them. And he was shot in the leg, you say?"

I nodded. "In the thigh, I'm pretty sure. It all went by a little fast."

"So, we'll call all the hospitals and see if they got anyone in tonight with a gunshot wound."

I exhaled and leaned back, closing my eyes. "It was just a graze, or he wouldn't have been able to run out of here. I can't believe they would go this far. I can't believe he was inside my house."

"How did he get in here?" Fowler asked. "Front door was locked, right? When Jean got here, she said it was still locked."

"Back door," I said. "It's been broken up. It's old, and one kick or even a mild push would have opened it."

"Might wanna get that fixed," he said.

I lifted my gaze and looked at him. "You think they'll be back?"

"I don't think they'll leave you alone till you stop talking, no. It's a dangerous game you're playing."

"But I can't back down now," I said. "These people are bad seeds; there's nothing worse than a corrupt cop. You have to agree with me on this. I have to clean up this mess."

He gave me another look. "Even if it means risking your family getting hurt? Because I have to tell you. I don't know what you're up against here, but it seems like they're willing to take it as far as they can. They're not backing down as long as you're not. Maybe you should consider backing off. I'm sure the FBI can run the case without you talking."

I wrinkled my forehead, then rose to my feet.

"How can you even suggest that?"

"I'm just worried about you, that's all," he said and rose to his feet as well. "I don't want you or your family hurt. You're risking losing everything, and I want to make sure it's worth it."

I shook my head in disbelief. "They're not gonna break me. I am not letting them win."

He threw out his hands. "All right, Hunter. The choice is yours. I'll make the calls and see if we can locate the cop who was in your house tonight and got himself shot. Until then, please be careful, will you? Stay alive for me. And get some sleep. You look terrible."

"Thanks," I said, smiling while letting him out. "I mean it."

Chapter 19

I PARKED the motorcycle in the alley and walked up to the backdoor of Al's building. She had moved locations since she recently had been attacked in her home, when I decided to hide Josie at her place, thinking she'd be safe there. She had only moved a few blocks further south, to a location just as remote as the former and even harder to find. It was the next morning after a night with next to no sleep. I had driven through town to get to her first thing.

Al was a former CIA hacker and the only one who could help me out. She was also slightly paranoid and kept herself hidden. From what, exactly, she had never told me, and I wasn't sure I wanted to know.

"Yes?" she asked over the intercom.

"It's Harry," I said.

"I can see that, you fool; there's a camera in this thing," Al said dryly. "What do you want?"

"Just let me in, will you?" I said.

"Last time I did, my place ended up like a warzone. Not only was I knocked out, but I was also compromised and had to move because of it. I want to make sure it won't happen again."

"I need your help," I said with a deep sigh. "I can't tell you the details in the street. Someone might hear me, and where will that leave us?"

"Okay. You make a valid point. Are you sure you're alone? Did anyone follow you here?" she asked.

"No. I'm sure I'm all alone," I said, yet still looked around me to be certain. It was more of a reflex than because I believed there would actually be someone there. "I rode here on my bike and took a couple of detours before I ran around the block three times until I was certain no one was following me. Just like you have instructed me to."

"And you're not bringing trouble my way?"

"That, I can't promise you. You know I can't," I said.

"At least you're honest," she said, then buzzed me in.

"Finally," I mumbled, and pushed the heavy door open, then rushed up the four flights of stairs. I knocked on the door and heard Al fumble with the many locks behind it before it was pulled open, and she peeked out through the crack.

"It's still me, Al."

"Just checking," she said, then opened the chain and the door and let me in before she closed it behind me and locked it thoroughly.

"Okay, you're in. What's up?"

I walked to her desk and wondered if she had gotten a few new monitors since I was last there. I counted at least three new ones. On one of them, it showed a place where it snowed, and people wore furry hats. I wondered if she was spying on some Russians. On another, they were all wearing masks inside of a supermarket, and I realized it had to be somewhere in Asia, maybe even China, where they had the outbreak of the Coronavirus. It had gotten pretty bad over the past few weeks, and the sale of masks had exploded even here in the States.

"I need you to take a look at this," I said and pulled out a small bag from my pocket. Inside it was the small device that Fowler had handed me in his office.

Al grabbed the bag and stared at it between her hands, studying it. "A microphone?"

"I need to know who owns this. Who installed it? I don't know how, but I thought maybe you could track it down somehow."

She stared at the small device, then nodded.

"I can do that."

Al emptied the bag and poured the microphone onto her desk, then picked it up with a pair of tweezers.

"Small one," she said. "A newer model. It's amazing how small they make them now, huh? Not much bigger than a pin. This looks like a pretty advanced model, though. This is not a cheap piece of equipment."

"That's what I was thinking," I said. "It's not something everyone can get their hands on."

"I'll look into it," she said, furrowing her brows beneath the dreadlocks while turning the device in the light.

"How's the family? How's Josie?"

I lifted my eyebrows. "You're asking about my daughter now? You never cared much before?"

She shrugged. "Well, you might say I feel closer to her these days. After what happened."

That made me smile. Al was far from as cold-hearted and uncaring as she liked to pretend to be.

"Josie's good," I said. "She's okay."

"And her heart?"

"No problems there. Her body seems to be accepting it well, and she's back in school."

Al looked at me, smiling wryly. "So, everything is back to normal? Then how come you didn't sleep last night?"

"Are you spying on me too?" I asked.

"No, you fool, I took one look at that face and knew. You have like no color in your cheeks."

"Ah, I see. Well, let's just say whoever put that microphone up has it in for me. They tried to attack us last night in our house."

"And I'm guessing it's all connected to what happened last month, to Josie's kidnapping and the refugees being smuggled in the appliances."

I wrinkled my forehead. "I never told you about that."

She smiled. "You don't have to. I have my ways."

"I know you do. That's why I'm bringing this to you. Not a word to anyone."

She lifted her eyebrows. "I never speak to anyone for that same reason. Except for you who keeps knocking on my darn door. Now, get out of here and let me work. I'll let you know when I have something."

Chapter 20

MY FINGER WAS SHAKING a little as I rang the doorbell. Not because I was nervous, but because of the many cups of coffee I had practically inhaled before I left the station. I had kept to myself all day while working, trying not to talk to anyone except Fowler in his office. Yet, I still couldn't help but see suspicious behavior everywhere and felt like all eyes were constantly on me. I kept listening in on conversations between my colleagues, trying to figure out if I recognized the voice from the night before. I was becoming paranoid, and it was about to drive me nuts.

I could hear someone coming down the stairs inside. The footsteps paused for a few seconds before they continued the rest of the way to the door.

A set of blue eyes landed on me as it swung open.

"Yes?"

"Kristin Holmes?"

She smiled politely. She had pretty eyes that looked up at me with wonder, reminding me of a child.

"It's Grant now," she said. "I took my husband's name when we married last summer. How can I help you?"

I showed her my badge. "Harry Hunter, Miami PD. I wondered

if we could have a little chat?"

Seeing the badge made her eyes begin to flicker, and she was suddenly slightly flustered. It wasn't an unusual reaction when I came to people's homes like this. They all worried if they could have done something wrong.

"I...I was about to leave...for yoga..." she said and rubbed her neck under the ponytail nervously.

"It won't take long."

I walked past her inside, and she closed the door, still slightly worried. "What is this about?"

"Can we sit?" I asked and pointed at her dining room table. She nodded, still fiddling with the small hairs on her neck.

"Sure. Do you want anything? Coffee?"

I smiled politely. "I don't think we have time for that if you don't want to miss your yoga class."

She shrugged. "I can make some real quick."

"Then I won't say no to that."

Kristin disappeared into the kitchen and came back with two cups of coffee. She placed a cup in front of me, spilling a little on the table as she did, then wiping it away with a paper towel and a nervous chuckle.

I sipped my cup. "Wonderful coffee."

She sat down in the chair next to mine while I opened the case file and showed her a picture of Kate Taylor taken ten years ago, just a few months before she disappeared.

"I believe you know her?"

She swallowed when seeing her friend. "K-Kate? Is that what this is about? But it was so long ago."

"I know, but the case was never closed," I said. "I take it you've heard about her son, Nick?"

Kristin nodded, warming her hands on the sides of the cup, even though it wasn't very cold in her house.

"Yes. Awful tragedy. I can't believe it."

"Well, it has me wondering too, and that's why I am here. I was hoping you could shed some light on the family. What would make Nick bring a gun to church and try to shoot his father?"

Chapter 21

"I...I don't really know much about them," she started, fiddling with her cup. "I mean, it's been so many years now, and I hardly knew much even back then. I'm not sure I can be of much help, to be honest."

I nodded. "I understand. I was just...well, worried that there was something we were missing here."

She sipped her cup. "Like what, Detective?"

I exhaled and folded my hands on top of the file. "I don't know. That maybe Nick tried to hurt his father for the simple reason that he knew he had killed his mother?"

Kristin stared at me, her eyes growing big. She shook her head. "Detective, I don't really think...why would you say that? He was cleared back then. He had an alibi."

I looked at the papers in the file. "He was at a conference, yes. In Atlanta."

She nodded and smiled. "Yes, that was it. He was very far away. I don't really see how he could have..."

"But what if he did?" I asked, deliberately provocative. "What if he somehow managed to kill her anyway? How was their relationship? You said in your statement that she needed to *blow off some steam.* Both you and your friend, Joan, used that same expression, oddly enough. But what does that even mean?"

Kristin stared up at me, her eyes searching mine, her tongue playing with the inside of her cheek.

"I guess it meant she wasn't doing very well in her marriage."

"Why not? Were they fighting a lot?"

"I...I guess. Or maybe she just found him to be extremely boring," she said.

"And she wanted out? You said she wanted to disappear, right?"

She nodded, sipping more coffee, her lips quivering slightly. "Y-yes. I think she killed herself. I think she got drunk that night then drowned herself."

I stared at her. Now, it was my turn to scrutinize her. "But why, Kristin? Why would your friend kill herself? Why not just get a divorce?"

"I...I don't know."

"I'll tell you. I'll tell you what I think. I think she was scared of him. No, more than that, she was terrified of her own husband, and she told you this on the trip. She didn't dare to leave him. And you're terrified of him too, aren't you? That's why you haven't told anyone that you, too, believe he killed her. Because he has been threatening you, am I right?"

She shook her head. "I...I don't really..."

"It's okay. You don't have to. It's not your job to figure these things out. It's mine. But if he really killed his wife, then I'm taking him down for it, one way or another, with or without your help."

I paused and sipped my coffee, not allowing myself to get too agitated. There was nothing worse in my book than a man abusing his wife. And this guy would even let his son go down before he told the truth.

I looked into the case file, then pulled out a piece of paper I had printed before getting here and showed it to her.

"Do you know anything about this?"

She looked at it, then shook her head. "What is this?"

"I found this in Nick's files. Apparently, the DCF had their eyes on the family. Back when Nick was four years old, his school reported that the boy was engaging in troublesome behavior. He had asked a girl to strip down naked for him in the bathroom, then told her to lick the toilet seat. The DCF investigated the family and found odd bruises on the child, and he told them stories of him being forced to punish himself when he was bad and cut his skin with razor blades, then being forced to spend an entire night in a small bathroom, only allowed to drink from the toilet bowl. The DCF supervised the family for months but found nothing and concluded it was just stories that the boy had made up. The parents had explanations for all the bruises since the boy got them riding his bike or climbing trees, and the cuts were some he had inflicted on himself, they said before they stopped him. DCF ended up believing them and left the family alone. Now, my question to you is this: Did you know, Kristin? Did you know this was happening in their home?"

Kristin was no longer looking at me. She was shaking her head and crying. "I knew the DCF had been on their case. Kate told me about it; she said the boy had told a bunch of lies and that it would all blow over eventually. Andrew was angry about it, and I sensed Kate was scared too, scared of losing the boy, but she just didn't want to admit it. I don't know. I just assumed she was right, that it was nothing but a bunch of lies that the boy had come up with."

"But deep down inside, you knew something was off in that family, didn't you? When you visited them, the way Kate never wanted to talk about them, how she seemed troubled at times. Did she have bruises too? Did she?"

Kristin swallowed, her head still bent. Then she nodded. "She had these cuts on her arm that looked like they were made by razor blades. I didn't know what to think. She didn't want to talk about them, so we just didn't. There was also the time she had bruises on her upper arms like someone had grabbed her, hard. There were other things too, cuts in strange places, like right on her bikini line when we went to the beach. She had excuses for all of them."

"And you pretended to believe her because it was easier that way, am I right?" I asked.

Kristin sniffled and nodded. "Yes. You're right. I'm not proud of it, but it's the truth. In the end, we barely noticed anymore. But it definitely got worse and worse."

"Do you still see each other? You and Joan? Are you still friends?" I asked.

She shook her head. "We haven't seen one another since…that trip. I heard she was divorced, moved, and got married to some other guy."

"That explains why it's been hard to track her down. So, you don't know where I can find her?"

She shook her head again, grabbed a tissue from a box, and blew her nose. "I'm afraid not."

I got up and looked at my watch. "All right. Thank you so much, Kristin. You've been a great help."

"You really think he killed her, do you?" she asked once again as I walked toward the door. "Even though he had an alibi?"

I nodded, halfway out the door, then paused. "I do. Somehow, he managed to get away with the perfect murder."

Chapter 22

"YOU WANTED TO SEE ME?"

I walked into Fowler's office, forgetting to knock. I had just gotten back from my meeting with Kristin Grant and bought a sandwich on my way back that I still hadn't eaten. I was holding it in my hand as I walked inside.

Fowler looked up at me, then pointed toward the two empty chairs.

"Sit."

I did. Fowler looked at me from across the mahogany table. He pressed the tips of his fingers against each other.

"I don't quite know how to tell you this."

"I'm a big boy," I said. "I can take it. Is it about last night? Any news about the guy who broke into my house? Have the hospitals called back? Have they found a guy who was shot in the thigh?"

"Easy there, cowboy," Fowler said, shaking his head. "I have had no luck finding him yet, no. But that doesn't mean we won't. He'll turn up sooner or later. I have a word out to all the stations, and they'll let me know the names of anyone who didn't show up for work today. We'll get him. One way or another."

I exhaled, annoyed. I had hoped for good news. I had no idea what to tell my family if I went back home and he hadn't been found. Josie was terrified that he was going to come back. And to be frank, so was I.

"So, what is this about? Why have you called me in?"

"It's about the boy."

"Nick?"

"Yes, him. His dad was here earlier. We had told him to bring in Nick's computer and his phone, so we could go through it all to find out if he had planned to bring the gun to hurt more people, or if he was fascinated by mass shooters and maybe frequented any of the websites where they chat and cheer each other on, you know stuff like that. Well, we didn't find any of that, but his dad presented us with some pretty damaging material. He said he knew we'd find it anyway, so he might as well show it to us. He had already gone through his son's social media accounts by himself in anger because he wanted to know what Nick was up to, and that's when he found all this stuff. He said he thought about deleting it because he wanted to protect Nick, but then decided against it since he believed the boy needed to take the punishment for his actions. It's about time he learns that his actions have consequences, he said."

"Really?" I said suspiciously.

"Yes, really. I know you believe your boy here is innocent..."

"I'm not saying he's innocent," I interrupted him. "I'm just saying that he shot his dad because he thought there was no other way. And I'm trying to find out why he felt that way. And, actually, I've been getting closer..."

"I'm gonna stop you right there," he said, "because what we have here is a gamechanger."

I wrinkled my forehead. "What do you mean?"

Fowler lifted a hand to stop me. He grabbed the phone and dialed a number, then spoke into it.

"Do you have it ready? Can you send me the files?"

There was an answer, and Fowler hung up. "I've had the IT guys working on it for the past few hours, and they have the files ready for us now. You might want to eat that sandwich first because after this, you'll have lost your appetite."

Chapter 23

A REDHAIRED GIRL looked into the camera on her phone. She was crying, her narrow, bloodshot eyes looking at us while she was pleading.

"Please," she said. "Please, don't make me do this."

Then she leaned over, placed her tongue on the toilet seat, and started licking, still while crying. Once done, she put her head inside the bowl and flushed while her head was still in it.

Crying, she lifted her head, then cried out: "I'm a worthless whore; please, take care of me, Daddy."

Clip to the next video. Another girl. This one was blonde. She, too, was crying while filming herself. She filmed herself naked on the floor of the bathroom as she peed into a plastic cup.

Then, she drank it.

The next video showed a girl cutting herself on the arm with a razor blade while crying. The letters she cut were shaping the word:

Whore.

In the last video, we watched a girl as she took a toilet brush. Then—crying heavily—she put it in her mouth.

"Okay, okay," I said and turned away from Fowler's computer screen, suddenly pleased I had listened to him and eaten my sandwich before we watched the videos. "I've seen enough. What in the world is that?"

"They call it *hurtcore*," he said. "Girls, who, against their will, are pressured into humiliating themselves while filming it."

"And you got these videos from Nick's computer?"

Fowler nodded. "And his phone. You can see the texts he sent to the girls as well. I made a transcript of one. Look here. You see how he tells her to kneel by the toilet and flush while her head is still inside of it. Then he tells her what to say, to call herself a worthless whore, and she's pleading with him to stop it. His only answer is that her pleading turns him on. He asks her to film herself while she's crying, then hit herself and strangle herself and tell herself that she's *just a stupid whore*. In one of them, he even asks her to put the toilet brush up inside of her and eat her own feces, but I thought that was a little too much for you to watch."

"And they do it?" I asked.

Needless to say, I was disgusted—on the verge of throwing up.

He nodded. "Yes. Because they have no choice, or they don't think they have. He meets them through Skype or messenger or on Instagram or TikTok, wherever he can find them, and they start out as friends. He tells them he likes them and grooms them slowly until they're ready. Then, he sweet-talks them into sending him nude photos of themselves or even videos. They do it because they have low self-esteem, and because they think he likes them. Then, as soon as he has the video or the photos, he starts pressuring them. He tells them he'll send the video or the pictures to her family and her friends. He threatens to post it on social media, so everyone will see, and that's when the humiliation begins. They plead with him not to, and then he can persuade them to do anything he'd like to see—humiliating themselves. These are broken girls, Hunter. You've got to be really broken down to do something like this. And some of these girls are minors. They're not much older than Josie, for crying out loud. It's sick! This guy is a pervert, Hunter. He's nothing but a predator, and I'll see to it that he is put away for a very, *very* long time. Mark my words. You are done trying to save him; do you hear me? Done."

Chapter 24

I HAD no idea what to believe. As soon as I was done at Fowler's office, I ran to the parking lot where I had parked my bike, then got on it and roared into the street. I drove it through town, zigzagging my way through traffic, going through what Fowler had told me in my head.

Could it really be true? Could the boy I had seen really have done those awful things to those girls?

It didn't seem possible.

Yet, the evidence was there. Right on Fowler's computer. Video after video extracted from the boy's computer and phone. Text after text where he degraded them to nothing but objects, dolls he could treat however he wanted.

Fowler was right; it was sick, and there was no way I could explain my way out of this. There were no more excuses.

I parked in front of the detention center and walked up to the back door. The woman behind the glass saw my badge, then called for someone to lead me down the hallway and back into the room with the barren walls and tables that were bolted to the floor.

I waited for about ten minutes until the door opened. Nick had a big bruise on his cheek as he approached me and sat down, his eyes looking at the floor, not at me.

I stared down at him, my nostrils flaring, the images still flickering for my inner eye, images and videos I would never escape.

"Look at me, Nick," I said, trying to keep calm. "Look at me."

The boy lifted his eyes.

"You remember me, right? You said so the last time I was here. I tried to help you in church, and I have even tried to help you out there, trying to figure out why on earth a young boy like you would shoot your own dad. And now they tell me you've been hurting young women online? What do you have to say for yourself, Nick!"

The boy looked at me, then shook his head. "I don't know what you're talking about.

I slammed my fist onto the metal table. "Yes, you do! Don't lie to me."

He crumpled down in fear, shaking his head. "No. I don't. What videos?"

"The ones they found on your computer of the girls humiliating themselves, doing only what you told them to do, what you blackmailed them to do, breaking their poor spirits."

"I...I don't understand," he said.

"They found them on your computer and your phone. Don't give me that innocent act. Was it because that's what your dad did to you? Because you went through the same thing in your childhood? And now you're just repeating it? In some sick vicious circle? Like people becoming molesters because their parents were? Did your dad do those things to you, Nick?"

Nick exhaled. His eyes were filling.

"Did your dad tell you to lick the toilet seat? Did he lock you in the bathroom, and have you drink out of the bowl? Did he tell you to cut yourself with razor blades? Did he, Nick? Nick? Darn it, Nick, talk to me."

Nick shook his head. "I...I don't know. I don't remember..."

"But the DCF suspected it. In your file, they said you told them those things. When you were four years old, you said these things were done to you. Were they right? Was it your father? Was that why you pulled that gun on him? Did he torture you and your mother and then kill her, did he? Nick?"

"YES!" he yelled, then bent forward like he was in pain, talking through a curtain of tears. "Yes, he did all of those things! I knew no one would ever believe me like they didn't believe me back then. That's why I shot him. There was no other way for him to be punished for what he had done."

"How did you know, Nick? How did you find out he killed your mother?" I asked, my heart pounding in my chest. Finally, I was getting somewhere in this case. It wasn't pleasant what was being revealed, but it had to see the light of day. "How did you realize it?"

Nick leaned forward like he was telling me a secret, and no one else could hear. But it was just us there, and the guard, who didn't seem to care even a little bit.

"I've always known but never dared to say anything. I suggest you ask his new wife."

Chapter 25

"ARE YOU DETECTIVE HUNTER?"

I had just walked out the front door of the building housing our police department on my way to my bike. It was late in the afternoon now, and I was running late for Camille's treatment. I almost rushed past him without seeing him. But as he addressed me, I recognized him right away. When someone gets shot in front of you, you tend to remember their face forever. Same goes when they're the main suspect of your investigation.

"Mr. Taylor? What are you doing here?"

He was smaller than I remembered him yet seemed bigger because of how well trained he was underneath his suit. He had a sharp jawline like his son and big bushy eyebrows that I suspected Nick would get one day too.

He exhaled. His flaring nostrils, along with the vein in his forehead, told me he was agitated. I stayed a few steps away from him. He pointed a finger at me. I didn't move. His gesture was aggressive, and I didn't want him to think I was scared of him. I was twice his size.

He spoke through gritted teeth.

"It has got to stop."

"Excuse me? What has got to stop?"

He growled angrily. "This. You. Whatever it is you're doing."

"I don't know. What am I doing?"

I looked at my watch. I was so late for my appointment with Camille and had put my hope in traffic being light enough for me to make it anyway. Now, we were going to be late if I didn't break a few traffic regulations on my way home.

"My son is sick, Detective. Don't believe anything he says."

I wrinkled my forehead. "What do you mean he's sick?"

"He's a pathological liar, Detective. He does this. He's been doing it all his life. Ever since he was a kid, he'd lie to his teachers and tell them these stories."

"So, you're telling me he's lying when he tells me he was abused as a child?" I asked bluntly, then waited for his reaction.

It came pretty fast. His eyes went blank for a second, then fired up in rage. I could tell he was trying to keep himself composed, but failing miserably. Everything inside of him exploded while he bit down, trying to stifle it by clenching his fists. He lifted one up toward me, but it barely reached my face.

"I...How dare you!"

"How dare you...sir? Torturing a little child? Murdering your wife?"

Andrew Taylor stared at me. The fist came down, and he pulled back. It was obvious he was taken aback by my words. That was the point. I wanted him to know that I knew what kind of a person he was and that I was going to expose him.

"Is that what he told you? And you...you believe him? How? Why? The boy is not well. You must know this. Didn't you see the videos from his computer and phone? Didn't you see what kind of a sick monster he is? How he abused those girls and humiliated them? That is the kind of person he is. You saw it with your own eyes. He tried to kill me, Detective. I'm the victim here. He's sick, just like his mom was too. My son belongs behind bars. I hate to admit it, but that is where he should stay, and I suggest you keep it that way. Don't you understand? He never liked the fact that I remarried. He hates my wife, and now he's trying to get back at me this way, trying first to shoot me, then tell anyone stupid enough to listen that his dad is an abuser and a murderer. Don't tell me you're actually buying into it? Are you that stupid, Detective?"

I looked down at the man in front of me in the blue suit and yellow tie. Yes, I wanted to slap him across the face; I wanted to hurt him. For what I believed he had done to his son while growing up, and how he had abused and probably murdered his wife. But this was not the time or place. Justice would come soon enough. And that's when he'd be taken down.

I lifted my arm and looked at my watch. "I have somewhere to be. If you'll excuse me, I don't have time for this."

Andrew Taylor scoffed as I pushed my way past him, hitting my upper arm against his shoulder, pushing him aside.

"You're a fool for believing him, Detective; don't you see? He's using you!" he yelled after me, but I was no longer listening. I got on my bike, then roared it to life and put my helmet on, ignoring him. As I rode it across the parking lot, I could still hear him yelling, his voice growing smaller and smaller behind me.

Chapter 26

WE WERE FIFTEEN MINUTES LATE, and Dr. Kendrick wasn't very pleased with us as we rushed inside, me pushing Camille in the wheelchair even though she didn't need it that much anymore and walked mostly on her own. She still couldn't run, at least not yet.

"I am so sorry," I said as she gave me that look, arms crossed. "Something came up at work."

"You have been late to every afternoon treatment for the past week now," she said. "That means other patients' treatments who are scheduled after her will be pushed too."

"I know. I am sorry."

Dr. Kendrick sent me a compassionate smile. "I know it's not easy to have to come in twice a day."

"I wish we could just do all of it at once," I said while the assistants helped Camille get in the chamber and closed the lid with a low shush. Camille's eyes locked with mine as it closed. I knew she didn't enjoy the claustrophobic feeling right after it was locked, knowing she couldn't get out, but after a few minutes, she would usually calm down and be able to relax.

"Why can't we just do an entire week of treatments at once?"

Dr. Kendrick nodded. "I get that a lot. But we can't leave her in there for too long. Wouldn't be good."

"What would happen?"

Dr. Kendrick pushed a button on the instruments, and the air hissed in the steel cylinder. "Well, we have to do this with oxygen at high atmospheric pressure, so at first, it would damage her ears… possibly burst her eardrums, and we won't want that to happen. It could also change her vision or collapse her lungs. Oxygen toxicity or poisoning could occur; too much oxygen in the body's tissues can cause convulsions and other complications. It can damage the central nervous system, and in severe cases, cause death. So, that's why we're very cautious. But I am so happy to see the big progress in your wife. It's truly remarkable. We'd like to write her story for a medical paper after we're done here. Would she be willing to participate in that?"

I smiled and glanced at my wife inside the chamber. Her eyes were closed now, and I knew she was resting.

"Why don't you ask her yourself?" I said. "She is capable of answering for herself now."

It was true. She had been speaking more and more over the past week or so, and she was able to use entire sentences now. It was like she was finally truly coming back to us…like she was slowly becoming herself again.

Dr. Kendrick smiled and nodded. "Very well. We'll do that when we get closer then. Her story is truly remarkable, and we're trying to get this treatment FDA approved for brain injury, so I am hoping her story can help that process and maybe speed it along so other patients can get it too and maybe even get their insurance to pay for it. So many come here knowing this is a chance for help, but they can't afford it, and they leave emptyhanded. I hate to see that, knowing I can actually help them. It's heartbreaking."

"I can understand how it must be," I said, then sat down in my usual chair, pulling up my computer and placed it in my lap. Camille's treatments had become a time for me to really dig into my work, and I was beginning to enjoy those little moments of quietness in my life. I still thought about the meeting with Nick's father earlier and shivered when thinking about what the boy had told me at the detention center. I opened the case files and looked through them again, then reached into my briefcase and pulled out the old file on the murder case of Kate Taylor. I had asked to have her autopsy sent over from the ME's office in Key West and needed to go through it. As I read through it, one line, in particular, grabbed my attention and wouldn't let go. I kept reading it over and over again, then stared at Camille inside her chamber before returning to it. I flipped a page, then looked at the next one, searching for another detail, then found it. I stared at the words on the page, wondering if I had just discovered the proof that she was, in fact, murdered, and how it was done.

The problem was that it made absolutely no sense to me.

Chapter 27

"AND THEN YOU look up at me with those big brown eyes of yours, and you say to me, *you do realize you have it in your hand, don't you?*"

Camille burst into laughter, and Josie joined in, laughing wholeheartedly. It was becoming an everyday thing for Josie to ask her mother to tell her stories from back when she was just a young child during dinner. And I had a feeling it was one of Camille's favorite moments of the day as well. To me, it was more than that. It was everything. Watching them reconnect was my favorite thing in the whole world.

"I can't believe you did that, Mommy," Josie said and ate her noodles. We had brought home Chinese food today. We had been eating a lot of take-out food lately since it was impossible for me to make it to Camille's treatments and cook dinner as well, so even though it meant we ate a lot of the same food, it was what was possible these days. And it worked fine. Gave us plenty of time to talk till Camille got tired and needed to get back into her bed.

"It's true," I said. "I was there. I'm a witness."

Josie gave me an endearing look. She had been so happy lately, and it was a joy to see. Being fourteen wasn't an easy age, to put it mildly. But ever since her mother got better, there had been less of those meltdowns, and the rolling of eyes and growling had subsided for a little while too. I knew it would be back eventually, of course, it would. Teenagers would be teenagers, and I just enjoyed the way things were right now until it changed back.

I rose to my feet and grabbed the plates, then walked to the kitchen to wash them off and put them in the dishwasher, while Josie asked her mother for another story.

"Don't forget your homework," I said to her. "Your mom needs to rest soon too, baby."

"Please, Dad?" she asked. "Just one more story. I only have math and science. It's so easy."

I chuckled. I didn't know of any other teenage girls who'd call math and science easy. And she was even in advanced classes in both subjects, yet it still seemed like it was almost too easy for her.

"All right," I said and closed the dishwasher. "Just one more story then."

"Yay. With pictures. I want to look at pictures too," she said, then rushed to the shelves in the living room and pulled down a photo album. She hurried back to her mother and opened it, then flipped a couple of pages till she found one she liked and pointed at it.

"This one. What are we doing here? How old am I?"

Camille glanced at the picture, then smiled warmly. As it turned out, remembering things from her past was very good for Camille's rehabilitation as well.

"That one," Camille said. "Is from our trip to Key West. You were…four, I think? Right, Harry?"

I nodded and wiped my hands on a dishtowel, then walked back to look at it over her shoulder. A very young Josie stared back at me from a white sandy beach, wearing goggles, a determined look on her face.

"You loved watching the fishies in the water down there," I said. "You could spend hours watching them."

"And your dad was fishing," Camille said. "But you didn't like that he would catch the fish, and you would always tell him to throw them back."

"I wanted to eat them, but you would hear nothing of it," I said with a light chuckle.

Camille flipped a page. "Look, there you are, holding a baby hammerhead shark. You caught that with your bare hands in the water."

"I think I remember this," Josie said. "I threw it back out in the water, didn't I?"

"You sure did," I said and looked at my beautiful daughter. This was one of those moments you just wanted to last forever. I was so happy in this very second that I paid very little attention to the screeching tires in the street outside.

Chapter 28

THE MICROWAVE BEEPED, and Jean got up. She pulled out her dish. It was supposed to be some kind of chicken and mashed potatoes, but she couldn't really tell which was the chicken and which were the potatoes, and the gravy seemed more greenish than brown. She stared down at the plastic tray and its contents, then decided to toss it in the trash. She made herself a sandwich instead, while glaring at the house next door, wondering what they were doing in there. She wondered what they were having for dinner and whether Josie needed help with her Spanish homework.

Let it go, Jean.

Spread out on the table behind her were listings for rentals in Savannah, Georgia. Jean had a sister living up there and thought it was time she moved closer to her. She had seen a couple of job listings searching for a nurse up in the area as well and applied for some of them. They weren't as exciting as the one she had working the ER in Miami, and they paid less too, but it was what she needed right now. She had to move on.

It was time.

Jean sat down and ate the sandwich while reading through the rental listings. There was a nice little townhouse in walking distance from the center of Savannah, close to restaurants. It had a nice porch outside and was built in that old Victorian style she loved so much.

Jean smiled and took another bite of her sandwich. She imagined herself living there, sitting out on the porch on the swing, or walking to downtown and going out to dinner or even just for a cup of coffee.

Jean had always been drawn to Savannah and knew that if she didn't live in Miami, that's where she'd go. Often when visiting her sister, who lived about half an hour outside of the town, she had taken trips to Savannah and loved just walking the streets there, looking at the pretty old houses with their wrought-iron porches and Spanish moss hanging from the trees. It would be a new start for her, a brand-new life, and it was exactly what she needed.

Get away from the old.

Jean walked to the window and looked out at her old street. She had lived there for almost twenty years now. She still liked it there; she had to admit. Yet she had that sense inside of her that she was done with it; she was done with Miami.

And with Harry Hunter.

Yes, she was going to miss him and Josie. It was going to be hard for the first couple of months, but it was better than staying here and having her heart broken every time she saw either one of them.

Anything would be better than here.

Jean finished her sandwich while looking into the street, thinking about the first time she and Harry had met when he and Camille had just moved in. Jean had not been very excited to get new neighbors since she enjoyed her privacy and being in her yard without anyone seeing her. The house had been empty for years, and she liked it that way. She avoided them for the first couple of days after she saw the truck arrive, thinking the last thing she wanted was to get tricked into having to help them carry their stuff.

But then one day, a young woman, pregnant on the verge of bursting, had knocked on her door, asking if she had a couple of eggs because she was baking. As soon as Jean had opened the door and looked into the woman's eyes, she knew she couldn't resent her.

As Harry came over later to give her the eggs back, she realized she was going to love those two forever. But mostly him. As Jean stood there thinking about it, she realized she had loved him from the second she stood face to face with him on that porch. She hadn't wanted to admit it back then because he was married, and she really liked Camille, especially after they began to hang out almost every day, drinking coffee or later having a glass of wine. Jean had kept it to herself that her heart beat just a little faster when he was nearby, or how she'd jump in happiness when hearing his voice.

You need to get out of here, fast, girl, she thought to herself as she looked into the street, a tear caught in the corner of her eye that she didn't allow to escape. She grabbed her phone and checked her emails, seeing if there were any responses from the jobs she had applied for or the rentals she had written to. She sighed and thought about her new life instead, trying hard to get excited about it, when she heard the tires screeching. She lifted her eyes and saw the car drive into the road, then rush past Harry's house, opening fire.

Chapter 29

RA-TA-DA-DA. Ra-ta-da. Ra-ta-da. Ra-ta-da-da!

The sound was deafening, and it felt like it went on for hours, even though it was probably just for a few seconds—a few crucial and potentially fatal seconds.

Ra-ta-da-da. Ra-ta-da. Ra-ta-da. Ra-ta-da-da!

It kept going, on and on, for an eternity.

I had realized it too late. I had ignored the sound of the tires on the asphalt outside, thinking it was just some idiot burning rubber, showing off for his friends or some girlfriend he was trying to impress.

It had never occurred to me that this could happen. Not to me, not here, not in this nice neighborhood. But now it did, and as I realized what was really going on, I threw myself at Josie, pushing her to the floor, letting my big massive body cover her, while the sound of the bullets splintering the wood outside, tearing holes in the door and shattering the windows, drowned out her screams from beneath me.

Ra-ta-da-da. Ra-ta-da. Ra-ta-da. Ra-ta-da-da!

I screamed at the top of my lungs, and so did Josie and Camille.

Camille had fallen to the floor and lay flat, face-down on the wooden planks next to us. But she was in the open, not covered by furniture the way we were. She was exposed but paralyzed by fear, unable to move. She stared at me, scared out of her wits, then reached out her hand toward us and grabbed Josie's in hers.

And then she screamed.

A bullet ripped through the tip of her shoulder, tearing the flesh open with a loud, almost whistling sound.

"MOM!" Josie screamed when seeing this. "MOOOM! NOOO!"

Meanwhile, the sound continued outside. Endlessly.

Ra-ta-da-da. Ra-ta-da. Ra-ta-da. Ra-ta-da-da!

Another bullet whispered through the air and hit Camille on the floor. Seeing the blood, and how her body spasmed, I screamed.

"NO! Camille! No!"

Camille withered in pain. Blood was gushing from her wounds, soaking the wooden floor beneath her.

I yelled through the rain of bullets while crawling toward her, making sure Josie was covered behind the couch.

"I am not losing you once again!"

I wormed my way across the floor, reached out my hand to grab Camille's, and pulled her, sliding her body across the wooden floor, when a bullet smashed through the window closest to us, whistled through the air and grazed her neck, then continued and ended in the wall behind us.

Crying, I pulled Camille behind the couch, next to Josie, but then realized my shirt was soaked. I gasped and stared at her neck, where blood was gushing.

"Oh, dear Lord, no!"

As the sound of gunfire subsided as quickly as it had started, I pressed my hand against the wound, trying to stop the bleeding, while screaming at Josie.

"CALL 9-1-1!"

In the second I had yelled the words, the back door burst open, and someone stormed inside. A heartbeat went by, and I held my breath.

NO OTHER WAY

Jean's shrill voice cut through the air.

"Harry? Josie?"

A sigh of relief went through me, then fear set in—the fear of losing Camille all over again.

"In here. We need help. Please, help us!"

Chapter 30

I FELT like we had become regulars at the Jackson Memorial Hospital the past few years. I, for one, had spent enough time in there, waiting for news of my loved ones, paralyzed with fear, with no other tools to help me but my prayers.

I was bent over, mumbling under my breath, pleading with God not to take Camille away again when I felt Jean's hand on my shoulder.

"I'm sure she'll be okay."

I lifted my head and looked at Jean, then at her bloody clothes. The front of her white T-shirt was completely soaked, and Camille's blood was smeared on her arms and face. She even had some in her hair. Jean had managed to stop the bleeding using a dishtowel and applying constant pressure to the wound before the ambulance came. The paramedics had told me they believed that might have saved Camille from bleeding out and maybe even saved her life.

Again, she came to our rescue. How could I ever thank her enough?

"It was scary," she said.

Jean's frightened eyes lingered on me.

"When will this ever end, Harry?"

NO OTHER WAY

I shook my head in disbelief. "When I shut up."

She leaned back with a deep exhale. "I can't believe they'd…I mean…come on!"

I nodded in agreement. It was, by far, one of the scariest minutes of my life. Luckily, both Josie and I had made it through without a scratch. She was sitting in a chair on the other side of me, eyes staring blankly into the air, in a state of complete shock. I put my arm around her and pulled her close. Her body was shaking in my arms, but she wasn't crying. She was just staring into thin air, barely even blinking, hardly breathing.

"Maybe it's time I cave in," I said, addressed to Jean. "Maybe I've reached my limit now."

She sat up straight and gave me one of her looks, reminding me of my mother the time I had told her I was going to quit playing baseball because someone on the team was picking on me. I had trouble running fast because I had grown so much very fast and become clumsy and unable to control my long limbs almost overnight.

"You listen to me," she had said back then, giving me that exact same look. "If you give in to a bully, you empower him. You give him complete power over you. Instead, you show them what you're made of, Harry. You become the best and the fastest."

And so, I did. Once I realized those long legs could be used for running really fast, I had become the star of the team within months, and no one bullied me again. I still knew this to be true; you shouldn't give in just because you go through resistance or because people were pushing against you. But this was different. This was becoming dangerous.

"Don't you dare even say that," Jean said. "I will not hear those words leave your lips again, Harry Hunter."

It was always serious with Jean when she called me by my full name. That's when she meant business…when she wanted to be sure I was listening.

"I have to think about my family, about Josie," I said and glanced down at her in my arms. "I don't think I can justify this any longer."

"You listen to me, Harry Hunter," she said. "These people almost killed you and your entire family tonight. You don't let them get away with this, you hear me? This is not you. This is the fear talking. Don't let fear do the talking for you. Fear is a coward. Faith is the warrior, and you're a warrior, Harry. Have faith. And then do your part. Bring them down, all of them this time."

"But how?" I asked, throwing out my hands. "How am I supposed to do that? I'm talking to the FBI. I'm helping them all I can, but even they keep running into walls of silence. No one dares to rat on their colleagues. They've tried to follow the money trail and so far, arrested a couple of officers from our district, but they've only just scratched the surface. I have a feeling this goes way deeper. If only there were something else I could do…"

She nodded, then pulled out her phone from her pocket. "Maybe this can help."

She found a video and played it for me. "I was on my phone right when it happened, checking emails. I saw the car, driving fast down our street, tires screeching loudly. I don't know why, but something compelled me to do it. I turned on the camera and started recording right before they began shooting. Look."

She turned the video on, and I watched as the blue car rushed down the street, then slowed down right in front of my house, and some type of automatic rifle was pushed out through the window, then began to shoot. It all went by so fast; it seemed impossible that it was the same incident that I had experienced inside my house. Being in there, fearing for my family's and my life had felt like an eternity…like it would never stop. In the video, it took less than a minute.

But the picture was very clear of the car, and as I looked in through the window, my heart began to beat so fast I feared it might explode.

Chapter 31

I DECIDED to stay the night at the hospital, while Jean took Josie home. Jean drove Josie to my dad's place, where she'd spend the night while a forensics team took care of our house. Josie needed her sleep, and there was no reason for her to stay. The doctor had told us Camille was going to be okay. She had lost a lot of blood, and they had to stitch her up on her shoulder and neck, but she was going to be fine. They were all superficial wounds, and there was no severe damage done or any fractures. She had been very lucky, he said. Also, to have an ER nurse as a neighbor to stop the bleeding in time.

"It was all just a very happy ending," he said.

I didn't know about happy or ending since I had a feeling this was far from over yet.

I waited until Camille was out of surgery around three a.m., then went with her into the room they gave her and waited for her to wake up from the anesthesia. Around four a.m., she was fully awake, her brown eyes looking at me. I couldn't – for the life of me —understand how she could look so beautiful even with what she had been through. But she did. She was gorgeous, as always. She parted her lips like she wanted to speak.

I shushed her while pulling up the covers.

"You need to rest, Camille. We'll talk later."

She put her hand on my arm, then squeezed it to stop me.

"No."

I paused. "What do you mean, no? You're beginning to sound like your teenage daughter; do you know that?"

She looked at me, her eyes strained, painful.

"I...need to tell you the truth. About me. I owe this to you. You've been nothing but good to me."

I shook my head. "Nonsense. You don't owe me anything. I don't need to know. At least not now. We can talk about it later."

I looked away, biting my cheek. I realized my hands were shaking. I had wanted answers, but now that she was offering them to me, I wasn't sure I wanted them anymore. I was terrified of what they might do to me, how I might react. I wasn't even sure I wanted to know anymore.

Because I feared it would destroy everything. Destroy me and my family.

"But I need to," she said. "I need to tell you the truth, no matter what it might do to me, what it might do to us."

I shook my head. She sent me a weak smile.

"It's time, Harry. No more lies. No more secrets. These people almost killed me a second time tonight, trying to shut me up, wanting to shut both of us up. But it was mostly me because I have the knowledge to take them down. I am dangerous to them, and we both know this."

I stared at her, my nostrils flaring, not knowing what to do. I grabbed a chair from the corner of the room and sat down next to her bed, holding her delicate hand tightly in mine, pressing back my fears, bracing myself for what was about to hit me.

"All right. I guess we're doing this, then."

Chapter 32

"GROWING up in the Dominican Republic, all people ever dreamed about was coming to America. Where I grew up, sexual abuse was like second-hand smoke. It was everywhere. You couldn't escape it. You knew one day it would catch up to you. I was exploited by a couple of my father's friends, and he let them do it, even received money from them. He was a pimp, not just for me, but for numerous other girls in our neighborhood. It was normal. My granddad was a pimp, and when my brother turned thirteen, he was told he was going to be a pimp too. It was just the way things were where we lived. I knew that I had only two choices. Either I became a prostitute, or I became a pimp. There were no other possibilities, no other way. I remember seeing the people involved in trafficking in their new cars, their big houses, throwing money around downtown. They were living the life. So, I decided I didn't want to live my life as a victim anymore. When I turned eighteen, I decided I was done being exploited, and I wanted to make a life for myself. And I was good at it. I would approach girls in the street or at the mall, and they'd let me because I was a woman, a beautiful woman. I was nice, and why would some nice woman not be someone you could trust? I would pick the prettiest girl, sitting by herself. I'd tell her she had beautiful eyes. If she said thank you, I'd leave. But if she told me, 'No, I don't,' I knew I had her. I looked for the broken ones, the ones easy to persuade, the ones who would want a new life for themselves. So, I told them I could get them a modeling job and told them to come with me to the harbor, where my brother waited with the rest of his team. They'd stack them in boats and transport them to the U.S. coast. I would get my share of the money, and I began saving up. I wanted to get away. I wanted to travel to the U.S. I wanted to go to university, a real American university, FIT. I wanted to become an engineer. And this was my way. It was the only way. There was a lot of money to be made this way. And it wasn't just young girls. We helped families fulfill their dreams of going to America, of starting over. We helped them get there, and that made me feel good about myself. They were achieving what I could only dream of. Every time I watched that boat leave at night, I would dream of it one day being me onboard, fulfilling my destiny. The power of the dream was so strong, it became a longing, a yearning, and I would often lie awake at night fantasizing about it, wanting it so bad I could scream. One day, when I had enough money, I told my brother to put me on board his boat. I handed him all my savings and told him I wanted to go. He looked at me, then shook his head. You know what he said? He said, "Can't do it. You're the best one we've got." He wouldn't let me go because he didn't want to lose me and what I could do. It would be bad for his business. So, you know what I did? I went to his competitor, another guy whom I knew smuggled out refugees, and paid him instead. He took me on his boat along with maybe a hundred other refugees, with nothing but the clothes we wore and the dream in our minds. He took me to the coast of America, and then they threw us overboard, telling us to swim the rest of the way. So, we did. Not many made it. I did. I remember sitting on the beach north of here, holding the white sand between my fingers, thinking I made it, I finally made it. I also remember a body that had washed up close to me, then realized it wouldn't be long before they'd come for us. So, I ran. I ran and hid and became a homeless person in Miami. Living in abandoned buildings, I met many people. One of them told me he could help me make money. And it wasn't prostitution. He took me to the harbor, where I met with Ferdinand, the guy from your work, and that other man, Wolfe, was there too. Ferdinand said he had work for me if I wanted it. They wanted me to go back and forth between the U.S. and Santo Domingo in the Dominican Republic, and help with the transport. I had an advantage because I was local, and they needed someone they could trust to handle the other side. I didn't have to stay there, just go once or twice a month. If I did this, he would be able to give me a social security number and a passport. I would become an American. I didn't even think about it for one second. I had to get off the streets. I had to make a life for myself. So, I did. I eventually made enough money to pay tuition for FIT, and I started there. I kept telling myself it wasn't bad what I was doing. *Everybody does it*, I told myself. *If I don't, then someone else will.* These people, most of them, wanted to go. They didn't know what awaited them once they got here. Usually, it was working in a field or a factory; for some, it was prostitution, but for most of them, I truly believed they were given a better future. I told myself I was helping them. They wanted to go. Or they wouldn't be willing to pay all that money for us to take them on a dangerous trip across the ocean. They knew the risks it involved. That's how I justified it for myself. But I was suffering. Deep inside, I was hurting. Seeing these people getting stowed away, hundreds of them in small compartments, was awful. So that's why I started doing drugs. I met a guy at FIT who introduced me to crack, and I took it without even questioning. Here was finally something that gave me peace, something that made me at ease and made me forget. And for about a year or so, I was doing great. I flew back and forth between Santo Domingo and Miami once or twice a month. I kept them on a schedule and made sure they paid our people in Miami and didn't keep the money for themselves. I ran a tight ship, and no one dared to defy me. When I went back there, I drove a big car. I was the queen of the island, and no longer a victim. I felt important. People knew who I was, and they respected me. It felt good. But once I was back on American soil, it didn't feel good anymore, and the more drugs I took to subdue it, the more I messed up. I was thrown out of FIT, and soon they found someone else to run the trafficking operation for them. I was cast out and found myself on the streets once again, alone and with no money, only craving my next fix. That's how fast it can go."

She sighed and placed a hand on my arm.

"Then, I met you—my savior. You picked me up in an abandoned house down in Overtown, where I had been living for months. I barely knew what year it was. You took me to rehab and paid out of your own pocket. No one had ever been so good to me. You came to see me every day and showed me so much love, it was overwhelming. I had never had anyone love me like that before. So, I decided to leave my past behind, and, once we got married, I believed it would actually happen. I was finally living the dream. When your colleagues, Wolfe and Ferdinand, realized who you were going to marry, they got scared. They came here, came to our house shortly after we married, when you weren't there, and threatened me. They told me if I ever said anything to you, they'd kill our daughter and me. I promised them I wouldn't. They came by at least once a year to make sure I wasn't talking, throwing all kinds of threats around and humiliating me, telling me what scum I was, what a whore I was, and that no one would believe me anyway. They said they'd let me take the fall, and I'd go away for the rest of my life. Stuff like that."

I looked up at Camille. I had listened while looking mostly at the floor below, my heart pounding in my chest.

"So, why did they try to kill you three years ago? What changed?" I asked, my voice shaking. I felt so repulsed by what I had heard; it was hard even to speak.

Camille exhaled. Her eyes filled and a tear escaped, then ran down her cheek.

"My brother came. He came to my door five years ago. After that, everything changed."

"Your brother? He was here?"

She nodded, closing her eyes briefly. "He said I owed him money. He had brought a couple of guys, and they threatened to reveal that I was an illegal immigrant if I didn't pay up. I had made it to America because of him, he said."

"But it wasn't him?" I asked. "He didn't bring you here?"

"Doesn't matter. He wanted money. So…I…well, I only know one way to get money…"

Camille looked away.

My hand slid out of hers, and I felt myself recoil.

"So, you…went back?"

She nodded, closing her eyes, tears streaming down her cheeks.

"I contacted Ferdinand, and he got me working the malls here, finding girls. I told him that's what I was good at, finding the girls that were broken. They trusted me, I told him. It was easy for me to get to them. They always walked with me willingly. So, I started working for him again and gave all the money I earned to my brother. It was tormenting me, but I couldn't see any other way out."

I stood to my feet, pushing the chair across the floor behind me, making a screeching sound.

"You…you were out of it. We had a great life and still you… went back to…that?" I could barely get the words across my lips. "We had everything, Camille, and still you…I can't believe you. Why didn't you come to me? Why didn't you ever tell me anything?"

"Don't you understand? I couldn't. Not only would they kill me and perhaps my family back in Santo Domingo, but I would also… lose you. You'd look at me the way you are now and yell at me like you just did. And I would lose Josie. I couldn't bear that. I was finally happy. I thought I could stop at any time, that I could just tell Ferdinand I was done once I had paid my debt, but they wouldn't let me. When I told them I was done, I wanted out because it was tormenting me to be lying to you, they came to our house one afternoon. They broke in through the back door, then injected me with drugs so I overdosed. They knew my story and knew to make it look like I was just some addict who had slipped. But they hadn't counted on me surviving. And now, they're trying to kill me again. These people, Harry…You don't know what you're up against. They're dangerous and powerful. There's no stopping them. They're everywhere."

I stared at her, my nostrils flaring violently, my fists clenched. I could feel pain in my jaw and realized I had bitten down so hard that it was hurting me.

"I…I can't believe this," I said, going back and forth inside the room.

Camille was crying heavily, sobbing, and I felt nothing. I couldn't make myself feel sorry for her, even if I tried. She had chosen this. She had made the choice for her and for us. She had exploited young, innocent girls and sent them into prostitution—sent them to slavery. She could justify it all she wanted. She could tell herself it was okay, that everyone did it, that these people wanted a better life, that she was helping them fulfill their dreams. She could say that she had no choice as much as she wanted to, but the fact was that these were nothing but excuses. She did have a choice. She had a choice back in the Dominican Republic, and she had a choice here. She most certainly had a choice after marrying me. Yet she still went back to it, and that made me angrier than anything.

How could I ever look into her eyes again and feel anything but disgust?

How could I ever forgive her?

"There might be no way of stopping them," I said, pointing at her. "But you're gonna help me do it anyway. Even if it costs us our lives. It's the only way for you to redeem yourself; do you hear me? You and me, we're taking them down, all of them. You're gonna tell the FBI everything you just told me. You're gonna give them names; you hear me? You're gonna give them all the names they need, leaving no one out. If you ever want to see Josie again, that's how it'll go down. Are we clear?"

Chapter 33

JEAN COULDN'T SLEEP. It wasn't exactly a surprise. How could anyone sleep after what had happened? After seeing a drive-by shooting of your neighbor's house, of the man you loved, fearing for his and his family's lives. After saving Camille's life, fighting to stop the bleeding, then rushing her to the hospital? No one would be able to sleep after that.

The fear still lingered in her throat and felt like a lump. Jean realized she wasn't going to get any sleep, so she got up and walked downstairs to the kitchen, where she grabbed herself a glass of water, then went to the freezer and pulled out a bucket of Ben and Jerry's. She ate it with a spoon while looking into the street, tears running down her cheeks, her hand shaking as she dug the spoon into the ice cream.

It didn't help, though. Not as much as she wanted it to. She still felt terrible, and there was nothing that seemed to make her feel better. There was only one thing left to do.

She grabbed her phone and called her sister. Anna didn't pick up till her third try when a sleepy voice sounded on the other end.

"Jean? Is something wrong?"

"I'm sorry for calling like this," Jean said. "I know you were sleeping. I just needed someone to talk to."

"Hold on. Give me a sec. I'm going down to the kitchen, so we don't wake up the kids. Okay, I'm here now. I'm all yours. What's going on? You're scaring me, sis. You never call like this."

Jean grabbed another spoonful and plopped it in her mouth.

"Is that ice cream?" her sister asked. "Is it that bad?"

"It's worse."

"It's him again, isn't it? Harry, right? I've told you he's bad news, sweetie. He'll never leave his wife, and you're gonna end up hurt. I've said this from the beginning."

"I know. I know. It's just that…today was really bad."

"What happened?"

"Someone tried to kill Harry and his family. A drive-by shooting. I watched it all from my house. I was so scared, Anna, you have no idea."

Anna shrieked at the other end.

"A drive-by shooting? Are you kidding me? Tell me it isn't true. I always said Miami was a dangerous place for you. I never liked you living there, but geez. I'm telling you this because I love you, Jean. You need to listen to me. You have got to get out of that town."

"I knew you'd say that," she said. "I'm still thinking about it. Like we talked about the other day. I'm looking at listings and have applied for a couple of positions in your area."

"No, nah-ah. We can't wait for that," she said, getting her big sister tone on. "You've got to move faster than that. Tomorrow, Jean. Tomorrow you pack up a few things, and then you drive up here. We'll send for the rest of your things. I don't care that they need you at the hospital or that Harry needs you. You have to get away now. You come up here. We'll find you a place to live and a job. You can stay with me, Mike, and the kids till you find something else. We have a guest room; you know this. I'm not asking, Jean. I'm telling you to do this now. Are you listening?"

Jean nodded, pressing the phone closer to her ear. She loved her sister so dearly and couldn't understand why she had lived so far apart from her for so many years. Why had it taken her so long to realize how important family was?

"Okay," she said with a sniffle. "I'll come."

"Tomorrow."

"Tomorrow."

She hung up, feeling slightly invigorated. This was a good thing. This was the right thing. Now was as good a time as ever. She could start over. It was possible to forget and move on.

Jean stared out the window at Harry's house next to hers, then exhaled, thinking about what it could have been, but never was.

We came so close, Harry. So close.

Then she went upstairs, found her old suitcase, and started packing. She was going to leave first thing in the morning. She might as well, she figured. Just call the hospital and tell them she quit—that she was leaving town.

Would she tell Harry?

You don't owe him anything.

Still, she'd sent him an email. Yes, she'd do that. Or a text. A text was a little more personal. She'd thank him for all he had been for her and tell him it was time they both moved on, then wish him luck. She had all the sentences ready in her mind and knew exactly how to write it. She carried the suitcase down by the door, so it was ready for the morning. Anna was right. She could send for her things later.

Then, she sat down and started writing the text to Harry, trying to frame it properly, wondering how exactly one said goodbye to the man you loved when you were still in love with him.

That's when the phone rang. When it was still between her hands, and she had written the first words,

Dear Harry…

His name appeared on the display, and her heart sank.

Why was he calling her now? It had to be important, she thought, then picked up.

He sounded agitated and maybe a little scared. His breathing had a desperate sound to it.

"Jean? I'm so glad you picked up. I was afraid you wouldn't."

"Harry? What…"

"Oh, Jean," he said, sounding almost like he was crying. "I need you. I'm so sorry to call you like this, but I really, *really* need you right now."

Jean closed her eyes and exhaled deeply. Her sister's words rang in her head from back when she realized Jean was taking care of him and his wife, who was in a vegetative state. Jean had told her she was just helping out a little bit until they got into the routine—until they got things figured out. It was just for a month or two tops, she had told her, even though she knew it wasn't true, even if part of her hoped it would be longer.

"He'll never stop asking you to do stuff, and he'll only pay you back with a wounded heart. You won't be able to say no to him because you're in love with him, and he'll end up hurting you even worse. Break it off now. Make it fast. Less pain that way."

Make it fast.

"Harry…I…" Jean began.

"She told me everything," he said, crying, breaking down.

Jean held her breath. She couldn't stand even the thought of Harry crying. It broke her heart to pieces. She loved him too much to ignore him being sad.

"Camille did?" she asked, surprised. This wasn't what she had expected.

"Yes," he said. "Please, Jean. I don't know what to do with myself. I'm a mess. I need you."

She exhaled, biting her lip, a million voices in her head were telling her not to do this, that it would only end badly.

"Stay where you are. I'll be right there."

Chapter 34

I LEFT Camille at the hospital. I couldn't stay in that room with her anymore. I couldn't be anywhere near her. I met with Jean in the parking lot, and I got into her car. We drove back to her house in silence, while I stared out the window, trying to gather myself at least enough to be able to tell Jean everything.

I waited until we were in her house, drinking coffee at her kitchen table. Then I told her everything Camille had told me, every last detail. I needed to get it out. I guess it was a way for me to digest it, to talk about it, and let it sink in properly. I also needed her to understand. I needed her to realize that Camille and I were over. There was no way I could stay with her.

I was done.

"Wow," Jean said when I finally stopped talking and both of our coffees were almost gone. "For real?"

"For real," I said, nodding slowly. "I'm not making this up. I mean, you can't really make up something like this. But it makes a lot of sense to me now. She never wanted to talk about her past or her family. When I asked, she'd brush me off quickly and turn to something else. I just assumed she had a terrible relationship with her parents or something, or she was embarrassed about her background. I could never have imagined this. And then, later on, she was always so secretive when I asked her what she had been doing all day. I kept asking her if she didn't want to go back to school, if she wasn't bored at the house after Josie had started school, and she just said she kept herself busy. Now, I know with what." I chuckled angrily at that last part. I still could hardly believe this story, or that I had been such a fool.

"Luring young girls into slavery?" Jean asked, fingers tapping on the side of her cup. "I can't believe it. I thought I knew Camille. This is insane."

"Now, you know how I feel."

Jean looked up, and our eyes met. "I am sorry, Harry. This must feel awful. I can't even imagine…"

"I am done with her," I said, locking with Jean's eyes and not letting go. "I can't go back. Not after this."

Jean swallowed. Her eyes scrutinized mine. Then she nodded swiftly. "I can't blame you. This is a lot to take in, for anyone."

I took Jean's hand in mine. We both looked down at our hands, then I leaned forward, grabbed her face between my hands, and pulled her into a kiss. The kiss was soft and gentle and absolutely wonderful. It was all I had dreamt of and even more. And for the first time, it didn't fill me with this deep nagging sensation of guilt because I had nothing to feel guilty about anymore.

I was free. I was finally free to love Jean.

"Harry…I…," she whispered as our lips parted.

"Shh," I said. My forehead was leaning against hers. Her breath was on my skin. I didn't want to talk anymore. I wanted to enjoy the moment, make it last. When I opened my eyes to look at her, they fell on something behind her. Something standing in the living room next to the front door that I hadn't noticed when we walked in, but now I did. Now, it was all I could see.

"What's that?"

I pulled away abruptly.

"What's what…?"

She turned to look, then sank into her chair.

"A suitcase?" I asked, my voice trembling slightly as the realization sank in. At first, I told myself that she could, after all, just be going on a short trip to see her family or just a vacation, even though I knew she rarely did that, if ever. But as I turned my head, I saw papers in a stack on the kitchen counter, close to where I was sitting, close enough for me to see what they were.

"And listings? Those look like rental listings and job listings for…" I leaned over and looked closer. "Savannah?"

"Harry…I…"

I looked at her, startled. "You're leaving? For good?"

"Well…not just yet…"

"But soon, right? The suitcase is by the door. It's all packed, right? You were going to leave in the morning, weren't you? Just leave us without saying a word? Not even a goodbye?"

"I was going to tell you."

Jean reached over and removed the stack of papers, putting them in a drawer, trying to hide them. But it was too late.

"It's nothing," she said.

"Nothing? You were planning on leaving. That's not nothing."

"I am sorry."

"But… How? How will I survive without you?" I asked, suddenly feeling hopeless. "You…you can't leave us, Jean."

"That's not fair, Harry. I need a life too," she said with a sniffle, then walked to the window, turning her back on me. "I need to move on."

I looked down. It all seemed so futile now. What was I even doing here? Why was I spilling my guts out to Jean when she was about to leave?

I rose to my feet and grabbed my phone from the table.

"I'll let you go then. I understand."

I walked to the door. She turned around.

"Harry, I…"

I paused, hand on the doorknob.

"No, Jean, I haven't been fair to you. You're right. I need to sort out my mess on my own from now on. I wish you luck and hope you'll be very happy up there. Believe me, I do want the best for you, and this is it. I'm not good for you; I'm trouble."

I stormed out the door before I could break down and cry, then rushed to my own house, ducking under the crime scene tape, and walked inside where all the bullet holes were marked with numbers, tears running down my cheeks, wondering how I could have been such a darn fool. I had thought she'd wait for me forever. But of course, she couldn't. Now, I didn't understand why I thought she would. How had I not seen what I was doing to her, how she was hurting in all this?

I had been so selfish.

Chapter 35

I STAYED UPSTAIRS ALL NIGHT, wandering about in my bedroom. Every now and then, I daydreamed, looking towards Jean's house, thinking about what could have been, but for the most part, I researched. I dove right into working on the case to keep me from thinking about Jean and how much I had screwed up…how I hadn't realized time was running out.

I sighed and went through the autopsy of Kate Taylor once again, looking closely at the details that I had wondered about earlier, that frankly had startled me quite a lot. I still couldn't figure out the pieces, how they were connected, but there was something here that didn't add up.

I walked to the window and looked down into the street. Part of the area in front of our house had been blocked off, and a piece of crime scene tape was blowing in the wind. The crime scene techs had worked until late and would be back the next morning to finish, they had told me. I knew me being in the house was tampering with the scene of a crime, and I wasn't supposed to be there at all, but I didn't know where else to go, and I needed my computer and files to do my work. I would make sure to be out of there by the time the crime scene bus arrived in the morning.

Staying in my old house wasn't exactly comfortable, and I wondered if I would ever live here again. It had been our house, mine and Camille's house that we bought together. There had been so many happy moments shared here. And now it felt like it had all been a lie.

Was none of it real?

Once we started the process of the divorce, we'd have to figure out all those things. Did we keep the house? Did I simply buy her out and stay here with Josie? Or did we sell it and split the money? I still loved this house, and it was Josie's childhood home, but after tonight, I wasn't sure we'd ever be happy here again.

Especially not if Jean wasn't our neighbor anymore.

I also wondered what would happen to Camille. I was going to bring Agent Jackson to her tomorrow so she could tell her story to him and give him the information he needed, especially the names. The FBI would most likely cut a deal with her if she promised to testify against them. But would they try to kill her again? And would she have to serve time herself?

Probably.

I sighed and thought about Josie and how she'd once again have to miss her mother. We'd share custody, so that once she got out, Josie would be with her half of the time, if Josie wasn't an adult already and could choose for herself when to see either of us. The thought terrified me. How would she ever survive in this brutal world? Would it eat her up like it had her mother?

I shook my head and decided I didn't want to think about it. Instead, I thought about my visit with Nick Taylor and then his father, Andrew Taylor, and how angry he and been when addressing me. Why did the boy tell me to ask his new wife? Was he just a typical angry teenager trying to get his new stepmom in trouble? Because he hated her? Or what did he mean?

I sat down at the computer, then did my research. It didn't take me long to find tons of information about Andrew Taylor, the State Attorney.

As I scrolled down all my hits, I came across a picture from his wedding with his second wife. I couldn't believe what I was looking at. I couldn't believe *who* I was looking at. But seeing this, everything suddenly made a whole lot of sense.

I had finally found my missing piece.

As I pondered this new information, my phone buzzed in my pocket, and I pulled it out.

An unknown number usually meant it was Al.

Chapter 36

I WAS WAITING OUTSIDE of Fowler's office as he came to work the next morning. He stopped when he saw me, jaw almost dropped.

"Hunter? Are you okay? I heard what happened last night. What are you even doing here?"

"I had something important to tell you. I've solved the murder of Kate Taylor."

Fowler lifted his bushy eyebrows. "That old thing? It's ten years old, Harry."

"But never closed. I know who did it. Let me show you."

We walked inside, and I didn't sit down for once. Instead, I spread out all my papers, opened all the files, and started to explain it all to him, going into each and every detail. I told him my plan and how to take down the killer, then left in a hurry. I drove to the hospital, where I met with FBI Agent Jackson outside in the parking lot.

We shook hands, then walked inside, where I showed him to Camille's room. I listened in as she told him everything, every little detail about the trafficking ring and her own part of it, making sure she got it all out, even how deeply involved she had been. The agent recorded everything and took notes while she spoke. I was very pleased with how thorough she was. Most of the names she threw on the table were no surprise to me, but some of them most certainly were.

"And you'll testify to all this?" Agent Jackson said as she had finished.

She nodded. "Yes."

"And you do realize this means you're incriminating yourself as well, right?" he asked.

Camille closed her eyes and nodded again.

"Yes."

"We can probably ask the DA to look for a reduced sentence and get you a good deal," he added, "if you show up in court and tell them these things you've told me today."

She swallowed. She was exhausted, but the doctor had said she was well enough to do this. I wanted to strike while she was still willing to talk, fearing she might regret it if we waited too long.

"We could also apply to get you into the witness protection program," he said.

Camille's eyes landed on mine.

"But…Josie?"

"You wouldn't see her again," I said.

"Or she'd have to go with her," Agent Jackson said.

I shook my head. "I am not losing my daughter too."

"You are married. You could both go," he said. "You could start over in a safer place."

The thought was appealing. It really was. Right now, there wasn't anything that made me want to stay in Miami. But I couldn't leave my job, and I couldn't move somewhere else and start a new life with the wife I didn't love anymore. It was simply not possible.

Agent Jackson gathered his things and rose to his feet. "Think about it…both of you. Once this is over, you'll have made a lot of enemies. It might not even be a choice anymore. It might be a necessity."

ONE WEEK LATER

Chapter 37

"YOU READY FOR THIS?"

Fowler looked at me. He was wearing his Kevlar vest the same as I was, along with a helmet. We both had our weapons in our hands.

"It's not every day you get to take down a murderer," he continued.

I nodded, feeling satisfied, yet still nervous, as was typical in the situation. We had no idea what the outcome would be. Hopefully, we'd get the killer, and no one needed to be hurt.

But that wasn't always how these things panned out, unfortunately.

"I'm ready."

Fowler grinned. "Then, let's do it. Perimeter is set up; we have the house surrounded. Let's go."

Fowler went in first, and I followed. We found him in the living room.

"Police!" Fowler yelled. "Hands where I can see them."

Andrew Taylor was on the floor fast, arms over his head, wearing his PJs. A cup of coffee was on the floor and had spilled the black substance in a puddle, ruining the nice beige carpet. It was

Saturday morning, and he had probably thought he'd be able to enjoy his morning coffee in peace and quiet.

I wasn't sorry to have ruined that.

"Andrew Taylor," I said. "You're under arrest for the murder of Kate Taylor. You have the right to remain silen…"

"What's going on here?"

The woman at the top of the stairs looked down at us, her eyes were petrified. I smiled and pointed my gun at her.

"Just the person we were looking for. Would you please come down here, ma'am? Slowly and keep those hands above your head, where I can see them, please."

"But…"

She did as she was told and walked down with her hands stretched above her head.

"What are you people doing here? What are you doing to my husband?"

As she approached me, I smiled again. "We're arresting him. For the murder of his ex-wife. Or rather for conspiracy to. Because he didn't exactly kill her himself, did he? You did that."

Her eyes met mine. I saw confusion in them and defiance. "I…"

"Save it," I said. "We know you did it."

"Don't say anything, Joan," Andrew Taylor said.

"I don't intend to," she said, walking closer to me, looking into my eyes.

Those were the last words said before we dragged them away. We let them sweat it out for few hours before they were taken into an interrogation room, Fowler and I doing the interrogation together.

"I didn't do anything," Andrew said. "I had nothing to do with it."

"Okay," I said, placing the files on the desk in front of them, then taking out the pictures of Kate Taylor from when she was pulled out of the water. I placed them so they couldn't avoid looking at them. "Then tell me about Kate. I'd like to hear about her from both of you."

Neither of them said anything. Not that it was a surprise.

"Okay. Let's do this another way. I tell you how I think it all went down, and then you can stop me if I got it wrong, okay?"

I looked first at one, then the other. No one said anything.

"I need my lawyer," Andrew Taylor said. "I'm not saying anything until he gets here."

"Of course not," I said. "Until then, I'll just talk a little bit if you don't mind. You can always correct me if I get things wrong."

They didn't make a sound.

"So, when did you two start seeing one another?" I continued. "When did you fall in love? When did your affair start?"

Still nothing.

"See, I have a feeling you planned this for a very long time, didn't you? Because you had fallen in love, you and Andrew. But Kate didn't want to give you a divorce, am I right? So, you wanted to get rid of her. It was easily planned once you got started. Joan invited her to celebrate her birthday with your third friend, Kristin, thinking it was a great alibi. Especially since you chose a weekend where Andrew was at a conference in Atlanta, providing him with a rock-solid alibi, and he would be the first suspect. We all know that. And it went down perfectly. No one suspected foul play from her good friends. But what got to me first was the fact that no one had seen Kate with you down there. When interviewed afterward, the bartender said he remembered seeing both you and Kristin, but not Kate. Now, the investigation was mostly focused on that guy, Matt, and finding him, and no one had seen him either. None of the guests in the bar or anyone working there had seen them. Not Kate nor Matt. And it took me a while to figure it out, but I realized that Matt doesn't even exist. Kristin panicked, didn't she? When she was interviewed by the police, she thought she should come up with something better than what you had planned. So, she made up some guy Kate might have met, someone the police could focus on investigating, a possible killer. But since it wasn't planned, you didn't talk about him until the detective mentioned him, realizing Kristin had to have talked about him. During the rest of the interview, both of your stories were a complete match, a little too much, to be honest. Using the same sentences, like she needed to *blow off some steam*, or she *wanted to disappear*, she was *bummed out about her marriage*, stuff like that was the same, word for word. And that smells like you two talked it over beforehand, getting your stories straight. But Matt was only in Kristin's memory because she made him up while sitting there at the sheriff's office, thinking it would be better, it would be more plausible if she painted a picture of Kate as being loose, as wanting to sleep with another guy, and then maybe he could have killed her. It was a better story than her simply vanishing out of the blue like you first planned, hoping they'd think it was suicide. But the fact was, no one had seen Kate in Key West because she wasn't there. She was somewhere else, wasn't she? She was suffering a slow and painful death."

Chapter 38

THE ROOM WAS EERILY QUIET. The two of them didn't even move, barely blinked. Not even a raised eyebrow.

"Anyone have anything to add?" I asked, sipping my cup of coffee, praying their lawyer wasn't going to burst in anytime soon. Fowler was staring at them, leaned back in his chair, letting me run the show.

"No? You don't have anything to say for yourself?"

I put the cup down, my eyes lingering on both of them.

Finally, Andrew Taylor lifted his eyes and met mine. "It wasn't like that. You don't understand."

"Oh, really? Then tell me. What did I miss?"

A look from Joan made him lean back and clam up.

"Okay," I said. I placed my fists on the table and leaned forward, getting close to Andrew Taylor.

"Then, let's try this. She hurt your son. That's why you did it."

The look in Andrew's eyes told me I was on track.

"See, at first I assumed it was you who did it, that you had abused Nick. But then I realized that it stopped. There were no more reports, and when I called the school, they said it had stopped after DCF was put on the case. After that, Nick never had bruises again. Because his mom was dead. Kate was the one who tortured your son, wasn't she?" I continued. "And you knew you could never get her out of your life otherwise. DCF had been involved, but they dismissed the case. How could you make anyone else understand what was going on if they wouldn't? They'd only think you were the one abusing him because let's face it; it's more likely the father would do such a thing."

Andrew leaned forward. "I didn't know how bad it was until DCF told me what Nick had said. The details of how she made him lick the toilet and cut himself were unbearable. I had to do something at least. After DCF dismissed the case, I tried to solve it myself. I kept an eye on her when she was alone with him. I went out of my way to make sure they weren't alone. One day, I walked in on her as she pushed his head into the toilet bowl and flushed. That's when I knew I had to do something. But I didn't have the guts. Not till I asked Joan for help and told her about it. She suggested it; she suggested we get rid of her."

Joan let out a small angry snort, and Andrew gave her a look, then bowed his head. "They know," he mumbled. "It's not like I'm telling them anything they don't already know."

"Just stop," she grumbled.

I continued. "So, she came up with how it could be done. Because after her divorce, Joan had gone back to working again, back at the hyperbaric treatment clinic where she worked before she married her first husband, who didn't want you to work, am I right? That's where I met you when I brought in Camille. But your name is Joan Kendrick now, not Joan Smith, like the woman in the files, the one who reported her best friend missing. You took your maiden name after the divorce. And you never took Andrew's last name since you tried that once when you were married before, and it was too much trouble to change your name once again. That's why I never made the connection. Not until now, at least. So, here's what I believe happened. You chose a weekend Andrew would be away at a conference in Atlanta, and his alibi would be solid since he would be the first one they looked at. You don't have to watch a lot of crime shows or even be the State Attorney to know this. You brought Kristin along. She was your best friend. You could trust her. You told Kate you could help her with something she had trouble with. I found her medical records and realized she was diabetic, and she had a foot ulcer that wouldn't go away—a type of condition many people came to your clinic and received treatment for. You promised her free treatment if she came on the weekend, out of normal operating hours. She crawled inside the chamber, and you turned it on. And then you simply just left her there, knowing no one else would come in all weekend when the clinic was closed. I read the autopsy, and that's when it occurred to me that she hadn't drowned. Her eardrums were popped, and there was permanent scarring, called fibrosis of the lung tissue, a symptom of oxygen toxicity that can lead to death, as you yourself have taught me. You also taught me that it is one of the side effects of being inside a hyperbaric chamber for too long. It was a risk, you said. So, I thought, what about an entire weekend? What if she was left in there for two whole days? Knocking on the sides, suffering, screaming for help, but no one hearing her? Unable to get out? After that, you could have taken her dead body out, driven her down to Key West, where you placed her in the water, making it look like she drowned. Then you went to the police station and told them your friend had gone missing, after making sure your stories were straight. What I can't figure out is why Kristin was willing to go along with it."

I saw a hint of a frown between Joan's eyes.

"Unless…" I said, scrutinizing her. "Unless she had something…" I flipped a few pages and returned to the initial interview with her. "Kristin wasn't married. Why was that? Did it have something to do with Kate?"

Joan's nostrils were flaring, and I could tell I was getting closer.

"What did Kate do?" I asked. "What did she do to Kristin?"

"She slept with him, okay?" Joan said, spurting it out. She was like a pressure cooker that had finally reached its limits. "Kristin had met this sweet guy that she really liked, and Kate kept telling her that he'd cheat on her. When Kristin came home and found the two of them in bed together, all she could say was: I told you so. That's the kind of woman she was."

"But that wasn't all, was it?" I asked. "There has to have been more for you both actually to want to kill her."

Joan sighed deeply.

"What did she do to you? You've all known each other since college. What did she do that made you want to kill her to revenge yourselves?"

Joan swallowed. I could tell she was debating with herself what to say next. She wanted to tell me; I could see it in her eyes. She wanted to justify herself. As I stared into her eyes, it suddenly occurred to me. There was a detail I had missed. Her eyes. Her piercing green eyes.

"Oh, dear Lord," I said. "Nick is your son, isn't he? He's not Kate's?"

That's when she finally broke down and cried—leaning forward, mouth half-open, her upper body convulsing.

"Kate couldn't have children of her own," I said.

"Sh-she forced me to give him to her. When I got pregnant."

"Because he was Andrew's child. Because you had an affair with Andrew. Why did you agree to it, Joan?"

"Andrew persuaded me and told me it was best for the child. I know now he only did it out of fear of Kate. They'd raise the child like it was theirs, they said. I had recently married and didn't want an affair to destroy everything, so I agreed to it, even though it was the hardest thing I have ever done. I told my husband I was doing an internship overseas for nine months, then left. Kate and Andrew came over and took the baby home. I came back different. I never became the same woman again. And for all these years, I had to watch him grow up with her as a mother. It was pure torture."

"And then when you realized that the abuse was happening, you knew you had to get rid of her. But it wasn't that easy. DCF believed her and not the child, and she refused to give Andrew a divorce. She would take Nick with her, and then you'd lose him completely."

"The woman was insane," Andrew said. "You must understand

this. She was abusive to anyone in her proximity. It was impossible to get out of her claws. It was her friends, her family; all experienced her evilness. She was nothing but pure evil. She'd even cut herself to make it look like I was abusing her. She'd hurt herself to make her friends feel sorry for her and think I was the bad guy. I would even see her do it. Once, we were having a fight, and she grabbed a knife and cut herself on the throat, then yelled that she'd call the police and tell them I did it. I know how the system works. The police would have to arrest me no matter what I told them, and the press would be all over it. I didn't have the guts to leave her. She'd ruin my life, she said. Make sure I never saw Nick again. Destroy my career by telling the world I had abused Nick and was a child molester. I'm the Miami-Dade County State Attorney. It would have ruined me. She had the power to destroy me completely, and she would have done so if I hadn't stopped her. She would have completely ruined my son too, and I couldn't let her do that."

"But he was already damaged. You realized it when you found the videos on his computer," I said. "That's why you wanted him to stay behind bars. You feared he'd become like his mother. He had been abused, and now he was abusing others. It was better for you if he stayed there—if he went to jail. You were scared of what he might do if he got out."

"I told you he was a liar. Just like his mother, he manipulated and lied constantly. When he pulled that gun out in church, it was just part of his show. He wanted you to think I was abusing him, but in fact, he was abusing others. I had told him the night before that I'd go to the police with what I had found, showing them how he had humiliated those girls, that's why he brought the gun. To take me down, not to kill me. But to make it look like he had no other way. He was going down and dragging me down with him. That was his plan. And I guess he succeeded. I never told him the truth about who his birth mother was. There never really was the right time." Andrew glanced at Joan briefly. "He hated her guts, and it tormented her daily. Now, I guess it's too late. It's simply too late."

"It is, for both of you," I said.

I closed the file, then stopped the recording. I folded my hands with a deep sigh. "I think I've heard enough."

"Me too," Fowler said, then rose to his feet.

As he walked to the door, he shared a look with Andrew Taylor that for a second made me think they knew one another, but then it was gone.

Chapter 39

WE STAYED at my dad's place, further down the street. Our house was still a crime scene, and to be honest, I wasn't sure I'd ever feel comfortable there again. I considered selling it once it was all over, but who'd want to buy a house full of bullet holes? One way or another, I'd have to fix it up first. And I really didn't want to.

I hadn't seen Camille for several days. She was taken into the FBI's custody as soon as she was released from the hospital, and I didn't know where they were keeping her. If we'd ever see her again, I didn't know either. For me, it wouldn't matter much, but for Josie, it still did.

My dad had made spaghetti and meatballs for us, and we sat around the table, eating in silence.

"I solved my case today," I said and took a second portion.

"Really?" my dad said. "Well done."

"We got a full confession and everything. Three people were involved in planning it. We have two of them; the third will be taken in tomorrow, and we'll need her confession too. But it looks like we'll be able to close it soon."

"I bet that feels good," my dad said and leaned back. "Serving God by serving the people."

"It does," I said. "Even though it's never as black and white as you'd like it to be."

"You mean the murderer is actually human?" he asked.

I chuckled. "Yeah, something like that. I always want them to be these vicious, mean people that belong behind bars. But they're never that. Still need to do their time, though. I don't feel bad about it."

"But you're human too," he said. "So, you understand them."

"I don't really understand them killing a person, but I guess I understand their pain if you know what I mean. I don't know. Is anyone having more? I can eat the rest if no one else can."

Josie shook her head. She had her phone under the table and was obviously not very present because of it. She thought I didn't see it, and I pretended not to. I didn't want us to fight. Not tonight. She had been through so much the past few months and years, even with her mother being sick and all. I could cut her some slack.

"So, Josie, any plans for the weekend?" I asked. "Josie?"

She looked up from her phone. I smiled, and she put it away, looking embarrassed. "The weekend? It's only Thursday, Dad."

She said it in that teenage way like I didn't even know that it was Thursday.

"I know, and I wanted to ask you first because I wanted us to do something together this weekend."

She made a face. "Something? Like what? Please don't say something lame like going to the Everglades. I hate that place. Or the beach. I can't stand all that sand. It gets everywhere."

"It's nothing like that," I said. "I thought maybe we could go swim with dolphins in Key Largo. I know you've always wanted to do that."

Josie's eyes grew huge. She dropped the fork from her hand. She let out a small shriek. "Really? I thought it was too expensive? You always said it was?"

"It is, but I think we deserve it, don't we?"

"Oh, my God, Dad. Are you being serious right now? I have dreamt about this since I was a baby."

"I know you have," I said. "And now, it's time. Now, do your homework."

Josie almost danced up the stairs to the temporary bedroom my dad had given her. I smiled and turned to look at him, sitting next to me.

"Feeling pretty good about yourself there, aren't ya'?" he asked.

"Yes, as a matter of fact, I am feeling good about this. I always wanted to take Josie down there, to this rescue center where they take care of injured dolphins and where you can get in the water with them. It's extremely expensive, but I think it's worth it."

My dad nodded. "And it certainly isn't a way for you to buy her happiness because she might never see her mom again? Or a way for you to create a diversion, so you won't have to tell her?"

"Maybe," I said.

"Don't you think you owe it to her to talk to her about it, at least? To tell her the truth?"

I swallowed. "How can I? I'm not about to tell her what her mom has done. It would break her heart."

"True, but it will break her heart either way. If her mom takes the witness protection program or goes to jail, either way, she'll be out of her life. She needs to know."

I grabbed my plate and rose to my feet with an annoyed movement. My dad was right, as always, but I didn't want him to be. If I wanted to take my daughter swimming with dolphins to avoid questions about her mother, then so be it. That was my issue, not his.

Chapter 40

I WAS FEELING PRETTY confident and good about myself as I entered the station the next morning. Josie had been the happiest girl all morning, and I had to admit I was enjoying seeing her like this for once. Ever since the shooting incident, she had been so down and sad, and she had slept terribly at night. Most nights, I had slept with her, to be there and hold her when she had nightmares. This night was the first that she slept through without even waking up. It gave me hope that she'd get past this too. I had found her a therapist that she was going to see for the first time today since I wasn't sure I could deal with it all by myself.

I sat down at my desk, then opened my computer, ready to finish my report on the Kate Taylor murder, but for some reason, I couldn't find it. I searched the entire database, but it simply wasn't there. All there was, was the old case file from Key West; none of my work was anywhere to be seen.

I was starting to sweat now, and my hands were getting clammy as I searched for the audio file from the interrogation.

It wasn't there either.

It was gone.

Vanished.

"What in the…?"

I kept searching, going through everything, my fingers tapping the keyboard, my heart pounding in my chest, but still, nothing turned up. No results, it said. I then walked to the cabinet behind my desk to find the paper version that I always kept there.

It was gone too.

"What the…?"

I turned around to look at my desk, but I hadn't left it there either. I searched my bag, my drawers, everywhere.

Nothing.

All that was left were the old case files. It was like I had never done any work on this case at all.

What is this? I can't believe it?

I called down to the detention center and asked if they still had Andrew Taylor in custody.

"He was released last night," the woman said.

Released? He hadn't been to court yet; he couldn't have had a judge set bail yet?

"And Joan Kendrick?"

"Also released."

"On what grounds?"

"Case was dismissed," she said. "Charges were dropped. That's all it says in the papers."

"Who signed the release form?" I asked, my voice shaking with anger and frustration. I couldn't for the life of me figure out what was going on, how this was possible. How could this have happened?

"That would be Abraham Fowler," she said. "Major Abraham Fowler."

Chapter 41

HE WAS on the phone when I rang the doorbell, and as he opened the door, he finished his conversation.

"I gotta call you back. There's something I need to deal with here," Fowler said, then hung up. He gave me a look. I couldn't tell if it was concern in his eyes or resentment.

"Hunter? What are you doing here?"

I pushed my way past him inside, and he closed the front door behind me. The amount of marble on the man's floors and walls gave the place a cold feel.

"You let them go?" I asked.

Fowler let out a deep sigh. "So, that's what this is about. I should have known. Please…Hunter, sit."

"Oh, I prefer to stand," I said.

"You're mad. I can't blame you. But you know how it is, Hunter."

I shook my head. "No, I don't. Not this one. We did everything correctly. We had a warrant when we went in. We Mirandised them properly. We had a full recorded confession. He admitted to conspiring to kill his wife. His new wife admitted to actually killing her. We had them both. Now, I hear that you let them go. Why?"

Fowler threw out his arms. "Because I couldn't let you take them down. At least not him. He's too important."

A frown emerged between my eyes. "Important? Because he's the Miami-Dade County State Attorney?"

Fowler's eyes met mine, and the dime finally dropped. I took a step backward, startled.

"You have got to be kidding me. You let him go because you needed him? Because he's part of it too? The trafficking ring. I should have known. A guy like him is very good to have on hand. He knows what's going on, but you pay him to look the other way. The very same person who is supposed to be trying to combat trafficking is on your payroll. Clever. You run that whole darn operation, don't you? I didn't want to believe you did; I didn't want to see it, but of course, you do. It makes a lot of sense. Now, you can't risk him being in custody since he might reveal what he knows. Maybe he'll even try and make a deal. Am I right?"

Fowler's expression changed. His eyes were angry now.

"Am I right?" I asked again, slamming my fist onto his kitchen counter. "At least be honest with me."

"Yes, you're right," Fowler said with a snort.

"I can't believe you," I said. "Those…young children, those families who were being transported…you did that? You made money off that?"

"It was good money, okay? More than that, it was millions. Man, Hunter, you have no idea how much money it was. And you could have been in on it if you hadn't been…well, you. Besides, we did them a favor. They wanted to come here; they wanted to come. We made that possible. If it hadn't been us, it would've been someone else. That's the way the world goes. It used to be drug trafficking that was the most lucrative around here, but this is where the money is. So, there will always be someone doing it, taking that money. Might as well be us. Don't you see?"

"You broke the law. Human trafficking is a serious offense, and you know this. You subjected those poor people to great danger. And what about the girls that were kidnapped, the ones Camille lured in, huh? What happened to them? Did they end up on the street somewhere, drugged out of their minds, and raped by hundreds of men? Did you ever stop to think about them?"

Fowler stared at me, his fists clenched. He was looking for something that could justify his actions, but not finding it.

"These people…your people tried to kill my family," I said.

"You kept getting in my way, Hunter. I tried to warn you. I tried to get you off our backs, but you kept coming back. The others wanted to get rid of you long ago, but I kept telling them you were harmless. I protected you, Hunter. People are pissed at you, and I can't hold them back anymore. I love you like a brother, Harry, but I'm afraid it ends here. I'm not letting you ruin what I spent years building up. I'm sorry you had to find yourself in the middle of all this, but it's pure business. You can't stop it now."

I looked down at him, the man I had known since we were both in our early twenties. I thought I knew him. I thought we were on the same side.

A smile spread from the corner of my lip.

"I'm sorry; I'm afraid I already have," I said.

"What?"

"No, wait…I'm not sorry," I added. With a swift movement, I pulled up my shirt so he could see the wire I was wearing.

Fowler went pale, his eyes blank.

"W-what?"

"Say hello to Agent Jackson from the FBI. He has been listening in for quite some time now, waiting for you finally to confess. Remember that microphone that you told me you had found in your office? Thinking it would lead me somehow to whoever put it up, I went to Al. She traced it for me, and the digital footprint led her directly to your computer. You made up that story about your office being bugged because you knew I suspected you when they found Josie, and you were the only one who knew where she was. But by giving me that tale about the microphone, you believed you had lied your way out of it. But the thing is, there's always a footprint, and Al found it. So, I went to Agent Jackson and told him my suspicion. Ever since, he's been listening in on all my conversations, especially with you. Camille then later confirmed our suspicion when she started naming names. Now, if we use the recordings from today, from right now, along with her testimony and the video my neighbor Jean recorded of you driving the car during that drive-by shooting, I think we have evidence enough to put you away for quite some time, don't you think?"

Fowler stared up at me. He didn't even blink and barely breathed.

"I can't believe you did that. I can't believe you'd do that to me. We were friends, Hunter. We were like family."

"I can't believe any of the stuff you've done, so I guess we're even," I said. "Now, I'm afraid I have to put you under arrest."

Fowler pulled out his gun and pointed it at me. I lifted my hands. Sweat was springing to his forehead.

"I can't let you do that, Hunter. Don't move! Don't come anywhere near me, or I will kill you."

"Whoa," I said and stepped back. "What do you think you're doing with that? The FBI is waiting right outside. They came here with me when I told them I was coming to see you. You wanna kill me and add murder to the list of crimes? You don't want to do that, Fowler. Don't be a fool."

He shook his head. He looked confused. "Stay where you are. Down on your knees and stay there."

I did as he told me. He then asked me to bend my head down, and I heard his footsteps move across the marble tiles, then a door slide open. A second later, I heard an engine start.

No!

The front door burst open, and Agent Jackson stepped inside, flanked by two others in full uniform.

"You're too late," I said and rose to my feet. "He took the boat in the back."

Chapter 42

SHE HADN'T LEFT. The suitcase was still in the living room by the door, ready for whenever she was. But so far, she hadn't been ready. Jean wasn't sure she'd ever be. But then, what was she supposed to do with herself?

She had called in sick at the hospital. The flu, she had said. That would give her at least a week before they began asking questions. That week had passed now, and she still hadn't gone back there. She hadn't left either. Jean had simply stayed in her house, while wondering what she was going to do, not coming up with any solution.

Harry had told her he wanted her, that he was done with Camille. It was everything she ever wanted. But was it enough? Was it too late?

Jean held her coffee cup tightly between her hands while staring at the red suitcase. On the kitchen counter, her phone was vibrating, lighting up. She reached over and grabbed it, then looked at the display. It was her sister again.

Anna had called non-stop every day since Jean was supposed to go up there and never made it. Jean had sent her a text, telling her she was having second thoughts, that she needed time, but apparently, Anna wanted to hear it from her in person or at least talk to her. Jean didn't want to talk to her since she knew just how persuasive her sister could be, and how she'd end up convincing her to go anyway. And she wasn't ready. Jean needed time to think. Think about her life, her future.

What did she want?

Jean felt her eyes fill again. She had been crying so much this past week; it was amazing there was any tears left. The phone went dead again at least for a few seconds before it lit up once more. Her sister always tried twice. In case Jean had been too far from the phone on the first try and not made it in time. Anna liked giving people second chances.

Darkness was settling upon her small street outside now as the day was about to end—yet another day where she had done absolutely nothing and made no decision. She had received an email the day before from a nursing home in Savannah. They wanted to see her for an interview next week. There was a number she was supposed to call and say if she'd be able to make it. Jean hadn't called that number yet.

Now, it was too late. At least for today. She'd call tomorrow. Probably.

Jean took her phone in her hand, then found Harry's number and stared at it. She called it, thinking she needed to talk to him; she had to know what his plans were. But he didn't pick up, as usual, and she heard his voicemail begin, then hung up.

Jean walked to the sink and put her coffee cup in it, then looked at Harry's house next door. They hadn't been there all week, and the technicians had been working over there every day, their many cars blocking the street. Except for today. Today, Harry's house had been completely quiet. Jean wondered if they were finally finished. She had no idea this type of work took this long. On TV, they always made it look like it took a few hours, and then they had the case all figured out. But it was the same with series taking place in ERs. It always seemed so simple, yet being a nurse required so much more from you. Sometimes, you were holding the hand of someone about to die; other times, you were assisting in childbirth. It was all aspects of life. And she loved that. She loved not knowing what the day would bring when she got there. It was going to be very different, working at a nursing home, where the patients were all the same till they passed away.

It'll be steady. Steady is good for you right now.

That's what her sister would say, at least.

Jean sighed. She had hoped that Harry would move back soon, but she couldn't blame him if he never wanted to. The house was a mess after what happened. The porch and the wood on the outside were completely destroyed; several windows were shattered too. It looked like something out of a war movie.

He's never coming back, is he? Nothing will ever be like it was.

No, he needs to move on too, just like you.

Jean looked at the suitcase again, then decided it was time to go. She didn't have to wait until the next morning. She could drive all night and make it there early. Determined finally to do it, she grabbed her phone, and was about to call her sister back, then put the phone in her pocket, when suddenly she heard a noise coming from the back. She walked closer to the door as the screen door slammed shut.

"Hello?"

The feeling of the cold gun against her temple made her shiver. She turned to look at the man holding the gun, then gasped. She knew those eyes staring down at her from the many barbecues at Harry's house, even though he looked different, stirred up, frightened even.

"F-Fowler?"

"That's right, my dear. I need you to come with me."

"W-why?" Jean asked. She spoke while fiddling with the phone in her pocket, frantically tapping the display, hoping to call someone, any number. As Fowler pulled her arm, forcefully, her hand slipped out of the pocket again.

"Because you matter to him. He cares about you."

Chapter 43

I FELT DEVASTATED. I had failed. I should have known Fowler would try to run. I thought he was smarter than that, knowing that most criminals that ran ended up in the morgue. But apparently not. Apparently, he thought he could be the one to break the statistics.

The fool.

I had no idea where he was, where he had run to. We had searched the canals behind his house that led to the river for hours and hours. We had the marine patrol alerted, searching all the waterways; the FBI had put a helicopter in the air and dogs on the ground. And yet we still hadn't found him. We thought we had, on several occasions, when stopping a boat similar to his, but it wasn't him.

Now, as darkness had fallen, we were lost. He could have gotten to Key West by now if he wanted to, or the Bahamas if he made it out on the open waters. I had this feeling that he hadn't gotten that far, that he would stay close. But that was just a feeling.

I sat at the docks, staring out at the Intracoastal waters, while the marine patrol officers packed up their gear. I had been out on their boat all day and felt like the ground was still moving beneath my feet. My face had gotten sunburned, and I was very tired. I was thinking about Josie and getting home to her at my dad's place when the phone vibrated in my pocket. I pulled it out, and immediately, my heart sank.

It was Jean.

I hadn't heard from her in more than a week, ever since that day at her house, when I realized she was going to leave. I hadn't called her since I wanted to give her space. If she wanted to start over somewhere else, then so be it. There really wasn't much I could do about it. I had refrained from thinking about her all this time, well almost, as much as I was able to. But I was pretty sure she was in Savannah, and I didn't really want to talk to her right now. I let the voice mail answer it. Once she had hung up, I could see she had called more than once. I stared at the name on the display, a deep sadness washing over me.

Had I been wrong in giving her space? Hadn't I fought enough for her? Did she want me to?

I bit my cheek, contemplating this, when the voicemail showed up on the display, letting me know she had left a message. It took me a few seconds before I finally decided I wanted to hear it, and I pressed the screen.

At first, I thought it was a mistake. That she had probably just butt-dialed me since there was no voice, no one saying anything. Except, when I listened closer, I could hear a voice, one that made my blood run cold.

It was Fowler. Fowler telling her to move, while Jean whimpered and pleaded for him to let her go.

I stopped breathing while listening to this.

As the message ended, I replayed it, this time listening even closer. There was something there, a sound that I recognized. The sound of a gate slamming shut that I knew a little too well.

It was the gate to our neighborhood dock. It was located at the end of our street, and if you paid a monthly fee, you could keep your boat there. I kept a couple of kayaks in the shed down there, which I often took Josie out in, especially when she was younger. I knew the sound of that gate slamming because it always did so with such force that I feared it would crush Josie's small fingers.

"He's still here," I said and leaped to my feet. I looked at the marine patrol officer, Officer Bryant, who was packing up.

"I know where he is," I said. "We're gonna need to go back out."

Chapter 44

IT WAS hard to see anything in the darkness. The light from the marine patrol cruiser only reached a limited space out in the deep dark waters after the sun had set completely.

I had asked them to take me to our dock behind our neighborhood. Of course, Fowler was no longer there, but it was the last place I knew he had been, about half an hour or so earlier.

You could get pretty far away in half an hour in a boat, especially when hugged by darkness.

Where are you, Fowler? What have you done to Jean?

I cursed myself as I told them to try and go down the river. Why hadn't I reacted faster? Why hadn't I been better prepared for my meeting with him? I had let my feelings run away with me, let them blind me. I was angry, furious. I had felt betrayed, and it made me not think straight.

And now, Jean's life was in danger.

Why are you such an idiot!

I was surprised that Jean hadn't left since I had thought she'd be in Savannah by now, starting her new life. But Fowler had to have known that she was still there somehow, or maybe he had just taken the chance.

He knew my weak spot, my Achilles heel.

"It's almost impossible to find anything out here at this time," Officer Bryant said.

"Just keep looking," I said. "We can't give up now."

The guy shook his head, then sighed. "As you wish."

My heart was throbbing in my chest as I worried about Jean alone with Fowler. What was his plan with her? To keep her with him as collateral to make sure I wouldn't harm him? Or did he want to hurt her to get back at me? Just how desperate was he?

I didn't know.

I stared down at my phone when it finally rang—unknown number.

"Al, talk to me."

"I traced her phone," she said.

A wave of relief washed over me, and my shoulders came down slightly. I was so scared for Jean; it was unbearable.

"And?"

"I've got her on my screen now. They're heading north of the Intracoastal waterways."

"North?" I said. That was a surprise. I was so sure he'd try and go south, getting out into the ocean and maybe heading for the Bahamas. But, of course, he knew I'd think that, and that was why he was going in the other direction. This way, he could make it up to central Florida if he sailed all night, and disappear somewhere up there, while we searched the waters south of us and maybe even went to the Bahamas.

"Yes," she said. "He's not far from Bay Harbor Islands."

I signaled to the marine patrol officer to turn around, and he did. He made a huge turn, then sped up. I kept Al on the phone as we raced across the water, the warm moist air hitting my sunburned face, wiping away the few tears that escaped my eyes, tears of worry and fear.

If anything happened to Jean, I would never forgive myself.

Chapter 45

SHE WAS LYING at the bottom of the boat. He had tied her hands behind her back. Luckily, he hadn't been smart enough to search her, and Jean prayed that they could trace her phone somehow, that someone knew she had been taken—hopefully Harry—and that they could use her phone to trace her.

But the chances were slim. She knew this much. Harry probably thought Jean had left for Savannah a week ago, so he wouldn't even be over to check on her. He would have seen that she had called, though. He would know something was up, wouldn't he?

Oh, Harry, I need your help now.

It was dark out, and Jean had no way of seeing where they were going. Water splashed down on her, raining on her face and hair. She was getting tired of the bumping. She kept knocking her head and shoulder hard against the deck every time.

Where are we going? What's he going to do with me?

Fear rushed through her, and she groaned behind the gag. Fowler towered above her by the wheel, wind blowing in his hair as he rushed the boat across the choppy waters. Jean whimpered worriedly. They had been going at it for at least an hour. Where could he be taking her? Were they going north or south?

She didn't even know.

Jean tried to fight the strips around her wrists. They were cutting deep into her skin and hurt like crazy. She kicked her legs and screamed behind the gag, but couldn't even hear herself over the roaring engine and the sound of the boat hitting the water. It didn't matter how much she screamed; Fowler couldn't even hear her.

But as she kicked her legs, her right foot hit something. She looked down and saw a stack of life jackets. She had kicked them, and now they had fallen and revealed something that was hidden beneath them, something Fowler hadn't realized was there, almost within her reach.

Jean's eyes grew wide as she looked again. She lifted her glance and glared at Fowler to make sure he hadn't seen what she was up to. He was deep into his world, steering the boat along, and didn't even notice her.

Jean wormed down toward it, slowly, her eyes steady on him, making sure he didn't suddenly turn his head and look down at her. But he was busy and, in the distance, Jean could hear the sound of another engine. Another boat was there, closing in on them.

She'd have to signal them somehow, she thought, then wormed downward. Once close enough, she stuck her foot inside one of the life jackets, then lifted it slowly into the air. She paused when she thought Fowler was about to look down at her and figure out what she was up to, but he only looked behind him, then yelled.

"Crap!"

Jean swallowed as he made a sharp turn, and she realized someone was following them, but Fowler was trying to lose them in the darkness. She lifted the life jacket and slid it up against the side, then let it dump into the water.

With a small gasp, she looked up to see if he noticed, but he was too busy looking behind him to even think about her.

So, she stuck her foot into the second life jacket, then slipped that one overboard as well.

Chapter 46

"I THINK WE LOST HIM," Officer Bryant said. "I can't see him anywhere."

I stared into the darkness, which felt like an abyss. We had been so close. We had followed Al's directions and caught up to a boat that had no lights on. But the boat had spotted us too early and made a sharp turn. Now, it seemed to be gone. I could hear the engine in the distance but couldn't figure out which way it was going. Could he have gone into one of the canals? It would be impossible for us to find out which one if he did.

I put the binoculars close to my eyes and tried to look again, but was met with nothing but darkness until there was something else. Something was bobbing up and down on the surface of the water.

"I see something," I said. "On our port side. If you can get a little closer."

The marine officer did and then slowed down as we approached something in the water. It looked like a piece of clothing, but as I stuck the push pole in the water and pulled whatever it was out, I realized it was something different.

"It's a life jacket," I said and pulled it up on the deck. "What's it doing in the water?"

"I think I see another one," Officer Bryant yelled from behind the steering wheel. He turned the boat left. "Over there!"

We approached it, and I picked that one up as well. Then I glared into the water when I spotted something a little to our right side. "Over there. There's another one. Looks like it's a trail!"

"Like freakin' Hansel and Gretel," Bryant yelled, turned the boat, and went in the direction of the jacket, fast, this time passing it since we spotted another one ahead of us.

"It's Jean," I said to myself, smiling as he sped the boat up, and I felt the strong wind in my hair. "It has her written all over it."

We followed a couple of jackets more, praying she wouldn't run out of them, then finally spotted the boat ahead of us.

"There he is," I yelled. "Don't lose him this time!"

The officer pressed the boat to its maximum, and soon we were closing in on Fowler, fast. I pulled my gun out to be ready, hoping I wouldn't have to use it on an old friend. But ready to, if it came to that.

Officer Bryant was in close contact with the chopper, and as he told it our coordinates, I could hear it approaching in the distance. I could see its lights coming up behind us as we came close to Fowler and his boat. Officer Bryant yelled into the microphone for him to stop, but, of course, Fowler didn't. He took a sharp right turn, trying to escape us when another boat joined us from that side. It was another marine patrol that had communicated with Officer Bryant. A third one came from his port side.

Fowler was surrounded.

He made another sharp turn, and now I could suddenly see Jean in the beam of light we were shining on their boat. She had lifted herself up on her knees, and with her hands tied behind her back, she was now lifting something and turning around. I narrowed my eyes to see what it was, then realized it was a gun.

Not a gun-gun, but a flare gun.

With it clutched between her hands, she turned around, so she had her back turned to Fowler before she fired the gun straight at him.

The bright red light that followed blinded us all.

THREE WEEKS LATER

Chapter 47

"DO you need more wood up there?"

I looked down at my dad in my driveway. He was wearing overalls and held a hammer in his hand. The driveway was packed with wood we had bought at Lowe's to fix up the porch and façade, leaving no room for our cars. So far, we were doing pretty well, and it wasn't looking too shabby.

Josie was in the back with Camille, talking. My dad and I were giving them their space, moving along with the fix-up. I was planning on moving back into the house a week from now, and since I was on leave from work while the investigation of Fowler and the trafficking ring was being brought to an end, I thought there would be no better time than this to get my house back to its own beautiful self. I had realized I loved this house, and now that Fowler and the rest of his goons were gone, I believed I could feel safe in there again. It was, after all, Josie's childhood home, and I'd had many wonderful memories there. I believed there were more to be made. Many more.

"Yes, hand me that big one over there," I yelled.

My dad grabbed a plank and slid it up toward me. I placed it on the porch. My dad walked up to me, wiping his forehead with his hand. He handed me a soda from our cooler box.

"Thanks," I said. "I needed that."

It was getting really hot outside. It was April, and the temperatures most days were in the mid-eighties. Not a perfect time to do house renovations, but hey, this was Florida. Any day would be too hot, right?

I drank from the bottle and ended up gulping down almost half of it.

"Looks pretty nice," my dad said, studying our work so far.

"Still a lot more on the inside once we're done out here," I said.

My dad nodded and drank.

They had come for all of them. They had arrested them at their homes, some even at the station while their colleagues watched. The FBI had taken them all down, one after another. Fowler had talked like a schoolgirl after her first kiss as soon as he was able to after being hospitalized with third-degree burns. He had spilled everything, probably making one heck of a deal with the FBI if I knew him well. They wouldn't let me in on the details. But the fact was, the ring was taken down—each and every one who had been involved, including Andrew Taylor. And the media was naturally all over it. I had even been able to re-gather everything in Kate Taylor's murder case, and Al had found the original recordings of their confession, even though Fowler believed he had deleted them. Nothing ever disappears in the digital world, as Al said. And that had proved to be to our advantage once again. Kristin Grant had been arrested too and would be charged with aiding and abetting a murder. Joan Kendrick was being charged with murder. Andrew Taylor faced charges in both cases. So far, twenty-two more people had been arrested in the trafficking ring. Meanwhile, Nick Taylor would be tried as an adult and was facing attempted murder charges along with charges for being in possession of—and producing—child pornography.

"We'll get to the inside soon enough. Maybe do a complete make-over of the living room?" my dad said, looking in through the window that he had replaced a couple of days ago. My dad was an excellent handyman and had even built the church he had been the pastor at back in the day. It had lost its roof after the last hurricane, but other than that, it was still standing after all these years. I was lucky to have him in my life.

A car with black tinted windows drove up the street, and my heart dropped. It stopped, and Agent Jackson stepped out. He smiled and approached us. I walked down the stairs, wiped my dirty hands on my jeans, then shook his.

"Looking good," he said and nodded toward the house.

"It's getting there," I said. "Can I offer you anything? A soda?"

He gave me a look, then shook his head. "No. I'm afraid we have to get going. Is she ready?"

"She's in the back with Josie. Let me get her," I said.

I walked around the house and found them sitting in the chairs on the back porch, deep in conversation. Josie saw me, then shook her head violently.

"No, Dad, no."

"It's time."

"Already?"

I exhaled. I wanted this to happen as little as she did. "I'm afraid so."

"Please, Dad, can't she stay a little longer?"

I shook my head. "It's time, Josie."

Her face darkened. Camille put her hand on her shoulder.

"It's okay, Josie."

A tear escaped our daughter's eyes. "No, it's not. Why does she have to leave and not come back?"

"Because I did some stuff, bad stuff, and now since I have told what I did and what a lot of other people did, those people want me dead."

"I know what a witness protection program is," Josie said. "I meant, why can't you come back here. To visit?"

I exhaled. This was the tough part. Camille had accepted to enter the witness protection program to start over, but it meant she wouldn't see Josie anymore. I didn't understand how she could ever make such a decision, but that was just me. For Camille, it was important to be able to create a new life.

Agent Jackson had given us these few hours to say our goodbyes.

"You ready?" he said as we walked out on the other side of the house. Camille glanced back at Josie, leaned over and kissed her forehead one last time, then nodded.

"I'm ready."

Josie whimpered, then leaned her head against my shoulder. I put my arm around her.

"We just got her back, and now she's going again," Josie said with a sniffle. "It isn't fair, you know?"

"I know, sweetie."

Camille walked up to me, lifted herself on her tippy toes, and kissed my cheek.

"Goodbye, my handsome husband. I would tell you to take good care of our daughter, but I already know you will. You'll both forget me soon enough and move on with your lives, as you should."

She then nodded toward the neighboring house, where Jean was standing on the porch. "I heard you call her when I was in my hospital room, the day you ran away from me. I see the way you two look at one another. I think you'll make a cute couple."

With that, she turned around on her heel, walked up to Agent Jackson, and let him take her to the car. She got in, and the door was closed while Josie clung to me, her body shaking. I put my arm around her, and we watched together as the car disappeared down the street, Camille waving from the rolled-down window.

That was it. She was out of our lives forever. From now on, she'd have a new name, a new place to live, and we wouldn't see her again.

Josie wiped her tears away, then hugged me tightly. "At least I got to say goodbye this time," she said.

"Are you going to be all right?"

She nodded. "Yes. Eventually."

"How about we grab us some ice cream?" my dad said from behind us.

Josie smiled vaguely, then nodded, wiping more tears away. I turned to face my dad when he nodded toward the fence where Jean was now standing.

"Not you. Just me and Josie," my dad said.

Josie sent me a look, telling me she knew what was going on, and that she approved. I knew she had just said goodbye to her mother, but she loved Jean. Her lips mouthed, "Go," and so I did.

Here goes nothing.

I ran a hand through my hair, then approached Jean. She looked adorable in her pink shirt and denim shorts. But I guess at this point, she could have had a bag over her head, and I'd think that.

"So, she's really gone, huh?" she asked.

I nodded, my eyes fixed on hers.

"You must be devastated. How's Josie?"

"I have a feeling she'll be all right," I said. "In time."

Jean smiled. "That's good."

"And you?"

"What about me?"

"Have you decided if you'll stay here or go to Savannah?"

That made her smile widely with a glint in her eyes. "I think I might stay for a while. See what happens."

I stared at her lips till it became awkward, and then I decided just to go for it, realizing that, at this point, I had nothing to lose. If I wanted her, I had to go for it; there was no other way.

So, I leaned over, grabbed her in my arms, and pulled her into a kiss.

THE END

Afterword

Dear Reader,

Thank you for reading these stories about Detective Harry Hunter.

This is the first three books in a planned series of shorter, more fast-paced mysteries. I loved writing these stories, and I hope you enjoyed reading it as well. I hope to write many more books about Harry.

As usual, some of the things in this story are taken from the real world.

BOOK 1:

The rape in the beginning was inspired by a real rape that happened at a high school dance, where tons of kids saw it happen, and the guy even called the dad afterward.

You can read more here if you want to.

https://www.huffpost.com/entry/richmond-high-gang-rape-victim_n_3389573

The story of the Philippine gang and the divers on Jeju Island is real too. You can read about these amazing women here:

Afterword

https://ich.unesco.org/en/RL/culture-of-jeju-haenyeo-women-divers-01068

BOOK 2:

I know this story is a little extraordinary, and it might be hard to believe, but something like it actually happened. An eight-year-old girl received the heart of a ten-year-old girl who had been murdered. Later, she began having frequent dreams of someone being murdered. The girl was taken to a psychiatrist, and it was later concluded that the girl was talking about a real incident, going into details she couldn't possibly know. After contacting the police, they were able to provide clues like time of death, murder weapon, place, clothes worn by the murderer, and what the little girl had said to him before she died. All that led to the arrest and later conviction of the murderer of the eight-year-old girl.

It's on the verge of being supernatural, but actually, it isn't, according to the scientists and doctors. There are, in fact, scientific reports written about this, and about all the accounts of transplant receivers experiencing a change in nature afterward and dreaming things that their donors lived through. A Dr. Pearsall has collected the accounts of seventy-three heart transplant patients and sixty-seven other organ transplant recipients and published them. You can read more here. This article also goes into possible explanations for the phenomenon. It's very interesting:

https://www.namahjournal.com/doc/Actual/Memory-transference-in-organ-transplant-recipients-vol-19-iss-1.html

You can also read more here:

https://www.iacworld.org/the-scientific-mystery-of-transplant-cellular-memory-projectiological-hypotheses/

Now, the story about refugees being smuggled hidden in appliances is also taken from the real world, believe it or not. Border control between Mexico and the U.S. recently found eleven Chinese migrants inside the furniture and appliances in the back of a truck. It never ceases to amaze me how they keep finding inhumane ways to smuggle people and what refugees will subject themselves to in order to make it. You can read more and see the pictures here:

Afterword

https://www.cnn.com/2019/12/10/us/california-border-migrants-hiding/index.html

BOOK 3:

I was so happy finally to give you the end of Camille's story. Now, as usual, a lot of the things I put in my books are taken from real life. I recently made a new friend, and her husband works in Hyperbaric medicine. He told me about this amazing field of medicine that I had never heard about, and I started to research it more. I found this story of a young girl who nearly drowned and was dead for two hours. Once she woke up, the doctors realized she had a severe brain injury. She started treatment in a hyperbaric chamber, and months later, she was almost a normal kid for her age. It's truly remarkable. You can read more here and watch a video of her progress. It is also true that the treatment isn't FDA approved for treating brain injury, at least not yet. I, for one, hope it will be soon.

https://www.newsweek.com/eden-carlson-brain-damage-reversed-drowning-638628

Now the term Hurtcore, where someone humiliates another person and forces them to do stuff while filming themselves like Nick did to these girls, isn't something I came up with either. I wish it were. It's so awful; I really wish it was just my imagination. Recently a 22-year-old British man was arrested for doing this to a number of young girls; eleven of them were just children. He got twelve years in jail for what he did. It's apparently something that takes place all over the world, and it's nasty. You can read more here:

https://www.bbc.com/news/uk-england-merseyside-43962411
and here:
https://www.vice.com/en_uk/article/59kye3/the-repulsive-world-of-hurtcore-the-worst-crimes-imaginable

You might think that I went overboard with the trafficking ring reaching so deeply within the police department and involving the State Attorney and all that, but it actually isn't too far from a true story that recently emerged here in Florida. Doctors, lawyers, and

Afterword

deputies, were all arrested in a human trafficking sting. You can read about it here:

https://www.nbc4i.com/news/u-s-world/doctors-and-cops-among-277-arrested-in-human-trafficking-online-prostitution-sting-in-florida/

As always, I am so grateful for all your support. Please leave a review if you can.

Take care,

Willow

About the Author

Willow Rose is a multi-million-copy bestselling Author and an Amazon ALL-star Author of more than 70 novels.

Several of her books have reached the top 10 of ALL books on Amazon in the US, UK, and Canada. She has sold more than three million books all over the world.

She writes Mystery, Thriller, Paranormal, Romance, Suspense, Horror, Supernatural thrillers, and Fantasy.

Willow's books are fast-paced, nail-biting page turners with twists you won't see coming. That's why her fans call her The Queen of Scream.

Willow lives on Florida's Space Coast with her husband and two daughters. When she is not writing or reading, you will find her surfing and watch the dolphins play in the waves of the Atlantic Ocean.

To be the first to hear about **exclusive new releases and FREE ebooks from Willow Rose**, sign up below to be on the VIP List. (I promise not to share your email with anyone else, and I won't clutter your inbox.)

- GO HERE TO SIGN UP TO BE ON THE VIP LIST :
http://readerlinks.com/l/415254

TIRED OF TOO MANY EMAILS?
Text the word: "willowrose" to 31996 to sign up to Willow's VIP text List to get a text alert with news about New Releases, Giveaways, Bargains and Free books from Willow.

FOLLOW WILLOW ROSE ON BOOKBUB:

https://www.bookbub.com/authors/willow-rose

CONNECT WITH WILLOW ONLINE:

AUTHOR WEBSITE:
Http://www.willow-rose.net
EMAIL:
madamewillowrose@gmail.com
AMAZON AUTHOR PAGE:
https://www.amazon.com/Willow-Rose/e/B004X2WHBQ
FACEBOOK:
https://www.facebook.com/willowredrose/
TWITTER:
https://twitter.com/madamwillowrose
GOODREADS:
http://www.goodreads.com/author/show/4804769.Willow_Rose

Copyright Willow Rose 2020
Published by BUOY MEDIA LLC
All rights reserved.

No part of this book may be reproduced, scanned, or distributed in any printed or electronic form without permission from the author.

This is a work of fiction. Any resemblance of characters to actual persons, living or dead is purely coincidental. The Author holds exclusive rights to this work. Unauthorized duplication is prohibited.

Cover design by Juan Villar Padron,
https://www.juanjpadron.com

Special thanks to my editor Janell Parque
http://janellparque.blogspot.com/

To be the first to hear about **exclusive new releases and FREE ebooks from Willow Rose**, sign up below to be on the VIP List. (I promise not to share your email with anyone else, and I won't clutter your inbox.)

- Go here to sign up to be on the VIP LIST :
http://readerlinks.com/l/415254

Tired of too many emails? Text the word: "willowrose" to 31996 to sign up to Willow's VIP text List to get a text alert with news about New Releases, Giveaways, Bargains and Free books from Willow.

Follow Willow Rose on BookBub:
https://www.bookbub.com/authors/willow-rose

Connect with Willow online:

AUTHOR WEBSITE:
Http://www.willow-rose.net

EMAIL:
madamewillowrose@gmail.com

AMAZON AUTHOR PAGE:
https://www.amazon.com/Willow-Rose/e/B004X2WHBQ

FACEBOOK:
https://www.facebook.com/willowredrose/

TWITTER:
https://twitter.com/madamwillowrose

GOODREADS:
http://www.goodreads.com/author/show/4804769.Willow_Rose

Printed in Great Britain
by Amazon